FEAR NO EVIL

Robert Burslem

First Published 2013

Robert Burslem
rburslem@fsmail.net
2 Castle Park Road
Sandycove
County Dublin
Republic of Ireland

DEDICATION

THIS BOOK IS DEDICATED TO MAUREEN GUTKIN

MAUREEN, MY PARTNER HAS BEEN MY INSPIRATION, MODERATOR AND MOTIVATOR. SHE HAS SAT THROUGH COUNTLESS DISCUSSIONS OVER THE PLOT AND SPENT TOO MANY HOURS TO COUNT EDITING AND CORRECTING MY MISTAKES. WORDS CANNOT EXPRESS MY HEARTFELT GRATITUDE.

THANKS AND ACKNOWLWDGEMENTS

Special thanks to my good friend Joe Mullane for reading and checking the final manuscript.

Thanks to all my friends for the kind words of encouragement I have received.

Thanks to my family for their patience when I was writing this especially Clare, Paul, Ashleigh, Aidan & Phoebie

Preface

As I write these words North Korea is threatening the United States with nuclear weapons. In truth it most probably does not have the ability to make good its threats never the less America is moving anti-ballistic missiles into defensive positions. Perhaps more worryingly the Iranians are developing their own nuclear weapons and they constitute a real and credible threat. Not that long ago Western countries went to war with Iraq on the (wrong) assumption that country possessed weapons of mass destruction. Who knows what 'rogue' entities will emerge in the future with similar weapons? The subject matter of this book, South Africa's nuclear weapons, is very real.

I first heard about South Africa's nuclear arsenal in 1982. At the time I was working in southern Africa, in what was then known as the 'Front Line States' (African governed countries that shared a border with 'Apartheid' South Africa). It was a very 'tetchy' time and when we got the news we all immediately knew it was a real game changer.

In my opinion Nelson Mandela has been one of the most impressive men to have walked on this earth. But we didn't know what he was going to turn out like in 1982. At that time he was in prison, convicted of terrorist offences which he did not deny. His organisation, the ANC, had links to hard line communist countries, rogue states and major terrorist groups.

World opinion had completely turned against Apartheid South Africa and it was becoming increasingly clear that Nelson Mandela and the ANC would form the first universally elected government in South Africa. But we knew then there was no way that the United States and other Western countries were going to allow nuclear weapons to come under the control of what was then an unknown political entity.

Fear No Evil is a fictional story but there is a lot of fact included. The political background is correct, the dates are right, the bombs as described were manufactured, the places are real and many of the events actually occurred. I have had to simplify the story in some respects and make adaptions to fit in with Duncan Murdoch and his colleagues. The book is the result of several years of research and the story is in no way farfetched.

Notwithstanding the above it is a story and the contribution of my imagination should not be underestimated. I hope you enjoy the read.

Any similarity with real people, apart from the obvious, is coincidental.

There are some author's notes at the rear of the book.

Robert Burslem
Chester, United Kingdom
April 2013

Prologue
Outside Pietermaritzburg, South Africa 1959

Peter and Johannes led the group of six boys as they walked along the dusty track that connected the isolated farm houses that were their homes. The afternoon sun hung in a clear blue sky, its heat mitigated by a cooling breeze that wafted across open fields. The boys wore identical khaki school uniform; shorts, short sleeve shirt, knee high socks and floppy bush hat. They chatted in Afrikaans, the language of the Boers, the descendants of the Dutch that had first settled in South Africa more than three hundred years previously.

Mr Joubert their history teacher, who had just taught them their last lesson of the day, was very old. Thin, stooped and grey haired, the deep lines in his face bunched when he spoke. Normally Mr Joubert's lips were curled downward as if in a scowl. But this outward appearance belied his true ability. When he spoke about the history of his beloved country it was with passion and infectious enthusiasm. His pupils would sit mesmerised, transfixed by his piercing blue eyes. To Mr Joubert history was a series of stories that he brought to life and told in such a way that the boys believed their teacher had been there and was merely giving an eye witness account of events.

That afternoon Mr Joubert was to have taught them about the history of agricultural development in South Africa but the boys had pleaded with him, behaving not like their sixteen years but more like small children, begging to be re-told their favourite fairytale. Mr Joubert needed little encouragement.

Although already knowing the story well, the boys sat captivated by the tale of how the British, motivated only by greed and jealousy, had marched into their beloved Transvaal, right into Pretoria and declared the province a British colony, how the Boers, outnumbered and poorly armed had tricked the British commanders to enter forbidden Zululand and provoke the Zulu's, led by the great Cetshwayo, who had thrashed the British at the battle of Islandwana in 1879.

Mr Joubert told them how the Boer leaders, having weakened the British invaders by guile, had issued an ultimatum: leave the Transvaal voluntarily or be forced out. The British had of course stupidly rejected the ultimatum and the First Boer War started. It was a short lived affair, from December 1880 to March 1881 and culminated in the Battle of Majuba Hill. The British, occupying the high ground, were well manned and armed but had been humiliated by a rag-tag army of Boer farmers equipped only with hunting rifles and limitless determination. They had crawled up the hill on their bellies, under a hail of enemy fire and, when they finally got to the plateau at the top, had blindly charged the British defensive line which quickly collapsed; all the British were killed or ran away.

Mr Joubert straightened his back and spoke the final words with steely pride. "And the British, then realising they were beaten, had surrendered their claim to the Transvaal. The South African Republic was born under our great and historic leader Paul Kruger."

Now, as the boys walked home, they were fired up, each imagining that they were among the brave 'Volk' that were clawing their way up Majuba Hill. It was then, as they approached an Acacia tree with its spreading branches, they saw the two African boys sitting, eating oranges.

Thaba and his younger brother Moswen should have been at school that day but when they'd arrived at the thatched rondavel, with its dirt floor, that served as a classroom, the teacher was absent. That day there would be no rote reciting of the times tables or scratching letters of the alphabet with chalk on to slate tablets whilst sitting cross legged on the ground.

They knew their mother would be angry. She had paid for the lessons and even scraped enough cash together for the uniform of sky blue shirt and navy shorts. Unfortunately her efforts had not been enough to purchase shoes for either of her two boys. Thaba knew at fourteen he was fortunate to have a mother that allowed him to attend school when he should really have been working in the fields. Because of that he decided not to return to his village. Instead he went to the De Koch farm. It was orange harvest season and he knew the Bossman would pay him a rand if he and his brother picked enough fruit during the day. So for six hours Thaba and his younger brother had picked oranges. The bossman had been happy and as well as the one Rand he'd given them a small bag of oranges to take home. It was these oranges that the brothers enjoyed in the shade of the Acacia tree.

Johannes was going to walk past the Africans but Peter stopped.

"You two, you're supposed to stand in the presence of your superiors."

Thaba and Moswen didn't move. They looked down to the ground as they'd been taught. They knew it was better not to look the white boys in the eye, it would be seen as insolence or, even worse, a challenge.

"Get up!" said Peter.

Johannes stopped. "Leave them alone Peter. They're doing no harm.

Peter ignored Johannes and walked over to Thaba and tugged at his shirt sleeve. Thaba got slowly to his feet, Moswen followed suit, clinging on to his bag of oranges.

"What are you doing here? This is a white area," Peter spoke in Afrikaans.

Thaba and Moswen made no reply.

"Do you understand me? Do you speak Afrikaner?"

Thaba kept his gaze down. "English, no Afrikaans."

"You don't speak the language of the country you live in?" responded Peter in English. "You Zulu's really don't have any respect or gratitude for what you have."

"Not Zulu," replied Thaba. "Xhosa."

The other boys had grouped around.

"Fucking Xhosa. A tribe of thieves. You come here to steal."

"Leave them alone Peter, they're not doing any harm," interjected Johannes again.

Peter grabbed at the bag of oranges that Moswen held. "I bet you stole these." The little boy resisted. Peter grabbed at the tiny black arm and tried to force it to let go of the bag. Thaba in turn grabbed Peter's arms, protecting his little brother. Instantly, the boys came forward as one and grabbed the black youths, two holding Moswen and three Thaba, who struggled to get free. Thaba had broken a golden rule; under no circumstances could a black boy interfere with a white one.

Peter finally got the bag of oranges. "Look the oranges are too good. They weren't grown by an African farmer. They must have stolen them."

He turned his attention to Moswen and shouted into the little boy's face. "Where did you steal them from?"

Thaba struggled against the restraining grip of the white boys. No longer keeping his eyes lowered, he looked Peter straight in the eye. "You are a coward. You are only strong because there are more of you. You would lose if the fight was equal."

Johannes smiled. "Now there's a challenge for you," he said.

"I'm not going to fight with a dirty kaffir just to prove something we all know already," responded Peter.

"Okay," replied Johannes, "Your choice, we believe you can beat him but he will always believe you are a coward."

The other boys joined in. "Come on Peter; show him what you can do. Teach him a lesson."

Peter had no choice if he was to save face. The two boys squared up to each other in the grassless area under the shade of the Acacia's branches. For a long time the boys circled each other, their fists raised as if they were following the Marquess of Queensbury's Rules. Thaba made a couple of feints, sudden movements as if he were about to attack. Each time Peter stepped back in alarm. The boys laughed. Frustrated, Peter let out a kick that connected with Thaba between the legs. The African reeled backwards with the sudden burst of pain. Peter, taking advantage of the opportunity, came forward and started reigning blows on Thaba's head. It was all Thaba could do to cling on to his opponent and drag him to the ground in a tight clench. For a while the two boys rolled around in the dirt, neither inflicting punishment on the other. Peter, trying to break the impasse bit into Thaba's shoulder. The burst of pain forced him to release his bear like grip. In a second Thaba was on his back and Peter was astride his opponent, pinning his arms to the ground.

"Hit him Peter," shouted one of the boys.

Peter let hold his grip of one arm and raised a fist, preparing to bring it down into Thaba's face. But he was too slow. Thaba, as quick as lightening, struck upwards with a clenched fist and connected with the bridge of Peter's nose which immediately split open. For a split second Peter was frozen by the shock of the sudden blow which allowed Thaba to heave Peter's body to one side. Free he started to get to his feet, anger flashing in his eyes. Peter knew the fight was lost and tried to regain his footing and run away but Thaba was too quick and pounced on Peter's back and he went face first into the dirt. The African grabbed Peter's head and shoved it into the dust, twisting and pushing at the same time. Peter could feel the sandy grains mixing with the blood, filling his nasal passages and going into his mouth. The flame of heroic courage that Mr Joubert had kindled in Peter's heart was fast diminishing. As he choked all Peter could feel was terror, and with the paralysis brought on by that terror Peter thought he was going to die.

He came from behind. Thaba didn't see Peter's friend come forward. All he felt was the point of the shoe connect with his ribs and the breath suddenly being expelled from his lungs. The second kick was enough to make him release the grip on his opponent and roll over.

The fight was over. Thaba struggled back to his feet as Moswen, now released, ran forward to join his brother. It took Peter more time to get up. When he did he stood looking at the two blacks with contempt. Moswen was the first to laugh but Thaba soon joined him.

"What are you blacks laughing at?" demanded Peter wiping the mix of blood and sand from his face.

They didn't answer, they continued laughing.

Johannes stood a few steps behind, the others clustered around him. Peter turned to face them. "What are they laughing at? What is so funny?"

Johannes was the first to laugh, quickly followed by the others. If felt like an eternity to Peter, as he stood there with everybody laughing. "Why are you laughing?" he demanded.

Johannes eventually pointed. "Peter, you pissed your pants."

Peter looked down towards his crotch; the wet stain stood out on the khaki. It was clear for all to see that fear had made Peter lose control of his bladder.

"How bad is that Peter?" said Johannes, "A kaffir made you piss your pants. Some hero you are. You're never going to live this one down. It'll be with you for the rest of your life!"

Peter ran, ran to get away from the chants of 'piss pants, piss pants."

Johannes could never know it but his last words were going to be prophetically true. The scare that Peter van Stardan retained from that day was not on his face, it was on his heart, like an indelible engraving.

BOOK ONE
Puma Game Lodge, Kruger National Park, South Africa
Saturday 23th March 1963

A Lee-Enfield was not Peter van Stardan's first choice in rifles, not for the task in hand, not for anything really. He preferred his ancient bolt action Mauser. But then again he was prejudiced, he didn't like anything English. He wouldn't have chosen soft nose hunting rounds either. He preferred more precise and less messy jacketed bullets. But he understood why he had been instructed to use the Lee-Enfield and soft bullets. He knew that attention to detail was important.

The dawn sky was a dull red, the tip of the sun threatening to break the horizon heralding the birth of another day in the South African bush, another day indistinguishable from others that had preceded it for countless millennia. It seemed to Peter van Stardan that time moved at an imperceptibly slow pace in the bush and this was the evidence that God had given his people the land for eternity. But for Peter van Stardan's companion, this day would not be ordinary.

It was time. Van Stardan had to work quickly. Even so he trod carefully in the shadows looking where he placed each foot, conscious of every tiny sound. Half crouched, to lessen his silhouette, he moved forward between the scattered thorn bushes closing in on the herd of antelopes that were drinking at the watering hole directly ahead. He knew that the antelopes would be alert; their ears raised, twisting like radar, eyes darting looking for even the tiniest movement, their noses twitching, seeking stray pheromones in the air. The watering hole was a dangerous place for them. Peter focused his gaze on the lush elephant grass for a moment checking wind direction; he had to stay down wind of the animals.

To his right he heard the gentle snap of a dry twig. He froze, eyes fixed on the gracious animals, watching for signs of alarm. There was nothing. The antelopes continued dipping their long barbed tongues into the murky water, quenching their thirst in anticipation of the long hot day to come. Peter turned his head in the direction of the sound. Matthew, twenty yards to his right, was crouched still as a statue. There was just enough light for their eyes to meet. Matthew gave a gentle shrug before cautiously taking another step forward. Peter went down on one knee. "It is time", he thought. Slowly he operated the worn bolt action of his weapon, the action he had cleaned and oiled that morning. The sound of the round sliding into the barrel and the hammer going back was almost silent. He raised the rifle and pushed the stock tightly into his shoulder. He didn't use a scope; at this range it wasn't necessary. He took a final measured look at Matthew, triangulating the shot in his mind. He picked out an animal from the herd, a small doe-eyed Springbok and closed his finger on the trigger, taking up the slack from the less than precision firing mechanism. He felt a twinge of shame for targeting the tiny harmless animal, the national emblem of his beloved South Africa.

He drew a deep breath and held it for a moment, long enough to calm himself and eliminate the tiny tremble of anticipation. Steadily he came to his feet and shouted, almost screamed, his companion's name, "*Matthew*!" The herd needed no further warning. In unison the animals stampeded, heading for the safety of the bush and thick thorn. The tiny Springbok that had been in Peter's sights leapt high into the air every third pace, making it an impossible target. Simultaneously hundreds of birds, previously unseen, rose from hidden nests in the long grass. They screeched a deafening cacophony of warning, further shattering the dawn silence. Matthew too stood erect. Bewildered he turned to face his stalking partner.

"Full frontal, thank you," thought Peter. He swung his rifle around in the direction of Matthew. He hardly had to take aim. Without hesitation he pulled the trigger. The crack was lost, drowned out by the din of the animals. Matthew recoiled from the initial impact of the bullet, stepping backwards, wavering for a while before collapsing to the ground. The .303 bullet had done its work well, but it wasn't a clean kill.

Matthew was conscious but unable to move. As he lay on the ground and tasted blood his brain raced trying to make sense of what was happening. He watched as Peter slowly walked towards him. Peter van Stardan looked down and calmly prodded the entry wound in Matthew's chest with the muzzle of the Lee-Enfield. "Slightly to the right," he mumbled, annoyed that he'd not done better. Matthew's chest heaved as he coughed; a trickle of blood ran from the corner of his mouth. With a grimace of pain he exposed his once white teeth that were now blood red. Peter thought he looked comical. Mathew's last intelligible word was "Why?"

"Because I was ordered to," replied Peter. For a second he was tempted by a flash of pity to fire a second shot into Matthew's head and finish the job, just as he would have done for any animal but he resisted the temptation almost laughing to himself for considering such a foolish thought.

"How could I claim an accidental shooting if Matthew had two bullets in him?" he said to nobody in particular.

Frank Plumly came running from behind as fast as his dumpy middle-aged legs would carry him. "For Christ's sake, what have you done?" he gasped as he knelt beside the motionless body and felt for a pulse.

"He crossed in front of me. He came between me and the quarry," replied van Stardan calmly. "It was an accident."

"Rubbish," replied Frank, "I can see he kept his line perfectly."

"It was an accident," repeated Peter van Stardan flatly.

Frank Plumly worked frantically on the body hoping to rekindle a spark of life. "Fetch the Land Rover. Let's get him back to the camp, let's try and do something for him."

"I don't drive," replied van Stardan. "Not in the bush. Besides he's dead. There's no hurry."

"Don't you realise you'll be in big trouble for this?"

"No I won't be. It was an accident, you saw what happened," said van Stardan lighting a cigarette. "You get the Land Rover. For your own sake remember what I am telling you. It was an accident."

Frank Plumly had been happy with his lot as Warden of the Puma Game Lodge on the edge of South Africa's Kruger National Park. He'd been secure and content - until a few days ago. Now, as he hurriedly stumbled back to the Land Rover his mind raced.

The booking he'd taken for a hunting trip was not unusual, nor was it unusual for one of the hunting party to make a preliminary visit to sort out the details. South Africans took their hunting seriously. But there was something odd about Alfred Smidt. This client didn't quite look the part. He was not athletic, too big, a city type.

The conversation had begun innocently enough as Frank Plumly showed his customer the cabins the party would be occupying.

"You like your job?" Alfred Smidt had started with a rhetorical question. "I can see it has its attractions. You look comfortable with your life."

"Who wouldn't be?" replied Frank. "This is God's country and he's entrusted me to take care of this small corner of it. What more could a man ask for?"

"You're married, family?" asked Alfred although he already knew the answer.

"Yes. I have a wife and two children, a boy and a girl. We live in the main lodge."

"Your children must love it?" led Alfred.

"As much as me; sometimes I think even more. They don't know anything else."

"You're from England." It was a statement. "I suppose it would be hard on your wife and kids if they had to go and live in the old country," continued Alfred.

"They wouldn't go. Not under any circumstances."

"Not even to be with you?"

"I'm definitely not going back," Frank replied emphatically.

"Sometimes people don't have choices," said Alfred more seriously.

"What do you mean?" asked Frank sensing the change in tone.

"In my experience the past has a habit of catching up with people when they least expect it."

"I'm not following you," responded Frank even though alarm bells were beginning to ring in his ears.

"Most people have a skeleton in the cupboard somewhere." The two men had stopped walking now and were facing each other. "What are you getting at?" demanded Frank.

"Nothing really," said Alfred sure in the knowledge he'd shaken Frank Plumly. "My philosophy is to let sleeping dogs lie. Now let's talk about the hunting trip. I need a little favour from you."

"What kind of favour?" asked Frank Plumly the bristles on the back of his neck standing.

"My colleagues are a lot younger than me. I think they'd appreciate a bit of private early morning hunting, a bit deeper in the bush than normal, off the beaten track. Can you organise that?"

Frank Plumly thought for a bit, looking for the catch. "I do that sort of thing for a lot of people. What's so special about your colleagues?"

"They just enjoy their privacy. That's all. They'd like the place to themselves. Just take them out of the way and let them do their own thing."

Frank couldn't get the conversation out of his head as he drove as fast as he could back towards the camp. Intuitively he knew there was a problem. The Land Rover jumped about on the rough track and after each bump Frank looked back over his shoulder at the body that lay limply in the back, draped in an old gray army blanket, a blood patch soaking through. Peter van Stardan sat beside him, silently staring ahead.

Alfred Smidt had a headache, a bad headache; his whole head was throbbing and it felt like it was going to burst but he knew he couldn't rest, there was important work to do. He heard the Land Rover entering the camp. With deliberation he folded the copy of the Pretoria Post that had been resting on his lap and slid it into the wicker paper stand. He raised his large frame, pushing hard on the arms of the chair and made his way to the door of the hunting cabin. Alfred Smidt was a calm measured man not prone to panic and it was his disposition that made him move slowly and deliberately now despite his discomfort. He left the cabin. The Land Rover was stopped in the middle of the compound, the dust not yet settled after Frank Plumly's frantic drive. Alfred walked quickly and intercepted Frank before he reached the hunting lodge. Frank tried to side step Alfred but was too slow.

Frank looked into Alfred's eyes. "You knew what was going to happen. That was murder out there. I will not be a part of it, I'm calling the police."

"Hold on a second," replied Alfred, almost whispering into Frank's ear. "You have to call the police, that's clear. But if that was murder what is to stop the police thinking you were part of it? Only the word of Peter and myself. You need to be careful in what you say." Alfred smiled. "But I'm sure it was not murder. It was just a tragic accident and you were the witness."

"When I report the murder they will know I'm not involved."

"Perhaps, but even if the police believe you, you can look forward to a trip back to England. The British Army has a long memory. I'm sure they would like to talk to you. Be careful what you say. It was just a tragic accident, that's it. They happen all the time." Alfred turned away sure he'd done enough.

Frank Plumly's last few steps to the office were completed more slowly, his mind racing, flashing back in time.

Frank's life journey was unusual. Born immediately after the 1st World War in the grim and impoverished industrial Potteries of England's west midlands he was destined for a life at the kilns, baking the ceramics that the area was famed for. He was brought up being told the best he could hope for was a job at the prestigious Wedgewood works. The toil and the sweat were the same as in other factories but the money was a little better because Wedgewood got a premium for their quality wares. Frank, even as a child, resented this pre-ordination of his life and it was during rain sodden overcast Saturday mornings that his aspirations had been raised and hope born.

On Saturdays he'd meet friends in a doorway close to the cinema at Hanley. The lads would pool their scant funds to purchase a single cinema ticket. The chosen one would sit in the cinema until the feature had started and then sneak to the toilets at the rear, release the latch on the emergency exit door and allow his waiting mates in. Once inside Frank would sit trance like, eyes fixed on the window to another world. He liked and laughed at silent Charlie Chaplin, Buster Keaton and the Keystone Cops but the big influence was the talkies and Tarzan. From the first time he saw his hero swing through the trees he knew he was going to live in Africa. He just didn't know how he was going to get there.

When he was fifteen years old he got a job as an apprentice furnace builder. Five years later he qualified, just in time to be called up for the Second World War which he spent almost exclusively in Ceylon on idyllic garrison duty, protecting Mountbatten's headquarters and the port of Trincomalee. Frank didn't have a bad war; in fact he had a really good one and in many respects he was disappointed when it ended, but end it did. In January 1946 orders came to ship out. He embarked on a troop ship at Madras, bound for Liverpool, demobilisation and back to civilian life. The prospect of a return to the furnaces of the Potteries was not particularly alluring.

The troop ship went the long way around the Cape of Good Hope stopping at Durban to refuel and pick up more troops surplus to the Empire. Most of the soldiers were happy to be returning to England but not Frank. His sadness on departure turned into deep depression on the two week run from Madras to Durban. It became too much for him. Whilst the troop ship swung on its anchor in Durban Bay Frank got himself assigned to a shore party collecting supplies. The sergeant in charge of the shore party had his suspicions and was waiting when

Frank made his move. The confrontation was short and more violent than the sergeant had anticipated. Frank hit the sergeant, knocked him to the ground and then gave him a couple of kicks for good measure. The sergeant lay on the floor motionless, Frank ran, ran as fast and as far as he could.

He became an official deserter from the Army. He wasn't too bothered about that at the time but he did think about the sergeant every now and again. He made his way north to Kruger National Park, the Eden on earth he'd read so much about. With enthusiasm as his main qualification and a fair amount of lies he begged a job in the Game and Wildlife Department. His desertion from the British Army remained a matter of record only, a fact dimmed by time and almost forgotten by Frank, until Alfred Smidt came along and fanned the dying embers of his memory.

Frank picked up the phone in the lodge and dialled the police post. It seemed a long time before there was a response. A woman picked up.

"This is Frank Plumly, Puma Game Lodge. There's been a hunting accident."

The police inspector arrived within an hour. The body was still in the back of the Land Rover. The Inspector lifted the blanket.

"Single chest shot," he said without emotion.

"Died almost instantly," said Frank. "He could never have survived that wound."

"I should go to the scene," said the Inspector.

"It's quite a trek," replied Frank. "And there's nothing much to see. But if you really want to go I'll take you."

"I suppose there's little point. One bit of bush is much the same as another. Where's the shooter?"

"Here. He's pretty shaken," Frank pointed to Peter van Stardan surprised at how easily the lies tripped from his mouth.

"What happened?" asked the Inspector looking van Stardan directly in the eye.

"We were stalking antelope at the watering hole," began Peter. "We'd agreed our positions but Matthew crossed into my field of fire, concealed by a thicket, I had no idea it was him. I just heard rustling, I didn't know if it was a warthog about to charge or even a lion. I let go a warning shot. Matthew shouldn't have been there."

"Have you been hunting before? Do you normally shoot blind? That's a dangerous practice," said the Inspector.

"It was a split second decision," defended van Stardan. "Matthew was a good friend. I'm really cut up."

"Did you see it? Is that what happened?" the inspector asked Frank.

"Yes," he replied shocking himself with the reply.

"I'll need detailed statements from both of you then. Come down to the police post later," said the Inspector. "Get yourselves sorted out first."

An hour later Peter van Stardan sat with Alfred Smidt in his darkened cabin. For a long time they were silent. Peter was waiting for Alfred and Alfred was waiting for the pain killers to kick in and relieve his splitting headache.

The plan had been a long time in the making but in the end had been swiftly concluded. The three men Alfred, Peter and Matthew, had arrived at the camp the previous afternoon. They'd spent the evening together eating and drinking under the African stars. The conversation had been benign. Alfred's mood was good. He'd smiled and was pleased because although Peter knew what was expected of him he was able to speak easily with Matthew, arousing no suspicion. Alfred had needed Peter to pass this test because the task in hand, the one he had chosen him for, would affect every man woman and child in South Africa and perhaps even the world. Matthew, for his part, had remained ignorant of his impending fate believing that the trip was just another part of the Broederobond or Brotherhood's assessment process, for Matthew, no less than Peter was a member of that secret and pervasive organisation that controlled the levers of power in South Africa.

Matthew had slept easily that night, Peter not at all; not because of his conscience, but because he'd lived the plan over and over in his mind and didn't want to fail. In the pre-dawn darkness the two colleagues had met their guide Frank Plumly in the yard next to the Land Rover.

Alfred eventually rose from his chair and walked to the window. He pulled back the curtains letting in the bright shafts of sunlight. He looked at his protégé and spoke gently in Afrikaans, the only acceptable language of the Brotherhood.

"You acted well and completed your task. Do you have any questions for me, is there anything you want me to tell you?"

Peter contemplated the question, wondering if this too was part of the test. He decided it wasn't. "Why did you want me to kill Matthew?"

"Oh that is not really important. Maybe one day I will tell you. What is important is that you did it. Was it difficult?" asked Alfred without emotion.

"Not as bad as I imagined," was Peter's factual reply. "It would have been easier if he were a black I suppose."

"I can understand that," answered the older man without irony. "Now tell me Peter, why did you shoot him?"

For a moment Peter was confused. "Because you told me to, that you ordered it is enough isn't it?"

"It should be and in this case it was." Alfred returned to his armchair. "For a long time I have been looking for somebody to take on a special task, a task of immense importance. For years I have been seeking the right person and now I have finally found him. You are the chosen one.

I have watched and mentored you for the past years. From the beginning I hoped you would be the right person and so it was. But there could only be one and in a way Matthew surrendered his life for the nation. His sacrifice was your final test of loyalty and obedience. You should not think badly of Matthew he gave a lot to prove your strength and resolve.

Now that I am sure of you we can progress. You are young, only twenty-two," continued Alfred. "That is very important. I need somebody who is young because we, the Brotherhood, are embarking on a project that will take many years, even decades, to come to fruition and the truth is I will probably be dead and with our Maker before it is complete. It is a project that will ensure the continuity of our way of life here in South Africa for generations to come. It will be a heavy burden to carry but a burden for which I believe you are ready. Before I go further I have to warn you that we have passed the point of no return. You have by your actions demonstrated that you are prepared to dedicate your whole life to our cause, to put your country, our people and our organisation, the Brotherhood, before your own life. There is no going back. Do you understand?"

Peter did not hesitate in his response. "I am prepared to give all for my country."

Alfred nodded and smiled. "Tomorrow you will travel with me and we will begin."

Cape Verde Islands
Wednesday 27th March 1963

Peter van Stardan had never heard of the Cape Verde Islands before he'd started his journey with Alfred. Not many people had. Even now he didn't know much except that they were islands in the Atlantic Ocean, somewhere off the West African coast and were controlled by the Portuguese. But Peter van Stardan was having trouble taking in a lot of things at the moment. Up until now the Brotherhood had been a loose organisation, a fraternity that professed loyalty to the Fatherland. Now he was witnessing for the first time the extent to which the organisation's tentacles had spread, the grip it had on South African society and the resources that were at its disposal.

It had taken the combined and co-ordinated efforts of the South African Air Force and Navy to get Alfred Smidt and Peter van Stardan to the islands in three days. An executive jet belonging to the Air Force had taken them from Pretoria, in a circuitous route to an airstrip near Walvis Bay on the coast of South West Africa. A frigate of the South African Navy had sped them across the dead calm South Atlantic waters. It was just after 5am on the 27th March, in darkness, when the ship had dropped anchor in Praia Bay. The Harbour Master was on the waiting custom's launch. The formalities were cursory and swift. The visit was unofficial and would remain unrecorded in official documents.

Casa Negro, the "black house", was not actually black. It was white, a neglected dirty weathered white. Nevertheless the name was appropriate; the house had brought little luck to its numerous owners since it was constructed in 1922. It had been built in a flurry of false optimism, intended to be the centre piece of a massive and profitable vineyard. Whilst the land had the right aspect and the soil was basically good, the water supply from bore holes proved to be both too sparse and too saline. Vines could never flourish in such conditions. As the house changed hands it invariably left each subsequent owner poorer than when they arrived. Now it was a little used Government guesthouse.

The main building, a two story villa topped with undulating red terracotta tiles, badly needed a repaint. It sat in the centre of an expansive and sad looking cobbled courtyard where weeds, indifferent to the lack of water, forced their way between the sandy joints. A high wall surrounded the courtyard and the only entrance was through heavy wooden gates which were now firmly closed and secured by a drop in cross- bar. Inside the villa it was surprisingly cool. The design allowed a through draught, when all the shutters and doors were open, which needed little augmentation from the gently spinning ceiling fans.

Peter van Stardan was seated in a dark wood cushioned armchair, to the left and slightly behind the seat of Alfred Smidt. He allowed his gaze to wander, looking through the veranda doors at the lengthening shadows that were encroaching on the courtyard. They'd been in the room for hours but the day had gone fast and now the sun was swiftly descending in the late afternoon sky.

Alfred spoke. "Two hours and it will be dark. Then we will be able to leave safely."

With Alfred Smidt and Peter van Stardan were two other men, seated opposite in identical chairs. The business of the day had been accomplished in this informal setting that did not truly convey the gravity of the subject matter under discussion. Only Alfred had spoken for South Africa. Peter was there to listen and serve as a living memory of the meeting; there would be no official written record.

Even now when the main business of the day had been completed Peter maintained his silence. Principles had been established that day that were clear and easy for Peter to memorise. It had been agreed beforehand that the world should not know of this meeting but the participants knew that for sure the world would become aware of its consequences.

"Our boat will be in the harbour in just over two hours," said Alfred, "What time do you fly?" His question was directed at Isaac Klein, leader of the other delegation.

"We are guided by the need for security but hope it will be before ten pm. Otherwise we will not be back in Tel Aviv before noon tomorrow. When will you be back in South Africa?"

"We will be cautious. I plan six days. There is no hurry. Our ship will take us to Cape Town, just as if it were on a normal patrol. When people move quickly it tends to attract attention."

The four men were silent for a while, the silence eventually broken by Isaac Klein.

"Our business is concluded and it appears that we have some spare time together. It is not often that high representatives of sovereign states come together in such circumstances. From our discussions it is clear that we will be working closely together for many years so why don't you tell me why you think that our countries have been thrown into this partnership. Why does your country want to join us on this perilous journey?"

Alfred contemplated his answer carefully.

"It was a speech by a British Prime Minister that set us on our course. In February 1960 MacMillan came to my country and in front of our Parliament carried out the great betrayal. He said that a "*Wind of Change*" was blowing over the Continent of Africa. He implied that black men would take over the government of my country. By that he showed his ignorance of our history and depth of our feelings. It didn't matter that when my forefathers arrived in the Cape Colony from Holland, centuries ago, there were no black men living there. No matter that South Africa, a self governing Dominion of the United Kingdom had been amongst the first to join the fight against the Germans, no matter that we had not subjected and slaughtered the black population that had come to our land, as had other Dominions like Canada, New Zealand and Australia, or even America for that matter. He was casting us adrift. We were being abandoned by the Crown that we had loyally served.

For most South Africans that was too much. In 1961 we had declared our self a Republic and withdrawn from the British Commonwealth. We had washed our hands of our dirty connection with Britain. But events elsewhere on the continent were going against us. Colonies to the north were becoming independent; we could see the spectre of Black Nationalism drifting south like a dark cloud. We could see that one day it will be at our door step and it is for this moment that we prepare. We will demonstrate to the world that we are not just another underdeveloped African country. We will stand high as a member of the international community and those countries will have to take us seriously. We have already begun to make our mark. It is not an accident that the world's first heart transplant was carried out in my country. We encouraged and supported Dr Christian Barnard in December 1961. That one operation showed the world we are not just another backward African nation. We refuse, to the last drop of our blood, to be chased from our country by a bunch of uncivilised blacks who will use the land to scratch out a living at subsistence level under corrupt leaders."

"Strong words indeed, there is no doubting your commitment," said Isaac Klein.

"It is the truth. And what about you and your country?" asked Alfred.

"For me it is very simple," began Isaac. "The Jews that walked into the German gas chambers were the last Jews to die without a fight. If there is to be another holocaust we will not be on the receiving end. All that we do now is to ensure our existence and to take what God promised us. The new beginning was difficult enough. We had to expel the British from Palestine. Then we fought two wars just to establish our state of Israel. It is inevitable that we will have to fight more wars just to survive. I suppose it is an irony that a speech by another British Prime Minister set us on our present course. Do you remember the speech that Winston Churchill made in America in 1948? He spoke about an Iron Curtain falling across Europe. Churchill's speech signified the beginning of the Cold War, the realisation that only two superpowers will control this world. We will do all that we can to ensure that the stronger of the two powers supports us. But there is something else. In another part of the speech that went unnoticed by most, Churchill said nobody respects weakness. This is a lesson we have already learnt with the blood of our people. I assure you we will not be weak, we intend to be respected."

"It is good that we both feel so strongly," continued Isaac. "We are motivated to help each other. We in Israel already have the technology. Was it not Einstein, a Jew that made this possible? Was not the Manhattan Project driven by Jewish scientists? That will be our contribution. You have the deposits of uranium and the space to hide and test. Together we will go faster than either can go alone. Soon Israel and South Africa will be the fifth and sixth nuclear powers. Who knows, maybe we will one day find ourselves sitting together on the Security Council of the United Nations. By acting now we secure our States for future generations."

In the fading light of the courtyard the men bade their farewells.

Isaac spoke. "I am sure we will meet again but most probably not in this place. The current Portuguese Government is with us both at the moment but my people tell me that already within Portugal strong forces are on the move. When the Government in Lisbon falls, as it will, Portugal will cease to be a colonial power. You, in South Africa, would do well to look to your borders with Mozambique and Angola. One day South Africa will have hostile neighbours, just like Israel."

BOOK 2
Twenty-five Years Later
Stirling Farm, Okavango Delta, Botswana
Tuesday 1st March 1988

Despite the debilitating African sun, the squat grey vultures hopped about the fringes of the dusty clearing impatiently. They edged ever closer becoming more daring as each minute passed. The smell of death was in their nostrils. They were eager to close on their quarry and start their grizzly work. The structure was not as rickety as it appeared. Four stout, if not straight, poles acted as upright supports for the platform that was made from woven branches and saplings to form a flat surface six-foot clear of the ground. On top of the platform lay the lifeless body of Jomo, facing skyward toward the celestial home of his ancestors, the destination of this his final journey. Jomo's torso bore the regalia of his tribe and clan, his status as a warrior proclaimed by the presence of his asagi and shield, the same asagi and shield that had been presented to him at his initiation such a short time ago. He would need the weapons to prove his status when he stood in front of his forefathers for judgement.

A few paces back, Duncan Murdoch, now in his fortieth year stood straight and upright holding four year old Maggie in his strong arms. The child sensing the occasion clung uncharacteristically to her father, burying her head in the nape of his neck. Elizabeth, abandoning African tradition, stood next to her husband a protective arm around James who despite his nine years hid his head in the folds of her dress and clung tightly to her leg.

Duncan's broad square shoulders and chiselled handsome face betrayed no emotion; for Duncan emotion was not for public display. His austere Scottish upbringing had conditioned his mind to accept hardship alone and without outward display. The only person that ever got to see his true feelings was his beloved Elizabeth. She knew the grief he felt. But Duncan accepted and respected the African communal outpourings: wailing, howls and tears.

Elizabeth had chosen to wear a light coloured cotton dress that tastefully revealed the feminine shapeliness of her body. Only in European culture is black the colour of mourning. Her tight black hair was pulled back into a bunch enhancing the beauty of her high cheek bones and proud face. Even the solemnity of the occasion could not distract from the handsomeness of the couple. Never had black and white looked so natural together.

The ceremony was coming to an end, the men had withdrawn. Bare breasted women, their necks, wrists and ankles weighed down with bulging bands of colourful beads danced around the platform of death creating a din literally intended to wake the slumbering inhabitants of the heavenly home. This was the culture that Elizabeth had been born into but by dint of chance and fortune of war, had abandoned if not for something better then for something different. For those trapped in a single culture it would be hard for them to imagine that Elizabeth could be at home in both worlds. In this respect she was perhaps unique.

"It's our way," said Elizabeth quietly to her husband. "It is important for us. You have your God and we have our ancestors."

Duncan felt the flat of Elizabeth's hand gently rub his back. He whispered, "There is something really wrong with this. I think it is a mistake to dispose of the body till we know the facts. At the very least I would have liked a doctor, a professional doctor, to have had at a chance to help before he died. All I managed to get was soiled samples and I don't know if this is enough."

"My brothers Tembo and Morgan did not struggle to bring Jomo back in the hope of a cure. They brought him back to die amongst his own people and that is what has happened. That he was dying was never in doubt. We Africans know when the end is coming. We do not fight the inevitable. Let us just accept and watch quietly for a little longer."

Duncan felt the requested silence was not for Jomo. He knew that Elizabeth's mind was being cast back to the dark episode of her own father's death, the time when she had held his battered body in her arms and felt his last warm breath on her cheek.

When the women had finished their dance Elizabeth looked toward Duncan. "We should go now."

"What will happen to Jomo's remains?" asked Duncan.

"Till the next full moon and beyond he will lie here. The men will take it in turn to stand guard, to stop scavenging animals taking the body. The carrion alone will be allowed to pluck the flesh away. Over time the sun will dry and bleach the bones white. Only then will the remains be laid to rest in our special place."

The family quietly moved away.

The source of the Okavango River lies deep in the African interior. It twists and turns over the central African Plateau seeking but not finding an outlet to the sea. Finally accepting defeat it butts up to the northern edge of the Kalahari Desert and breaks up into smaller flows becoming an inland delta that soaks away into the porous land. In good years, when rainfall is plentiful in the interior, the delta is a lush oasis covering thousands of square miles on the very edge of one of the most arid deserts in the world. But only a trickle of water had arrived in the past four years. Pools that should have been overflowing were just baked mud. Low hills that should have been islands were just part of the dusty landscape. Failed rains make for a recurring natural disaster for both wildlife and farm stock.

Established commercial farmers built dams and sunk deep bore holes to get them over the worst of the bad years. But Duncan, Elizabeth and the clan never had the chance to get established. For five years there had been nothing but drought. They'd had no opportunity to build a reserve. Their enterprise, their experiment, tottered on the brink of existence.

Duncan, Elizabeth and the children walked slowly back to their house, a structure that came with the land and had been rescued from dilapidation by Duncan's own hands. For years it had been deserted by the original German settlers that had constructed it in the early twentieth century, settlers who had been chased away in the wake of the Great War when Germany had lost its colonial possessions. Elizabeth did not speak till they were near the farmhouse.

"Your God says that seven years of famine will be followed by seven years of plenty, but I do not know if we can wait two more years. Perhaps this is not the place for us. I know we meant well but perhaps it was a mistake to bring so many of my people with us to live here. Perhaps we should not be here at all. Perhaps there is worse to come."

Duncan knew that Elizabeth was constantly concerned for the 150 Matable that Duncan and she had moved from war torn Zimbabwe five years earlier to avoid their annihilation by their Shona enemies. He struggled to find words to reassure her.

"Elizabeth you know that we exist only by the grace of nature in this part of the world. Since time immemorial the rains have failed. We are just unfortunate that it happened so soon after we arrived. And all our bad luck follows from that. If there was work on the farm the boys would not have been forced to go and seek paid employment in the mines and Jomo would still be alive. There is nothing mystical about that. What we have here is our dream but there will always be difficult times. Together we will get over them. I will not give up our dream so easily. When the rains come and the river floods all will be well again, just you wait and see. Imagine if your people had stayed in Zimbabwe. They would probably be dead now, slaughtered or starved to death by a brutal regime. We are free of that. In Okavango there is a future for them and us."

Elizabeth sighed. Duncan continued "And believe me I have not given up trying to find out what happened to Jomo. There was something strange about it."

"And you think your friends in London will give you the answer you're looking for?"

"If what I think is true I'm worried about what it could mean. Now let's get home I want to play with the kids," said Duncan. "James and Maggie don't need this sadness."

Vastrap Military Airbase, Kalahari Desert, South Africa
Monday 7th March 1988

The pilot banked the Executive Lear Jet to the right and made a low pass parallel to the ill-defined concrete strip in the middle of the desert. He needed to get a better view before attempting a landing. He consoled himself with the knowledge that if the strip was not that prominent it was at least very long; designed for much bigger jets taking off in high temperatures. Unfortunately the last few days had been very windy. Sand had drifted to the very edges of the concrete and given all the support buildings a light dusting that was more effective than any camouflage. The passengers in the Lear were tightly strapped into their seats. They strained against the belts to get a view through the plane's circular windows. A tiny black hill stood out against the monotony of the desert beige. The younger one shook his head. Unlike the pilot he felt that the less that could be seen from the air the better.

The pilot completed his circuit and lined up on the runway choosing to make a long shallow approach. The decision for a shallow approach was not for the comfort of the passengers but rather to give him time to react should the mirage effect taint his judgement on his visual landing. Visual landings were just about compulsory at Vastrap, but not because the airfield lacked electronic navigation aids. In fact the airfield boasted some of the most sophisticated and advanced equipment available. It was just rarely switched on. The policy was to keep the electronic signature of the base as small as possible. Even VHF radio communications were kept to a minimum. Nothing was to be done that might attract attention to the site.

Alfred Smidt had never visited Vastrap previously but he knew every detail about the place, down to the last nut and bolt. Vastrap, and the events that were planned to happen there, would vindicate his life's work. He remained driven and would let nothing jeopardise its future.

Alfred Smidt rarely travelled now. The passing years had taken their toll. His obese body, abused by years of excessive alcohol and tobacco, was failing. But worse were the effects on his mind of the constant headaches that changed his moods so suddenly. On good days, in periods of lucidity, he displayed flashes of his once great strategic ability but too often events were becoming blurred and he was prone to lapsing into bouts of almost incoherent babbling. Despite this he remained the unchallenged leader of the Brotherhood.

Smidt knew that what had occurred at Vastrap in recent weeks could jeopardise the future of the project and that is why he and van Stardan deemed the circumstances serious enough for them to risk making the journey and attracting attention to themselves.

The southern Kalahari is arid. Just thousands of square miles of sand and rock which for most of the year is swept bare by scorching winds.

The largest part of the desert lies in the former German colony of South West Africa. When Germany lost the 1st World War they also lost their colonies and South West Africa was passed on to South Africa as a Protectorate. Unlike the other great desert of Africa, the Sahara, the vastness of the Kalahari was not even punctuated by the occasional oasis. Only on the very fringes of the desert did any form of human life exist; the Bushmen, living little more than a pre-historic hunter, gatherer existence. These people would pose no threat to the momentous event that was planned. The very concept of what was going to happen was beyond their imagination.

Vastrap had originally been built as an emergency landing location for South African Air force transport planes that crossed the Kalahari, ferrying men and supplies to the war that raged in southern Angola, an unreported conflict where the South African military was fighting a proxy war for the United States. In actual fact Vastrap had never been used for its intended purpose and now it never would be. All charts and maps that referred to Vastrap were being withdrawn from circulation. Any plane in trouble was going to have to make its own arrangements. Vastrap did not exist as far as the world was concerned.

The logistical effort needed to sustain the base had been a limiting factor in its development. Everything had to be brought to Vastrap, right down to the last drop of drinking water. But its very isolation, and the faultless strata of igneous rock that lay beneath the sands, made it a perfect site for Alfred Smidt's project.

The plane landed smoothly and was guided to a corner of the apron. The pilot shut the engines down. Before the doors were opened, ground technicians were tying canvass covers over the engine intakes to prevent wind blowing corrosive grains of sand into the turbines. Without the engine powered air-conditioning the temperature inside the plane's cabin began to climb dramatically. Beads of sweat were visibly forming tiny rivulets of perspiration on the brows of each passenger even before they had disembarked. Once outside the men felt dry desert air rake at their throats as they took the few steps to the prefabricated administration building, the building that had been all but invisible from the air.

Peter van Stardan followed Alfred Smidt into the air-conditioned conference room. Waiting were the two men they wanted to see, David Liebermann and Jan Kutz. The two men could not have been more different and may have even been considered a comedy duo in other circumstances.

Jan Kutz stood five feet eight at a stretch. At first glance it seemed as if his bulbous head was attached to his flabby and overweight torso without the benefit of an intervening neck. His sand coloured uniform of shorts and tunic was too small and exaggerated his Michelin Man appearance. Bulging arms strained the stitching of his short sleeve shirt. His belly hung flabbily over his hidden belt that struggled to fulfil its function of holding his sagging trousers in place. He removed his desert cap in the presence of Alfred and Peter revealing his close cropped hair and heavy sloping brow that protruded partially concealing sunken eyes that were too close together and connected by one single large eyebrow that stretched the width of his head. The apparition was not appealing. When he spoke it was in gruff tones through clenched tobacco stained teeth that rarely betrayed the glimmer of a smile from his thick cracked lips. Not that he had much to smile about at the moment.

"I have had the building secured as you requested," he grunted by way of greeting. "We will be able to talk freely." Without invitation and with surprising agility he squeezed his bulging rear end into a waiting chair.

The second man, David Liebermann, was lean and stood a more impressive six-foot two inches tall. He had the formal bearing and expression of an intense and humourless German academic. Despite his years in the desert his complexion was pale and wan, visible evidence that his life was totally devoted to his secret and hidden work, often underground. His rimless glasses did nothing to soften or hide his piercing and intense blue eyes. The light well fitting business suit was fresh, the crease in the trousers faultless. The top button of his impeccable white shirt remained fastened and his tie bragged membership of the Royal Society. When he spoke his words were well spaced, his tone emotionless offering little room for compromise.

"As Director of this facility at Vastrap I welcome you," he said offering his hand to both Alfred Smidt and Peter van Stardan in turn. His grip was firm and formal. "Please take a seat. I have arranged refreshments."

His self assured confidence verged on the arrogant and his appointment as director of the nuclear programme had been a difficult decision. It had been thought by some that picking a Jewish South African was a move designed to please the Israelis but this was not true. He was born to a German father and Dutch mother in Berlin. He'd followed in his father's footsteps and become one of the new breed of young quantum scientists that had been spawned by the pioneering work of the Max Plank Institute. Whilst his father was firmly in the camp of the theoretical physicists, David displayed an uncharacteristic practical ability and erred toward experimental and applied work and this is how he found himself working, as a junior with Niels Bohr in Demark during the Second World War. Fortunately for him in this sleepy backwater he'd avoided the wrath of the Nazi anti-Jewish pogroms; in fact with the exception of the 'Jewish Question' David found the philosophy of the Nazi's remarkably in tune with his own thinking.

David's father had been killed on the 25th August 1940 during the first ever air-raid by the British on the German capital. This unfortunate incident had the duel results of denying the Nazi's the opportunity of dealing with David's father and making David anti-British. After the air-raid David's mother went to South Africa, via Portugal, as an exile. When the war ended David, despite being Jewish, could not escape the ramifications of his Nazi sympathies and so joined his mother in South Africa. She died of a sudden stroke less than two weeks after his arrival. With his qualifications and experience David had been quickly identified as a prospective candidate for the South African nuclear programme. With no family he threw himself into his work.

Alfred remained standing. Either disregarding or ignorant of the possible sensitivities of David Liebermann, he put his hands together, lowered his head as he spoke aloud and signified the beginning of the formal meeting with a Christian prayer.

The Brotherhood was founded on deeply held Christian beliefs, to the unknowing a flawed version of Christianity that uniquely existed within the Dutch Reformed Church as practiced in South Africa.

David Liebermann sat expressionless. Alfred Smidt remained standing. Peter van Stardan knew that this was a bad sign – his Chief was about to ramble.

"This is the first time I have felt it necessary to travel such a distance for many years. It is not a journey I have undertaken lightly," said Smidt.

He began pacing the room as he spoke without addressing anyone in particular. "Our organisation, the Brotherhood, was founded in 1910 in reaction to our defeat at the hands of the British in the so called Boer Wars. The founding fathers of the Brotherhood realised that we could not defeat the English in a conventional military struggle. They had to find a different way to wrestle power from the English and so over the next decades they established a secret organisation, an exclusively Afrikaner organisation, an organisation composed of thousands of clandestine lodges throughout our beloved country. The members of the lodges had one objective only, to infiltrate and take over all the important organisations, both political and economic, within our country. Building on the foundations left by the founding fathers our achievements have been outstanding. Our political party, the Nationalist Party, rules strong today. Every Prime Minister of our country for the last fifty years has been a member of the Brotherhood. Most Cabinet Ministers are members, the captains of industry and the leaders of the civil service are part of us. Of course we accept the English or at least the capital they pump into this country. But the English only fool themselves in thinking that they have influence, never mind control, of our country.

There have been errors, unforgivable errors. Our biggest failure was to allow the English to drag us into the Second World War. Our natural position would have been to side with the Germans in 1939. They at least recognised the truth that not all races are equal. It is unforgivable that our pure Afrikaner blood was spilt defending the false cause of democracy. The only mitigation was that the Second World War left England so weak that their political reign in Africa was catastrophically damaged. This eventually enabled us to achieve our ambition of a true

Republic. Only then were we free to address the second great threat to our existence, the Kaffir.

Of course we cannot be stupid in this matter. We need the Kaffir in the same way as our forefathers needed oxen to pull their ploughs. Our masterstroke is the policy of Apartheid which allows the true leaders of this country, the Afrikaners, to achieve their destiny but also allows the black African to develop at his own pace, which everybody knows is at no pace at all.

We have beaten the English and confined the black man. Now we are ready to take our place on the world stage. For this to happen we must have real physical power. History has too often demonstrated that the meek do not inherit the earth. And so it is in this project that our hope rests. Once the project is complete we will stand amongst the strongest as equals. Like the United States, Britain, France, Russia, China and Israel we will be a nuclear power and our voice will be heard loud and clear."

Alfred Smidt stopped pacing and turned to face the conference table. "Nearly twenty-five years ago we embarked upon this journey. We have come a long way and are now at a critical point, on the cusp of success. But recent incidents have jeopardised that success. Explain to me what happened and what you are doing to rectify the situation." Alfred Smidt finally took his chair.

"I will begin by summarising the programme," began David Liebermann, "As you are well aware we now not only have the theoretical technology to build nuclear weapons but we also have most of the necessary equipment and materials. Specifically we have increasing supplies of good quality highly enriched uranium. But no matter how good our technology or how diligent our manufacturing process we actually need information on how a device will work in practice and that kind of information is not actually available in the public domain. The only information we currently have on actual tests came from Israel who got it second hand from the French. The French no longer pass on this important information. So as it stands, both Israel and South Africa are desperately in need of test results and the only option is to carry out our own tests. It is impossible to carry out tests in Israel. So it falls on South Africa to provide the venue for the test programme and that is what Vastrap is, a nuclear assembly and test site.

Nuclear powers have tested devices in the air, on the surface, underground and even underwater. Because of the clandestine nature of our operation the only option open to us is an underground test because that is the one that is most likely to escape the attention of other nations.

Today, as we sit here, we have almost completed digging our shafts deep into the earth and we are beginning the process of assembling and arming our test device. In the last few weeks materials have been brought to this site and work has begun on the assembly of the devices.

Now to the current problem. The basic "explosive material" we use is highly enriched uranium. Some of our stock comes from Israel. The balance is produced in South Africa. Highly enriched uranium is radioactive and handling it is delicate and dangerous work. Some weeks ago we discovered that several of the men were showing signs of radiation sickness. Because the monitoring equipment was faulty we lost valuable time identifying that the sick people all worked in the underground assembly facility. Eventually we identified the source of the radiation leak to cracks in the protective shields on the transport pods. The technical solution was relatively simple and has been successfully carried out. Unfortunately a number of people have already died and several more are suffering from radiation exposure. We have isolated the sick people in our small hospital but are expecting more deaths. We estimate that about twenty people are affected."

Peter van Stardan spoke for the first time. "You realise if the outside world discovers that people are suffering from radiation sickness it can only come to one conclusion?"

"I do," replied David Liebermann. "This is why we have tried to be so careful in isolating those that are sick."

"But you have not been completely successful in this?" asked Peter van Stardan.

"This is not a question for me," responded Liebermann. "I must refer you to the person responsible for the security of the installation." He turned to Jan Kutz.

A curled lip that passed as a feeble smile was the Security Chief's immediate response. When he spoke his speech was laboured.

"The dead have been buried deep into the bedrock and covered in concrete, just as we were instructed. The same will happen to the others as they die." Jan Kutz offered no more.

Peter van Stardan pressed. "I believe one man is not accounted for. Is this correct?"

The Security Chief continued. "One man is unaccounted for, an African labourer. He was sick and in isolation but he disappeared one night. The doctor says that he has had a fatal dose of radiation and will certainly die. He most probably wandered off into the desert. We're looking for his body. The matter is under control."

"I do not believe it is under control," interjected Liebermann. "The same night the victim disappeared two men from the main camp also went missing, friends of the victim I understand. I think it more probable that the sick man and his friends escaped the camp. That is potentially dangerous."

"If one dying kaffir escapes from the camp how dangerous can that be?" defended Jan Kutz. "Radiation sickness is not contagious is it?"

"No, it is not," replied Liebermann. "But let me explain to you, again. Radiation sickness is clearly recognisable and the remains of the body will continue to be radioactive for a very long time indeed. Even the man's excrement will be radioactive."

"Excrement, what's that?" asked Jan Kutz.

"Shit to you," replied Liebermann, barely able to disguise his sarcasm.

"If anybody does discover his radioactive body they'll just think he worked in one of the uranium mines. You do know that South Africa is one of the biggest exporters of uranium in the world?"

Liebermann didn't try to hide his exasperation. "A different kind of radiation! To put it simply, there are three types of uranium: uranium ore, the material that is mined from the ground, enriched uranium, the fuel used in power stations and finally there is highly enriched uranium, the type that is only used for nuclear bombs. One test on the body of the sick man will tell the world that South Africa has an atomic bomb or is at least working on producing one. You need to get the body back. I cannot be more explicit." Liebermann sat back in his chair and looked up at the ceiling.

After a long pause Alfred Smidt spoke, his words unambiguous, "You will get the body of the sick man back or you will face the wrath of the Brotherhood. Is that clear enough for you?"

Jan Kutz was shaking. He was aware what a threat from the Brotherhood meant.

Peter van Stardan added, "You will also eliminate the two men that escaped with him. We want no witnesses."

Foreign and Commonwealth Office, London
Tuesday 29th March 1988

It was just over twenty-five years since the Israelis and South Africans had first met on Cape Verde, a fact that would have frightened the people at the Foreign and Commonwealth Office had they known. Today the location was less remote but the people just as secretive. Stuart Cameron had left his office in Century House, Headquarters for MI6, south of the River Thames and walked along the Embankment, crossing the river at Westminster Bridge. Midway across he'd stopped and looked towards the riverside terrace of the Houses of Parliament. It was a fine spring day and the sun had coaxed a few members of parliament into the daylight, away from the dark murky corridors that was their usual habitat. Stuart Cameron was a man born into the establishment. He could have chosen a career in politics and been on that terrace now. He was glad he wasn't. What he disliked was not so much the insincerity and shallow self-promoting motives of the average politician, it was more the absolute inability of a run of the mill politician to influence anything that was meaningful. Parliament was no place for a man of practicality; he was glad he'd chosen the Army to begin his career and gone on from there.

He continued his walk threading his way through the throngs of tourists to Parliament Street. He flashed his security pass as he entered the Foreign and Commonwealth Office, a grandiose building constructed at a time when Britain was a great Imperial power but currently inhabited by people who fought relentlessly to exercise some influence on world affairs when their credibility was in continuous decline.

A prim looking secretary led Stuart towards the dark stained office door. Inside Sir Basil Parker Smythe was waiting. Sir Basil was as pretentious as his name implied; dignified, late fifties, tall but overweight, square shoulders, impeccably groomed, immaculate Savile Row suit, glistening black shoes and the obligatory diagonally striped blue and red tie announcing his old-Etonian pedigree.

"Ah, Stuart, welcome, come in, come in. Have you met young Ralph here? He'll be taking the notes. He's cleared to the highest level; father was a colonel in the Guards you know."

Stuart felt Sir Basil was more concerned with his assistant's background than his ability. He sat at the embossed leather topped meeting table. Sir Basil and young Ralph sat opposite. Ralph opened his secretary's shorthand notebook.

"Tea?" offered Sir Basil.

"Do you have coffee?" asked Stuart.

"Sorry, its morning coffee and afternoon tea here, tradition you know. Never mind let's get on with things."

"That's fine," answered Stuart, "I'm keen to find out how I can help you."

"Not so much help," replied Sir Basil, "but I thought it would be both timely and appropriate if we had an exchange of information. Bit of liaison never hurt eh? Don't want a right hand, left hand situation developing do we?"

"Fine," answered Stuart mentally translating Sir Basil's words into 'real speak'. Something was going on and Sir Basil didn't have a clue. He was hoping Stuart and MI6 might be able to enlighten him.

"I'll open the batting shall I?" said Sir Basil. He didn't wait for Stuart's reply. "Very dynamic world situation at the moment. Let me explain."

Stuart settled into his seat. Sir Basil, like most civil servants liked to talk.

"The Cold War is at end game. We've won although not all the Soviets believe it yet. They're going to pull out of Afghanistan before long. What do you think about that then Stuart?"

"That's good news," replied Stuart. "I'd heard similar. I just hope we don't end up filling the vacuum. Our track record in Afghanistan is not that good."

"I can't see any circumstances where British troops will be operating there. North West Frontier and all that is a thing of the past. Eh?"

"Hopefully."

"Polish Pope proving to be no bad thing, destabilising the Polish Communist Party. Bit of contagion taking place in Hungary. We're doing our bit to fan the embers, quietly of course."

"Of course," nodded Stuart.

"The Americans are busy around the Pacific, recently forged a promising alliance with the Chinese, potential to split international Marxism further."

"Yes I've been reading the newspapers." It was Stuart's way of saying he was being told nothing new. "I would say though," continued Stuart, "I think it was Churchill quoted an old Chinese proverb "*beware the sleeping tiger*". Churchill was always worried about the potential of China. He said if they ever got their act together they could take over the world."

Sir Basil tipped his head back and laughed. "Not much chance of that old boy, not in our life time. They are definitely division two and not set for promotion. Churchill didn't get everything right you know?"

Stuart was getting bored and wondering when Sir Basil was going to get to the point.

Sir Basil continued. "Then there's the Pershing and cruise missiles being deployed here. And the Americans have got a big new project underway; call it the Strategic Defence Initiative, mirrors in space and all that science fiction guff."

Stuart cut in. "I'm fully aware of all of that."

Sir Basil was quiet for a while, as if thinking. Ralph's pencil came to a halt as he finally caught up.

"Just say it," prompted Stuart.

Sir Basil took a breath. “The Russian communists want a quid pro quo before they throw in the towel, a face saver so to speak. The Americans have agreed. They think it could be in their interest too. They’re putting a bit of pressure on us.”

“So?”

“They want a win in South Africa. An end to Apartheid, black votes and all that. They are even calling for the release of Nelson Mandela would you believe!”

“Well it’s going to happen in the end. Maybe not the release of Mandela, he could die in prison, but the rest will. All that is up for discussion is the number of people that get killed before the inevitable happens.”

“Stuart, you’re missing the point. South Africa is in our sphere of influence. Nothing to do with the Americans. We’ve been there a long time, generations. Why my own family have vineyards in Stellenbosch. This could be a disaster all round.”

“Oh, sorry,” said Stuart. “I didn’t realise the magnitude of the situation. Your holiday home is under threat.”

Sir Basil’s face was puffed and red now. “That’s unfair Stuart. This is important. It’s not a personal matter. I know a lot of good people in South Africa.”

“White ones?” asked Stuart.

Sir Basil turned his attention to Ralph. “Are you writing this down?”

Ralph looked up with a smile. “Yes, I am.”

“Well don’t you stupid boy. Have you no gumption. Whatever happened to discretion? Get out.”

Ralph got up to go.

“Leave your notebook,” said Sir Basil.

Ralph put the notebook and pencil on the table and turned to leave.

Sir Basil shook his head. “Ralph?”

Ralph turned to look at his boss, a glimmer of hope in his eyes. “Yes.”

“Take your pencil!”

Stuart was the first to speak and break the silence. “The Americans may be thinking that South Africa is a low cost for the end of the Cold War. But there is a potential problem.”

“What are you talking about? The strategic position at the tip of Africa? The mineral wealth of the country?” asked Sir Basil.

“Potentially worse than that,” replied Stuart. “I wouldn’t be too keen to turn the country over to an unknown, possibly radical, leadership. The South Africans have been working with the Israelis for years. Now whilst we don’t have any hard and fast evidence we think the South Africans may be close to developing a nuclear weapon.”

“Oh fuck,” said Sir Basil with an uncharacteristic slip into base language, the repercussions immediately apparent to him. “Every African state has fallen into chaos after independence. Independent African countries inevitably end up in the hands of some radical *“tin pot”* dictator.

We can't allow someone like that to have an atomic bomb to play with! This could be a game changer. Better tell me what you know."

Stuart was quiet for a while as he decided how much he would disclose. He put both his hands palm down flat on the table. "It's as I said; not quite common knowledge but certainly a given in my circles that the Israelis and the South Africans have been building atomic bombs."

"What! Are you saying the Israelis have the "bomb" too?"

"Yes certainly. They deny it but we know they have nuclear weapons. The Americans have even coined a new phrase to describe the Israeli policy; it's called "*Plausible Deniability*".

Sir Basil cut in. "You're mistaken or exaggerating the situation. The Israelis have a civil nuclear programme. We know about that. They even have a power station; I think it's called Demona, somewhere in a remote desert. It's all above board. The Americans do regular checks and issue reports that they share with us."

"Well you're partially right," said Stuart. "It's actually all above ground. At least the civil programme is. The military development takes place underground, directly below the Demona reactor. You have to admire the Israelis. What better place to hide a military installation than below a civil one? I could do some delving and get more detail for you."

"What can I do in the interim?" asked Sir Basil. "The Americans are indicating they are going to put pressure on the South African Government quite soon."

"Play for time, stall them. But keep it under your hat for as long as you can."

Stirling Farm, Okavango Delta, Botswana
Wednesday 30th March 1988

Elizabeth was standing by the kitchen window when she noticed the lights in the distance. For a moment her heart lifted. Perhaps Duncan had changed his plan and decided not to overnight in Gaborone. Despite being close to the Kraal, the traditional African compound where her family lived, she always felt a little uncomfortable when it was just her and the children alone in the farmhouse. That is why her twin brothers, Tembo and Morgan, had agreed to stay in the farmhouse with her; she knew Duncan would be pleased to see them there. She dried her hands and walked out on to the stoop. Through the darkness she saw the lights veer off to the left away from the track, heading deeper into the scrub. It was after eleven, too late for any normal caller. She could only think it might be game hunters. Morgan and Tembo joined her outside.

"They are not good hunters," said Morgan. "They are the type that like to dazzle animals with halogen lights and shoot them when they are mesmerized and defenceless."

Elizabeth nodded. She knew Duncan didn't like this kind of hunter either. This was not sport; the animals didn't stand a chance, it was just slaughter.

"It is not as if the hunters want the meat for food," added Tembo. "They just chop off the head for a trophy. Sometimes if they bag a big cat they skin it and leave the carcass to rot."

Most Africans still had trouble coming to terms with people who killed just for the fun of it.

"You could have been out there to greet them," mused Elizabeth as she returned to the living room.

"Lovemore and Tanzari will know to keep out of their way," replied Morgan.

Women from the Kraal had collected sufficient wood for Lovemore and Tanzari to keep the fire burning through the hours of darkness. There was enough to keep animals away. All Lovemore and Tanzari had to do was stay awake, ensure the flames danced and keep the earthly remains of Jomo company. It was an important but not arduous task, a task shared by all the initiated men of the Kraal. They had been glad to step in for Morgan and Tembo whilst they stayed with their sister in the farmhouse. The death of Jomo had been more poignant for Lovemore and Tanzari than others because they were the same age. All three had grown up together and been initiated into manhood at the same time. They were brothers in more than spirit.

Because the vehicle approached from behind raised ground, they heard the engine of the Land Cruiser before they saw the lights. They were already on their feet when they were caught in the powerful beams. Blinded they tried to shield their eyes with cupped hands. They made no move to escape. Danger did not normally come from men in this area of the Okavango. The vehicle came to a halt. Over the noise of the engine they heard a door slam shut. A moment later the driver killed the powerful roof mounted spots, leaving the more manageable dipped beams on. Gradually Lovemore and Tanzari's eyes adjusted to the light and they were able to see the Remington rifle pointing at them. It was clear there was no point in attempting to run.

The driver joined his companion. He carried a pistol and was shorter than his companion with the rifle. Both were dressed in safari suits and wore floppy bush hats.

"Just as they said in the bottle store," said the short one to his companion. Their accents were unmistakably South African. "We couldn't have asked for better."

"Who is on that thing?" asked the tall one, pointing to the death platform with the barrel of his rifle.

"It is our brother," said Lovemore. "We are sitting with him till he is ready to go to our ancestors."

"What happened to him?" asked the short one.

"He had been away working but got sick and came back here to die," replied Tanzari.

The South Africans looked at each other and smiled. "That's what we wanted to hear."

The short one went to the back of the pickup and returned with a thick plastic body bag. He threw it at the feet of Lovemore and Tanzari.

"Put what's left of him in this," he ordered.

"You will stop him joining the Spirits," responded Lovemore.

The tall one raised his rifle and clicked the safety to off. "Do it or you'll be joining the Spirits sooner than you expected."

Lovemore picked up the body bag and walked towards the platform. Tanzari followed and shinned up one of the supporting poles on to the platform. Minutes later Lovemore and Tanzari were carrying the body bag containing the half decomposed body of Jomo to the Land Cruiser. As carefully as they could they placed what was left of Jomo into the back of the vehicle.

The two Africans faced their assailants. "It is a bad thing that you do," said Lovemore.

"Don't worry.....," said the one with the pistol as he raised the weapon and shot Lovemore in the forehead. He immediately turned to Tanzari and pulled the trigger again, "...you'll see your brother very soon."

Both men laughed.

"Quickly search them for papers," said the driver. "Then let's get out of here."

It was mid-morning when Duncan drove up the track and the farmhouse came into view. He could see something was wrong. A throng of Africans from the Kraal were milling around the garden and a

Botswana police car was parked on the hard standing. As he got closer the crowd turned to face his approaching car. Elizabeth broke free from their midst and ran towards him. He pulled to a halt and got out of the vehicle to catch Elizabeth as she fell into his arms tears streaming down her face.

Aldermaston Biological Testing Facility, Berkshire, England
Thursday 26th May 1988

"So what's the big deal?" asked Dr Stanley Pendleton.

"That," replied Dr Susan Aitkins, pointing to a pile of yellow plastic covers that were in reality aprons, the type of heavy lead lined aprons worn by radiologists in every X-ray department in the country. "Or what's wrapped in the aprons that is."

The two scientists stood in a small laboratory that occupied a tiny part of the giant Aldermaston establishment. The name plate on the door of the laboratory read *"Compliance and Forensic Studies Section"*.

"Tell me," said Dr Pendleton.

"A package came to us yesterday. Apparently it has been lying in some Police Forensic laboratory in London for some time. They got it from some chap in Foreign and Commonwealth who in turn had gotten it from a mate of his in Africa who is investigating an unexplained death. All a bit woolly really."

"What exactly is it Susan?" asked Dr Pendleton.

"It's a sample of excrement from a dead man!" replied Susan. "Not the type of stuff we normally work on here. But it gets better. The police chappies did their thing, all the conventional stuff including toxicology. They found nothing much except that there appeared to be raised levels of iodine in the blood that was trapped within the samples. That in itself would give no indication of the cause of death and so they sort of lost interest. That was until some graduate trainee got involved. He'd been reading how iodine in tablet form can protect people who have been exposed to nuclear radiation; specifically it reduces the incidence of damage to the thyroid. He managed to get hold of a Geiger-counter and ran it over the sample and hey presto, the sample is in a lead container and on its way here *post haste*."

"And what have you got so far? I hope it's something to make my trip worthwhile."

"Oh I think so," replied Susan. "The sample was definitely radioactive – not dangerously so, but never the less radioactive. Now I know the sample's small and I can't be one-hundred percent sure at the moment but, wait for this, indications are that the person that produced the sample died from radiation sickness induced by exposure to uranium 235, most probably weapons grade!"

"Wow, that's not good. Better get me the name of the chap at Foreign and Commonwealth. Meanwhile see what else you can find. And well done!

Zodiac House, Church Square, Pretoria
Friday 3rd June 1988

A cold front from the Antarctic drove a stiff breeze that assured the noon sun was not going to add much warmth to the day even though the sky was clear. A few visitors milled around Church Square but few lingered longer than was necessary to walk quickly around the formal gardens and take a picture of the Paul Kruger monument. The Square, a central tourist attraction, could have been magnificent. It was surrounded by many fine period buildings but planners, as they are apt to do, had allowed a national treasure to be tarnished by granting planning permission for contemporary structures that somehow just did not complement what already existed.

Zodiac House was just such a contemporary building. Reaching eighteen stories and constructed from grey concrete and glass, it added nothing of architectural interest to the area. Its only redeeming feature was that it was so bland that, despite its size, few people even noticed it. This dubious quality had not gone unobserved. The first sixteen floors were occupied by a collection of commodity traders, international bankers, lawyers and accountants. The top two floors, only accessible by a specially coded lift, were occupied by the Brotherhood. Not that they advertised their occupancy. Casual enquirers would have been hard pressed to discover their presence. "Central but anonymous," had been Alfred Smidt's comment as he'd signed the lease.

Peter van Stardan's corner office was on the seventeenth floor. The two exterior walls were almost entirely glass and afforded magnificent views. Peter stood at the windows and looked down into Church Square, his mind not on the scenery.

For years he had shadowed Alfred closely and wasn't allowed to make a significant decision on his own. But as time passed more of the day to day responsibility for the running of the nuclear programme had fallen on him. The apprenticeship had indeed been a long one but Peter always had the reassurance that he could 'bounce' any awkward questions off his boss - until recently. Of late Alfred had been difficult to get hold of even when he was just sitting in the office one floor above. As a result Peter often had the dilemma of deciding if he was to take immediate action on some point or hang on till Alfred was ready to see him. Now was one of those moments.

Peter fingered the two dirty cardboard identity cards and looked at the typed letter lying in front of him, hardly able to believe what he was reading. "Is there no end to their incompetence?" he thought to himself. "How could I have been so stupid as to have left something so important in the hands of that idiot Jan Kutz? I won't be making that mistake again." The incident had confirmed his worst fears about Kutz' ability. He'd waited two days to see Alfred, that was already too long. He was going to take action, now!

The phone on his desk rang. He scooped up the receiver. His secretary spoke.

"Mr. van Stardan I have the number you requested. It is on the private line." The secretary didn't wait for a response; the line clicked.

"Peter?" the male voice was familiar.

"Eric, good to hear your voice. Thank you for taking my call so quickly."

"Ah, always a pleasure to hear from you?"

Peter explained his problem.

"You should have come to me in the first place," said Eric. "Did they manage to get themselves caught?"

"No but they did manage to eliminate the wrong people."

"Whites?"

"No."

"Thank God for small mercies. It shouldn't attract too much attention then. Now what can I do for you?"

"Get the right people," replied Peter.

"Send me what information you have. Then leave it to me."

Van Stardan hung up. He hadn't wanted to involve BOSS, the Bureau of State Security. They were too independent and had a habit of 'going over the top' but he saw no alternative.

Stirling Farm, Okavango Delta, Botswana
Sunday 12th June 1988

It was designated a seasonal grass strip. Sometimes, in normal years, it was unusable due to water logging but just now it was not much more than a stretch of hardened and cracked mud with a wind sock. The twin engine Cessna circled to allow the pilot to get his bearings and make sure the landing space was clear of obstructions. Ground control and landing permission were unheard of concepts at this landing strip. If it looked okay from the air then the pilot could land.

As the wheels made contact with the ground a vortex of dust swirled behind the plane and quickly coalesced into a cloud that hung in the listless air. The pilot taxied to within a few yards of Duncan's battered Land Rover.

Long gone was the time when Duncan felt the urge to salute his visitor, the man who had once been his commanding officer. Their relationship was past that stage, now they embraced as friends.

"Good to see you Duncan," said Stuart Cameron. "I'm sorry it's taken so long for me to get here."

"Not as if you're around the corner," replied Duncan, "It's a shame your visit will be so short, but its good see you again. By the way, what are you now? Almost a general I suppose?"

"Not quite, but I'm working on it, replied Stuart with a smile. "But for this visit I'm just a civilian, a tourist if you get my drift." Stuart looked Duncan in the eye. "I've come because I have news about the package you sent and I really need to speak with Tembo and Morgan if that's possible."

Duncan nodded. "I thought as much."

"I'm sorry about what happened to your boys. I know how you feel about them. You must be cut up."

"It's worse for Elizabeth," Duncan answered. "Things were difficult enough before the shootings."

"What's the problem?"

"You'll see on the way to the farm. Come on let's get going."

As a junior Lieutenant Cameron had taken to the young Private Murdoch immediately, recognising something in him that others had not. Cameron had been devastated that his testimony had earned Duncan a life sentence in a Court Martial during the Aden campaign and he'd worked hard in the following years to rectify the situation. Not that Duncan bore a grudge – not now. He respected the man's integrity.

"Let me sort the plane out first," said Stuart turning to the pilot who'd just walked over to them. "I'll be back here in about four or five hours. Can you find something to do to amuse yourself?"

"No probs," replied the pilot. "I'm used to hanging about."

"The limousine is not up to much," said Duncan pointing to the Land Rover, "But it's not that far and I thought you'd see more this way."

Duncan drove slowly over the poorly made tracks that served as roads. It was clear to even the casual observer that the land was parched. Apart from a few straw-like clumps, the grass was non-existent and the cloudless sky offered no promise of rain and fresh growth. Stuart saw the groups of long horned African cattle, clustered under leafless Acacia trees, seeking shade from the relentless heat, sagging skin barely covering their protruding bones. They passed an individual cow that had lost the will to live and sat, collapsed on her haunches, fully exposed to the sun, head bowed, eyes dull and lifeless, as if willing on the relief of death. The men travelled in silence.

Duncan turned off the road on to the rutted track that ran a kilometre to the farmhouse and stopped the vehicle on a dusty patch adjacent to the house.

Elizabeth had seen them approaching and was waiting on the stoop.

"How's my Princess?" asked Stuart hugging Elizabeth.

She laughed.

"Welcome to my palace," she said with mock sincerity. "I hope you survive the experience. It hasn't changed much since you were last here. Still no air-conditioning, only fly screens and mosquito nets. No respite from the heat, even at night. Being royal doesn't confer many luxuries in this part of the world."

"Don't change it," replied Stuart. "You'd ruin my dream. You have a piece of paradise here."

"It doesn't feel like that at the moment," she replied. "But let's get you cooled down with a beer and then we can talk. Tembo and Morgan will be along soon."

Twenty minutes later Tembo and Morgan arrived and the five of them settled into wicker chairs on the stoop.

"Where are the children?" asked Stuart.

"At the Kraal," replied Elizabeth.

"They're just as happy there as here," added Duncan.

"I hope I'll see them before I leave," said Stuart. "It's great how you live here."

Duncan spoke. "The set up's the same as when you were last here. Elizabeth me and the kids live in the farmhouse. Morgan and Tembo live with the rest of the clan in the Kraal. They've made it a real African home; roundavals, stockade, cattle pens, the lot. They grow their own corn cobs and some ground nuts when they can."

"Is that enough to keep the place viable?" asked Stuart.

"No," replied Duncan. "We need to do a bit of commercial farming for cash. The land is not that good for crops; cotton and tobacco are out of the question. Rearing beef cattle is the best way of generating cash. But that's not too good at the moment."

"I noticed," replied Stuart. "Last time I was here it was so green and there was a watering hole, almost a lake in front of the house."

"That's long dried up. The only water we have now is from our deepest borehole and we don't know how long that will hold out."

"What are the prospects?"

"The rains that were supposed to fall in November over Angola totally failed and it's too late now: we're into the dry season. It'll be another six months at the earliest before we see any worthwhile water."

"Is that why some of the boys have been going away to get jobs."

"It is," replied Elizabeth. "We'd have been bankrupt without the cash they sent back. But now three of them are dead and it's a worse disaster."

"I want to talk about that, but first I want Tembo and Morgan to tell me their stories."

Morgan began. "Jomo was the keenest. He was the one who wanted to go. Really he shamed me and Tembo to go with him."

Tembo nodded his agreement.

Morgan continued. "He wanted to go and work in the mines. He thought we could earn good money in South Africa and it would help the farm. We got a bus to Gaborone and then another to Plumtree. We tried to get work at the coal mines at Hwange but there was nothing there for us. At the border we got a ride on a lorry to Kimberly. We thought there might be work in the diamond mines but we were unsuccessful again. It was there that a man told us that there was work in a new mine in the middle of the Kalahari. We laughed at first. Everybody knows there are no big mines in the Kalahari. But the man introduced us to an Afrikaner gang-master, a real old fashioned Boer."

Tembo took over.

"The gang-master agreed to take Morgan and me immediately but said Jomo was too small. We told him he had to take all of us or none of us. He agreed in the end. So it was our fault in a way that he died."

"I doubt that," replied Stuart. "Carry on."

"The gang-master put us in a hostel for a couple of days, till he had enough people to fill a truck. We drove for nearly two days in a covered wagon. It was very uncomfortable and it was a long time between food and fuel stops. We couldn't see where we were going; it was all strange to us. We just knew from the sun that we were generally travelling towards the West."

Duncan broke in, "Didn't you ask?"

"We were just told that it was a new mine and the location was a secret for commercial reasons. Even the big commercial prospectors keep their finds secret for as long as they can. It's not unusual. We arrived at a camp at the edge of a town at the end of the second day. It was a bit strange. It was more like an army base than a mining depot. We stayed for two days and then were herded onto more trucks one evening. They told us we were going to drive to the mine overnight because it was too hot in the desert during the day. We didn't like that because we know it's dangerous to drive in the desert at night. It's too easy to get lost. But we felt better when we found we weren't the only truck; we were part of a big convoy, maybe fifty trucks or so. All of them were painted sand colour and there was no company writing on them. We set off just after dark. It was a long journey. We went quite fast but even so we didn't arrive till the next morning. That is when we got our real introduction."

"What do you mean?" asked Stuart.

"As soon as we got there we could see it was not a normal mining operation," replied Morgan. "There were lots of guards – too many. It was more like a military camp. Our gang-master told us it was because they were digging where there was an old South African military airbase. We were hoarded into a hanger and had to stand in line in front of a couple of white boss men. Jomo, Tembo and I were standing together. A man came along the line. He was angry and complained that Jomo was too scrawny for the mining work and that they'd have to find something for him to do in the assembly plant. We said we didn't want to be split up but he ignored us.

Tembo and I were given beds in a dormitory together. Jomo was moved to a different billet. We didn't see much of him after that. We were just put to work."

"What work were you doing?" asked Stuart.

Tembo and I had to work in a huge covered hall. It was big although it didn't look much from the outside. They were sinking two shafts deep into the bed rock. We had to take turns down the shafts digging with pneumatic drills. The rock was really hard and the boss men were always complaining, trying to make us go faster. The conditions were bad."

"In what way?" asked Stuart.

"We had to work twelve hour shifts, seven days a week. The work was hard, the food rubbish, the bosses really unfriendly and we couldn't even have a proper wash when we finished our shift."

"Why?" asked Stuart.

"They told us they had to bring all the water to the camp by tanker and so it was rationed. Two minutes only in the communal shower at the end of our shift."

"If it was so bad why didn't you leave?"

"A lot wanted to leave believe me. But they told us we had contracts and we had to fulfil them. We couldn't run away because we were in the middle of the desert."

"Tell me what happened to Jomo."

"As I said we didn't see that much of Jomo," continued Morgan. "Once when we did see him he told us he worked in an underground factory. He said he was a cleaner there, that they were mad about cleaning, everything had to be spotless all the time. We joked with him that he'd got the good job and we'd swop our work any day for a bit of cleaning. Then one morning Tembo and I were on shift and alarms went off all over the place. It was the only time we stopped work on the shafts we were sinking. Everybody had to go to their billets and wait. Late in the afternoon one of the bosses came round and told us there had been a chemical spill in the factory but everything was okay. We were all given pills to take and we had to have showers. It was the only time we had showers when the water wasn't restricted. We were happy about that. All our work clothes were taken from us and replaced. Even our billets were hosed down.

We went back to work next morning and everything seemed fine. It was a few days later that rumours began to spread that some of the people that worked in the factory were getting ill. It was nearly a week before we found out that Jomo was one of the sick. By then we'd heard that some of those that were sick had died. We made enquiries about Jomo but they would not let us see him or even tell us how he was."

Tembo took over the talking. "We thought there was something really bad about the place and decided to get out. We knew that Jomo had been taken to the camp infirmary so one night we sneaked in and took him. He was really sick and could hardly talk but he did say he was dying and wanted to go home. We didn't really have a plan. We just carried him to where a return convoy was assembling. We hid inside the empty tank of one of the water tankers and the convoy set off. The next morning, when there were signs of civilisation, we got away from the convoy and came back here by bus. It took a long time but Jomo was determined not to die till we got back. You know the rest."

"Well, what do you think?" asked Duncan turning his attention to Stuart.

"First tell me what happened here, when you got back. About the two boys that were killed."

Elizabeth broke in. "Unfortunately I know this story only too well. I will leave you. I need to go to the Bottle Store. I'll be back soon."

"I'm sorry, am I driving you away?" asked Stuart.

"No," replied Elizabeth. "Tembo and Morgan normally go around this time. They pick up the bits and pieces we want and any post. It's only a couple of kilometres"

Tembo and Morgan looked disappointed.

"Don't look so sad little brothers," said Elizabeth. She looked at Stuart. " They drink a couple of beers and play chequers with the old men but think I don't know about it. They can miss their treat today. Duncan, give me the keys for the Land Rover."

"You really do drive that thing?" asked Stuart.

"Why are you so surprised? Now tell me are you chauvinist or are you prejudiced. Is it because I'm a woman or because I'm black, or maybe it's a little of both?" Elizabeth wagged a naughty finger at Stuart, a sign of their comfortable relationship that they could joke in such a way. Nevertheless Stuart blushed. Elizabeth smiled, feigning indignity as she went into the house. The others laughed.

"Better get back to what I am good at," said Stuart. "Tell me about the shootings."

Duncan began. "I was away from the farm. I was in Gaborone, dropping off your package at the British Embassy. So it's better if Morgan or Tembo tell you."

Tembo began, "I suppose Morgan and I were lucky. We were staying in the farmhouse to keep Elizabeth company whilst Duncan was away."

"Why was that lucky?" asked Stuart.

They heard Elizabeth start the Land Rover.

"Because it was actually our turn to watch over Jomo's remains that night."

Elizabeth pulled away and steered the Land Rover onto the track.

"Did anybody know you were with Elizabeth?"

"No," replied Tembo. "Everybody thought we were watching Jomo. We even came back from the bottle store early for our duty."

The rear of the Land Rover bounced down the track.

"You do realise that you two could have been the intended targets!" said Stuart.

Tembo and Morgan raised their eyebrows in surprise. "Why?" they asked in unison.

The image would be indelibly fixed in Duncan's mind. The ground under the Land Rover rose 'dome like' before it burst in a giant eruption. The Land Rover itself lifted clear of the ground and was thrown into the air as if weightless. The sound of the explosion arrived a millisecond before the shock wave hit the stoop knocking everyone to the ground. A mushrooming ball of smoke and flame unfolded above the now burning and twisted remains of the vehicle that had slumped back to the ground and settled into the newly formed crater. The explosion was deafening. It took a few seconds for everybody to get back on their feet. They stared motionless, trying to take in what had happened, as shards of glass and bits of metal fell all around.

Duncan let out a piercing scream *"ELIZABETH!"*

The plane had left the grass airstrip a little late that day, Stuart was not on board. It was the third day before Duncan realised that his friend had not gone. The intricate details of the explosion were sharp in Duncan's mind but the context and implications a haze. Sometimes he expected to see Elizabeth in the house but mostly he lay on the bed hugging his children. James and Maggie struggled to understand but they knew something bad had happened and remained subdued. Stuart had handled the Botswana Police and the investigation. Women from the Kraal provided comfort to Tembo and Morgan and took care as best they could. Whilst Stuart knew he had to do something to stop Duncan sinking deeper into a whirlpool of despair, he decided he could help best by concentrating on the practicalities of the situation. For some reason Mary Scobie came to mind.

Mary was the wife of Jimmy Scobie, the sergeant who many years ago had taken the teenage Duncan under his wing when he'd enlisted in the British Army. She'd taken care of him and brought him into her family. The bond had been cemented when Jimmy died in Duncan's arms after being fatally wounded in a shoot -out in the alleys of Aden Town. Mary and Duncan had been united in grief before. It had not been a hard decision for her. The only question was the plane fare and Stuart had paid that. There was not much to leave behind in her lonely Glasgow council flat.

On the fourth day she arrived. Mary had the straight back and square shoulders of a woman much younger than her near sixty years. Through her own adversity she had learnt how to deal with tragedy in a practical manner. She knew that life must go on; she too had been left alone to tend young children when her husband had been shot. She knew there was a house to run, food to cook, clothes to wash and most of all children to love and cuddle. She knew when soft smile and gentle touch was required but was also aware when it was time to make Duncan face reality.

Eventually Duncan came out on to the stoop and took the chair he'd occupied when Elizabeth had died. He looked to where the explosion had taken place. Men from the kraal had filled the crater and removed the debris. There was little evidence of what had happened. Stuart had supervised and made sure of that.

"Now that's better isn't it," said Mary after she'd cajoled Duncan to put on the fresh clothes she'd laid out for him and made him shave and shower. Although still drawn and pale, he was beginning to look better. She poured coffee and placed it on the table in front of him. "Drink that. I'll get you something to eat."

Stuart joined him on the stoop. "How did she get here?" asked Duncan.

"I didn't know who else to call. She's the nearest to family that you have. As soon as I told her she just wanted to come. She's what you and the children need at the moment."

Duncan nodded and the two men sat in silence for a long time. Mary came back to the stoop. Eventually Duncan broke the silence. "I just can't imagine life without Elizabeth."

Mary put a reassuring hand on Duncan's shoulder. "The fact is you're just going to have to." The firmness of her Scottish accent was extenuated. "What's happened has happened and it can't be undone. James and Maggie have their entire life in front of them and it's up to you to be strong for them. They can't see you moping around forever. You'll just have to come to terms with what is."

Although it felt harsh Duncan knew it was true but he also knew it could not be that simple. He drew a breath. "I need to know why this happened. I need to know who did this. I'm angry. I need to avenge her death. Until that anger is gone I will not find peace."

"All in good time, you have other priorities for now," replied Mary.

"Please heed Mary's advice." said Stuart. "In the meantime if it helps I think I've pieced together part of the jigsaw. I think it would be better if Tembo and Morgan hear what I have to say. We'll talk this afternoon."

That afternoon Duncan and Stuart walked, they were joined by Tembo and Morgan. Stuart spoke most of the time, the others listened.

"It appears that Tembo, Morgan and Jomo stumbled on to something that was very sensitive. I would guess that the South Africans are developing some kind of nuclear capability and that they, Tembo, Morgan and Jomo, got work at some secret facility. It appears that Jomo was somehow exposed to nuclear radiation and it was that, that killed him. From the samples that you sent to London it was possible to determine that the nuclear material to which Jomo had been exposed was actually 'weapons grade' uranium. I would also hazard a guess that the two shafts that Tembo and Morgan were working on are for a nuclear test.

Because Jomo's bones provided tangible evidence that South Africa is building a nuclear bomb they needed to get his body back. You, Tembo and Morgan, need to be killed because you are witnesses and might even be able to tell people where the site is and what is going on there. What I find astounding however is the South African's ineptitude in making not one but two blunders; firstly they shot the wrong men at the burial platform and then they blew up Elizabeth. They must know that they have now attracted attention to themselves."

"So how did they come to kill Elizabeth?" asked Morgan.

"The South Africans were undoubtedly watching the farm. They most probably got information about your movements at the bottle store. Operatives from BOSS, the South African secret service, had most probably expected you and Tembo to be in the Land Rover. They'd buried a huge charge in the culvert that runs under the dirt track leading from the farm and set it off most probably by delayed time pressure pads or even by radio signal from a long distance."

"So our sister died for us?" asked Tembo.

"I know it's a tough message but yes, that is what I believe and what's more you may still be in danger. If they've tried to kill you twice it is possible they are stupid enough to try a third time. You must be very careful."

"I make this promise to my sister," said Morgan, "I will find the people who did this thing and I will extract revenge."

"I am with you on that my brother," responded Tembo. "I will not rest till her killers have paid in full for what they have done."

Duncan spoke for the first time. "The people who blew up the Land Rover were just foot soldiers. For my part I will extract payment from the people that gave the orders."

"I understand what you are saying and why you are saying it," replied Stuart. "I must tell you that what has happened has implications far beyond this family. When news of this gets out governments will get involved. It won't be easy for you to fulfil your promises. All I can say for my part is that if it falls within my power to assist you then I will."

Zodiac House, Pretoria
Tuesday 14th June 1988

It was dark outside when Peter eventually left his office. He'd been sitting all day contemplating the second blunder, the mess up BOSS had made. He knew he had to tell Alfred. Instead of taking the lift to the underground car-park and heading home he strode up the one flight of stairs and walked along the corridor toward Alfred's office suite. He tried the handle and was surprised it opened. He went in. The reception desk in the outer office was vacant. The wall clock said seven pm. "Gone home," he thought, but the oak panelled double door that led to Alfred's inner office was ajar and he could see a light beyond.

At one time Peter would have been comfortable just going through, but now, with Alfred's increasing withdrawal he was not so confident. Privately Alfred had assured him that his unavailability was a personal matter and that he should not take offence and Peter had taken him at his word. Peter never called unannounced now, but this evening he felt it was different. Gently he pushed the heavy door. The well oiled hinges moved silently and easily to reveal the back of his Chief's leather swivel chair.

"Alfred," he said gently.

The chair rotated slowly until Peter could see Alfred Smidt, see him as he'd never seen him before. Gone was the plump and ruddy smiling face and in its place was a ghostly grey apparition, an old face, wrinkled and contorted with pain.

Peter stepped forward, "Alfred what's wrong?"

Alfred raised a hand signalling Peter to stop. He almost gasped the words, "Give me some time please. Sit and wait."

Unsure if he should obey the instruction Peter hesitated.

"Just a few moments," Alfred pleaded.

Peter sat on the edge of the chair. Gradually the grey hue faded from Alfred's complexion but his expression remained drawn, his eyes closed. He gripped the arms of his chair tightly. On the desk, was an open bottle of tablets lying on its side, a few tablets spilled out, a half full glass of water beside it.

After a while Alfred spoke, his voice tired and husky. "It's getting better now. You can speak but it will be some time before I will be able to answer you."

Peter thought for a moment before going on to explain about the mistake in the Okavango and how he'd taken the decision to pass the matter on to BOSS.

When he had finished there was a short silence before Alfred responded. He spoke without opening his eyes or slackening his grip on the arms of the chair. "That was a mistake. BOSS are ham fisted. They were sure to make a mess of it; they make a mess of everything."

"I tried to see you before I made the decision but I couldn't get hold of you," apologised Peter.

"I know," replied Alfred. "I think you now know the reason I have been unable to see you."

"You are sick," said Peter, "You should be at home in bed. At the very least you need some time off."

"Time is a commodity that is in short supply for me and rest will not help with my problem."

"Have you seen a doctor?"

"Much more than that," Alfred half laughed through the pain. "The best medical practitioners in South Africa have pronounced on me. They say the tablets will work for now but soon they will be of little help. I'm glad you're here. It's time for you to know."

"Know what?"

"I realise that for a long time that you must have believed I have been losing my mind, possibly getting senile and a lot of other things. Maybe you thought of dementia or the like."

Peter shook his head in false denial.

"You're not fooling me for a second. If you haven't noticed you're not the man I think you are. Let me tell you straight out it's not dementia. I have a tumour, an inoperable brain tumour and it's growing. Sometimes it affects my thinking and behaviour. The tablets reduce the pressure for a short time, but that is all. Eventually, in weeks or at most months, pressure from the tumour will cause a blood vessel to rupture, an aneurism I think they call it and then the end will come quickly."

Peter sat quietly taking in the words.

Alfred continued. "Don't be shocked. We are all going to die and there are very few pleasant deaths. My Maker is calling me. He is waiting for me and soon I will be with Him. But there are things that need to be done first, important things that concern you.

You already know you are my chosen successor. You will take this chair when I am gone and I must better prepare you. For many years I have left you alone with your project because in that project I saw the best chance for our country but now it is time to show you something else. I have a surprise for you. You are to learn the final details of what you can achieve by sitting in this chair, how the levers of power work and what is available to you. Tomorrow we will travel and your next lesson will begin. It will probably be our last long journey together."

"We should have flown," said Peter taking his eyes off the road for a moment to look at Alfred. "It would have been much quicker."

"No, the doctors have told me my days of flying are over, something to do with the cabin pressure acting on my brain. It's too much of a risk. Besides I want to talk to you and the drive will be a good opportunity."

Juana Maria de los Dolores de Leon Smith was the Spanish born wife of Sir Harry Smith, the British Governor of Cape Colony from 1847 to 1852. At that time it was a customary honour to name something, usually a new town or settlement, after the Governor's wife. Sir Harry's wife's name was a bit of a mouthful so when a suitable place was identified it was simply called Ladysmith. The town nestles in the largest South African mountain range, the Drakensberg and is about two hundred and thirty miles south of Pretoria along the N3 highway which continues on to Durban. It was along the N3 that Peter now drove, headed for their overnight stay at Ladysmith's Royal Hotel. In the morning they would complete the journey, high into the Drakensberg, along little known and unmarked tracks, climbing through steep sided gorges until they broke through to a secret, well hidden, flat bottomed valley with green pastures.

"Do you study history?" asked Alfred.

"A little," replied Peter.

"Tell me then, when did Hitler lose the Second World War?"

"That's easy. The 8th May 1945," replied Peter.

"Incorrect," said Alfred. "The date you give me is when Germany officially surrendered. Hitler had been dead for a few days by that time. The truth is Hitler actually lost the war in the first few days of December 1941!"

Peter thought for a little while. "Do you refer to the Americans joining the conflict after Pearl Harbour?"

"Partly. A less well known disaster befell the German military a day or two earlier. The Germans were on the cusp of taking Moscow when the Russians released their last reserves of crack Siberian troops. The Siberians not only stopped the Germans but also pushed them back. With that Russian attack the Germans had lost the initiative in the East. The combination of failing to beat the Russians and the United States joining the conflict sealed Hitler's fate, and he knew it."

"Then why did he carry on?" asked Peter.

"Because he believed. He believed in his cause and hoped that fate would intervene. But there is more. In 1944, when the Allies were closing in from the West and the Russians were fighting on German soil he still carried on, carried on until the Russians were knocking on the door of the bunker in which he was sheltering. Why did he do that?"

Peter didn't reply.

"Hitler knew that the flower of Germany had died defending the cause," continued Alfred. "He knew that what was left of the German people was not worth defending and he was not going to give the ultimate victors the pleasure of enjoying the spoils of war. If he could not have the Germany of his dreams, then he was determined there would be no Germany for anybody else to enjoy. That is what was truly great about Hitler, his total commitment. That is the commitment I see in you, that is why I have chosen you to be my successor. Promise me Peter you will fight to the end to make the South Africa of our dreams come true."

"I made a commitment to you and my country many years ago. Nothing has changed. I will not waiver."

"Good," replied Alfred. "Of course I realise that desire is simply not enough. You must also have the means, the tools, the resources, to succeed. Tomorrow I will show you what I have prepared. Now let me sleep as you drive."

The previous night Alfred had retired to his room almost immediately leaving Peter to eat alone in the grandeur of the Royal Hotel's dining room, the dining room that was part of the fabric of South African history. In this room British Army Officers had once dined in luxury before retiring to soft beds and crisp sheets whilst their troops had bivouacked in canvas bell tents, cooked on open fires and swatted mosquitoes. But it had not always been good for the British. During the Boer War the British military elite had been shaken to the core. During the infamous siege of Ladysmith the bedrooms and the dining room had became a makeshift hospital through which most of the three thousand casualties suffered by the British had passed. Whilst the siege had eventually been lifted by a relief column it had always been viewed as a resounding display of defiance by Nationalist Afrikaner's. Peter van Stardan took inspiration from the surroundings.

Now, in the early morning light, Peter watched as Alfred worked his way painfully into the back seat of the waiting Range Rover that had come to collect them for the final leg of their journey, high into the Drakensberg. At first the Range Rover made good speed on the tarmac roads but progress slowed when the surface changed to pressed gravel and quarry dust. The vehicle climbed higher and higher, twisting and turning. The sides of the valleys closed in and soon they were crawling through narrow gorges. For the last mile they travelled slowly through a dramatic pass, sheer cliff walls towering above them on either side blocking out the sunlight. Then, as if by a miracle, they broke out into brightness and laid before them was the hidden expanse of a broad flat bottomed valley carpeted in lush green meadow.

The driver spoke unsolicited words. "In the beginning this used to be a deep valley with a lake at the bottom. Over thousands of years rivers carried rock particles down the hillsides and the lake silted up to produce this beautiful hidden space."

They drove across the valley for more than half a mile along a barely visible strip road before arriving at a small cluster of green camouflaged buildings.

"Welcome to our base," said the driver. "These are temporary buildings; the entry to the cavern is over there." He pointed to what looked like an entrance to a train tunnel that disappeared into the mountains. "We have prepared for you."

The driver halted the Range Rover within a few yards of a raised dais that was shaded by a green and white striped awning that flapped gently in the light breeze. Two grand carved chairs stood waiting on the dais. An escort opened the car door and led both men to the chairs. They sat. Almost immediately, from unseen speakers blasted the resounding beat of marching music and from the tunnel entrance a column of soldiers in black uniforms marched perfectly in three abreast formation and came to attention in front of Alfred and Peter. The colour sergeant, with unsheathed ceremonial sword, stepped to the front and saluted. Alfred came to his feet, tugging at Peter's cuff for him to do the same. Peter, following Alfred's example, bowed his head in response to the display. The colour sergeant turned and promptly marched the welcoming ceremonial guard back towards the tunnel entrance.

"Now we have to wait for a while," said Alfred.

"What is this?" asked Peter. "Who are these soldiers?"

"This is the surprise I promised you. I should have made you aware of this force a long time ago, then you would have found no need to involve BOSS in our affairs. But it is too late to worry about that now.

More than two thousand years ago the Emperors of Rome realised that even though they ruled the mightiest civilisation ever to have existed, their power could always be challenged. As a precaution they established a group of men, very special men, men of fanatical loyalty willing to sacrifice themselves for the ideals of the Roman Empire, men who obeyed orders without question. The Emperors called them the Praetorian Guard.

The Roman Empire endured for centuries. I believe it was not a coincidence that it only went into decline after Emperor Constantine dissolved the Praetorian Guard in the fourth century

What you have just seen is my version of what the Romans had, a force of just five hundred men that is worth more than an entire army. You know I am not a romantic but I could not resist taking and twisting the name used by the Romans. The capital of our great South Africa is of course Pretoria, named after our national hero Peter Pretorius. I have therefore called this elite group the New Pretorian Guards, or NPG. The ceremony today is to introduce you to them and for them to acknowledge that you are their leader in waiting. When I am gone this group of men will do your bidding to the death, without question. Regard them well.

Now I think they are going to carry out a display to demonstrate their skill to you."

BOOK TWO
Diego Garcia, US Airbase, Indian Ocean
Sunday 6th November 1988

Taking off in a tropical thunderstorm is not advisable but is possible and sometimes necessary. The plane was standing ready, engines idling. Visibility was less than three hundred yards and rain lashed against the windscreen of the stationary Orion P3 maritime surveillance aircraft. The crew of eleven were strapped in tightly as the pilot opened up the four turboprop engines. They were all nervous and not just because of the take-off. When full thrust had been achieved the pilot released the brakes and the plane moved forward, quickly gaining momentum. The crew were pushed back into their seats. Four turbulent, dark minutes later the plane broke through the cloud cover into a clear blue sky. The pilot eased back on the throttle. The rest of the climb, to cruising altitude, would be carried out at a more sedate pace; they'd need all the fuel they had for the planned sixteen hour mission. The crew unbuckled their harnesses and settled down for the long journey.

The pilot knew the crew thought the briefing was bull-shit. They'd been told some crap that a new hole in the ozone layer had been found and somebody in the US met office wanted data to determine its extent and severity. The crew weren't stupid. They knew that didn't explain why there was such a panic forcing them to take off in the middle of a tropical thunder storm and fly half-way around the world. But the pilot had his orders and these included not telling the crew the true story.

After twenty minutes the plane reached its cruising height.

The pilot spoke to the co-pilot. "Okay we're going in the right direction, just about south, next stop Southern Ocean. Shut down and feather one and four. Engage auto pilot. You take control. I reckon about five and half hours till we're on station."

The Orion P3 had many variations. This version was used primarily by the Air force for meteorological research but it also had submarine detection capabilities. For long missions it was routine practice to shut down one of the engines, normally number one because it had no electrical generator fitted. This extended the endurance of the plane considerably, at minimum risk. Flying on just two engines increased the plane's efficiency further but at the expense of safety. This plane had had the standard bomb bay doors removed and an extra fuel tank was fitted where the bomb load would normally have been carried. It had no attack or defence capability in its own right but it carried a lot of sophisticated measuring equipment. It just collected information; lots of information.

Exactly five hours and twenty eight minutes later the plane was on station. The pilot initiated the prearranged plan, a copy of the standard grid sector search pattern. Only they would not do it once. They'd cover all sectors at 35,000 feet, then they'd drop 5,000 feet and repeat the search pattern, then drop another 5,000 feet and do the same again. They would carry on all the way to 10,000 feet. In the back a technician would be busy. A small scoop had been extended out of the plane's underside. It passed external air along a pipe, through a fine fibre filter before exhausting it out of the rear of the plane. Minute dust particles from the atmosphere would get trapped in the filter. Just before a change in height the pilot would tell the technician to change the filter. The technician put a new cartridge in the slot and popped the used one into a purpose made aluminium tube container with a screw top. He wrote the mission number, height and time on the side of each canister with a felt pen.

The pilots and the technician were kept busy. The rest of the crew had little to do. They'd been told to leave their observation equipment switched off because the pilot didn't want too much energy drawn from the main electrical buzz; it would reduce the plane's efficiency.

Ricky Bott was twenty-two years old and designated the number two Electronics Specialist for the mission. As a kid in the mid-West he'd been a pain in the arse for his parents. He was into everything. His concerned mother had taken him to see an analyst once. The analyst concluded that Ricky was of about normal intelligence, had good powers of concentration and had an empathetic and kind nature. He was a very active child, verging on hyper-active, but his behaviour was not disruptive enough for the child to be diagnosed with any clinical condition. The analyst just advised that the child should be kept occupied at all times. And that's what the thoughtful parents did. They kept him on a gruelling schedule right up to Junior High, a schedule that would have been impossible to maintain had there been any siblings. When he wasn't at school he was playing sports or in some club or other. In the summer he went to summer camp, in the winter he got involved in model making. He specialised in making scale models of US Military aircraft, down to the last detail. It was no surprise when he told his parents he wanted to enlist in the US Airforce at the earliest opportunity. They'd said they were looking forward to him going, they'd enjoy the rest, but the truth was when he went they felt their life was pretty empty and they'd have loved him to come back.

Ricky, qualified for the past three years, sat in his flight seat staring at the bank of blank cathode ray tubes. Not a light flickered on the console to keep his attention. It was driving him mad just sitting there with the prospect of doing absolutely nothing for the endless hours of the planned mission. Ricky knew that if he switched on any of the main kit it would register on the flight engineer's consul in the cockpit, right behind the pilot. So that was a no go. He'd only be able to turn on kit that would not register in the cockpit. It was a 'no brainer'. The radiation monitoring equipment had an inbuilt battery backup. His hand stretched up to the toggle switch on the top left hand corner of the consul and threw the switch from “main buzz” to “backup power”. Then he pulled the main breaker. Immediately he got a loud high pitched tone in his head phones. Quickly he turned down the volume and adjusted the squelch. The tone persisted.

The radiation detection equipment had its shortfalls. The sensor, which was only one of an array of sensors that protruded from the plane’s belly, picked up gamma radiation from particles in the air. The concentration of the particles was heavily dependent on variables such as particle size and weather conditions. The sensor could be rotated and should have given a rough idea of which direction the radiation was coming from, so long as the prevailing wind direction was taken into account.

Ricky rotated the sensor through three hundred and sixty degrees and watched the indicator carefully. The dial was graduated by a coloured bar that changed from green through yellow and orange to red. The needle now hovered between orange and red. It didn’t budge throughout the sensor’s rotation. This meant that the gamma rays weren’t coming from any particular direction; the plane must be in the middle of a radiation cloud. Ricky thought about telling the pilot but decided to hang on a while. He wanted to be sure about his facts. He’d most probably get a kick up the arse for switching the equipment on without authorisation. He’d look pretty sick if it was just an atmospheric “hot spot” they were going through. He picked up a pencil and started recording readings on his note pad. Before he’d finished writing the first column he felt the plane start to descend, dropping another five thousand feet. For the next four hours he took manual readings every thirty seconds. It was tedious work but it kept his mind busy. The needle never went completely into the red; it was even beginning to drop a little over time.

The tropical storm had moved on by the time the plane got back to Diego Garcia. The landing was smooth and uneventful. The plane was parked in its usual spec on the apron and after final shut-down checks the crew exited the plane and began the short walk back to the briefing room. The Technician carried a canvas bag containing the aluminium tubes.

Ricky quickened his pace and came up alongside the pilot. “Hey Skip, can I have a word?”

“Yeah, what do you want Ricky?”

“I know it was against instructions but I got a bit bored during the flight so I took some readings. I made some notes. I thought you might be interested.”

“What kind of readings Ricky?”

“Radiation levels Skip.”

The Pilot grabbed Ricky by the arm and pulled him to one side. The other members of the crew slowed. “You guys carry on, me and Ricky will catch up.”

“What the fuck do you think you were doing?” demanded the pilot.

The colour drained from Ricky’s face. He didn’t get time to answer.

“Who else knows about this?”

“Nobody Skip, I just made some notes and was going to give them to you.”

“Hand them over. You say jack-shit to nobody over this or you’ll find yourself in a dark place you’d rather not be. Understand.”

“Yes Skip.”

Lieutenant Colonel Chuck Collins leaned back in his leather swivel chair, hands behind his head and looked through the enormous picture window that dominated his office. He didn’t take in the natural beauty of the turquoise lagoon that had recently been designated a place of special scientific interest. What he saw were the six giant battleship grey freighters of the US Navy that swung on their anchors in the afternoon sun, freighters that held enough provisions to keep two brigades of the United States rapid deployment force fully supplied in the field for a period of two months and stood ready to sail to any flashpoint in the Southern Oceans on twenty-four hours notice.

Major Brian Shapiro knocked on the Lieutenant-Colonel’s door and walked straight in. “Got a minute Chief?”

“Yep, what have you got?” answered Collins looking at the sheaf of papers in the Major’s hand.

“The report on yesterday’s reconnaissance flight is ready to send to Langley. Do you want to go over it?”

“No, I don’t want to delay it. I read the draft. I reckon we better get it to the spooks in Washington fast. They’ll be interested. Code it and ‘flash’ it over straight away.”

“Do the Brits get to see it?”

Collins thought for a second. “No. We’ll keep it to ourselves.”

“They might be pissed off.”

“It’s a request from CIA at Langley, not strictly speaking military intelligence. We can argue it’s outside the protocol,” Collins said looking out across the lagoon at a Union Jack that fluttered on a distant flagpole.

The volcanic archipelago that makes up the islands of Diego Garcia was home to a major American military outpost but did not belong to the United States. It was a legacy of colonialism and part of the dwindling British Indian Ocean Territories. All that the United States had was a fifty year lease and a co-operation protocol. After the Second World War the United Kingdom was tired and more importantly broke but still had aspirations to play on the world stage. Stretched militarily, it suited the British to let the US have a base on Diego Garcia and they went to a lot of trouble, including shipping out the entire population of the archipelago, to make the Americans happy. Of course the British maintained a military presence on the islands but it was dwarfed by the US contingent. The protocol said that both countries would share military information but as the years passed the flow of information became decidedly one way. This irritated the American commanders on the islands and the relationship could become tetchy at times.

"Come in," shouted Major Philip Penrose in response to the knock on his office door. He didn't enjoy the same panoramic view as his American counterpart on the islands and his office was little more than functional.

Staff Sergeant Stanley Acton entered the room, came to attention in front of his commanding officer and stiffly saluted.

"At ease sergeant," said the Major not lifting his head from the papers he was reading.

Unseen by the Major, the Sergeant raised his eyebrows in annoyance at his words, only '*at ease*' and not '*stand easy*'.

"Sir. We have intercepted a priority coded message from our cousins across the lagoon that's not on the exchange list. Shall I lodge a complaint?"

"I don't think so," replied the Major. "We didn't get much of a response the last time we complained. Perhaps we should just send it to GCHQ. It will give them a bit of practice on decoding and if there is anything interesting I'm sure they'll pass it on to the appropriate department."

Sergeant Acton came back to attention and saluted before turning to leave the office.

"Sergeant, best if our cousins across the lagoon don't know we've got the message," Penrose added almost as an afterthought.

"Sir."

GCHQ Cheltenham, England
Friday 18th November 1988

The security guard placed a wooden tray in front of Stuart Cameron. "Empty your pockets, everything please Sir." The West Country accent felt inappropriate in the situation. It was a sound that Stuart associated more with yokel farmers and cider drinkers rather than high security. In his mind it took from the guard's credibility and he smiled at what he considered a slightly surreal situation.

Stuart had set off from London early in the morning speeding westward along a nearly empty M4 motorway and arrived in Cheltenham before 10am. His high level security pass was good to get him into the car park but not much more. Clearing GCHQ security proved to be a tedious drawn out affair.

Jacket off Sir, spread your legs, raise your arms. The security guard went through the jacket pockets and felt the collar and lapels for lumps before proceeding to run his hands over Stuart's stretched body.

"Everybody gets treated the same here Sir," said the security guard as he gave Stuart's groin area a slightly rougher than necessary frisk that wasn't surreal in any way and effectively removed Stuart's smile.

"That's fine Sir," said the security guard, now smiling himself. "If you'd like to get your things together and sit over there your escort will be along shortly."

The British consider themselves to be particularly good at intercepting information and code breaking. This assumption is not entirely without foundation. They've been in the business a long time. Mary Queen of Scots was beheaded after a secret message of hers, encouraging rebellion, was intercepted and decoded in 1587. Since that time the English Government have continuously maintained some kind of code breaking capability. More recently, during the Second World War, the exploits of Bletchley Park, the cracking of the German Enigma Code and the development of Colossus, the world's first computer, had significantly shortened the conflict.

In the Cold War the British had reorganised and built on the foundations of Bletchley Park. GCHQ was moved to Cheltenham, not far from Bristol. Starting in a commandeered stately home, the facility had been continuously expanded with programmes of priority building and now employed thousands of people many of whom would be amongst the intellectual elite of the country. And it was one of these elite that Stuart was now visiting.

The escort arrived, a uniformed soldier. "If you'd like to follow me Sir I'll take you to your appointment."

Stuart got up and eyed the escort's holstered sidearm.

"Don't let it concern you Sir. I haven't had to use it yet," the escort commented noting Stuart's gaze

They set off at a brisk pace twisting and turning down a labyrinth of corridors and covered walkways between a mix of permanent and pre-fabricated buildings. Eventually they came to a halt outside a solid wooden door halfway down a darkened passageway. The plaque on the door read 'TULIP'. There was a camera entry system and also a push button coded entry. The escort knocked.

A speaker clicked. "What?" said an irritated female voice.

"Mr Cameron for TULIP," replied the escort.

The door opened.

"Off you go Sir," said the escort. "They'll call me when it's time to take you back."

It was not what Stuart had envisaged. The windowless reception office was dull and cluttered. Around the walls were innumerable battered bottle- green filing cabinets. Facing him was a tiny wooden receptionist's desk and a vacant rickety chair that had the appearance of having been retrieved from a dump. On every flat surface were piles of untidy buff folders. Standing to the left, at the open drawer of one of the filing cabinets was a woman, her appearance in stark contrast to the surroundings.

Mid-30's she was pretty, she was sleek and she was fashionable. Her thick sandy hair was pulled back into a pony-tail, revealing sculptured beauty, an unblemished coffee complexion and a slightly furrowed brow.

Stuart spoke. "I'm here to see TULIP. I believe he's expecting me."

"Wrong!" was the quick-fire response.

"I don't think I am," said Stuart. "The appointment was confirmed."

"No, you're wrong, it's not a he it's a she and it's me. I'm TULIP. Bear with me a moment. I'm looking for a piece of paper." She stuck her head back into the drawer of the filing cabinet.

Jane Ashton aka Tulip clearly didn't come out of a standard jelly mould. But then most of the people at GCHQ didn't. She'd been born on the Wirral in the North West of England. Her father was her first mentor. He was a machine shop foreman who existed in an environment well below his intellectual capabilities and so he'd projected his unfulfilled ambitions on his daughter. Her mother was a nurse of the old school whose salary, almost in its entirety, went on sending the couple's only child to Mostyn House, an expensive private school on the Dee Estuary. The school itself was an anachronism. With an ethos based on fading moral values, it emphasised success by examination and defined ethical lines. The headmaster had stood against concepts such as child centred education, continual assessment and, as he saw it, pandering to the emotional needs of children. In an increasingly liberal society the establishment was bound for extinction, fortunately not before Jane had completed her education.

Classical Greek and Latin were compulsory subjects from year one. The values of Plato, Aristotle and Democrates were soon digested. Jane had initially been taken with the free thinking philosophy of Diogenes until she found out that her hero's test to prove the achievement of freedom from inhibition was to masturbate in public. That was too much for her adolescent mind. Nevertheless it was in the roots of Greek and Latin that Jane's interest in modern languages was kindled. Languages were not Jane's only forte. She was also a natural with figures. Unfortunately the school was not blessed in the mathematics department. In fact it was quite dismal, but that didn't stop Jane. With the aid of a private tutor and a lot of personal effort she ended up with top grades in her 'A' levels. Jane was not however your typical bookworm. Good looking, even beautiful as she matured, she had an athletic build and participated in all school activities with blind enthusiasm. What little sadness there was in Jane's schooldays came from her failure to develop the personal relationships she desired. Perhaps because she was different her contemporaries struggled to relate to her. As far as the headmaster was concerned she was a certainty for Head Girl but Jane failed dismally to secure the necessary votes in the student election. By the time she'd left Mostyn House she'd formed many shallow relationships but no deep friendships. If anything this failure did not thwart her ambition but made her more independent.

She had chosen Swansea University because it offered a combined degree in languages and mathematics and because she didn't feel comfortable she would fit in at either Oxford or Cambridge, both of which would have welcomed her with open arms. Before the first year was over she had been singled out by the head of the Math faculty as an interesting prospect. When it came to the final year there was no series of interviews on the 'milk round' looking for a job. Her career path had long been decided. She went straight into training at GCHQ's Cipher Department. Steadily, over a decade and a half she'd developed a particular savvy for Cold War communications and untangling political intrigue. With unerring clarity she was able to distinguish between the genuine and the Machiavellian. She progressed so far that her work became recognisable by the opposition and so, for her own safety, had earned her own code name; she was 'TULIP' and TULIP's assessments were not unfamiliar in the highest echelons. However it wasn't the beauty of her mind that was captivating Stuart's gaze as he waited for her search to be completed.

Finally she retrieved the document she was looking for. "Right we are. Come through Mr. Cameron. You now have my undivided attention."

Stuart followed her through the door into the main office, which was a larger shambolic version of the room they'd left. His eyes ignored the mess and remained transfixed on her womanly features.

She sat behind her desk and pushed a pile of folders to one side so she had a clear view of her visitor.

"It appears we have been thrust together," she said. "How do you think we should begin?"

"A cup of coffee would be good," was his reply.

She smiled. "I'm afraid I don't have that facility. But I'll take you to the canteen later, after we've made some progress. And if it's okay with you I'll call you Stuart and you may call me Jane. You begin."

Stuart went on to tell the story of Jomo, Morgan and Tembo. He explained Duncan's suspicions about Jomo's illness and the sample he'd sent to London. He told her about the theft of Jomo's remains, the killing of the two young warriors and his own visit to the Okavango. Jane heard about the death of Elizabeth with genuine sympathy. To conclude he told her about his meeting at the Foreign and Commonwealth Office and his understanding of the general political situation.

Throughout Jane nodded her encouragement. Whilst listening attentively she was also making her own personal assessment of the man in front of her, deciding if she could work with and more than that trust Stuart. She only spoke when he had finished and had sat back in his chair.

"Do you think you can locate the intended test site?" she asked.

"Not with any precision," replied Stuart, "but I think I could extrapolate the approximate area within a given arc. I know where they started from and know how long they travelled by lorry and the rough direction."

"Good, if you could do that for me I'll see what I can do to pinpoint the location exactly and, if we're lucky, get some photographs."

"You can do that?"

"Possibly, and if I succeed I will let you know. But let's go to the canteen and I'll tell you what I've got. It looks like we have a picture emerging and it's not a good one."

Her personal assessments were always quick. She felt she could trust him. Her intuition was razor sharp and had never let her down. She was ready to share information with him.

The restaurant for established staff was light and airy and the space between tables large by design. Jane and Stuart sat alone in a corner. He ate roast beef and she picked on a salad between sentences, for it was Jane that did most of the talking now.

"You're well aware that the UK and United States share a lot of secret information," she began. "In the Cold War we're supposed to be indivisible, two sides of the same coin, although it's hardly a secret that the Americans view us very much as the junior partner. It was actually not that long ago they suggested that there should be a permanent representative of the US Secret Service in GCHQ. When we counter proposed a reciprocal arrangement, that one of our chaps take up residence with DEFRA in Cheyenne they went cool on the idea. So our main high level line of communications remains a liaison office and that office has been fairly busy of late.

It all started a couple of weeks ago. Our main radio telescope, Jodrell Bank in Cheshire which is part of NATO's early warning system, picked up some communications from a US spy satellite called Vela 2. The signal suggested that the satellite had detected a double flash in the South Atlantic, somewhere between South Africa and the Antarctic. A double flash is the unique signature of a nuclear detonation above ground. The message we'd received was relayed immediately to the US. This signal should have set alarm bells ringing all over the world. To our surprise it didn't. So twenty four hours later we sent a polite note of enquiry to our American friends. The response took two days coming and the explanation was improbable if not impossible. The Americans told us that the camera lens in the Vela 2 satellite had been hit by not one but two microscopic bits of space dust at just the right time interval. The statistical probability of that is just about zero but if it had happened the camera lens would have been damaged. We've seen pictures taken after the reported incident and they are perfect. No damage to the camera lens. So clearly the Americans lied to us. I got involved at this stage."

"I intercepted a report from our station at Diego Garcia. Our personnel there noted a bit of a 'kerfuffle' going on. The place is subject to regular anti-cyclones that disrupt routine operations. In the middle of one of the worst storms recorded in recent history a 'routine' observation flight took off on what turned out to be an endurance mission. The flight, the Orion P3, returned safely and the Yanks were pretty quiet about it but our chaps picked up an increase in 'unshared' data transmissions from the Americans, all in high cipher. A particularly long coded message landed on my desk. In summary the Americans, despite what they told us, believe that the Vela photographs are genuine and that a nuclear device was detonated in the South Atlantic, either in the air or on the surface. We then looked for independent supporting information. Our radio interception team identified a series of short wave transmissions to and from a Japanese trawler operating in Antarctica. The captain of the trawler sent a message to his base saying the crew had seen a bright flash in the sky at about the same time as the Vela satellite had taken its photographs. The trawler got a message back from Japan instructing the Captain to tell his crew that it was just the Aurora Borealis, the Southern Lights, that they'd seen."

"You think the Americans got at them?" asked Stuart.

"Probably not, I personally believe the trawler was illegally fishing for whales and they didn't want to risk an inspection. So best to stay stum."

"It's mainly supposition," commented Stuart.

"A lot of my stuff is. There are other bits however," continued Jane. "On Diego Garcia word is that one of the crew of the Orion P3 is in a bit of hot water. He's been isolated and is apparently waiting transfer orders.

They are moving him to one of the polar early warning stations, the American version of sending someone to Siberia!"

"If there was a nuclear explosion there should be evidence, say residual radiation?" suggested Stuart.

"In theory yes. We had HMS Endeavour at Port Stanley in the Falklands. She sailed immediately but only makes about 450 nautical miles per day. By the time she got to the right area there was nothing to detect."

"That's good in a way isn't it? No radiation, no bomb. Maybe the Americans are playing with a straight bat after all," said Stuart.

"Not really. It makes us more worried. There may be no detectable radiation because the radiation had a very short half-life, say like in a Neutron bomb!"

"That can't be," responded Stuart. "Even we don't deploy neutron bombs. Only the US has that kind of technology."

"Exactly. Another nation with such a weapon would worry the Americans and it becomes understandable why they are playing their cards so close to their chest.

"Ah!" said Stuart.

"Exactly," repeated Jane. "As the Americans might say, having an ordinary nuclear device gets one into the ball game. Having a neutron bomb puts one at the very top of league division one. That's why our Lords and Masters want us to get involved and they want to keep it away from main stream MI6. It's just you and me and we have a free hand on this one."

Stuart sat back and looked around. The restaurant was deserted, even the staff had disappeared.

"Damn," he said. "I still didn't get a coffee."

Jane smiled. "There's a machine on the way back to my office. But first let me ask you something."

"Go ahead."

"This Duncan Murdoch chap, your contact in Africa. I've read all there is that's written on him. He's sounds like an interesting character. I'd like to hear your assessment of him."

"Now you're asking something with no simple answer."

"Have a go."

Stuart puffed. "I could simply say he's the best explosives man I have ever met. I think from a child he was interested in explosives. In the Army he trained as a combat engineer and during the Rhodesian war he had plenty of opportunity to put his skills into practice. He's also worked in civil environments, mines and quarries. What he doesn't know about explosives isn't worth knowing. As a soldier I'd go anywhere with him: tough, cool, decisive, and intelligent. He also worked undercover for us for many years. There aren't enough adjectives in my book."

"A good technical man then," mused Jane.

"That's not half the story. He has qualities that can't be learnt; integrity, honesty and a sense of right and wrong. He was unjustly convicted of murder by the British Army and imprisoned. He had every reason under the sun to hate the Services and indeed me yet when push came to shove he worked for us not because he'd forgiven the Establishment but because it was the right thing to do. Many people owe their lives to him. And he's totally selfless. His wife Elizabeth was originally his domestic servant in Rhodesia. He almost lost his own life rescuing her from near certain death."

"So she's a trophy of war?" quizzed Jane.

"No not really. They lost contact for a few years. When they met again after the war they fell in love. Elizabeth was a tribal princess and didn't want to be parted from her clan, particularly as they were under threat. So when they married Duncan spent every penny he had buying some land in Botswana and moving the whole tribe lock stock and barrel there. It's an amazing set up."

"Elizabeth must have been some kind of woman too."

"She was. As well as mothering two fine children she had other responsibilities. Her father was a famous Chief. She was the eldest child but had younger twin brothers, Tembo and Morgan. When her father died the eldest of the twins should have been made Chief. Only Elizabeth knew which of the twins was oldest. The twins are so close they didn't want anything to come between them so they begged Elizabeth not to say which of them is the eldest and she didn't. The three of them, with a little input from Duncan, lead the clan."

"I see what you mean," said Jane. "Even the twins sound interesting."

"Absolutely. They were trained by the Russians and were guerrilla fighters of some renown. They are very funny, like mischievous kids, but they're solid in a tricky situation."

"How do you know?"

"I fought alongside them."

"Tell me about it."

"Another day," said Stuart glancing at his watch. "It's time I left."

He never did get his coffee.

Filton near Bristol UK
Friday 18th November 1988

"Mutton dressed as lamb," thought the newspaper seller standing in the evening darkness on the corner outside the George V pub in Little Burton, an area crammed tight with tiny Victorian terraced houses two miles from the British Aerospace factory at Filton.

She had a good figure alright but that was it. Her shocking pink six inch high stiletto's made her too tall, her red skirt was too short and too tight and her bust was stretching the buttons of her lace blouse, giving sight of her undersize bra and bursting cleavage. She walked up to him and he struggled not to smirk at the apparition of too much eye make-up, shoulder length bleached blond hair and scarlet lipstick.

"A bit on the side, that's all she's good for," he thought. "I'd give her one alright, just to teach her a lesson, arrogant cow."

She looked the paper seller right in the eye. "Hiya Igor. If you got the dosh I got something you want," she spoke in a less than perfect Bristolian accent.

He hissed back at her. "Don't call me Igor you stupid bitch, my name is Desmond. Do you want us to get caught?"

"You dick-head Igor, everybody knows who you are. You got twenty copies of that fucking commie Morning Star newspaper under your arm. I think you should buy me a drink as well," she said pulling a folded A4 envelop from her black patent plastic handbag.

"Fuck off," he replied.

"Okay I will," she turned and started to walk away. She got less than five steps.

"Wait, what have you got?"

"Drink first."

They went into the pub and sat down in a quiet corner. "Port and lemon Igor, that's what ladies drink."

He left his papers on the table and shuffled off to the bar returning with a port and lemon and half a bitter. He sat down opposite her.

"Give me the envelope," he demanded.

"Ten pounds, in advance Igor. This is good."

"How fucking much," Igor raised his voice nearly shouting.

"Not so loud Igor, you don't want to attract attention now do you?" she smiled revealing lipstick stained teeth.

He spoke more quietly now. "I've never given you more than a fiver, you know that."

"Ah, but this is good, I know it is because everybody was so excited in the office when it arrived."

"So what's so important then?"

"How the hell would I know Igor, I don't read the fucking stuff. I just know they got worked up when it arrived and that means you want it."

"I'll give you six quid as a favour."

"You're getting pigging deaf. I said ten."

"If you don't give it to me I'll take it and you'll have nothing."

"I'll scream the fucking place down if you try it. Tenner or I walk."

"Wait", he said and went off to the toilet. He returned two minutes later and slipped her two blue five pound notes under the table. She passed over the envelope and swigged the dregs from her glass.

"With your bloody attitude I don't understand how you keep your job in that code place."

"GCHQ to you love, and you best be thankful they think so highly of me there. I'm the best cleaner in the place and I know it."

"If this isn't any good I'll ring your scrawny fucking neck," he hissed tucking the envelope into the folds of the last newspaper in his pile.

"It's good," she said walking off wiggling her arse at him."

An hour later the woman got off her third bus. She'd taken a difficult route, one that was hard to follow, but easy for her to notice if she was being followed. She was happy she was in the clear and headed for the Temple Park area of the city. She found her new Ford Cortina in Ben Nevis Road, just as she'd left it. She drove off, heading back towards Cheltenham. When she'd cleared the built up area she relaxed and allowed herself a genuine smile. With a sweep of her arm she whisked off the blond wig and glanced at the mirror. Jane Ashton was pleased with her night's work. Poor Igor never realised that he'd actually been looking at lamb dressed as mutton and it had been her that had 'given him one'.

Simons Town Naval Base, South Africa
Tuesday 20th December 1988

Peter van Stardan stood on top of the Martello Tower at South Africa's Simons Town Naval Base and looked out over the bay as a small flotilla slowly made its way to the military docking facilities. He had more than an hour to wait and so killed time by looking at the commemorative plaque and boards that were dotted around and filled with historic information. If he'd been concentrating he would have learnt why the British built Martello Towers to defend coastal towns and facilities throughout its empire. But van Stardan was not taking in what he read; his mind was fixed on a present day maritime encounter, one that could jeopardise his life's work.

Seventy two hours earlier, in the dead of night, the Israeli Defence Force Ship Haifa-al, was making a sedate fourteen knots as it patrolled the vast sea area between Africa and the Antarctic. It was due to stay on station for another week. The decision had been made to send the two support vessels it had been guarding back to their Israeli home unescorted. The Haifa-al would not begin its own long return journey until its provisions and fuel had been replenished at sea from a tanker that was making its way from Eilat. Never had the Israeli Navy undertaken such an audacious secret mission so far from home. The task had been completed and most of the men began to relax, but not all of them.

In a quiet corner deep in the dark interior of the warship one man listened intensely. Nothing was showing on the green screen of his oscilloscope, however on his high-fidelity Motorola headphones he could just detect the tiniest of blips. The frigate might be old but the passive sonar equipment was brand new and as time passed he became more certain of what he heard. Removing his headgear he spoke by phone to the Officer of the Watch on the Bridge.

"I'm sure I am not mistaken sir. A submarine is following in our wake about 600 yards astern, depth ninety feet, most probably electric because it is so quiet."

The Officer of the Watch called the Captain who spoke to the sonar operator directly and informed him of the plan.

Ten minutes later the Captain gave the order, "Full astern". The Haifa-Al juddered violently. Fifteen seconds later the Captain ordered "All Stop" and the ship was suddenly quiet. The Captain and Officers on the Bridge waited in silence. The phone from the sonar room rang. The Captain answered. "What did you get?"

"One hundred percent confirmation Sir, you caught them napping. They had to go emergency astern, their propeller cavitatied like a church bell."

The Captain spoke to his Number one, "Now they know we know they are there. Maintain the general heading but run on a tight zigzag, two nautical mile legs. That'll keep them on their toes and get me a current fuel status report quickly. All I have to do now is figure out who they are."

"It's a South African submarine," said a voice from behind.

The Captain turned to face the Admiral who'd just arrived on the bridge resplendent in white tropical uniform and crossed sword epaulettes. He saluted.

"Sonar reports it as a diesel electric boat," continued the Admiral. "Neither the Soviets nor the Western Powers would operate a diesel electric boat so far away from their home ports. They'd use nuclear subs. Besides I am sure this is not a military manoeuvre, it is the South Africans sending us a political message. They are displeased at what we have just done. They did not like us carrying out a nuclear test so close to them."

"Are you happy that I take evasive action?" asked the Captain.

"Absolutely, you are the Captain of this ship, it is your command. Within your orders do as you see fit, I have seen what I came here to see."

Number one returned. "Fuel situation Sir, it is very tight. We can only engage the turbines for about two hours at full speed, then we have to revert to the diesel if we are not to run out of fuel before the supply vessel arrives. I don't think there is enough for us to be able to outrun the submarine even if we make thirty-five knots for the full two hours."

The Haifa-al was not a new ship to the Israeli Defence Forces. It had been purchased second-hand from the British and the design reflected this. At the time the Hafia-al was built the British had an Empire to defend spanning the world, so their ships had not only to be fast in combat but also have a long cruising range. That's why they had two propulsion systems, a diesel engine for long endurance and twin gas turbines that could be engaged for high speed manoeuvring in combat. Now the Haifa-al ran on its diesel engine.

The Captain pondered a few moments. "Thank you Number One. Advise the engineers we will need the turbines soon and get the ship ready for sudden severe manoeuvres."

An hour later in the early morning light the captain ordered the turbines engaged but speed maintained at fourteen knots. He spoke to the sonar operator directly. "What distance do they maintain?"

"They keep tight within 400 hundred and 700 yards Sir."

"Are they sharp, do they respond quickly to our movements?"

"Not really Sir."

"Good," the Captain smiled. "Then we'll give them a surprise. I'm putting you on the Bridge Loudaphone and I want you to constantly give me bearings and distance to the target."

The Captain took his seat.

"Are you ready for manoeuvres Number One?"

"Yes Sir."

"Signal the engine room maximum speed both propellers."

The ship responded to the sudden increase in power. It felt like the bows were lifting themselves out of the water. The Captain looked at his stop watch and counted down the two minutes he'd allowed.

"On my instruction Number One rudder full to Port execute one-eighty degree turn. Port engine full reverse, starboard propeller maintain full ahead. As you bear go straight for the submarine as if you intend to ram."

"Are we going to ram Sir?"

The captain ignored the question. "Are you ready Number One?"

"Yes Sir."

"Good, then on my mark... three....two...one...execute," the Captain pushed the start button on his stop watch.

The First Officer barked his instructions; the bells of the ship's telegraph rang their orders to the engine room. The ship reacted suddenly and lurched violently to port. The list was so severe water washed over the port gunwale and flooded the deck. Many of the crew thought the ship would capsize and some below hurriedly made peace with their maker. The bow of the frigate came around quickly. The First Officer, hanging onto a stanchion for support, watched the compass intensely. The sonar operator constantly repeated the submarine's bearing over the Loudaphone: bearing 223... bearing 222...bearing 221... The compass passed bearing 220, then 210 then 205.

As soon as the frigate was pointed directly at the submarine the First Officer shouted his orders. "RUDDER MIDSHIPS, FULL AHEAD BOTH!" The Hafia-Al had righted itself and was now running on an even keel heading directly for the submarine that was dangerously close to the surface.

The submarine's Captain was old and experienced. Before his South African command he had been in the German Krieg's Marine, brought up in the tradition of the finest submariners the world had ever seen. He knew almost every trick in the book and was not the type to panic. Unfortunately even old sea dogs must answer the call of nature. The young lieutenant that had been left momentarily in charge of the submarine did not come from the same pedigree. The two vessels were now heading towards each other at great speed and as the submarine's Captain struggled to get back to the control room, the young lieutenant had to make a decision. It was the wrong one. "Hard to starboard!" he shouted.

At the same instant on the bridge the Captain of Haifa-el was getting ready. He looked at his stop watch whilst listening to the sonar operator. When he heard two hundred yards he barked his order, "Hard to port."

The frigate's Captain was confident that every mariner from the greatest admiral to the lowliest sailor knew the first rule of sailing was to give way to port. He knew that the Haifa-al and the submarine must come close but they would surely miss as both ships would go to port. He hadn't taken into account the inexperience and panic of the submarine's lieutenant.

The submarine's Captain pulled himself back to the control room, grasping the handrails tightly as the boat rolled alarmingly. Back at his post his sharp eye immediately saw the lieutenant's error and he shouted fresh orders.

"Hard to port, full reverse engines, flood all ballast tanks, emergency dive!"

Well drilled ratings of the South African Navy responded immediately. The submarine's bow began to dip, as it rolled violently from side to side. The reversed propeller thrashed in the water before its blades began to bite. It was the turn of the submarine's crew to feel fear as the vessel was pushed beyond its design limits. Worse was to follow.

The submarine's Captain knew it wasn't going to be enough. "More power!" he barked almost begging the boat to try harder. The propeller finally found purchase in the water but as the blades rotated a vacuum was formed on the back side of each individual blade. The vacuums could not be sustained and collapsed generating a horrific sound, like a clap of thunder that resonated the full length of the submarine. Sustained cavitations were every submariner's nightmare. There was no escape for the crew; it was like being trapped inside the bell of Big Ben when the hammer struck – time and time again. The crew had to decide if they were going to hold on to the handrails or cover their ears and vainly try to alleviate the acoustic pain. Some screamed as ear drums ruptured and for some tiny trickles of blood ran down their necks.

Both Captains clung to a spark of hope that by some miracle the two vessels would miss each other. It was close, very close but inevitably the listing conning tower of the submarine slammed into the rear of the frigate. The conning tower slid along the last few yards of hull before smashing into the fast rotating starboard propeller and finally hitting the rudder with such force it bent the central shaft.

And then it was over. All was calm. The submarine was taking in water but managed to blow its ballast tanks and bob to the surface. The helmsman on the frigate shouted "Ship not responding." The frigate's captain ordered slow ahead but the vessel was reduced to sailing in circles on a single propeller.

Van Stardan watched from the Martello Tower as three vessels approached; in front was the submarine with its damaged conning tower, missing periscope and twisted communications aerials. Following was a black and white ocean going tug, belching clouds of smoke and labouring to pull the third vessel, the grey frigate with no identification marks or fluttering flag. It was a sorry sight.

Leaving the tower he made his way on foot towards the quays. Simon's Town had been an important naval base for nearly two hundred years. Originally settled by the Dutch, the British had recognised that its location on the southernmost tip of Africa, where the rough waters of the South Atlantic Ocean butted up against the gentle warm waters of the Indian Ocean, making it one of the most strategically important places on the planet. It was the main reason the British had come to South Africa and chased away the Dutch.

Peter left the old, now defunct, area of the port that had been built from giant blocks of limestone hewed out of the nearby hills and laboriously levered into position by thousands of sweating blacks. He quickly arrived in the modern naval base, with sturdy piers resting on concrete piles, asbestos clad portal frame warehouses, goose neck cranes running on tracks and wide roadways for the multitude of fork lift trucks and tractor units that darted to and fro. By the time he got to the berth the submarine had tied up and engineers were clambering on board to inspect the damage. Further down the dock the gangplank was being put into position on the frigate and the tug was already sailing away having completed its task.

An officer in full dress uniform passed the main deck of the frigate waiting for the gangplank safety net to be secured. Peter sized up his adversary noting his formal square stature and stern facial features. When the net was fastened Peter didn't wait to greet the ship's officer but turned and made his way to the redbrick flat roofed building with a large observation window that was the base of the Harbour Master but had, on this occasion, been cleared in advance in anticipation of the forthcoming meeting.

A few minutes later the ship's Officer arrived escorted by a rating of the South African Navy. This was a deliberate snub by Peter van Stardan to show his annoyance and set the tone for the forthcoming encounter. But it was a mistake. Inwardly seething Peter knew he had to contain himself, to exercise restraint, but he was unable to mask his anger.

Van Stardan was sitting when the Officer arrived. He could barely force himself to stand and shake the hand of his adversary. The Officer removed his white peak cap. Peter noted the gold braid and insignia of an admiral. The Officer sat down without invitation, his expression fixed and severe.

Van Stardan paused for a moment as he formulated his first words. The pause was enough. The Admiral seized the opportunity and began his tirade.

"I wish to make a formal complaint about the careless and dangerous seamanship exhibited by submariners of your navy that has resulted in severe damage to a ship of the Israeli Defence Force. I expect and demand emergency repairs to be carried out so that I may safely return my ship to Israel. Furthermore I serve you notice that my government will undoubtedly seek full financial recompense.

My ship was patrolling in international waters when our sonar indicated that we were being followed by an unidentified submarine. The Captain of my ship acted quite properly. He altered course several times, he speeded up and then slowed down. He took measures to identify the submarine. Only after taking such measures did the Captain conclude the submarine was hostile. He then executed a turn and sailed towards the submarine."

Peter interjected. "So you admit you tried to ram our submarine?" "You admit that yours was the first hostile action?"

"If my Captain had wanted to ram your submarine be assured it would be at the bottom of the ocean at this point in time. The submarine failed to follow the basic rules of seamanship."

"The incident is open to interpretation," interrupted van Stardan.

"Let me explain simply," continued the Officer. "Your submarine collided with the rear of my ship, damaging the rudder. I am not sure what common practice is in the South African Navy but in Israel our captains are taught that ramming is most effectual when using the front end of the ship, the sharp bit! The Officer's sarcasm was undisguised. "My ship was sailing away when your submarine hit it. And may I add your submarine commander was exceedingly reckless with the lives of his own crew, the vessel was fortunate to survive the encounter."

Van Stardan, no seaman, knew he was at a disadvantage on questions of maritime practice. He changed the subject, quickly moving the discussion away from the collision.

"Your vessel was taking part in an illegal operation that was bound to have detrimental consequences for my country. Israeli actions were not in accordance with our agreements. That is far more important than the collision."

"I don't know what you are talking about," replied the Officer.

"It is my turn to speak simply," said van Stardan attempting to imitate his adversary's style. "Using facilities kindly made available by the South African Government, and without our permission, Israel carried out a nuclear test in waters off the South African Coast. This is totally unacceptable."

"I deny that Israel was involved in any such incident."

"That is a preposterous denial," replied van Stardan struggling to maintain his composure.

"I understand you claim this so called nuclear incident occurred midway between your country and Antarctica. As an impartial observer I would suggest to you that this area is a long way from your territorial waters. However if you are insistent on pursuing the matter you should take it up with the United Nations." The Officer knew that South Africa dare not approach the United Nations on the matter without attracting attention to its own nuclear programme.

Van Stardan countered. "For decades our countries have worked together. Now, when we are on the verge of carrying out our first joint test your country pre-empts the situation and explodes a device of its own on our door step and without warning. You do realise that what you have done could jeopardise all of our work at Vastrap? If the Americans get involved it could be the end of our project. Israel could also end up without an atomic bomb."

The Admiral laughed. "Times have changed my friend. Technology has marched on. The weapon you speak of, that we develop together, is primitive. In my country we are far beyond what is being produced at Vastrap. We only continue because we have given you our word and we will keep to our word – unless you force us to break it. As for the Americans you need not worry on our account. Do not underestimate the strength of the Jewish lobby in American politics. People in high places are working for our cause. I may be mistaken but I don't think your country enjoys such a relationship with Washington."

"This is treachery," mumbled van Stardan hardly able to digest the words he had just heard.

The Admiral smiled. "My country has the final part of our agreement to fulfil and will comply with our contract to the letter, that is unless you would rather we end our relationship now?"

Peter knew the implications. "No, we wish to complete the project. We await the final parts," he replied struggling to conceal the desperation in his voice.

United Nations New York
Thursday 5th January 1989

The theory was fine. The Nuclear Non-Proliferation Treaty was going to make the world a safer place. But like anything entrusted to the United Nations the admirable concept was dragged into the cesspit of political duplicity. Whoever put the word united in the name United Nations must be having a good giggle. In practice the representatives of the various countries believed themselves to be members of an exclusive club, membership of which confers many privileges and few responsibilities. Wise members of the club did not 'rock the boat' unnecessarily.

Vladimir Letchcan, the USSR's ambassador to the United Nations considered himself one of the wise. He'd slotted well into his New York based assignment. His perpetually smiling face, fat bald head and short dumpy body gave him a jolly image that he tried to live up to. As part of the Russian political elite champagne and beluga caviar were no strangers to his lips but to him they somehow tasted much better at Manhattan society parties. The only thing he really feared was the dreaded 'recall' to Moscow. For protection he'd developed a system; every so often he'd stamp his feet and thump the table in Security Council meetings and once or twice a year he'd make a rousing speech to the General Assembly extolling the virtues of the communist system. This kept his Kremlin bosses happy. The rest of the time, when not wallowing in Western decadency, he skulked around the corridors and meeting rooms of the United Nations building playing 'hail fellow, well met', unless something came up that is.

Today Vladimir sat at his desk and pondered the message from Moscow. It was setting him up for conflict, which he didn't like because that led to the protracted conflict resolution procedures which in practice amounted to countless wasted hours of boring meetings and debates. Better to avoid the conflict in the first place he thought, but he'd have to act quickly. The Non-Proliferation Committee was meeting Thursday and today was Monday. He decided the ambassador's dining room on the top floor was the best place to begin.

The US ambassador to the UN, John 'Buff' Cartwright was not like the other ambassadors. The USA had been instrumental in establishing the United Nations during the frenzy of moralistic self-congratulation that followed World War Two. The US Government had quickly become disillusioned with the institution it had spawned when it realised that the member countries had not only somewhere to express their views but also a platform to verbally attack and even humiliate America. US administrations quickly lost interest. The role of US ambassador to the United Nations quickly became the 'in joke' of Washington's political elite. Successive administrations had appointed ambassadors, sometimes to provoke and cajole, but more often than not just to get a politically painful individual out of Washington for a few days a week. John 'Buff' Cartwright fell into the latter category.

A middle aged short wiry man with rimless glasses, he had a painful expression permanently embossed on his face. He didn't smoke, he didn't drink, rarely laughed and went to bed at nine p.m. whenever he could. One insider joked, "Well he must do something, he's got eight children."

One thing everybody agreed on was that his hard line fundamentalist Christian views were not bringing him much personal happiness. He also had another known characteristic, born of his near obsessive compulsive personality. He was a person of strict habit.

Vladimir Letchcan arrived in the restroom of the Ambassador's Restaurant at exactly twenty-eight minutes after noon. Buff Cartwright walked in at half past, as he always did, intending to wash his hands thoroughly before eating his usual midday meal alone. Vladimir offered Buff a small sealed envelope.

"Don't worry;" said Vladimir, "It's not a condom. It's a friendly tip."

Hesitatingly Buff accepted the envelope and pocketed it.

After his lunch, at precisely one minute past one pm Buff was back at his desk and opened the envelope. Inside was a single white piece of paper. On it were written a series of numbers, the same numbers that the newspaper seller in Bristol had paid £10 for a few days earlier. At the bottom of the page was a single hand written sentence: *"Act before Thursday."* Buff looked at the numbers and recognised them from his army service days as a series of global grid references. He immediately faxed the sheet to the State Department in Washington.

The mission was hurriedly put together and only just possible. The President had withdrawn funding for the project and most of the planes had been mothballed or destroyed before Congress reversed the President's decision. As it was, there were only two SR71 Blackbird long range strategic reconnaissance aircraft in existence in the world and they were both based in the United States.

Once the mission had been authorised it had been relatively easy. Outbound the Blackbird had been refuelled mid-air by a KC 135Q Stratotanker out of Ascension Island. The Blackbird pilot had crossed the coast of Africa at over eighty-thousand feet cruising at Mach 3.2. The South African air defence radar picked them up but was powerless to do anything but watch. It couldn't get a lock-on because of electronic countermeasures but even if it could it wouldn't have made any difference. The Blackbird was simply too high and too fast for anything they had to throw at it. The plane did three passes with its Itek Operational Objective camera clicking away. Following another quick sub-sonic refuel over Ascension Island the Blackbird flew back to the US. A couple of hours later a full set of high resolution photographs were on the desk of the Secretary of State in Washington. The evidence was conclusive.

The White House issued a press statement on Wednesday evening:

> *'The US Government is in possession of evidence that clearly indicates the Republic of South Africa has been independently developing a nuclear weapon. This development if allowed to continue will change the balance of power on the Continent of Africa and is in breach of the sentiment and spirit of The Nuclear Proliferation Treaty. As an ally of South Africa the United States cannot tolerate this situation. The Government of the United States will make immediate representations to the leadership of South Africa in the strongest terms."*

A few hours later Vladimir Letchcan sat in his penthouse apartment overlooking Times Square sipping a large Jack Daniel's, a newspaper on his knee. He felt a warm glow. He would not have to surprise the representatives of the United States at the next morning's meeting. He'd already got what his masters in Moscow wanted, the condemnation of South Africa by the US Government.

Meanwhile in Bristol Jane Ashton looked forward to receiving her copies of the photographs from the US as part of the "*Mutual Co-operation Intelligence Agreement*". She hoped they'd arrive soon so she could fulfil her promise to Stuart Cameron. All she had to do was get ready for her trip to Africa.

Igor was not outside the George V pub selling his papers that night. He was inside drunkenly expounding the virtues of true socialism to anybody that was foolish enough to listen to his ramblings. He hadn't heard the news, not that it would have meant much to him anyway. He would never know his part in exposing South Africa's nuclear secrets. He was just happy that he'd turned his £10 investment into £25 by selling the envelope to a man he knew and regularly met at Bristol's Temple Meads railway station and who was, unknown to Igor, the Cultural Attaché attached to the Embassy of the Union of Soviet Socialist Republics in London.

Stirling Farm, Okavango
Saturday 28th January 1989

In a practical way Mary Scobie did what she could; she cleaned, she cooked she washed and cared for the children. But she knew there was little she could do for Duncan's morose mood. She had experienced tragedy in her own life and knew that the recovery process was slow. It took time and inner strength to find a way out of the endless rut of despair that was bereavement.

For the children he put on a show but most days he would just disappear into the bush for hours on end, un-provisioned, unarmed and caring little for the effects of the blistering sun. Too often his mind would drift back to his lonely childhood and he'd yearn for the strange security he'd got from his secret place, the lea of an anonymous rock on a barren Scottish hill side – his rock. When things were bad as a child he'd go there and sit alone drawing something from that ancient stone. In a strange way that place had made him strong enough to be alone. In the depths of his despair he thought it would have been better if he had never met Elizabeth, had never experienced the happiness and joy of love, of sharing; that it would have been better if he'd never surrendered his independence. Sometimes he just wanted to be alone again.

But he knew he wasn't alone. Somehow he always ended up back at the farmhouse, never returning purposefully, just arriving there. With head down and eyes fixed on his buff felt boots as he walked, he would look up to see the farmhouse in front of him. His feet had somehow returned him once more to his starting place.

One such Saturday, arriving back he stepped on to the stoop and pulled at the unlocked front door. It was strangely quiet inside and it frightened him.

"Mary!" he shouted, "James, Maggie!" There was no reply. His stomach felt hollow. He was used to seeing Mary standing on the stoop waiting for him with her warm and sympathetic welcoming smile. She was now his rock, his hope, passive and statuesque. He knew he would never think of women as the weaker sex again. Now that Elizabeth was gone he realised that it was she that had been his strength.

Duncan searched the house, yard and garden without success. He began to fear for James and Maggie, imagining how much worse it would be if they were not there and suddenly he realised how strong they had been. Their loss was great, no less than his own, yet they did not indulge in self pity.

He felt shame, shame that he could not display the same strength as his children. Undoubtedly they missed their mother. James often asked about her and he was not fooled by the stories of her now being with the angels. He was strong enough to face the truth without hiding. He never complained. Duncan cried, sometimes for Elizabeth, sometime in self pity but mostly for what had been taken from his children and, although he would never say it, somewhere in the depths of his mind he knew he could not be whole again until the matter of Elizabeth's murderers was resolved.

Duncan's initial fear was turning to panic. He headed for the Kraal. The once well trodden path was showing signs of abandonment. The family of Elizabeth, the clan, even Tembo and Morgan, had kept their distance believing that Duncan would have to fight the demons in his mind alone, but they knew there would be a time when Duncan would return to them.

It was only a couple of hundred yards to the Kraal but it was well hidden, shielded not only by trees but also an undulation too small to be called a hill. Even before the cluster of Africa roundavals came into sight he could hear excited voices and laughter. It shocked him. Laughter was a sound he'd almost forgotten existed and for a brief moment he thought it was a sound that desecrated the memory of Elizabeth.

He stopped short of the Kraal, concealed by the last of the bushes. As he watched he saw James running around in circles pursued by his cousins, the children of the Kraal. He was laughing as a child should. Maggie, sat in the middle of the circling group, smiling. Across the clearing stood men of the Kraal, in front of them was the Nanga, the witchdoctor. She wore the headdress of her office and gyrated her body as she wildly shook a bushy tail that had once belonged to an antelope but was now attached to an intricately carved stick and was her totem. Duncan didn't realise that the ceremony was for him and that the medium, with her incantations was asking the tribal ancestors for the return of the lost one.

To the left was the noisiest group. The women were crowding around something hidden from view, the ones on the outside pushing and standing on tip-toes to get a better look. There were occasional gasps of surprise from the women followed by shrieks of high pitched laughter.

Duncan stepped into the open. The first to see him was the Nanga. She raised her hands and howled an incomprehensible sound in thanks to the Spirits. A silence fell over the compound; even the children had a sense of the moment.

From the huddle of women, an older one stepped forward, one who obviously favoured her food. She waddled her way towards Duncan. Smiling but without words she took Duncan by the hand and led him forward. As they got closer the women silently parted to reveal the subject of their attention. Mary Scobie, sitting crossed legged on the dusty ground looked sheepishly up at him.

Momentarily Duncan stood in silence looking at the apparition before him.

"What is happening?" he eventually asked quietly, his question directed at Mary.

"I have a new family," replied Mary opening her hands expansively to the surrounding women. "And for the first time in my life, I have a sister,

Mafutzi," said Mary proudly pointing and smiling to the one that had fetched him by the hand.

Mafutzi smiled at Duncan revealing the only two, lonely yellow teeth that remained in her head.

"Why are you sitting on the ground?" he asked.

"Ah," replied Mary, "that's a long story. This morning Tembo, Morgan and Mafutzi came to see me. They told me that it had been six months and it was long enough for me to be alone with you. They said that I had proved myself, that I had shown I loved you as much as they did and that therefore I was now one of them. They brought me and the children here to the Kraal and we have been here all day - having fun."

"But why are you sitting on the floor?"

"Well the women got me a welcoming present. They thought I looked strange in the clothes I'd arrived in from Scotland but they decided they would not ask me to wear African clothes. So they went to the store and asked for clothes that a 'white woman' in Africa would wear. The shopkeeper gave them T shirts and shorts, look."

"But why would they buy them and then laugh at you?" he asked.

"They're not laughing at the clothes," replied Mary with a smile. "It's my legs. Firstly they've never seen such white legs before, but more than that they've never seen varicose veins like this." Mary pointed to the raised blue veins that ran like a network of roads on her exposed calves and thighs. They're daring each other to touch them. They think there are snakes beneath my skin and they're scared they might get bitten."

For the first time since Elizabeth had gone Duncan began to laugh. Mary held out her hand, Duncan pulled her to her feet. She embraced him and whispered in his ear. "There is nothing for me to go back to in Glasgow. I will stay here as long as you need me if that's all right with you?"

Tears filled Duncan's eyes, not tears of sorrow but tears of hope. The women gathered around and held him. Tears flowed, and when the salty drops fell to the dusty ground they took with them some of the pain that had been inside him for too long.

Mafutzi broke from the huddle and her voice boomed. "We will celebrate in the best way I know – we will feast."

Mary replied. Her voice loud, and unequivocal and mocking, a tone that transcended cultures. "You might be my new family but don't expect me to eat that rubbish you call food."

Mafutzi laughed, "You'll eat it in the end. I'll cast a spell."

Duncan shook his head no longer attempting to withhold his smile. He stood back and looked at Mary in her new clothes, her bared arms and legs were already reddening in the sun. "You are going to have to watch your skin, the sun can be fierce.

"We have good muti," said Mafutzi.

"Yes," added Mary. "They're going to get me some medicine for my skin. It sounds like a sun tan lotion. I think they call it Hello Vera or something like that."

Duncan screwed up his face. "Do you mean Aloe Vera by any chance?"

"Yes, that's the stuff."

Duncan slept well that night for the first time in six weeks. However by early morning as he stood on the stoop his anger was back and once again he felt the need to walk, to escape into his solitude.

Mary came from behind him. "There's a truck coming," she said.

No sooner had the words left her mouth than a dust swirl became visible in the distance. Fifteen minutes later a decrepit Mercedes seven tonne flat bed bumbled its way up the track, loaded with, what appeared to Duncan, to be a miscellaneous pile of scrap metal and machinery.

"What's that?" he asked.

"My present to you," replied Mary. "And here's another bit." Mary handed Duncan a large shovel.

"You can't exist in a limbo. The children need to see there is a future and it's up to you to show them. So I was thinking, what with all this heat, that a swimming pool would be a nice addition to the farm. The children would like that. The money for my return ticket to Glasgow bought that lot," said Mary pointing to the cargo on the back of the truck. I got it very cheap. Now I can't go back to Scotland even if I want to.

I am assured that everything necessary for a swimming pool is on the back of that truck; pipes, filters, pumps, storage tanks and what not. I'm sure you'll figure it out.

I don't want to see you go wandering off alone anymore. You will dig a big hole at the back of the house with that," Mary pointed to the shovel. You can work out your anger doing something useful. And what's more I can keep an eye on you and the children will be able to join in.

"That's crazy," said Duncan. "It's not practical."

"Why?" asked Mary.

"Water Mary! We're in the middle of the worst drought in these parts for years and you want me to build a swimming pool!"

"You're a resourceful man. I'm sure you'll think of something," replied Mary.

Duncan struggled to think of a further objection. "What am I going to do with all the soil and stones from the hole?"

"I've thought of that," said Mary. "You're going to build me a beautiful rock garden and I'm going to grow my own Hello Vera!"

The first shovelful was the hardest, breaking the dry cracked crust. By the end of the day Duncan had dug a small hole that was waste deep. James and Maggie looked on. The second day James came to help with his toy bucket and spade. Duncan smiled. The third day Morgan and

Tembo joined in and the hole grew bigger. On the fourth day men came from the kraal. By the end of the week a ladder was needed to get into the giant hole and it was not only Duncan's physical condition that had improved.

Heathrow Airport, London
Thursday 16th February 1989

"Do you like it?" asked Jane waving her left hand under Stuart's nose showing off the ring on her third finger.

They were early for their 7.15pm overnight flight to Harare and were killing time with a drink in the business lounge.

"It's beautiful," answered Stuart truthfully, admiring the large diamond solitaire. "I didn't realise you were engaged. I never noticed the ring before."

"You wouldn't have, it's new."

"Well congratulations then." Stuart raised his glass by way of a toast. "Who's the lucky chap?"

Jane smiled. "You are."

"What!"

"I thought for where we're going and what we're doing a couple will be less conspicuous than an individual male and female," Jane explained, "It just looks better, more plausible."

Stuart looked at her with furrowed brow.

"Don't worry," she continued. "The ring is a fake. You're not my type and I know I'm not yours. You'll be quite safe."

"What about my reputation then?" Stuart mocked.

"Sacrifice it for the job."

"Seriously don't you think it's going a bit far?"

"You said it would be a good idea if I came on the trip?"

"Only after you suggested it about six times."

"Well be that as it may. It was also you that said that we'd have to cook up a story for my presence in some situations. All I've done is taken you at your word."

The Immigration Official at Harare Airport inspected the passports. He checked their names against a list. "These are no good, you cannot have entry."

"They're good passports," responded Stuart.

"But you are not on the visa list, so they are not valid," replied the Immigration Official confidently. "You need a valid visa to enter Zimbabwe."

"We don't need a visa if we are in transit to a third country for which we do have a visa. Those are your rules, not ours, we checked them out before we left," replied Stuart.

"You don't have a return air ticket."

"That's correct. We're not returning to the UK, not through Harare. We're in transit. Here is our car hire booking form and our reservation in the Victoria Falls Hotel. It is completely in order. We are entitled to entry by your own rules."

"Wait," said the Immigration Official.

Thirty minutes later they emerged into the daylight of the airport concourse. Stuart led the way to the once familiar car park across the road from the main airport building.

"That was a bit hairy," said Jane. "We could have got visas you know."

"Not unless I wanted a reception committee to greet me. Last time I was here we had a bit of fun at their expense. They might like to have words. This way I'll be in and out before they have time to put two and two together."

"Yeah, I heard about your fun," replied Jane with a smile remembering the report she had read.

They had lunch on the sun terrace of the Monomotapa Hotel, overlooking the park, in central Harare.

"Not what it used to be," said Stuart looking at the patchy un-mown lawns and bedraggled herbaceous borders. "Not that long ago the standard of those gardens was comparable to any English country garden."

"Well enjoy what's left. It's only going to get worse. I understand there isn't a decent public garden or park between the Limpopo and Cairo. Gardens and parks are colonial features, not priorities for new African governments," smiled Jane.

"A lot more Mercedes' saloons with government plates though," he shot back.

Jane shook her head. "There are connotations in those words that might be misinterpreted."

"What I mean is it wouldn't be so bad if the parks maintenance money had been diverted to say building a school. But it hasn't," replied Stuart. "Your average white Zimbabwean sees the parks fall into disrepair and then thinks what's going to happen to law and order and health care? They get scared."

"I know what you mean but the black majority cannot be denied the vote for some lawns and a few plants. All we can do is our little bit; keep an eye on the change process and make it as painless as possible."

"And look out for British interests at the same time," added Stuart. He changed the subject. "Come on let's go. I've only allowed four days for the drive and half a day of it's gone already. I want to be in Bulawayo tonight."

The drive had taken seven hours; they stopped along the way a couple of times. The Bulawayo Sun Hotel was tired. It needed a refurbish that could only be financed by more revenue. Customers were however becoming increasingly scarce and the prospects for the city centre hotel were decidedly bleak. Stuart's memory of their one night stay would not only be of declining standards of décor however. That night they'd been forced to share a room. Half the hotel was no longer habitable. It was a twin room, propriety was maintained but Stuart struggled to conceal his discomfort. As they walked the corridor to their room he'd lagged behind, Jane had brushed aside his reluctance with a crisp, "Come on don't be coy."

When he woke up he was relieved to see her bed vacant and the room empty. Quickly he showered and dressed. He found her in the dining room munching toast and scanning the Bulawayo Chronicle.

"Just getting a feel for the place," she said. "I've been for a little walk around town."

The drive from Bulawayo to Victoria Falls took place in silence. The landscape changed too. Gone were the vast commercial farms that dotted the highway, the irrigated crops of cotton and tobacco and the herds of Herefordshire cattle grazing in green meadows. West of Bulawayo there were few farms, just small native developments growing maize and millet. The few cattle were no longer of European pedigree stock but African Long Horns scavenging on semi-parched land. Even that agriculture soon faded. Within an hour or so there was just unfenced trees and bush, pushing right up to the road, their high hanging branches encroaching into the sunlight so that, at times, it was almost like driving through a tunnel of forest.

Stuart maintained a steady speed and they made good progress following the road that had only wide sweeping bends and no urban developments to slow them down.

"Good ambush country," Stuart eventually spoke.

Jane snapped out of her reverie. "My information is that guerrillas don't operate in this area anymore."

"They don't," replied Stuart, "but there are still occasional groups of bandits and they can be just as unpleasant. What were you thinking?"

"Just about our conversation in Harare. You don't think that the Africans are fit to govern themselves do you?"

"I think the days of white supremacy in Africa are over. I believe in democracy and think that Africans should govern Africa themselves. I am one hundred percent in agreement with the concept. It's just the reality that I struggle with. In black Africa all I have ever seen are falling standards for ordinary Africans and growing corruption."

"Democracy is not so perfect in Europe. We have to give the Africans a chance to catch up and develop the institutions," replied Jane.

"I admit there are slight differences between us," said Stuart. "Reality has tarnished my idealism but we most probably want the same outcome."

"I think the differences are bigger than you think."

The curtain of silence descended once more.

The Maitre'd stood erect as he welcomed Stuart and Jane to the formal dining room of the elegant Victoria Falls Hotel, a lone vestige of colonialism that the Government of Zimbabwe allowed to exist in all its grandeur because of the tourist dollars it brought in.

Stuart wore a light lounge suit and tie, Jane a low cut evening dress and diamond necklace that complemented her engagement ring and was made from the same paste.

"We have booked a table for four, eight o'clock," said Stuart.

"Yes Sir. Your guests have arrived and are already seated. Please follow me," he replied in an accent that would not have been out of place in any of Pall Mall's private clubs.

As they approached the table the two men stood. Both wore polyester slacks, broad check jackets and bright open necked shirts but it was their flat top crew-cuts with close shaved necks that gave them away as Americans.

"This is Jack Carter and I'm Burt Zimmerman," the taller one spoke.

"I'm Stuart Cameron and this is Jane Ashton," Stuart hesitated, "my fiancée - for this trip."

"You two engaged? That's great. You Brits really take team work to the limit."

They exchanged handshakes and sat, the Maitre'd gently easing Jane's chair into place before flapping the serviettes on to their laps. Seamlessly, in a well practiced manoeuvre, he took the red leather bound menus from an assistant who had miraculously appeared behind and passed them out, Jane first.

"Great idea to meet in this place," began Burt, "Boy you guys really know how to do things in style. I bet the ribs here are really good." Burt's appetite was proportionate to his waist line.

"Not sure about ribs," said Stuart "but I'm reasonably confident they'll do a nice rack of lamb."

Burt opened the menu. "Hey Bud," he said with urgency to the departing Maitre'd, "mine's in a foreign language!"

The Maitre'd continued as if he hadn't heard.

"I think all the menus are written in French," Jane said in a quiet voice. "It's most probably so they can charge more. But don't worry I speak French and I'll help you."

"Yeah, right, sorry, shu'da guessed that, thanks."

Jack Carter was more composed and business like.

"We're here for a reason so who wants to kick off?" he said looking at Stuart.

"Perhaps you'd do the honours," replied Stuart passing back the responsibility.

"Fine, but we'll talk in spades if that's okay with you two. We've been told via our controlling officer in Washington that we should talk with you, we presume you were told something similar. Our instructions are to co-operate and lay our cards on the table. So the US position is simple. South Africa is finished, they just don't know it. White supremacy is a dead duck. The State's view until recently was just to let things play out, let the blacks and whites beat up on each other for a while until the blockheads in Pretoria saw sense. But the game's changing now. We got a tip off from the Ruskies and it's sort of forced our hand. The South Africans have got *'the bomb'*. That won't play well domestically. The President has to take into account the feelings of the Afro-Americans."

"Especially when Presidential elections are on the horizon?" added Jane.

Jack ignored Jane. "Quite soon our President is going to give the President of South Africa two options. South Africa can run with Apartheid and a protracted civil war, which they will eventually lose, or it can give into democracy gracefully now and save a lot of lives. If they take the latter route we'll promise to assist them in negotiating a decent deal for the whites."

"What's the exact evidence you have of the bomb?" asked Jane.

"I thought you might ask." Jack removed a sheaf of tightly rolled photographs, held with a rubber band, from his inside jacket pocket and passed them to Jane. She rolled the rubber band off and smoothed the aerial photographs of Vastrap on the table. After a brief glance she passed them to Stuart. "As promised," she said with the trace of a smile. "My own copies haven't arrived yet."

"What does that mean?" asked Burt catching the gesture but not the words.

"Oh, just a private joke," replied Jane. "So what are your main concerns?"

"As part of the deal our President is going to offer the South Africans, they would have to eventually surrender their nuclear weapons. It's not negotiable. Nobody but nobody would be happy with the 'new' black led South Africa as a nuclear power. "

"We're on similar ground," said Stuart.

"We really don't know if the politicians will play ball. There are some pretty thick skulls in that part of the world and even if the politicians can be persuaded there are some tough hardliners knocking around the fringes that could rock the boat. We'd call them rednecks back home in the States. They might not like the idea of giving in so easy. Burt and I are going to recommend that as soon as political agreement is reached we grab their arsenal. We want to be ready to put feet on the ground straight away, account for their arsenal and keep an eye on it until the technical guys can be rounded up."

"So how do you think Her Majesty's servants can help?" asked Stuart.

"Well let's face it, this is your back yard. You have been dealing with them Afrikaners for a long time, even fought a couple of wars against them. You know the country and the people. We reckon you know better than most what's going on there," said Jack, "Besides you've got the biggest financial investment in the place; diamond, gold and all that shit and we ain't in the business of messing up our cousins."

"That's very thoughtful of you," said Jane.

"No problem. If you can't be honest with your friends who can you be honest with? Gotta trust somebody in this bad world. So are you in? Can we work together to make sure this damn bomb programme is properly neutralised?" Jack Carter finished talking and turned his attention to the melba toast that had just arrived at the table.

"Good of you to be so frank," began Stuart. "I'll try to return the gesture. What you are saying is that you're expecting an imminent informal political agreement between the US and South Africa but there could be a time delay between the negotiations and the signing of a formal protocol and rogue elements might 'try to pull a stunt' in that period?"

"Yeah that's right. It's gonna take time. Firstly the South African politicians got to sell the idea to their people and then we have to make it formal and involve the Canadians, the Frenchies and even China and the Ruskies."

"I understand that. So you think we, the US and British, should pool resources and provide the vanguard for inspectors from the Atomic Energy Commission, who we presume would have the job of dismantling the South African nuclear weapons programme. Our respective governments would know our role there but not the UN?"

"Yeah, but only when we get the green light from South African political leaders, if not the troops on the ground."

"I suppose that would give us a heads up on the South African programme. As you might say, we would be ahead of the posse?"

"Right. We need to keep the initiative. We don't want the Ruskies taking the lead here do we?" I got nearly fifty agents fired up and ready to go all over Africa to keep an eye on things. They're arriving at our base in Rwanda right now. We can watch a hell of a lot with that kind of manpower. What do you think you could throw into the pot?"

"Our contribution would be three people who would get support from myself and Jane here."

Burt Zimmerman could not keep the disappointment from his face. "We were hoping you'd do better than that."

"I'd suggest you don't worry too much about the numbers. They are three very knowledgeable and motivated people. They'll be pleased to assist and I can assure you that British troops on South African soil would not be acceptable to anybody."

"Okay!" said Jack Carter. "You're saying quality over quantity. That'll be fine."

The business over the four ate their meal with convivial conversation. Only Burt Zimmerman expressed disappointment with the size, if not the taste, of his rack of lamb.

The coffee finished and the last of the brandy drunk, the four were preparing to depart.

"I don't fully accept your reasons for involving us," said Jane.

Jack Carter stared at Jane for a moment before speaking with a tongue that might have been lubricated with alcohol but was nevertheless clear. He placed his hands flat on the table as if to emphasise his sincerity. "Do you want me to be honest, like straight between the eyes honest?"

"I thought you were being," said Jane without hesitation.

"We know you Brits think we Americans are loud and crude and even stupid. That's suits us sometimes and we sort of go along with it. But you do us a disservice at times. Our analysts in Langley don't have the evidence but they are pretty sure that the Ruskies were tipped off about Vastrap and they think it was you lot that did the tipping."

Stuart raised his eyebrows.

Jack Carter put up his hand to stop Stuart responding. "Please don't say anything. Let me finish. We think you did it because you were pissed with us for trying to slide a card under the table over the Israeli test, the Vela Incident in the South Atlantic. Which we did. Now bearing in mind that what's going down in South Africa will not only affect our negotiations for ending the Cold War but could also swing the result of the Presidential elections, our guys reckon it's better to have you lot in the tent pissing out rather than outside the tent pissing in. It's also our way of saying sorry. Friends?"

Jane and Stuart laughed in part at the explanation and in part at the expression of pained honesty on Jack's face. "Friends," they replied in unison.

"Now I got a question too. You guys have some kinda new secret organisation, a think tank or something, that we can't get a handle on, and we don't like things we don't understand. We know it's called TULIP but not much more," said Jack staring into Jane's eyes, "You wanna tell me about it? You guys aren't part of that Department are you?"

Jane laughed again. "No, not exactly part of it."

That night Stuart felt less uncomfortable going to bed; he had his own room. As he and Jane parted in the corridor Jane asked "Does Duncan Murdoch have any idea what you have in mind for him?"

"Not yet," he replied.

Washington DC
Friday 17th February 1989

Whilst the President's diary, as published in the Washington Post, was well scrutinized not many would have realised the significance of the curt entry stating that the President of South Africa, Stephen Duplessey, who was in the United States on a personal and private visit, was to make a courtesy call on the White House that afternoon. There was to be no follow-up press release or photo-opportunity.

The meeting was very similar to one that had taken place several years earlier, a meeting between the political leaders of Rhodesia and South Africa. At that time it was the President of South Africa who had done the summoning and it was Ian Smith, Prime Minister of Rhodesia who'd received the bad news. Ian Smith thought that he'd been called to Pretoria to discuss security matters. It was not long before he realised that there were to be no discussions, the fate of his country had been decided by others. He was only there to receive the bad news. The Rhodesian war had been lost not on the battlefield but in the far away offices of foreign politicians. The same fate awaited President Duplessey.

Mr Duplessey did not take the news well. Fearing the frailty of the aging South African leader, White House staff had taken the precaution of having a medical team on discreet stand-by in an adjoining office. It was a fortuitous precaution. As the implications of the message sank in, colour drained from his face. The US President would later say that he saw the man physically age before his very eyes. The doctors were called.

As heart attacks go it was quite minor and the prompt medical attention ensured that the Americans would not have the embarrassment of explaining why a foreign head of state had died in the Oval Office. Even so President Duplessey spent the next six days bed-ridden in the Presidential Suite of New York's Waldorf Astoria Hotel, which had been quickly turned into an impromptu intensive care unit. Continuous heavy sedation was part of the treatment and so it was left to the South African Presidential Aides to receive the message in detail from their US counterparts.

It was not that the Aides did not put up a fight. They threatened counter sanctions against the United States including the repudiation of debts, expelling of US warships from South African Naval bases and the withholding of strategic minerals such as cobalt and chromium. They even threatened to stop the export of the diamonds vital to the New York Jewish jewellery industry. But the threats were just brushed aside. The only choices for South Africa was a prolonged war and inevitable defeat or an immediate settlement, negotiated from a position of strength, with black political leaders and guaranteed by the United States and the rest of the international community.

The Aides were not empowered to conclude a deal nor did they despatch advanced reports to Pretoria or even fully inform the South African Ambassador in Washington. They decided that the news was best presented to an emergency cabinet meeting, face to face; even if this did risk a further Presidential heart attack. The President of the United States was disappointed not to have concluded matters.

As he recovered in his sick bed President Duplessey penned a personal handwritten note to the President of the United States who read it alone in the Oval Office. He disregarded much of the text as just the vitriolic jabbering of a sick man who had lost the plot. The last sentence though struck a note of truth as it confirmed what his agents on the ground in Africa were saying:

"Maybe you believe you can browbeat me into submission and bully my Government around to your way of thinking. Maybe you can make my people abandon a way of life that your own country advocated and embraced not that many years ago. But there are people in my country, unflinching people with power and influence that are not under my control. They will not accept your dictate and would rather see the coming of Armageddon, the end of the world, before they surrender what they consider to be their God given right. I have warned you."

Stirling Farm, Okavango
Saturday 18th February 1989

Digging a hole was the easy part of building a swimming pool. Pipe work, reinforced footings, walls, chicken wire, rendering, filters, pump and now finally tiling the deck; the man in the ironmongers at Maun hadn't explained all that to Mary. He was just happy to have sold a swimming pool to somebody in the middle of a drought. Not that she cared that much either because the project was fulfilling its primary purpose, the rehabilitation of Duncan.

Wearing only boots and shorts Duncan knelt on the ground concentrating on levelling the last bit of flat sandstone he needed to place into the wet cement; the stone that would become part of the path that surrounded the pool. Finally he got to his feet and arched his back to relieve the ache. He had been crouched for too long. But good things had been happening. Duncan's body was once more bronzed, strength was returning to his weakened muscles and his desire for life was rekindled. But more than that, he'd started smiling again. He hadn't forgotten Elizabeth, he never would but he knew there was a future and James and Maggie knew that they had got their Dad back.

"Time to stop now," shouted Mary from the kitchen door. "It's too hot. I'll get you a beer." The others had already gone, the friends that came from the Kraal everyday to help.

"I need some food," he growled in mock anger as he ran towards Maggie whose tiny feet were too slow to carry her away. He scooped her up in his arms and pretended to nibble at her neck. The child squealed with delight as she wriggled to break free.

Stuart went straight to the driver's door without thinking.

"You do that automatically don't you," said Jane. "Did you ever think I might like to drive?"

"It didn't cross my mind," he replied unlocking the door with the key.

"Well I would like to do some of the driving."

"Okay," replied Stuart, "But we've got a few obstacles coming up, we're going to cross the border into Zambia in about five minutes. It's a tricky drive and the guards can be difficult to deal with."

"I don't see how holding a steering wheel will help in negotiations with some border guards."

"After that it's only an hour or so drive through Zambia then we'll be in Namibia. The road is pretty straight and clear there. Perhaps it's best to wait till then," said Stuart climbing into the driver's seat without further discussion. Sullenly Jane got into the passenger seat.

"Perhaps you're right" she sighed," A straight stretch of wide road is most probably more suitable for a woman. They shouldn't be confused with bends and the like."

She slammed the car door, her sarcasm impossible to ignore. They drove in silence, crossing the Zambezi Bridge. Stuart gripping the steering wheel tightly, they entered Zambia without a problem, his concerns unfounded. He drove into the town of Livingstone and pulled up a hundred metres from the Livingstone Museum. He looked at his watch, "We're too early."

They finished the journey to the museum on foot and killed time by walking around the external exhibits. Stuart concentrated his attention on a Chipmunk bi-plane, a trainer of interwar vintage. Jane hung about the siege cannon that had been brought by ox cart from Cape Town in the 1890's by the vanguard of Rhodes' construction force. At exactly 11am the representative of the British High Commission to Zambia arrived, a lanky blond in her early twenties.

"Hope I'm not too late" she said. "I started early enough from Lusaka this morning but the drive was a bit of a bugger, roads full of potholes. Tyres will be in shreds before I get back to Lusaka." She handed over a folder to Jane. "That's the latest. We couldn't make head nor tail of the cipher. Perhaps it'll make more sense to you."

"That's great, thanks," said Jane taking the envelope. "Do you always drive yourself on long journeys?"

"I could use a pool driver but they want to stop every half hour to have a drink and talk with their mates. I haven't got time for that nonsense, rather get the job done."

"You have a nice drive back," replied Jane shaking the representative's hand before turning to walk back to their car. Stuart nodded at the representative and hurriedly followed Jane.

For the next couple of hours Jane's head was buried in the sheaf of papers she'd just received, Stuart concentrated on the road, and its bends. After an hour or so he saw the sign for a hotel ahead.

"Want to get a coffee or something?"

"Why? I'd rather we just kept going," said Jane never lifting her head from the papers. Most of the document was written in plain text but there was a section in field code that needed de-ciphering. Five miles before the crossing from Zambia into Namibia Jane told Stuart to pull over on a deserted section of road. She got out and burnt the papers she'd just received. At the border Jane used some disgusting public toilets and picked up a couple of bottles of Coke whilst Stuart stood in line for Immigration. By the time he'd completed the formalities she was back in the car waiting impatiently to start their journey along Namibia's Caprivi Strip.

The Caprivi Strip, an anomalous legacy of nineteenth century colonialism has enduring political implications. In the last decades of the nineteenth century, when the European powers were busy carving up Africa into colonies, boundary disputes were more likely to be settled in

London, Berlin or Paris rather than in Africa itself resulting in some strange agreements.

Britain was anxious to secure the sole trading rights in Zanzibar on the distant east coast of Africa. At the time the island was jointly occupied and administered by Britain and Germany. Initially the British offered to hand over Helgoland, a little island off the north German coast, if the Germans departed Zanzibar. The Germans weren't biting knowing that Helgoland was so close to Germany they could take it any time they wanted. Undaunted by the rebuff the British entered into a bit of duplicity. The Germans had two main colonies in Africa, Namibia and Tanzania, but they were unconnected which was inconvenient for them.

Aware of Germany's problem the British 'inadvertently' leaked a highly edited copy of a survey they'd just completed. The survey *'proved conclusively'* that the great Zambezi River that ran east from Victoria Falls ended up in Tanzania. It became patently obvious to the Germans that if they could get access to Victoria Falls, their two colonies would be united by one of the great African waterways.

During routine discussions the Germans nonchalantly mentioned that it might be nice if they had access to the most wonderful natural wonder of the world, Victoria Falls. The British delegation, as a *'fraternal gesture'*, agreed that it would be unfair to deny a cultured Nation like Germany access to such a place of natural beauty. The attendant cartographers quickly drew lines on a map, suggesting handing to Germany a sliver of remote unproductive land on the edge of a desert. In exchange, the British suggested it would simplify things greatly if there was a single administrative authority in Zanzibar: Britain. In a masterly stroke of flattery they even suggested that the ceded land be called the Caprivi Strip in honour of the then serving German Chancellor, Leo von Caprivi, the man who would have to endorse the deal. The Germans signed up as quickly as they could and commenced packing their bags in Zanzibar. A few weeks later the British released the full text of the Zambezi survey report. Whilst it proved to be true, the river did link German East and West Africa, unfortunately the river was so beset with rapids, cataracts and gorges it was totally un-navigable. The Germans had been sold a pup. The result however was that a tangle of international borders, all converging close to Victoria Falls had been created. The borders of Zambia, Botswana, Namibia, Zimbabwe and even Angola came together to make a mishmash that is all but impossible to police and is consequently a magnet for guerrilla fighters and bandits. It was in this area that Stuart and Jane travelled.

The sun was dipping, its edge brushing the horizon, when Duncan saw the car approaching. It was overdue but Duncan hadn't worried, Jane had phoned ahead from the hotel where they'd lunched. He'd thought their plan was overly ambitious. Travel itineraries need to be elastic in Africa.

He met them at the car. The two men embraced. As they parted Jane stepped forward.

"I'm Jane. It's good to meet you at last. Stuart has told me a lot about you."

"Then you have the advantage," replied Duncan.

The conversation on the last leg of the journey had concerned Jane's status. Stuart said that Duncan was a trusted confidante but Jane had been adamant.

"A cover is a cover and we will stick to it," she'd insisted. "I'll make up my mind when I get to know him. Besides he's not even on the payroll yet."

Stuart eventually conceded. He was dog tired, he'd driven all day. She'd refused to drive when he offered and as the day progressed he began to wish she'd take the wheel for a spell but she wasn't volunteering and he wasn't asking.

Duncan shook Jane's hand and smiled. "I was so surprised to hear of the engagement. I thought I knew Stuart but he's turned out to be the proverbial 'dark horse'. Welcome to Stirling Farm. I hope you feel comfortable here," said Duncan scooping up both bags.

"How did you know?" asked a surprised Stuart.

"Jane told me when she phoned."

"I'll take my own bags," said Stuart.

"You look more done in than Jane does," replied Duncan as he led them towards the farmhouse.

Jane allowed herself the luxury of a contrived smile in Stuart's direction as she fell in behind Duncan leaving Stuart to bring up the rear.

Mary had prepared food which was consumed with little more than mannerly enthusiasm by Stuart who just wanted to go to bed but dreaded the prospect of raising the subject, fearing that he would be forced to actually share a bed with Jane.

Mary settled the question. "We're a bit short on space since I've arrived and taken the guest room. So I've taken the children in with me and you two can have their room. Only single beds, I'm sorry!"

"That's fine," replied Stuart barely bothering to conceal his relief. "In fact I'd like to turn in now if that's okay. Perhaps you and I could spend a little time together in the morning?" were Stuart's parting words to Duncan. Jane followed shortly afterwards, allowing Stuart just enough time to get himself properly 'tucked in'.

In the morning, after coffee, the two men walked. Duncan showed Stuart the nearly complete pool. He told of Mary's inspiration and how she'd helped him through the darkness. The men walked to the spot where the explosion had taken place.

"I've only recently been able to do this," Duncan admitted. "I could only pass the place by driving quickly, but I'm slowly coming to terms with it."

Duncan led Stuart towards the small raised Kopje. They followed a worn stony path stopping just short of the summit.

"The farm's not that big in African terms, you can just about see all of it from the top. Elizabeth and I used to come here. This was where we made our plans. I suppose you could say it was our special place.

"It's peaceful," said Stuart. "Thank you for sharing it with me."

Duncan took the last few steps to the summit; Stuart followed and saw the rough hewn stones that had been carefully laid out and the flowers that were wilting despite having been placed there only the previous day.

"As a tribal princess she could have had a traditional burial but the elders said because she had decided of her own accord to make a life with a man from a different culture, it should be my choice what happened to her remains. I picked this place because of what it meant to both of us. From here she can see both the farmhouse and the Kraal." Duncan spoke as if she was standing there next to him.

They stood together for a while before returning slowly down the hill.

As they neared the farmhouse Stuart spoke. "When we last met I promised that if the opportunity came I would help you find whoever ordered the attack that killed Elizabeth."

Duncan stopped and turned to face Stuart. "Do you know who it was?"

"No, not exactly but I'm getting there," replied Stuart. "Things are happening that I am sure will lead to their exposure. Obviously our visit to southern Africa is not for pleasure. Jane and I are here for a reason. The situation internationally is delicate. We have to keep an eye on events and act if the situation requires.

I suspect you don't realise it but you have already had an influence on what is happening, even if it was inadvertent. The death of Elizabeth and Jomo started something big and to be honest, with your background I could do with you being on board. Would you make yourself available? Would you be part of it?"

Duncan thought for a few moments. "You haven't told me very much and I know you can't say a lot until I agree. I also know that for many weeks I indulged in self pity. I think I'm over that period now and ready to get on with my life. I have to trust you. If in your heart you think I should get involved go on, tell me. But before you make that decision for me just consider what Elizabeth would want. You knew Elizabeth as well as anybody."

They walked on a little further before Stuart replied.

"Elizabeth was not a selfish person; she was a person that thought of others. She was not the type that would expect you to be saddled with the burden of revenge. From her personal perspective I think she'd tell you just to get on with your life and accept what has happened. But if Elizabeth knew what I knew she would probably tell you to get ready to help. Things could go wrong, things that could have bad consequences for a lot of innocent people."

"Then I suppose you'll have to tell me more."

Two days later Stuart and Jane's car disappeared down the track in a swirl of dust as Duncan watched from the stoop. Standing with him were Tembo, Morgan, Mary and the children. Before their car was out of sight Duncan began to speak.

"I've agreed to meet them in Pretoria in ten days time. They think I can help them and also find out who was responsible for Elizabeth's death."

"Tembo spoke. "There is no doubting Stuart," he began, "but you must be wary of her. Her heart is good but her mind is muddled."

"You didn't understand her?" asked Morgan.

"I understand her but she doesn't understand us," replied Tembo. "She thinks bringing a black man to power is the same as liberation. She doesn't understand that oppression does not discriminate; white and black people can be equally oppressive. We took to arms and chased the white man from Zimbabwe and now have to live in exile ourselves. Liberation was not good for us. We have gained nothing and lost much."

"You don't think I should help?" asked Duncan.

"Oh yes you should help, but do not chase a false dream. Even I will dig up my gun, I will practice my shooting, I will put myself in danger. I will be ready if you need me, but not to fulfil a dream. I will help if it gives me the chance to avenge my sister."

"I am with you," said Morgan.

"For better or worse, the decision is made," said Duncan. "I'm getting ready for my trip. Mary, I hope what we're doing is right. I don't like leaving you and the children even if you do have the people of the Kraal with you."

Mary smiled. "Duncan you have to do what is right. You won't get peace of mind if you walk away. For my part it's nice to be useful again, I'd thought those days had gone forever. Besides, Tembo and Morgan will be here for now at least."

"But we will be ready when you call," added Morgan.

"And I will ask the Spirits to smile on your journey," finished Tembo.

Zodiac House, Pretoria
Monday 27th February 1989

"I don't trust them," said Peter van Stardan thumbing through a sheaf of telex communications. "They will not fulfil their part of the bargain."

Alfred Smidt shielded his eyes with his hand. Even with drawn blinds there was too much light. It made his headache worse.

"They are only playing with us. I know the Jews. It is true that they no longer need us. They have outstripped us in technology and possibly think the end is near for us and we are no longer reliable partners. They may make things difficult but they will always fulfil their side of the bargain to the letter, even if not in spirit, as long as the other side does the same. It is in their psyche. It would be against their God to do otherwise. Our agreement is very clear. We must be left with independent working devices. We must not give them any excuse to default."

"Then why all this?" replied Peter waving the papers.

"They are showing their displeasure because we damaged their ship, nothing more. The uranium ore they demand is in their minds compensation for the damage that was done. The parts we require will be delivered. We just need to meet their demands."

"I am doing what I can as quickly as I can. The delays worry me and all the extra communication is dangerous. Sooner or later somebody will discover our plans and even worse our vulnerability."

Meadow Vale Hotel, Pretoria
Tuesday 28th February 1989

"It's not that complicated," said Jane. "The Israelis send a message to a satellite, the satellite re-transmits the message towards earth and it's picked up by a South African ground receiver.

The Americans and Russians are spending a small fortune trying to intercept those messages but quite frankly we're out of that game. We don't have the money. We do something that is much less complicated."

"What?" asked Duncan.

"For South Africa it is quite simple. The messages from the satellite are received at a small military communications station on a hill to the southwest of Pretoria. Once received the South Africans relay them by microwave to an antenna on top of the Reserve Bank of South Africa, one of the most secure buildings in the country. The thing about microwave transmissions is that the sending and receiving stations must be in line of sight. Now the hill isn't very high and the buildings not that big either so the signal travels quite close to the ground. We just rented the top floor apartment in a high rise that is in the path of the signal and stuck a small bi-directional receiver on the roof. We get all their communications, outbound and inbound. There are slight difficulties though."

"What are they?" asked Duncan.

"The Israelis and South Africans don't have a unified cipher system. The nearest they have to a common language is plain English. Whilst we don't have a great deal to de-code they do use terms and phrases with which we are unfamiliar, and which may have serious implications! That's where you come in because we don't want to unduly alarm our superiors in London. Stuart knows you well and I've read your file. We do appreciate you're not a nuclear scientist but we believe you have a pretty good knowledge of what is required."

"There was a period when I had time on my hands and I studied as much as I could."

Duncan, Stuart and Jane all smiled knowing he was referring to the period he was imprisoned in Colchester.

"But that was a long time ago, I'm out of date now but I'll give it a whirl if you want. What have you got for me?"

Stuart spoke, "It's always been a bit of a mystery to us how things get done so quickly and so secretly in South Africa. Just consider their nuclear bomb programme. Many organisations are involved; ARMSCOR, that's the military procurement company, the civil nuclear power industry, the uranium ore producers, the army, the air force and that's just the big ones. None of those organisations seem to get bogged down in normal bureaucracy. Things just happen for them. It's like a scissors is always there to cut through the red tape. We are convinced there is an informal organisation that wields power and we think it is some kind of secretive off-shoot of a cultural organisation called The Brotherhood. What's worrying is that they appear to be operating independently of the Government and they are in play now."

"Jane and I have just come back from Cape Town. A couple of weeks ago a US freighter docked there expecting to load about five thousand tonnes of uranium ore, ore that the US wants for its own weapon's industry. The shipping agents were suddenly told that the ore was unavailable, even though it was clearly lying on the docks.

We went down there and saw the ore being shipped out of the docks at Cape Town by trucks. We followed one truck to Simons Town military dockyard, which is not that far away. The ore was then loaded on to a Monrovian registered freighter. We hung around for a couple of nights to see what we could pick up but got nothing. The crew of the freighter were confined to the ship, no shore leave.

London checked the Monrovian freighter out on the Lloyds Register of Shipping and they tell us that the ship is registered to a Cayman Islands' company that we believe is ultimately owned by the Israeli government."

Jane came in seamlessly. "That ties in with our intercepted communications. The South Africans and Israelis are not getting on all that well at the moment. It appears that until the Israelis get the uranium ore, they are holding onto something that the South Africans badly want. We are just not sure what it is other than that it's connected with their nuclear bomb programme. We're hoping that you might be able to help on that score."

"Give me the relevant papers and then leave me alone for a couple of hours. Go and get yourselves some lunch or something," said Duncan.

When Stuart and Jane returned two hours later, with coffee and a sandwich for Duncan, he was standing at the window looking over the city.

"How did you get on?" asked Stuart.

Duncan returned to the table and took a gulp of the coffee and a bite from the sandwich before he spoke.

"I think I was able to glean a bit."

"Well go on then," coaxed Jane not masking her curiosity.

"The first nuclear bombs used uranium as a fuel. We, that's the West and the Russians, don't use uranium any more. We found better stuff, like plutonium. The good news is that the South Africans don't appear to have any plutonium. They're only capable of building fairly primitive low yield uranium bombs."

"Can you tell if they have more than one device?" asked Stuart.

"From what I can gather they have built or are in the final stages of building between six and ten devices."

"Shit!" replied Stuart. "That really doesn't sound too good. What stage are they and how did they get there?"

"Where do you want me to start?" asked Duncan.

"The beginning," said Jane.

"Okay, you asked for it. As I said the South Africans are using highly enriched uranium as the explosive."

"Just a second," said Jane. "What is highly enriched uranium exactly?"

"Well, to put it as simply as I can, uranium ore is dug out of the ground. Ninety percent of it is standard uranium atoms. They're called uranium 238. The other ten percent is made up of a slightly different type of uranium, an isotope called uranium 235. It's the 235 that is useful. Enrichment is a complex process but it basically means increasing the percentage of 235 in the uranium: enriched uranium has about forty percent 235 atoms and is used in power stations; highly enriched uranium has up to eighty percent 235 and is used for bombs. That's it."

"Okay, got that," said Jane.

Duncan continued. "If you put enough highly enriched uranium together it will self destruct all on its own. The lump is called a critical mass. In a bomb they have two bits of highly enriched uranium, both smaller than the critical mass. The two little bits are joined together and become a single lump that is bigger than the critical mass. The atoms start to self destruct, very, very quickly. That's a nuclear explosion."

"Well now I know," said Stuart.

"So what does that mean to us," asked Jane.

"I think the South Africans have built a barrel type bomb. That's simply a metal tube with a lump of highly enriched uranium at each end. With normal explosives they shoot the two lumps towards each other and they meet in the middle of the barrel and hey presto.

"The big problem is that the two conventional charges need to go off at exactly the same time and when I say exactly I mean exactly, to within a millionth of a second. That's so that the two bits of uranium are pushed together properly. That kind of accuracy is very difficult, I would say impossible, to achieve with ordinary detonators.

The Americans had so much trouble when they built the first devices in Los Alamos, they had to invent a new kind of electrical detonator. They called it an 'Electronic Bridge Wire' detonator. These detonators are extremely difficult to make. A lot of people would say it's easier to make the bomb than make the detonator. The technology is highly classified."

"So?" asked Jane.

"Simple. There are lots of references to EBW 1773's throughout the papers you gave me to read. To me that means Electronic Bridge Wire model type 1773. My guess is that the South Africans may have manufactured bombs but they are depending on the Israelis to supply the detonators and the Israelis are now playing silly buggers. Possibly they are holding out for a few thousand tonnes of uranium ore? That might explain your ship in Simon's Town."

"You said earlier that the South Africans might have up to ten devices. How did you get to that figure?" asked Jane.

"They're buying the detonators in pairs. That tells us it's barrel type devices they're building. They mention twelve pairs. That equates to one test without a nuclear core and one full underground test. That leaves ten pairs of detonators. Of course some might be spares. I'd say between six and ten working devices."

"I take it we should be happy that they only have these barrel type devices?" asked Stuart. "You said they're low yield."

"That's true; they're unlikely to be much bigger than the Hiroshima or Nagasaki bombs. Incidentally the bombs dropped on Japan were most probably manufactured with South African uranium; they were exporting a lot to the United States at the time."

"I think you're suggesting that if we stop the South Africans getting hold of the detonators it's game over," said Jane.

"Perhaps pressure can be put on Israel to stop the shipment?" suggested Duncan.

"We can try and warn the Americans," said Stuart. "The problem is that the Israelis will just shrug their shoulders. We all know they are in it up to their necks but their official line is they have no interest in nuclear weapons. They'll just deny any involvement."

"I think there is more to it than that. I asked myself the question, why have the Israelis suddenly gone cool on the South Africans after so many years of co-operation? To me the only logical answer is that they've been told to. I think the Americans have warned the Israelis that they're about to abandon South Africa. That's why they're distancing themselves and more than that I think because they know that the present regime in South Africa is sunk they took the opportunity to use South African facilities to carry out a little atomic test of their own and get the South Africans blamed."

Stuart smiled, "I suppose that's why we use you for analysis."

"So," continued Jane. "We'll get no help from the Israelis or Americans so what about doing something this end, ourselves?" asked Jane.

"Intervene over here?" asked Stuart. "That's risky and outside our remit. Firstly the South Africans are a 'friendly' nation. They haven't actually done anything to suggest that they won't disarm and secondly it would be illegal under our own laws."

"I thought President Duplessey was openly warning that his government could not control the nuclear programme. Doesn't that give us the right to interfere? My analysis of the situation is simple. South Africa does have an elected government, for what it's worth. The elected government has decided upon a course of action but may not be able to deliver because of rogue elements operating within the country. By identifying and interfering with the rogue elements aren't we actually helping a friendly nation?"

"That's one interpretation," Stuart conceded, "but we still can't do anything over here without permission. You know the rules."

"So get permission," said Jane.

Stuart pondered for a moment.

"I can ask but I know what the answer will be. You can't explain something like that in a telex message. It will require face to face meetings."

"So get on a plane. Talk to the Foreign Office face to face."

"I'll see what I can arrange," conceded Stuart.

**Hoedspruit Military Airbase, Limpopo Province, South Africa.
Wednesday 1st March 1989**

Hoedspruit Airbase was built to a classical 'Cold War' design with a long runway, dispersed buildings, grassed over hardened plane hangars, two of which had direct entry to the main runway by side slip taxi ways. The two side slip hangers permanently housed six ready to go SAAB JAS 39 Grippen interceptor fighters. These planes constituted South Africa's primary air defence and could be airborne less than four minutes after being scrambled. Capable of more than three thousand kilometres per hour they could meet any threat from their northern neighbours. The planes carried the latest Sidewinder air to air missiles and Maverick air to surface missiles. Some thought this was overkill as none of South Africa's potential enemies had anything that could not be dealt with by the Grippen's single twenty-seven millimetre cannon.

It was not however the defensive or offensive capability of the aircraft that interested Peter van Stardan. It was the security of the airbase itself. There was no airport in South Africa that was more secure than Hoedspruit.

The ranking terms within the South African Air force were borrowed from the Army. Base commanders were normally Lieutenant Colonels but at Hoedspruit the base commander was a full Colonel, reflecting the importance of the installation. Colonel Erik Andres was alone as he made his way to an underground control bunker, the one normally used at times of high alert. He thought it was the best place to receive the expected incoming secure phone call in private.

Peter van Stardan picked up the phone in his office and waited for his secretary to make the connection. He'd eliminated the use of the airstrip at Vastrap for the delivery without much thought. It didn't have the turnaround facilities for a long-haul military transport. He'd seriously considered the nearest major airport, Upington on the Orange River. It had excellent facilities and an extra long runway but Upington was primarily a civilian airport and the appearance of an Israeli military transport plane would attract too much attention. Despite the distance Hoedspruit was the best option. Besides he'd checked out the base commander, Erik Andres. He had the right credentials. He was a trusted member of the Brotherhood and wouldn't require an order from the Air force High Command to do what was required.

A voice came on the line, "Hello, Andres here."

"Good morning. Do you know who I am; do you require any further verification?"

"No, I am satisfied. I know who you are."

"Good. I want you to prepare to receive a transport plane from a foreign country. The plane will make a delivery, a single wooden crate. It is not large. The contents of the crate are most important to the Republic.

Take great care of it until I arrange collection. You will refuel the transport plane and encourage it to leave immediately the delivery has been made. Do you have any questions?"

"Who will collect the crate, who will I release it to?"

"That has yet to be arranged."

Zodiac House, Church Square, Pretoria
Thursday 2nd March 1989

It was going to be a rare visit but there was no indication that there was any need for concern.

The black ministerial Mercedes with darkened windows glided into the underground car park of the Zodiac Building on the junction of Church Street and Church Square in Pretoria. It was directly followed by a security service BMW. Four men from the close protection unit jumped out of the BMW and took position around the Mercedes. The lead protection officer scanned the empty car park. When he was satisfied he signalled the driver of the Mercedes who got out of his car and opened the rear door of the Mercedes for his boss.

The passenger of the vehicle, Andrew de Kluge, held two official posts; he was both Deputy Prime Minister and Minister for Homeland Defence. The Minister stepped out of the vehicle. Slim and relatively young for his elevated position there was still a spring in his step. The close protection officers surrounded their charge and quickly marched him the few steps to the waiting elevator. Andrew de Kluge was too well known to make anything but an overt visit to the Zodiac building. De Kluge stood silently as the elevator ascended. At over six-foot three he was not only the youngest but also the tallest member of the South African Cabinet, but it was not only his height that drew attention. Only forty one he was the best looking of the political elite. His handsome smiling face crowned with a head of thick blond hair was in stark contrast to the jowly scowls that typified his greying balding cabinet colleagues. It was in no small part due to his physical characteristics that people saw freshness and hope for the future in him. But in truth what really differentiated him from his colleagues was more than looks; he possessed the dual qualities of intelligent pragmatism and strength of character. His real skill was the ability to distinguish political reality from the emotional rhetoric and pig headed dogmatism that had for so long dominated South African politics.

The elevator doors opened at the top floor revealing the welcoming party of Alfred Smidt and Peter van Stardan. Smidt had taken his tablets that morning, lots of them, probably too many. The strain of the past weeks had accelerated his decline but he wanted to remain clear and focused for this meeting. In reality as each successive week passed his intellectual capacity diminished an increment yet he needed to maintain his image as the dominant figure of the Brotherhood until Peter van Stardan was ready.

Alfred led his visitor to the conference room. He had made it clear to Peter that he wanted him to come to the fore at this meeting. When news got back to the Cabinet he wanted Peter van Stardan's position as heir apparent consolidated. Smidt had briefed and advised van Stardan, "Be proud of what we have achieved and promise more and better for the future."

Alfred and Peter sat on one side of the table facing Andrew de Kluge. De Kluge took some papers from his briefcase and placed them flat on the conference table.

"I requested this meeting for a special reason," began de Kluge. "What I have to say will most probably come as a surprise to you."

It was as if Van Stardan hadn't heard those first few words when he spoke. "I'd like to speak frankly." he began.

"I intend to do the same myself," replied de Kluge. "But I believe it would be better if you let me have my say first."

Van Stardan ignored him "In my experience politicians appear when there is good news and make themselves scarce when there is bad news. Therefore I would guess you have come so that you can be associated with the good news that we are about to bestow on our country."

De Kluge persisted, his voice half an octave higher, "I appreciate you are on the verge of achieving your goal and that you consider this to be good news, but I too have what I believe to be good news although I fear that you may not see it in the same light."

Both Alfred and Peter felt the first twinge of concern.

"Let me start by passing on the congratulations of the Cabinet to you both. The Government fully appreciates your dedication to the cause of South Africa. Your achievement has put us into a strong negotiating position."

"We are not quite finished yet," said van Stardan. "A test bomb is almost ready and several working devices are being assembled as we speak. We are now making advance plans for the next phase of our project. I want you to be the first to know that our ambition is to develop," he paused a moment for dramatic effect, "a hydrogen bomb, a thermo nuclear device!"

The announcement did not bring the expected outburst of enthusiastic surprise. It didn't even raise a smile.

"It is my turn to be frank," said de Kluge. "I can tell you now; there will be no next stage. As far as the Cabinet, this Government of South Africa is concerned, you have more than achieved all that is required of you."

"I don't understand. Exactly what do you mean?" asked van Stardan. "Having a working deliverable weapon is only the beginning for us. It is only our ticket to the top table. Now the real work begins."

"You have fallen into the trap of believing in your own fanaticism. You ignore reality," replied de Kluge. "Firstly how do you propose to deliver the weapons you have manufactured?" De Kluge didn't wait for an answer. "We have only Buccaneer and Canberra bombers strong enough to carry our bombs. Any '*freedom fighter*' with a hand-held missile can easily destroy such old planes. Our own missile programme has failed dismally and your latest proposal to buy Jericho 2 missiles from Israel would quite simply bankrupt our country. That is the simple practical truth. Let me ask you have you ever considered who these horrible weapons will be used against? Again de Kluge didn't wait for a response. "Would you bomb landlocked Zambia or impoverished Angola? What about the Congo jungle? The truth is we never could or never would use the weapons you have produced."

Peter laughed. "So why for the past twenty five years did you let us work on this project?"

"Because the weapons you produced have a political value. They are simply political capital and what is more we, the Government, are being forced to cash in that capital. In reality the West, our friends, knew we would never use such weapons. We would be finished, shunned by the entire world, if we used nuclear weapons against out defenceless neighbours. Their value lies in the fact that the West are terrified of them falling into the hands of others. By just having made the weapons you have to accept that you have completed your work."

"Our work has only just begun," protested van Stardan.

"No. It is over. We are coming to terms with the West," said de Kluge. "It is soon to be agreed. It is possible that soon you will have to start to dismantle your weapons, most probably under the supervision of the UN. When that task is complete we have to look forward to a different South Africa; a South Africa without Apartheid, a South Africa where all its people live in peace."

"You propose to give away everything!" van Stardan's voice was rising. "I do not believe it."

"We are in the middle of negotiations but it is clear we will have to surrender our nuclear weapons. In exchange for our weapons we will extract promises, promises that the whites can continue to live in this country in peace. It is obvious to all that eventually we will share this country with the black man but we must act now to secure the future, the future of the white minority. We need that future to be guaranteed by the West."

The voice screamed, almost hysterical with anger, but it was not van Stardan's. Alfred Smidt was now on his feet. His mind galvanised by De Kluge's words, his uncontrollable anger erupted.

"You have no right to give this land away. It was given to us, the Boers, by God. It is not yours to give away. May the wrath of the Almighty fall on your head for this treachery. We would not live under British masters so how could you think we would live under black ones? It is madness, sheer madness."

De Kluge sat passively although the outburst was more than even he had expected. He waited patiently until Alfred Smidt had finished and then he tried to reason again.

"We only exist in the modern world because of the support of the United States and Britain. They needed us on their side in the Cold War, but the Cold War is ending. The United States can no longer justify their support of the white regime to black American voters and Britain is only interested in maintaining its investments. Our choice is to fight a long guerrilla war and eventually lose everything or negotiate now from a position of strength. We, the Government of South Africa, have chosen the latter course."

"No, no, no. How can getting rid of our best weapon leave us in a position of strength? I will never accept this. Get out of this office. You are finished with the Brotherhood, you are finished altogether. Go before I kill you with my own bare hands and tell that idiot Duplessy he will not get away with this."

Alfred thumped the table with clenched fists.

De Kluge returned the papers to his briefcase and got up to leave. "What I have told you today has already been decided by the Cabinet. The Government stands above the Brotherhood. Soon orders will be given and they will be obeyed."

"We will see," shouted Smidt.

De Kluge left the room. He did not see Alfred Smidt slump back into his chair. He could not have known that, under pressure from the tumour, a blood vessel in Alfred's head had ruptured and the man had only minutes to live. But before that final blackness descended there was to be a period of relief from pain. The ruptured blood vessel momentarily released pressure but Alfred knew the end had come. His last moments would be lucid and calm.

Peter went to his Master's side and listened as the old man whispered his final words.

"What we have heard today is a blasphemy against God. It is the end of the world for South Africa. It is our Armageddon. Jesus, when he left this world for heaven left behind Peter, a rock to continue his work. Now I am departing I leave you to complete my work. Peter, an evil snake lurks in our country. Cut its head off and teach the enemies that lie without that they should not interfere. Destroy the sons of the antichrist that now control this country and threaten us from afar. Destroy the traitors if you want to keep alive the dream of our nation. We must have what God has promised us."

Even before Andrew de Kluge had left the underground car park Alfred Smidt was dead and Peter van Stardan's mind was racing. He knew he had to get the detonators from the Israelis to drop the final piece of the jigsaw into place but before that he had a more important task to complete. Peter looked out of his office, across Church Square, to the statute of Paul Kruger founder of the Nation and made his plans.

London
Thursday 2nd March 1989

Page four, The Daily Telegraph:

In a surprise move the Foreign and Commonwealth Office has lifted its banning order on the African National Congress (ANC). The ANC has long been regarded as a terrorist organisation dedicated to obtaining black majority rule in South Africa by force of arms. The ANC is now free to open an office in London and operate on a semi-official basis. Its most prominent leader, Nelson Mandela, remains incarcerated in a South African prison.

Some commentators believe that the action was taken to pacify disquiet within the Commonwealth following the recent disastrous Nairobi conference when Britain alone vetoed the imposition of sanctions on the Apartheid South African Regime. Others believe that this could be a first step in a far reaching plan to resolve the impasse that currently besets South African politics.

A spokesman for the Foreign and Commonwealth Office said that the move falls well short of official recognition of the ANC by the British Government. He added it is part of a continuing policy of constructive engagement. He went on to say he hoped the move would encourage the ANC to abandon its armed struggle and concentrate on peaceful political means to achieve its objectives.

The ANC remains a proscribed organisation in the United States.

The venue had been carefully selected. It was in Lancaster House that the renegade Rhodesian Government had finally capitulated in 1979. It was in this very room, in which the South African delegation was now sitting, that the final treaty that had established an independent Zimbabwe had been signed.

The message that the ANC representatives were to take away today was clear and simple. The Governments of the United States and Britain wanted the ANC to distance itself from its communist roots. If the ANC publically embraced a democratic, capitalist and free-enterprise model for the future South Africa, a model which safe -guarded the rights of the white minority and foreign investments, then the Governments of the United Kingdom and the United States would deliver the freedom of Nelson Mandela and free universal elections. The ANC would not have to fight to win its objectives.

At the same time as the representatives of the ANC received the news in London a Canadian diplomat, making a routine *'humanitarian'* visit to Nelson Mandela in his South African prison cell, passed on the same offer. He reported back that the offer had been ‘welcomed with interest’.

Meadow Vale Hotel, Pretoria.
Friday 3th March 1989 (morning)

Jane was rushing. She'd been longer on the phone than she'd expected and now she was late. She grabbed her bag and dashed out of the hotel room slamming the door behind her.

Duncan sat in the foyer bar. He'd been there for an hour, ever since he'd returned from dropping Stuart off at the airport for his London trip. He'd chosen a seat facing the lifts and ordered a beer as he waited for her. She arrived at the same time as the beer. The waiter hung on.

"Sorry I'm late," I came as fast as I could.

"No problem. What do you want to drink?" he asked.

"Just a coffee," replied Jane as she plonked herself on the seat opposite.

"So what's the rush?" asked Duncan.

"I've got news. I think I know when and where the detonators will be arriving," she smiled.

"Yeah, so come on tell me."

"The ship sailed from Simon's Town in the early hours. I didn't expect anything to happen before that but had alerted GCHQ to keep an eye out for any unusual air movements just in case. That's easy nowadays because all flight plans are filed on a central database. I couldn't believe it when they came back to me so quickly. An Israeli military transport lodged a flight plan, from Jaffa over Eilat, down the Gulf of Aqaba, the length of the Red Sea and then a refuelling stop in the Seychelles. The final part of the flight plan – wait for this – is only to the most secure South African military airbase, Hoedspruit. It has to be the detonators!"

"So what's the next move? I suppose we have to get the news to Stuart in London pretty quickly."

"We will of course have to try and get the news to Stuart, but he's coming back here as soon as he can."

"I suppose its bad news really," said Duncan. "It means that Stuart is travelling all that way on a fool's errand?"

"It was a long shot for Stuart in any event. The Israelis don't take instructions very well. The good thing is we've got something to work with now."

"Even if you're right, all that we really know is where the fuses are arriving. They could move them to anywhere in the country almost straight away. I don't really see any advantage."

Jane smiled. "What if we get ourselves up to Hoedspruit and take a look?"

"Poking around something that is so sensitive is dangerous," said Duncan. "But we can talk about it when Stuart gets back."

"There's no time to wait for Stuart. We need to move straight away and don't worry we won't stand out that much. The airstrip is on the edge of the Kruger National Park. There are loads of Game Reserves and hunting lodges in the area to provide perfect cover. We will just be two more tourists."

"That's really a full blown observation mission you're suggesting. That requires authorisation."

"Don't be a prude Duncan; we're only going for a few days break. I've already booked us a nice place to stay. That's why I was late getting here."

"What do you mean?"

"I've booked us into the Puma Game Lodge from tonight. Go pack, we're on our way."

Drakensberg
Friday 3rd March 1989 (afternoon)

Peter van Stardan didn't stay in Ladysmith's Royal Hotel this time. He drove straight to the secret NPG camp in the Drakensberg Mountains. There was no ceremonial welcoming guard of honour. It was a visit with purpose. Van Stardan needed to consolidate his position, needed to gauge the loyalty of NPG to him now that Alfred Smidt was dead. He also wanted to give the NPG their first orders.

Although only a few men, the NPG considered themselves to be a credible force. The Commander, Daniel Okra, a short spindly man didn't have a natural military bearing. His sunken cheeks and eyes made him less than handsome and he looked older than his thirty-five years. His blind allegiance, uncompromising attitude and a ruthless streak were his main qualifications. When Smidt had appointed Okra as leader he'd chosen the rank of Lieutenant Colonel for himself, a rank commiserate with a battalion commander in the regular army. Peter van Stardan was wise enough to realise that he had to respect Okra's self given rank and status, he'd even hinted at the prospect of 'promotion' in return for obedience and success.

Okra escorted van Stardan from the grassy valley floor into the tunnel which was the remains of a mine started in the 1850's. Prospecting miners of the era had been enthused with the hope of a big diamond find, another Kimberley. They had dug into the side of the mountain over a hundred years ago. The miner's optimism had proved to be unfounded and that optimism had gradually turned to despair with every yard the miners slowly dug. Finally admitting defeat they'd abandoned the workings. For thirty years the place had been forgotten. Not until the Second Boer War, at the end of the nineteenth century had another use been found for the place. The Boers quickly discovered they could not beat the British Army in a prolonged conventional conflict and so they developed special tactics. From secret hiding places bands of mounted soldiers would hurry forth and wreak havoc behind British lines before disappearing faster than they had materialised. The abandoned mine in the Drakensberg had been one of their secret hiding places. The tactics proved successful and the British, although claiming victory, were forced again to the negotiating table to agree on a compromise settlement. A young Winston Churchill had witnessed the campaign and when he became the British wartime leader he emulated the Boers tactics, choosing the same name for his newly established military units as the Boers had used. He called them Commandos.

The workings had remained secret after the end of the Boer War, partly as an insurance policy against British duplicity. Periodically work had been carried out. Jagged rock edges had been smoothed and the walls spray painted cream. The cement floor was painted red and fluorescent light fittings ran along the roof, electricity supplied from a hidden generator.

Okra led van Stardan down the tunnel for fifty yards before the great chamber opened up; a space blasted and hacked out of the basalt rock. Brightly lit, the domed space was big enough to house crates of supplies and even a few vehicles. Around the edge doors led into minor chambers, spaces that had been hewn out of the rock to form rooms.

"We have a kitchen, dormitories, an armoury, a field hospital, meeting and training rooms. We even have a suite set aside for your private use. We can lock ourselves in this redoubt for months without support or detection," said Daniel Okra with pride.

The men were gathered, ready for van Stardan. The parade began in the usual manner with prayers. God was asked to bestow his blessings on the Republic of South Africa. Daniel Okra went on to ask The Maker to accept the soul of Alfred Smidt and provide him a befitting resting place in heaven. Finally he asked The Creator to bestow his blessings on their new leader, Peter van Stardan and provide him with divine guidance so he could lead their beloved country through troubled times.

"Amen," said the men in unison.

Peter van Stardan spoke in a firm voice at the conclusion of the prayers.

"Men, I pledge to you, that to my last breath my life will be dedicated to our Fatherland. This is no idle promise on my part and you too, by the oath you have made, are obliged to the same commitment no less than I. The dying words of Alfred Smidt were of defiance, defiance in the face of a new and mortal threat to the existence of our country as we know it. In memory of Alfred Smidt we will do what he requested.

I am reassured by what I have seen. I know that your actions will live up to the promise. I am confident with the three plans that Lt Col Okra has devised. Each plan has a particular purpose. One is an act of justifiable retribution for wrongs that have been done to the Republic; the other is an outwardly simple task but one of great importance and the third is an insurance policy for the future of the Republic. These tasks will be your first tests and the ones that not only I but also future generations will judge you on."

Puma Game Lodge, Kruger National Park
Friday 3rd March 1989 (evening)

The layout of the Puma Game Reserve hadn't changed much in the previous quarter century. There was still the same Ranger's House with the attached office and a cluster of lodges that stood in a great circle around the dusty, unpaved courtyard. Sadly the lodges had barely benefited from the periodic refurbishments that mainly consisted of a lick of paint. But worse, in business terms, the ethos of the place had not kept pace with the rising expectations of a public that by the late 1980's demanded high standards of luxury in return for their eco-support. Discerning well-heeled customers no longer appreciated the basic rustic qualities of one of the oldest game reserves on the edge of the Kruger National Park. They noticed the absence of a decent restaurant and panoramic views from the bar.

"Back to basics," said Duncan. "Almost home from home for me, I like it."

Jane pulled the car into one of the parking places that were marked with lines of small white washed stones. She'd driven most of the way from Pretoria. Duncan had been an uncritical contemplative passenger, his mind focused on the wisdom of the journey rather than on her driving skills.

Mark Plumly was in the reception office working his way through a pile of accumulated paperwork that he had ignored for as long as he dared. He lifted his head and smiled as the two visitors entered.

"Jane Ashton and Duncan Murdoch. We have a booking," said Jane.

"Yes, I was expecting you. Have a good drive?"

"Excellent," replied Duncan, a comment which elicited a quiet smile of satisfaction from Jane.

"Got a bit confused with the booking," said Mark, "wasn't sure if you wanted two separate cabins or a two bed roomed cabin. It's all the same to me. We're quiet at the moment."

"Two separate cabins," said Jane without hesitation.

"Fine, I'll sort that. Now what about hunting, you didn't book anything?"

"We won't be doing any hunting," quipped Jane. "I don't like the idea of killing for killing's sake."

"I have to be honest, we do shoot here," said Mark, "but we eat just about all our kills. What's not eaten in the camp goes to the local Africans. Are you into photographic shoots instead?"

"Most probably we'll do that."

"A photographer. That's great. You can help me out. I'm looking around for a camera and what I know about the subject could be written on a budgie's beak."

Duncan looked at Jane and wondered how long she'd keep digging.

"Actually," she said, "I'm writing an article for tourists, nice places to visit and that sort of thing. Duncan here is escorting me and keeping me out of trouble."

"Oh God, a journalist, I wish I'd known. I'd have prepared a bit more. I'll have to take you for a couple of trips out into the bush as a minimum, show you the sort of game animals that live in these parts."

"No, you don't have to do that. We'll go for a couple of walks ourselves. I'm happy enough in the bush, been doing it for a long time," said Duncan

"If that's what you want," shrugged Mark. "Have you got a weapon with you? You can't walk around here without protection. There are wild animals."

"It was a last minute decision to come here. I was sort of hoping you might have something I could use," said Duncan.

"We do keep a couple of hunting rifles for use by the guests. Nothing very fancy I'm afraid. Do you have a gun licence?"

Duncan produced his gun permit and handed it over to Mark.

"Botswana? Don't get too many visitors from that part of the world. I suppose the permit will do but I will still need to test you on the shooting range, just to see for myself that you can handle a gun properly."

"That's fine by me. What about in the morning?" asked Duncan.

"Okay. Now food. There's no restaurant but we do family cooking here, nothing fancy. I can do a barbeque tonight and bring something from the house, unless you have other plans."

"Where's the nearest town? Is there a hotel around, say with a decent restaurant and bar?" asked Jane.

"Hoedspruit is the nearest big town, it's about a thirty kilometre drive. There are a few upmarket touristy places on the outskirts that have a good reputation. I could dig a couple of names out."

"I was thinking more of somewhere the locals use. I like to get a feel for a place when I visit," replied Jane.

"There's not much really. After game tourism Hoedspruit is known for its air base. There's only one place in town, The Herzhog Hotel and it really caters for air-force staff. I believe it gets a bit rowdy at the weekends."

"We're not driving bush roads in the dark," interjected Duncan. "We'd love the barbeque. Your wife does the cooking?"

"My sister actually, I'm not married," replied Mark. "Just me, my Mum and sister living here. Dad passed on a couple of years ago and I took charge and we carried on. It works for us. Mum wouldn't like to be anywhere else. The only thing is that you do feel a bit out of touch with things here."

Foreign and Commonwealth Office London
Monday 6th March 1989

By normal standards the meeting had been convened at an alarming pace, at least that was what Sir Basil Parker Smythe thought, but for Stuart the thirty hours since his arrival in London had felt like an eternity. The journey from Century House to Westminster had not been undertaken on foot this day, haste and rain had dictated the use of a black cab. On the way over no words had been exchanged between Stuart and his boss Estelle Dorking who was only half convinced by Stuart's arguments and had been deep in contemplation.

They had been greeted in the outer office by Sir Basil with an unsmiling face and limp handshake. His ruddy complexion was evidence of the discomfort the man felt when required to work under pressure. Stuart let Estelle go into the meeting room first. He followed with Sir Basil behind. Bringing up the rear Ralph almost trotted, gripping his notebook and pencil with excited anticipation. They all sat. Sir Basil looked up to the giant decorative plaster ceiling rose that surrounded the chandelier.

"Ralph."

"Yes Sir Basil." Ralph's response was sharp and attentive.

"Out!"

Sir Basil's protégé's face fell. He was unable to conceal his disappointment but knew better than to do anything other than obey his boss's command. With drooped head and rounded shoulders he skulked out of the room, at no great speed, clear that this would be the limit of his protest.

Sir Basil waited until Ralph had shut the door behind himself before he lowered his gaze and started to speak.

"You will note that I am alone. Our political masters have been informed about your information and request. Despite being invited to this meeting, not surprisingly no politician has elected to attend. I have also had a lengthy conversation with the Secretary to the Cabinet Office, he too declined the invitation."

"Won't be much of a conversation then," said Stuart.

"Exactly," replied Sir Basil. "Although time precluded me the opportunity of confirming your assertions with a secondary source, for the purposes of this conversation I will assume your report is correct.

Concerning your first suggestion, that somebody intercedes with the Israeli Government to stop the shipment of the detonators; the Americans secretly accept that Israel has nuclear weapons but publicly say it has no proof of their existence and, on an innocent until proven guilty basis, accept Israel's public denial. As a consequence, if the United States made a formal request to Israel not to export the detonators that would be tantamount to accepting that Israel is indeed in the nuclear weapons business and destroy their foreign policy in this area. The Americans will therefore not be approaching the Israeli

Government on the matter. Our Middle East policy is to follow the Americans. Therefore Britain will also not approach Israel. We did consider getting the French involved but on reflection decided it would most probably be firstly, a waste of time and secondly no better than taking out a newspaper advertisement.

I am surprised at your second suggestion. I didn't think that you would need reminding that South Africa is not only a friendly nation but also a key ally in the Cold War that occupies a geographically important location. The British Government will therefore not sanction covert operations or any kind of shenanigans in that country."

"Hold on a second," interrupted Stuart abruptly. "It was in this office that you, you personally, expressed your concern for the future of South Africa and it was you that actually got me running around the place to see what was going on."

Sir Basil raised a hand to stop Stuart. "I remember our last meeting well. In fact I have the notes that Ralph made at the time. I apologise if you misunderstood the purpose of our last meeting which was quite innocuous as far as I am concerned."

"There were no notes taken. You sent Ralph out of the room, just as you have done today."

"That I don't recall," replied Sir Basil.

Stuart exploded, "I hope the locusts eat your bloody vineyard at Stellenbosch."

Estelle put a hand on Stuart's arm to calm him. "No need to get personal."

Sir Basil continued. "There is also another factor that has come into play that you should be aware of. Our Government has decided, in its wisdom, to assist the Americans. That assistance means we have de-facto accepted the American proposals. The President of the United States thought it was premature for the US to recognise that Mandela chap and his ANC organisation but he wanted to give them an indication of what was on offer to them. Therefore, following a request from the US President our Prime Minister has decided to grant the ANC in London limited diplomatic recognition. This news has already been released to the press. It would be a brave man that would interfere in such a situation."

"Sir Basil," said Estelle, "I understand that everybody around here is expert at running for cover. All I will say is that the situation in South Africa is possibly going to become very unstable. We have an opportunity to take the sting out of the wasp's tail. The plan is worth serious consideration at least."

"That may be your opinion," replied Sir Basil, "It is not mine. Besides, as we speak and not a million miles from here, we are moving in conjunction with our friends from the American State Department. I am not at liberty to say more than that it is a very positive move on our part."

Estelle stood. "Come on Stuart, we're wasting our time. We might as well leave. One last word Sir Basil, if this thing goes 'tits up', as I suspect it may, I will remember this conversation and your part in it."

"Mrs Dorking, I am shocked and embarrassed by your language."

"Not half as fucking shocked and embarrassed as you're going to be," she concluded as she marched out of the room.

It was not so quiet in the taxi back to Century House. Stuart and his boss burst into laughter as the cab pulled away.

"Did you see his face? That meeting is going to go down in folklore." Stuart was barely able to stop the tears rolling down his cheeks.

"I have to say I did enjoy it. Those people are in a different world," replied Estelle. "Of course you know what this means though. We cannot do anything at all to intervene. It looks like they'll get a working bomb and we will just have to trust them to hand it over. All you can do is keep up your monitoring role and maintain liaison with the US field people."

"The sad thing is it's a dangerous game. I need to contact South Africa quickly and get myself back out there as soon as possible. They're putting together a plan and I don't want them going off half cocked."

"No don't let them do that, it wouldn't be good."

Puma Game Lodge
Saturday 4th March 1989

The shooting range wasn't up to much. Just a few old gallon paint tins filled with sand stacked in front of a giant termite mound. In the coolness of the early morning the two men stood forty yards from the paint tins, next to an old picnic table that was past its picnicking days.

"Are you familiar with this?" Mark passed the Remington P14 hunting rifle to Duncan. "It's not the best in the world but it's all we've got. It's not loaded."

Duncan took the rifle and pulled back the bolt to make sure the chamber was clear before pointing the barrel towards the ground and pulling the trigger. There was an empty click as the hammer struck home. He rested the gun on the palm of his hand to check the balance. Then he raised the gun to his shoulder and looked down the barrel towards the paint cans.

"I didn't bring a scope as you're not going hunting for anything specific, I didn't think you'd need it," said Mark.

Duncan loaded three .303 bullets from the handful that lay on the picnic table. He pushed the first into the chamber and swiftly operated the bolt action. "Middle can," he said as he raised the butt to his shoulder. The crack was crisp. He didn't wait to check his aim; he just pulled the bolt action again and quickly let off another round and then the last one.

"Three centre hits. That's good, you've shot before," said Mark.

"I was in the Army," replied Duncan.

"British or Rhodesian?"

"Both," replied Duncan honestly.

"You want to try the pistol?"

Duncan picked up the Taurus and examined it carefully. "Haven't used one of these before."

They're good value for what you get. A .38 calibre so a bit on the heavy side but will stop a baboon dead at close quarters. Nine round magazines," said Mark. "I only really keep a hand gun for visitors from the US; they always want a hand gun. Guess it's the John Wayne syndrome. Some don't realise it's only for close quarter protection. They actually try to hunt with it!"

"Can I have a go?"

"Be my guest."

Duncan slid a full magazine into the handle of the weapon and slipped the safety catch. He spread his legs for balance and took a two handed grip. He let his index finger run along the barrel and used his middle finger on the trigger. With extended arms he let off three rounds in quick succession. The rapport from the pistol was answered by three rapid metallic echoes as the bullets hit the paint tin.

"Wow!" said Mark. "That's amazing. At that distance I'd have been happy if you hit the termite mound never mind the paint cans."

Duncan smiled and pulled the magazine from the pistol.

"We'll that's an okay with me," continued Mark, "You can have what you want but you will have to leave a deposit, a signed cheque will do. I'm sorry about having to test you, you can't be too careful. There are a lot of accidents out here."

"Ever had an accident here?" Duncan asked more out of politeness than curiosity.

"No, I haven't had anything go wrong myself but a long time ago a chap got shot and killed when my father was in charge. It really affected my Dad, he was never the same after the incident, it changed his personality forever. Even when it was near the end for him, before he passed on, it was all he could talk about. He kept on saying it wasn't an accident. But I've said too much. I'm not supposed to talk about that incident. Come with me to the office, I'll sort out the paperwork and give you some ammunition. Do you want the pistol as well?"

"Might as well. It could be fun," replied Duncan sensing Mark's unease when talking about his father.

After stowing the weapons in his cabin Duncan joined Jane on the open terrace for breakfast. Mark was already with her, drinking coffee.

"What's your plan for today?" asked Mark. "If you're going walkabout in the bush I'll give you a map and suggest a trek for you. Then I know where to look when you get lost."

"We're not going into the bush. I thought we'd have a drive around the area," said Jane. "You're alright with that aren't you Duncan?"

"Bit of a waste of time me getting the guns, but I suppose if that's what you want."

"Here," continued Duncan holding his hand out to Mark, "Yesterday's newspapers from Pretoria. You said you felt a bit out of touch."

"Thanks," said Mark taking the rolled bundle from Duncan.

They drove away from the camp towards Hoedspruit. They only had a Michelin map but it gave just enough detail for them to circle the airbase. The perimeter covered a vast area. Some of the tracks weren't really suitable for a two wheeled drive car but Duncan drove and managed.

It was after two before they came into the town. The number of Saturday shoppers was dwindling and Duncan had little trouble finding a place to park on Main Street. They walked up and down taking in what little there was to see.

"I'm not sure I understand the point of this," said Duncan.

"If you don't look you don't see," replied Jane. "The plane with the detonators will have to come soon otherwise the flight plan will lapse. I reckon the delivery will be made in the next twenty-four hours."

"And so, what are we supposed to do then? We'd have been better off waiting for Stuart in Pretoria or at least waiting till we'd heard from him."

"Just treat it as a weekend away, a mini holiday," laughed Jane.

As they walked Main Street narrowed and the white marking disappeared from the road. Jane pointed to the other side of the road. "There's that Herzhog Hotel that the Ranger told us about, let's go and get ourselves a drink."

"I'm not sure you needed to do that," said Duncan as they drove back towards the Puma Game Park."

"What?" replied Jane spouting a smug smile.

"Come up with that story. Do they just come spontaneously into your head or do you spend hours concocting them in your mind?"

"Oh that was just a spur of the moment thing. I thought it would be a good way to get information and see the lay of the land. It wasn't hard to come up with; they did have a sign in the foyer saying that they catered for weddings."

"Well I can tell you one thing," said Duncan, "In real life you'll never get Stuart to hold a reception in a place like that. It's a dump."

Jane laughed and they drove on in silence for a while. Eventually Duncan spoke.

"You know Jane I have to say something to you and I hope you take it in the spirit it is meant. The types of people we are potentially dealing with are ruthless. They've been working on something for the best part of their lives and are not going to let go easily."

"Yes, so what are you saying?"

"I'm saying don't treat them as fools, they won't like it."

"You're too windy," replied Jane, "They don't even know we're here."

They completed the journey in silence.

When they'd entered the Herzhog Hotel Jane had gone straight up to the small wooden reception desk and was, after tapping the bell a couple of times, greeted by the proprietor, an apparition from a different era. It looked like his tiny aged frame could barely manage to support him. The man's back was curved and the resultant stoop reduced further his insignificant stature. His balding head boasted a few wisps of uncut grey hair, an attempted comb-over failing dismally to achieve its objective of improving his appearance. His black shoes were scuffed beyond the stage where a polish would help. He wore crumpled black and grey pants, the bottom half of a morning suit that had seen better days and his once white shirt, worn below a tight fitting waist coat, had a badly frayed collar. His sickly sweet smile exposed a row of stained crooked teeth.

"Yes dear. What can I do for you," he said wringing his hands together like some character from a Dickens novel, which is where he most probably belonged, as did his hotel.

Jane pointed to the faded sign on the wall that said *'weddings catered for'*. "This is a friend of my fiancé. He is showing me around. I'm getting married soon and I'm looking for a suitable venue for my reception."

The proprietor raised his bushy eyebrows. "Most people go to one of the new Safari lodges for that sort of thing nowadays."

"Oh, I like the old fashioned quaintness of this place. It's ... authentic. Could you show me around?" she asked.

"I can't show you any rooms. They're full tonight, some kind of military people, something to do with the airbase but I'll show you the grounds."

The old man hobbled in front, taking Duncan and Jane on a perfunctory tour. He obviously had no great conviction that he would take a booking. The tour ended with them walking through the bar area into the unkempt beer garden where men, mainly dressed in the blue uniforms of the air force, drank beer. Towards the back of the garden, clustered around two tables pushed together was a separate group of men in khaki shirts and shorts.

"That lot look different," said Jane nodding towards the men in khaki. Who are they?"

"They're the ones staying in the rooms," said the proprietor displaying a glimmer of optimism. "I'm expecting it to get busy here this evening."

The tour ended at the gate that led from the beer garden on to the street.

"Thank you very much for your time," said Jane. "I'll talk with my fiancé and get back to you."

"You're welcome my dear." The old man stood and watched them as they crossed the road and walked away. Returning to the beer garden he went straight over to the khaki clad men and whispered a few words to their leader. One of the men left the tables and carefully followed Jane and Duncan back to their car. He made a note of the registration number before returning to his friends.

They ate early at the camp, joining Mark and his sister on their veranda.

"That was fantastic," said Duncan wiping his mouth and hands with a serviette. "Unfortunately there's no pretty way of eating hog ribs, sorry."

"We're no better eaters than you," replied Mark wiping his own hands and mouth.

"Do you have all your guests to eat with you like this?" asked Duncan sitting back in his seat.

"No, we just don't get that many guests now. We're not fashionable anymore. When this place opened it was part of the Parks and Wildlife Trust. Now we're on our own. We pay rent and have to make a profit but frankly it's barely worth it. But it's all we've ever known, my dad came here in 1946."

"That's a life-time for you then. I'm sure there have been memorable moments."

"There have been, not all of them good, replied Mark. "I suppose it's a coincidence really, but do you remember I told you this morning we had a shooting incident here a long time ago?"

"I do," replied Duncan.

"Well I was reading the newspapers you gave me. Would you believe it, one of the chaps involved in it died recently and his obituary was in the Times."

"Is he famous then?"

"Chap by the name of Alfred Smidt. I don't know what he did. The papers didn't give much away. I guess he was just well connected."

"Did you meet him?" asked Jane.

"I didn't but my Dad did. He said he was an evil man. It was not in my Dad's nature to dislike somebody but that Smidt fellow must have pushed the wrong buttons somehow."

"Did he do the shooting?" asked Duncan.

"No, apparently there were two young chaps with Smidt and one shot the other when they were out hunting. It was put down as an accident but my Dad maintained to the day he died it was murder. He even went so far as to have an affidavit written up so that it could be used after he was gone."

"It must have really bothered him," said Duncan.

Jane yawned. "I'm really tired, do you mind if I go to bed?"

The men stood and Jane wandered off with a "Goodnight."

Duncan finished his beer. "Listen I'm pretty tired myself, I think I'll turn in too so I'll be fresh tomorrow."

Stuart was not known to suffer from bouts of worry brought on by irrational premonitions but just now he had a bad feeling in his gut, as he boarded the British Airways 747 bound for Johannesburg. He knew Duncan was sound; they had a common military background and way of doing things. They weren't risk adverse but liked to pick and choose when to take a chance. But he didn't have that much confidence in Jane's judgement. He thought she was from the 'let's poke the wasp's nest and see what happens' school of thought and mischief didn't have a place in Stuart's world.

He'd tried to phone her and Duncan in their rooms. He'd left messages at the hotel reception and he'd finally got somebody from the Embassy to go around and look for them. They'd just disappeared, gone off without leaving a message for him. He was strapped in; the plane completed its short taxi. The engines roared and Stuart was pushed back in his business class seat, more uncomfortable still that he was going to be out of contact for the next thirteen hours. He closed his eyes wondering what news would greet him on arrival.

Stanton Suburb, Pretoria
Saturday 4th March 1989

The exclusive suburb of Stanton, midway between Johannesburg and Pretoria, was home to wealthy business men and politicians. For much of the time many of the politician's homes were not occupied. South Africa's unique history resulted in the country having three official capitals: Johannesburg for the Executive, Cape Town for the Legislative and Stellenbosch for the Judiciary. Not only was the setup cumbersome it also meant that senior political figures had to maintain homes in more than one location and there was a lot of commuting, much of it during unsocial hours.

Andrew de Kluge was ready and waiting. He watched through the living room window for the ministerial car. As the vehicle pulled up he waved to the driver to acknowledge his presence. He didn't want him to knock at the door or ring the bell, it would wake the children. Quietly he tiptoed up stairs. He peeped into the bedroom of his two children and whispered a silent goodbye. He pushed gently at his own bedroom door and hoped the rustle would not stir his sleeping wife. But she was a light sleeper. She rolled over to face him. He could make out her sleepy features in the dim half light coming from the landing.

"Safe journey darling. See you Wednesday. Love you."

She hardly waited to hear Andrew's soft reply, "Love you too darling," before she turned over and went back to sleep.

The driver was waiting at the door. He picked up Andrew's travel bag leaving the ministerial briefcase for the Minister himself.

"Jan Smuts, fast as you like, I don't want to miss the first flight to Cape Town."

As Deputy Prime Minister de Kluge was entitled to use one of the private Ministerial jets but he liked to maintain his image as a man of the people, the white people, and travelled whenever he could on scheduled flights. He was known and respected for the practice.

"Yes Sir," replied his regular driver. "Bit of a rush today Sir?"

"I have to answer questions in Parliament on Monday and need time to prepare." Andrew settled into the backseat and opened his briefcase. He withdrew a bundle of legal papers and began to read. It was the signal for the driver to shut up and drive.

The beginning of the journey was through leafy suburbs as the driver headed for the motorway that connected Pretoria and Johannesburg joining it just as the sun was rising. It was twenty minutes before he signalled and took the long sweeping airport slip road. The driver slowed to a crawl and de Kluge lifted his head from the papers he was studying.

"What's wrong?" he asked.

"Motorway maintenance vehicle in front Sir, in the middle carriage way. Slowing us all down."

"I hope this doesn't make me late. You might have to phone ahead and get them to hold the plane."

The driver signalled and nudged his way into the left hand lane ready to join the approaching overpass that led directly to the main airport terminal. The raised road passed close to a block of flats. Andrew couldn't read anymore. He looked out of the car window and felt sympathy for the flats residents, living not more than a couple of hundred feet from the main road. In one of the windows he thought he noticed something strange but it didn't immediately register.

The RPG 7 rocket launcher was developed by the Russians to attack NATO main battle tanks. As armour improved and new tactics were developed it proved to be inadequate for its original purpose but this did not diminish the weapon's popularity. It had plenty of other uses and was particularly good in urban environments where its small size, single man operation and multitude of special warheads made it particularly effective. The RPG7 that Andrew de Kluge saw that morning, pointing out of a bedroom window, was fitted with a high velocity, armour piercing round that was deadly at over 500 feet, well in excess of the current 200 feet target range.

Andrew watched frozen in disbelief but his failure to react would not have affected the result. The round hurtled towards the car, striking the middle of the near side front passenger door. The soft nose of the projectile collapsed and a hardened spike shot forward piercing the door's metal. All Ministerial cars were armour plated, but the protection was limited to stopping small arms fire, not an anti tank round. Once pierced the metal of the door gave way and the charge came forward and entered the vehicle before it exploded.

The construction of the vehicle worked against the passengers now. When the explosives detonated the blast was contained and therefore magnified many times over. Later it would be hard for investigators to distinguish the parts of the driver's body from that of the Minister. What was mainly left was pulp.

A second or two after the explosion the maintenance lorry speeded up and disappeared in the labyrinth of roads that surrounded the airport.

Perimeter Hoedspruit Airfield, Limpopo Province, South Africa Sunday 5th March 1989

It was dark when Duncan was roused by the sound of a car engine starting. He was still drowsy as he heard the tyres crush the gravel as the car turned and headed down the track away from the camp. In the dark he fumbled for his watch on the bedside locker. The luminous paint on the watch's dial was not good enough for him to make out the time. He felt for and found the dangling string that switched on the wall light above his bed. He blinked at the sudden burst of light and waited for his eyes to adjust. "Three forty-five," he said aloud. He was going to turn out the light and roll over but mustered just enough effort to empty his bladder.

Stumbling back to his bed he pulled the edge of the curtain and looked into the courtyard. In the moonlight he could see the car was gone. Suddenly wide awake he quickly pulled on his trousers and made his way to Jane's cabin. He tried the door, it was unlocked and the bed was empty. "Stupid woman," he cursed under his breath as he decided what he should or could do.

Jane had made a number of assumptions before coming to her conclusion. She reckoned that the Israeli flight would arrive just before or just at daybreak. The flight plan would lapse within twenty-four hours, so it had to be today. She thought the Israelis would want to do the Red Sea and the east coast of Africa leg of the flight in the dead of night. She also reckoned that the transport plane would not continue directly on to the coast of South Africa but might take an unauthorised detour. If the plane turned right just before Maputo in Mozambique and made a quick dash across the country it would take several hours off the flight time and the Mozambique air defences were known to be non-existent.

She got out the car and leaned against the front wing, her eyes scanning the clear skies for signs of a plane. She knew daylight was approaching and began to fear she'd been wrong when on the distant horizon she thought she spotted a flickering light, a flicker that was too regular to be a twinkling star. She concentrated her gaze and watched as the plane's navigation lights came closer and became more distinct.

She'd picked her spot during the drive with Duncan, a dusty track about three miles from the airport perimeter on the approach path to the main runway. Even in the dark it would be easy, just by the sound, to tell the difference between a fast fighter and a heavy freighter.

Jane hadn't realised how good a spot she'd chosen. The land on the runway approach was a little higher than the runway itself so when the ground controller turned on the runway lights she not only knew that a plane was coming but also had a great view of the straight line of lights that the pilot would be aiming for. It was not long before she heard the steady drone of the four Pratt and Whitney turbo prop engines. The tone deepened as the pilot adjusted his approach speed by feathering the propeller blades incrementally.

As the plane got nearer it appeared to be travelling faster. Quite suddenly it was not more than a mile away and the engine sound was quickly turning into a roar. Then the unexpected, at least to Jane, happened. The pilot flicked on his landing lights, lights so powerful they lit the way for several hundred yards ahead of the plane, lights so powerful they could be seen from a hundred miles or more away on a clear night. Jane panicked as the sudden bath of light blinded her. Surely the pilot would see her and the car. The plane passed over her at an altitude of not more than a couple of hundred feet and just as suddenly as the light had come it was gone. The rhythm of her racing heart slowly began to return to normal.

Jane believed the detonators would not be kept at the airbase for very long. She guessed that they would be moved almost immediately and helicopter or road were the only two viable means of transport. A helicopter would be visible from almost any point around the airbase but a vehicle could use any of the airbase's entrances. But whichever entrance it used the vehicle would inevitably go south along the R40. The R40 was the main north / south road and north was the Zimbabwe border. It had to be south.

Jane drove from the dirt track and joined the tarmac road that led to the R40, passing the fenced off sprawling area of neatly laid out houses that was the dormitory suburb for the airbase's senior military staff. As she came to the outskirts of Hoedspruit she bore left and joined the R40. Soon the rail line began to run parallel with the road on the right. She only had to travel another mile before she found what she was looking for, a turn off, a spot to park where she could look out for her target. She reversed the car under the overhanging branches of a tree and settled down to wait.

Stuart was in a hurry, he wanted to find Jane and Duncan as soon as possible but it felt like events were conspiring against him. The plane had been half an hour late landing, clearing immigration had been a nightmare and now that he was finally out of the terminal the taxi was snarled up in a traffic jam that was going nowhere.

"What's the problem?" Stuart asked the white Afrikaner taxi driver.

"Terrorist incident," was the slurred reply.

"Bad?"

"It's on the radio."

"Can we listen?" asked Stuart.

With exaggerated effort the driver leaned towards the centre console and pushed a button.

"…was married with two children and was on his way to Cape Town where he was scheduled to address The House on Monday morning. A

police investigator at the scene said he believed the attack was probably the work of the banned African National Congress. A favourite weapon of the ANC, a Russian made and supplied RPG7, has been found abandoned at the scene. He said that members of the terrorist group had most probably gained access to the white's only block of residential apartments by posing as maintenance workers.

A Government spokesman in Pretoria said that this was a sad day for the Republic of South Africa but a message had been sent to liberals all over the world who campaign for one man one vote and demand the release of self confessed terrorists from our prisons. The ANC is a terrorist organisation that is not fit to be a part of any democratic process."

"Fuck," said Stuart aloud, trying to think what the ramifications of this act would have on British and American plans.

The taxi driver misread Stuart thoughts. "Yeah, I thought that too. Them Kaffirs are sneaky bastards. Won't fight face to face, they just blow innocent people up. We should hang the lot of them."

Jane didn't have the car radio on; she was concentrating on the road, looking out for likely vehicles. The early morning Sunday traffic was sparse and nothing had aroused her suspicions for the half hour she'd been watching. She got out of the car and leaned on the bonnet. Whilst her eyes remained focused on the road she allowed her mind to drift to her childhood. She wondered if Mr Grenville her headmaster at Mostyn House would ever have dreamed that one of his pupils would be involved in such an exercise. She thought, with his old fashioned sense of moral justice, he'd most probably be proud of her. She didn't have time to develop the thought further. Strong hands grabbed her hair and pulled hard. Surprised and off balance she fell to the ground and screamed with pain as she was dragged to the back of the car, out of sight from the road. When the grip on her hair was released she rolled over in the dust to look at her attackers, two white men dressed in khaki, like the ones she'd seen in the beer garden the previous day. She didn't have time to take in much more before a booted foot kicked her in the stomach and instantly knocked the wind out of her. For a moment she struggled to gasp a breath of air. It felt like her lungs were pulling against a vacuum. Dizziness swamped her mind and she lost consciousness.

When she opened her eyes she was face down in the dirt and didn't know if a minute or an hour had passed. She couldn't see her car. All she knew was that she was in a small clearing between thorn bushes. She didn't realise that her attackers had only dragged her a few yards away from the road into a space between the main R40 road and the railway line. The men spoke in Afrikaner. She could just about make out what they said. There were two voices belonging, she guessed, to the two men she'd glimpsed before. She heard the sound of another vehicle coming to a halt. A third voice joined in.

"We saw the car parked off the road. It looked suspicious and we recognised the registration from the hotel yesterday. We parked a couple of hundred metres down the road and backtracked on foot. We reckon she's the one the pilot of the plane reported seeing on his approach." one of the men said. "She's a spy or something. Give us some time and we'll get everything out of her."

The man who'd just arrived spoke with authority. "There's no time for that. We have to keep moving. Just shoot her after the truck passes."

"Shouldn't we take her with us? If somebody finds her here they might become suspicious," said one of the men.

"No leave her here. Make it look like a robbery. Take that ring off her finger and her watch and anything else you can find. If you want to make it look really authentic fuck her before you shoot her. Then they'll really think its thieving kaffers. Besides the newspapers aren't going to be bothered with this piddling story, not when they've got our other operation in Johannesburg to report on. That's going to keep them occupied for months to come."

Jane didn't move. She struggled to control her panic. She wanted to get up and run but she knew that it would be useless. She had to wait and look for an opportunity and although she professed in public that she 'didn't believe' she prayed silently for the first time since she was an adolescent.

"I'll take over the lead from you for now. Don't try and catch up too quickly, I don't want you attracting any attention to yourselves. Are you clear?" He didn't wait for an answer. "And don't shoot her till the lorry has passed."

Jane heard a vehicle start up and then pull away.

One of the men spoke. "That Okra's a cool bastard, no wonder he's the Lieutenant Colonel. Do you want to toss a coin to see who'll pull the trigger?"

Jane heard a light thud as the coin landed flat on the dirt.

"Awh shit, that's not fair, I've never shot anybody before. At least let me look her in the eyes when you pull the trigger. I wanna see if the lights really do go out."

"You're a sadistic bastard," said the other man. "I suppose you want to fuck her too."

"You arsehole," said the first man indignantly. "I'm married, what do you take me for? I'll keep an eye on her, you watch out for the lorry."

Jane heard his footsteps crunch away. She knew this would be her last chance to save herself. She braced her legs, ready to spring to her feet and dash into the undergrowth. If she got that far, she planned to just run and keep running. She started counting backwards from ten. She'd go on zero. Eight, seven, six, five, she slowed her count believing these could be her last seconds alive, four ... three...... two.......

Too late, the man returned.

"It's passed, come on let's get on with it."

Rough hands grabbed her hair and once again she screamed.

"She's been playing possum," said one of the men. "All the better, she knows what's going to happen."

Jane was pulled onto her knees. One of the men crouched down in front of her and looked directly into her eyes. "Say goodbye to this world," said his smiling face. Jane could not see the man behind her but she heard him click the safety catch and operate the slide action of the pistol that put a bullet into the barrel, her bullet. She wanted to cry out. Some unknown force stopped the tears but not the panic that ran through her body and she thought her last battle was going to be one of self-control. She fought to hold her bladder, clenching her buttocks. She desperately didn't want that to be her last memory. The cold metal of the pistol touched her temple. She closed her eyes; it was all she could do to frustrate the arsehole in front of her. The shot echoed in her ear. A split second later came the second shot. Still kneeling she opened her eyes and turned her head to look around. Both men lay on the ground, blood spurting from head wounds, soaking into the dry earth.

She didn't move, her eyes transfixed. From nowhere a strong hand grabbed her forearm and lifted her upwards.

"It's okay, you're fine. It's all over." Duncan, still holding the smoking hunting rifle, pulled her close and for the first time tears ran freely down her cheeks. He supported her as her knees buckled. She sobbed uncontrollably and held him tightly. Duncan could only think of Elizabeth and his failure to protect her as tears welled in his own eyes.

Stuart's Room, Meadow Vale Hotel, Pretoria
Tuesday 7th March 1989

Stuart was not normally fazed by air travel but he didn't feel good now. True a return trip to London was bad enough but it was really the trepidation he felt about what might have happened during his absence that stopped him sleeping on the return journey. And he wasn't feeling any better when he got to his hotel room in Pretoria. He sat at the small desk in his room pressing the telephone receiver to his ear talking to the man he'd just had the meeting with in London.

"This is an absolute catastrophe," said Sir Basil Parker Smythe.

"I agree. If the reports are true I don't see how our Masters in Westminster, let alone the Americans, can continue with their policy of relaxing their stance on the ANC," replied Stuart.

"Exactly," agreed Parker Smythe.

"Do you think it wise to talk like this on an open phone?"

"Needs must, just be careful," replied Sir Basil. "Firstly I need to know if your two friends have caused us any embarrassment. There are so many variables in operation at the moment we don't want any further complicating factors."

"I'm expecting my friends to return within a few hours. I have received a phone call from my man and an incident has occurred but I cannot comment on its nature or the possible ramifications. I can only say that our people are unharmed. The implications are, quite honestly, unknown at this point."

"Not good. I don't like surprises," replied Sir Basil. "Secondly, later today we will be having a meeting with *'interested parties'* that have recently been made welcome in the United Kingdom. The meeting will be in this office. At the moment they are categorically denying any involvement in the airport incident. Anything you can find out that could add to the debate would be greatly appreciated. I don't want our Masters to be making decisions based on flawed information although I have to admit it looks pretty clear-cut at this stage."

"I think I've got your drift," replied Stuart. "All I've got to go on at the moment is the same media reports and official announcements that you are getting in London over the wire. Once again I'll see what I can do. I going to put myself about a bit and see what I can glean."

"I'm sure you will Stuart, I'm sure you will." The line went dead.

Drakensberg
Tuesday 7th March 1989

Peter van Stardan waited impatiently. He mostly paced back and forth in the underground meeting room, occasionally making his way into the great cavern and along the tunnel to the valley floor, to stare in the direction from which the vehicles would come. The news on the radio was good, the first mission had been accomplished, the death of Alfred Smidt had been avenged and one of the traitors who was willing to surrender the Republic was at this very moment answering to his Maker who would dole out a punishment proportionate to the crime.

It also looked like the blame for the assassination had been left resting on the shoulders of the ANC, the evil would be usurpers of the South African nation. But what van Stardan wanted most of all now was the safe delivery of the nuclear detonators to this, his secret redoubt. Once he had the detonators he would be one step closer to controlling the weapons of Armageddon.

The detective sergeant had taken the stack of VHS tapes he'd collected to the South African Broadcasting Buildings in the Johannesburg suburb of Auckland Park. He didn't simply want to play back the tapes. He wanted the facility to freeze, magnify and roll back the pictures frame by frame and the best facilities were in the editing suite at SABC, which is where he now sat, accompanied by an editing technician. Together with the tapes he'd brought a lever arch file stuffed full of colour photographs and personal details of every ANC activist known to the police. He was sure he'd be able to identify the perpetrators sooner or later.

In the darkened room the technician ran the tapes at slow speed and projected the images onto a large screen. From time to time the detective called for the technician to freeze the picture or to zoom in or even to roll back a frame or so. It was painstakingly slow and tedious but never once did the detective need to refer to his file. After many hours and several re-runs he was satisfied. Finally he asked the technician to print off several nine by eight inch colour photographs. On inspection the definition was not always that brilliant, but it was sufficient.

Back at Police Headquarters he went straight to the incident room that had been set up to coordinate the investigation into the assassination of the Deputy Prime Minister. The Chief Investigating Officer was listening to a preliminary verbal report from the scene of crime forensic team. He interrupted and requested an urgent private meeting with his Chief Investigating Officer. They went into a private side office where the CIO listened without interruption. When the Detective Sergeant had finished the CIO asked a few questions to make sure he'd fully understood. Then, after swearing his subordinate to secrecy he dismissed the man. Left alone he picked up the phone and called the

Police Commissioner on his private line. The Police Commissioner listened attentively and as soon as the conversation was finished, he in turn called the Chief Secretary to the Cabinet Office. Three hours later the Detective Sergeant, the Chief Investigating Officer and the Police Commissioner were at Parliament House preparing to give those members of the Cabinet that could be quickly assembled a briefing on the investigation into the assassination of Andrew de Kluge.

The Chief Investigating Officer gave the verbal report. The Cabinet members listened in silence.

"Our initial suspicions lay with the ANC as the attack was not dissimilar to attacks that they had been credited with previously. However the evidence we have uncovered so far indicates that the ANC is not responsible. The weapon used was an RPG7 and it was recovered from an empty apartment overlooking the scene. The RPG launcher is a favourite weapon of the ANC. Crude attempts had been made to remove the serial number from the stock of the weapon. However we were able to recover the number using chemical enhancement techniques. It has been determined by cross checking our database that the weapon in question was one of a number seized when the Army intercepted a cross border weapons smuggling operation two years ago. According to our records the weapon was in storage in a Government armoury in Pietermaritzburg. When we made enquiries at the storage depot we were informed that the weapon is now missing from the inventory.

The assassination occurred close to the airport. This is a high risk area covered extensively by security cameras. I had the tapes collected and checked by one of my officers," the Chief Investigating Officer paused to point out the Detective Sergeant. "He has come back with the following photographs."

The Detective Sergeant passed around a number of photographic prints.

"You will note we have reasonable pictures of the Highways' Maintenance vehicle that was used to slow down the traffic and also less clear pictures of the RPG launcher sticking out of the window it was fired from. Whilst the pictures are not good enough to make formal identification possible it is quite apparent that the two men in the Highways' lorry and the man in the window are white.

Additionally, if you look at the last picture you will note the presence of an Army vehicle in the apartment block car park. The registration belongs to a vehicle assigned to the 5th South African Infantry Battalion. The vehicle was reported damaged beyond repair during exercises two years ago. The Battalion is normally based in Ladysmith but the bulk of the troops are currently on service on the northern Namibian border. The battalion commander is unable to explain the situation.

Furthermore another incident took place involving a 'non-existent' vehicle belonging to the 5th South African Infantry Battalion. Yesterday a farmer noticed an abandoned army jeep on the R40, near to the town of

Hoedspruit, in Limpopo Province. The farmer reported it to the police who discovered a couple of hundred yards away the bodies of two, so far unidentified, men both shot in the head by high velocity bullets. One of the dead men was clutching a loaded service pistol in his hand. We believe that this may be a connected incident but are not clear as to what the connection is at the present time.

Our preliminary feeling is that the murder of Andrew de Kluge was not the work of the ANC and that the real perpetrators may have an army connection. We will of course continue our investigation and keep you abreast of any further developments."

The Chief Secretary to the Cabinet came to his feet. "May I thank you gentlemen for the concise nature of your report. Needless to say the information disclosed at this meeting must be treated with the highest degree of sensitivity. Now if you would excuse us, I am sure the Cabinet Members would like to discuss the substance and implications of your report."

Duncan's Room, Meadow Vale Hotel, Pretoria
Wednesday 8th March 1989

Although Duncan was expecting the knock on the door he still looked through the spy hole before letting Stuart in.

"How's Jane?" Stuart asked without further greeting.

"Still shocked. It was a very close call. She's sleeping in the adjoining room at the moment."

The men sat down by the coffee table. "What happened?"

Duncan explained about Jane's excitement and insistence on the trip and how they ended up in the hunting camp and how she'd gone off alone in the dead of night.

"So what did you do when she disappeared?" asked Stuart.

"I had a good idea where she was going. I woke up the ranger and told him we'd had a squabble and she'd driven off in a huff and I was worried. He offered to come and search for her with me but I just asked to borrow his four wheel drive. He agreed and thankfully insisted I take the guns I'd hired with me.

I knew she'd go snooping around the airbase. I was cruising around and spotted an army jeep parked ski-whiff on the side of the road. A couple of hundred yards later I saw what I thought was our hire car part concealed under a tree. I drove on for a while and parked up myself. The railway line runs close to the road and is a bit raised and the sun was going to be behind me as well. So I decided to walk on the far side of the tracks, to keep my profile down and see what I could see. I took the hunting rifle with me. I walked a good way and didn't notice anything. I was about to cut across the waste ground and head for where I thought the hire car was parked when I heard a scream, I was sure it was Jane. I darted around a bit and saw them just in time. The gun was at her head and it was clear what was going to happen. I went onto one knee and took them both out. At that distance there was as much luck as skill in the shots. Thankfully I'd practiced with the gun the day before. But for that she'd be dead now.

She was in bits when I got to her. I couldn't spend too much time consoling her though. I forced her back to the car and made her set off back to the camp. She says she can't remember the journey at all, but she did arrive back safely. I wiped the tyre tracks out of the sand and followed after gathering up what I could."

Duncan fumbled in the top pocket of his shirt.

"By the way here's your engagement ring. I got it back from one of the dead men," Duncan laid it on the coffee table.

"Now that I've told you my story you tell me yours?"

"London was the damp squib we expected. I had a meeting with….."

"I don't mean that shit," said Duncan. "What's the deal with Jane?"

Stuart remained silent.

"Stuart I've been straight with you all my life and I think you've been the same with me – so far. Now what's the deal with Jane? You introduced her to me as your fiancée, and then she was present when you got me involved and by the time we get to this place she's virtually running the show. What's going on?"

"She's not my fiancée," sighed Stuart. "When we planned the trip we wanted it to look like we were a couple having a holiday together. It saves a lot of questions."

I understand that, but why continue the ruse with me? Don't you trust me?"

"No it's not that. Jane's not from my department, she's new to field work. It was her idea."

"What's her background?"

"She started off as a cryptographer and language specialist at GCHQ. But she has a great mind and has made a name for herself as a good situation analyst, so good in fact that she operates virtually independently and enjoys her own distinct code name. She's good. That's the truth and you breathe a word of that and I am goosed."

"Does she have any field experience at all?" asked Duncan. "As far as I'm concerned she's not a team player and is a danger to both herself and others – namely me in this instance."

Stuart shook his head in despair. "She has the theory and she is definitely on our side but like a lot of brilliant minds her brain's so full of good ideas there appears to be little room left for common sense. That's my opinion."

"In the light of what's happened I couldn't really disagree with your analysis," said Jane. Neither man had heard her open the door adjoining the two rooms.

Stuart stood up and placed a chair at the coffee table for her. "Sounds like you had quite a scare, sit down. I'll get some coffee ordered."

The two representatives of the ANC that had remained in London were now sitting in the anti-room of Sir Basil Parker Smythe's office in the Foreign and Commonwealth Building in Whitehall. Sir Basil kept them waiting as he went through the briefing notes that a messenger had just carried around by hand from Downing Street.

Ralph hovered in attendance awaiting instructions.

"This has all the makings of the shortest accreditation in history. I only welcomed them a day or two ago and now I'm going to have to expel them."

"Well perhaps they haven't signed a lease on a property or anything like that," chipped in Ralph.

Sir Basil shook his head in despair. "They're just about to be forced into a guerrilla war that could last decades and cost thousands of lives, but hey-ho there's a bright side; they didn't waste money on a lease. You just stick to the coffee and tea Ralph and leave the thinking to me."

"Sir," said Ralph pulling himself to attention.

"Give me ten minutes to compose my words and then show the gentlemen in and Ralph, once the meeting is started I don't want to be disturbed for any reason, any reason whatsoever. Is that clear to you?"

"Yes Sir Basil."

"How sure are you?" asked Stuart.

"Crystal clear," replied Jane.

"You were under a lot of pressure. It would be easy to have misheard."

"I promise you every word that was spoken is as clear as crystal in my mind. There is no mistake. They said that the operation their colleagues were involved with in Johannesburg would be dominating the news for a long time to come. My murder would attract no attention."

"Well the big event is the murder of Andrew de Kluge, a member of the Cabinet. This tells us two very significant things, firstly that the ANC were not responsible for his death and secondly it confirms there is some kind of faction or organisation that has considerable power and is fighting the South African Government. White fighting white at the highest level. What if the Government don't have or are too scared to exercise control?" asked Stuart.

Jane interrupted

"You said that our Government was about to throw the ANC out of the United Kingdom. What do you think their reaction will be? We're only just getting them onboard. The Soviets are not an entirely spent force. They would still dearly like to see their ships docking at Simon's Town and not ours or the American's. And if the Russians are too weak to pick up the cudgels, the Chinese are waiting on the side lines. Might be best if you got Whitehall to hang on a bit, don't let them burn their bridges."

"You're right. I need to speak to the Foreign and Commonwealth Office," said Stuart.

The meeting in Parliament Building went on for a long time. The Speaker of the House had been brought in. Whatever was decided in the room would have to pass through Parliament and his support and influence would be essential.

The President of the Republic of South Africa sat quietly letting the debate run its course. He listened as the Speaker summed up the general feeling.

"Others have presented us with a difficult decision. It was the Americans supported by British that have taken us to this point but their views are clearly a reflection of world opinion. It appears to me we only have a choice of route. The destination is the same whichever way we go. Recent events tell us we must act quickly and decisively. We must negotiate now from the position of strength we currently enjoy. Delay will allow powerful forces within our own country to overtake us. We must secure the best deal we can immediately.

Before I came into this meeting, as you gentleman were sitting here talking, reports have been coming in of gangs of white youths driving around African Townships shooting indiscriminately, killing innocent Africans because of the death of Andrew de Kluge. It will not be long before the black Africans start shooting back."

A murmur of muted agreement rippled around the room.

"I understand that Sir Basil Parker Smythe is about to commence a meeting, with the ANC representatives but I'm telling you that it is imperative that I get to speak with him immediately. It concerns the meeting."

"I'm sorry Mr Cameron I cannot put you through," replied the Secretary.

Stuart persisted. "What I have to say to Sir Basil is of great importance, he would definitely want to hear what I have to say. Now please, I do not want to have to resort to threats."

The secretary sighed. "I actually think the meeting has already started. The best I can do is put you through to his assistant, Ralph. Will that do you? It's better than nothing."

Stuart thought it wasn't much better than nothing but accepted the offer.

There wasn't time for pleasantries. "Ralph put me through to Sir Basil."

"I can't. He's in a meeting."

"I know. The call will affect the meeting. Put me through, now!"

"He won't pick up the phone. He'll just let it ring and get annoyed."

"Then take a message through to him."

"He told me he was not to be disturbed under any circumstances once the meeting had commenced. It's more than my job's worth."

"Is your job worth more than a child's life?"

"What?"

"Let me explain to you Ralph."

"The normal protocol is to stand during such an interview," began Sir Basil once the representatives of the ANC had been shown into his office. "However as your status is somewhat ambiguous and you are not the accredited representative of a sovereign state I think we can dispense with such formalities. You may take a seat." Sir Basil pointed to chairs in front of his desk.

"My Government, working in conjunction with its allies has been trying hard to find a resolution to the South African problem that is satisfactory to all parties," he began.

"We did not assassinate the South African politician," interjected the ANC representative.

"Your denial is noted," responded Sir Basil, disregarding the protest. "My Government accepts and hopes that one day normal democratic processes will apply in South Africa. We had identified your organisation, despite its terrorist credentials, as a potential major player in the democratic process."

"We did not kill him," interjected the ANC representative again.

Sir Basil did not even acknowledge the protest this time. "My Government made no demand for the ANC to formally renounce violence in return for bringing the organisation into the political process. However we expected that the ANC, if it was politically mature, to voluntarily abide by certain conventions."

"I repeat the ANC has neither authorised nor taken part in any violent operation since permission to open an office in London was granted."

"One of the conventions, a matter of common decency really, is that when warring parties are in peace talks they stop killing each other. It appears that your organisation is not aware of that convention."

The ANC representatives stood up. "How many times must I tell you? My organisation did not assassinate Andrew de Kluge."

Sir Basil, not wishing to be spoken down to also got to his feet and faced his opponent across the desk.

"My Government is convinced that there is clear evidence that the ANC is guilty of planning and carrying out acts of political terrorism and as such should once more be designated as a terrorist organisation that is illegal and banned from this country."

The ANC representative was near to bursting point, his voice raised, he shouted at Sir Basil. "You are totally mistaken. We have not broken any convention and what has happened to the British high and mighty principle of innocent until proven guilty? Answer me that."

In the brief silence before Sir Basil had time to respond there was a feeble knock on the door.

"Go away," he shouted.

The highly polished door handle went down and the door tentatively began to open. Ralph's head appeared.

"I warned you Ralph. Get out!"

Ralph gingerly entered the office and almost tiptoed over to Sir Basil's desk, his eyes cast downwards, as if terrified to make eye contact with his boss. Ralph placed a single sheet of paper in front of Sir Basil. Scribbled in pencil was the message, "Stuart Cameron says they didn't do it!"

Sir Basil looked at the message. "Ralph, look at me."

Ralph raised his eyes to meet those of his boss. Sir Basil noted a sudden change in Ralph's demeanour; he thought there was something different about him. He was standing a bit more upright, his shoulders a little squarer and his gaze unblinking.

"Is this correct Ralph?"

"Absolutely correct." Ralph turned and marched confidently, as one who had just crossed the Rubicon. Ralph left the room and slammed the door behind him.

"Please sit," said Sir Basil to the ANC representative. "Some new information has just come to hand that puts a different light on the situation and which I am sure you will find as pleasing as I do. Information has just come to my attention that suggests that the ANC may not have carried out the terrorist attack that I alluded to!"

The representative of the ANC just shook his head, not even tempted to say "I told you so."

An hour later, after Sir Basil had spoken with Stuart in private, and when the meeting had been concluded with tea and handshakes and a muttered 'all water under the bridge', comment, Sir Basil pressed the button on his intercom and leant back in his chair. "Tell Ralph to come in."

Before Sir Basil had a chance to open his mouth Ralph spoke.

"I've packed my things, my desk is clear I'm ready to go."

"What! Why? You just displayed an amazing use of personal initiative and decisive action. These are the qualities I knew that lurked within you. Well done, well done."

"Nevertheless Sir Basil, I think the saying is that one biscuit doesn't make a party. Overall my performance has not pleased you and it would be better for everybody if I just left. Of course it's nice to be leaving on a high note, the only high note of my employment." He turned to walk away.

Sir Basil did not take kindly to rejection nor was he used to requesting things he thought were his by right. But in this instance he made an exception.

"Ralph stop, turnaround. I don't think you should leave. In fact I will go so far as to say that I would like you to stay." The words stuck in his throat for a second, "I need you here."

"Really?"

"Yes really Ralph."

"Thank you Sir Basil," Ralph continued towards the door.

"Where are you going now," asked Sir Basil.

"I'm going to phone my father and tell him I did something right today."

Sir Basil spoke. "Indeed you will do no such thing. It would be crass. I'll phone and tell him. It will sound much better."

Ralph turned away so that Sir Basil didn't see him wipe the tear that was forming in the corner of his eye.

"You can go now Ralph. Ralph walked the last steps and grabbed the door handle.

"One last thing Ralph. You know you always refer to me very formally as Sir Basil. I think we've progressed a little beyond that stage now. I think in future you can just call me Sir."

Ralph shut the door behind him knowing that his troubles with Sir Basil Parker Smythe were not finished, but he also felt, for the first time since starting his job, that he just might be able to deal with them.

The maid had wanted to clean Stuart's room so they'd decamped to the hotel's pool area for coffee.

"So where does that leave us now?" asked Duncan.

"Despite our failure to intercept the detonators we have learnt a lot," said Stuart. "We know the South African government does have or is very close to having nuclear weapons. We also know they don't have full control of them and we are close to knowing the name of the man who does and we know he's ruthless, willing to carry out murder, even political assassinations."

"We know more than that," added Jane. "We can be sure that the Americans and South Africans are going to reach agreement sooner rather than later."

"I don't get that. How can we know when the Americans will act?" asked Duncan.

"Easy," replied Jane.

"Enlighten me," said Stuart.

"One of the motivations of the US President is to demonstrate to black American voters that he cares about their *'African brothers'*. The US election process kicks off mid next year. I'd say that he needs Mandela to walk free at the beginning of the year, so it's all going to kick off towards the end of this year. The real problem the President has is that if nuclear weapons fall into the hands of radical black nationalists he is likely to lose more right wing Republican voters than he gains black voters. The US needs to get hold of South Africa's nuclear weapons, or neutralise them at the least. And there is not much we can do till the Americans force the issue, except watch and wait."

"That's really cynical," said Duncan, "But why are we going to continue our involvement?"

"Because we're no better than the Americans," replied Jane, "We want the same things as the Americans but for different reasons. We're going to protect our interests. We might not rule South Africa but it is fair to say we own a good part of it but more than that, there are over two million British passport holders living in South Africa. A prolonged guerrilla war will result in a lot of them returning to the UK looking for the UK Government to support them. That's not going to happen. What we want is a nice pro-capitalist, non-nuclear, black majority government. Of course no British politician would admit to that. All they'll say is that the current regime is immoral and we are taking a stand on human rights grounds. Don't be too harsh on the Americans, we're most probably worse."

"I suppose we'll just have to be ready," said Stuart.

BOOK THREE
Lincoln Memorial, Washington D.C.
Monday 22nd January 1990

The South African Ambassador to the United States had re-read the long telex message he had received from President Duplessey's Office. It was the third time he'd read it. With the contents firmly embedded in his mind he folded the six closely typed pages and locked them in the wall safe of his office, the safe to which he alone had access.

As an ambassador Stefan Weiss was a thoughtful man, not prone to rash actions or decisions; a person preferring the gentlemanly ways of diplomacy, he thought more could be achieved by talking than warring. To him violence in general was ultimately futile. The type of battles he liked to fight were against the political elite, the battle ground the dinner tables of upper class Washington restaurants and the only barrage he would let loose was a barrage of words. The proof of his dedication to this philosophy was his forty-eight inch waist and 'type two' diabetes, courtesy of an excess of filet mignon and the finest French wine.

He collected his coat and hat. He would need protection from the cold wind that blew that day, weather in keeping with the chill task in hand. He left the embassy and hailed a yellow cab to take him to the Lincoln memorial. It was only a short journey. But the meeting would be defining. The future of his country would in all probability be decided there. When he arrived at the steps to the great building Senator Gene Barrymore was there, ready, waiting for him.

Senator Barrymore was an example of the new breed of politician that had started to infiltrate both Houses of Congress, smart, young can-do types not afraid to break the mould of traditional politics. Hatless but wearing a tailored herringbone overcoat he wrung his gloved hands to ward off the cold. The coat masked his superb physique, a physique that was primarily due to early morning five mile jogs and an hour's evening work out in the gym, every day except Sunday, when he attended church twice.

Stefan Weiss preferred the old type of American politician. The likes of Gene Barrymore were too crude, too abrupt, too smart by half for his liking but Stefan didn't have a choice. Gene Barrymore was the youngest member of the Senate Foreign Affairs Committee. However it was not that qualification that brought him to the meeting, it was the close personal relationship he enjoyed with the President of the United States. Gene's influence was based as much on his powerful early morning jogging partner as his performance in the Senate. Stefan knew that when the Senator spoke he did so with the approval of the Commander- in-Chief.

The Senator offered his gloved hand to Stefan Weiss.

"Thank you for seeing me like this," said Stefan.

"Always willing to oblige a friend," replied the Ambassador. "Shall we walk as we talk? I'm sure we can do both things at the same time."

Without waiting for a reply the Senator set off down the footpath that led to Constitutional Gardens, running parallel to the Reflecting Pond and on towards the Washington Monument.

"So?" asked the Senator.

"I'm sure you're aware my President made a private visit to the United States recently and during that visit he had a private discussion with your President where one or two options for the future of my country were suggested."

"Yeah I heard about that," replied Gene. "Pretty rough talks I understand. Your guy didn't take it too well I believe. How is he now?"

"He's fine, in good health. I think it was some kind of virus or something."

"Yeah right, I hope there's no recurrence."

"Over the past months my Government has carefully considered the suggestions put forward by your President. It is no secret that it was a bitter pill your President offered South Africa. However we are not oblivious to reality. Consequently my Government have asked me to investigate the possibilities in a bit more detail, and as I have always valued your opinion I thought we might have a confidential word to see the 'lay of the land' so to speak. I take it I can assume this conversation is taking place in the strictest of confidence?"

"You can and I think you can also assume that I have a very strong grasp of what is possible. You might even say I have an authoritative view. I assume the same is true for yourself?"

"Absolutely. Now to the substance of our meeting; recent events have made my Government speed up its decision making process."

"I heard about Andrew de Kluge's death. That's very sad. I'm sure my Government expressed its condolence appropriately?"

Stefan didn't respond to the question. "As I said my Government till now has been reluctant to accept American proposals for the future of South Africa. But after debate and consideration my Government is now more inclined towards a gradual, peaceful move in the direction of universal elections. But I have to warn you that the recent event we spoke about was not quite what it appears. It is this that has brought some urgency to the process."

"If what you're saying is that Andrew de Kluge was not killed by the ANC we already know that."

"You could not possibly know that!" retorted Stefan a little too hastily. "What I mean to say is what makes you think that the assassination was other than a terrorist attack by the ANC. Who do you think is responsible?"

"Actually we don't know specifically who did it but we know who didn't do it and it definitely wasn't the ANC. The Brits told us a couple of days ago."

Stefan was beginning to feel distinctly off balance by the blunt blows that were being landed. "Were the British involved?" he demanded.

"In the assassination? I don't think so," replied Gene. "But they've got a better grip than most about events in your country."

Stefan felt he was going down a blind alley and decided to change tack and get more directly to the point. "My Government thinks it would be best if there was general international agreement on the subject sooner rather than later. They would feel more comfortable if there was an agreement backed up by our allies – that is we would feel more comfortable if our friends, as part of the arrangement, offered us security, physical security."

They continued walking, passing the pond on the left and coming close to the memorial at the far end of the Reflecting Pool.

"See that construction?" asked Gene. "Know what it is?"

"War memorial I believe."

"Specifically it's the Korean War Memorial. When I look at it I remember all the Americans that died on the Korean peninsula defending a foreign people. After Korea lots of American lives were lost defending another foreign people in Vietnam. They are both salutary lessons that our current President takes heed of. Now your country has been a good friend of the United States and we're not going to abandon you but don't think our support is unconditional. We're not going to end up fighting in South Africa. Let's cut to the chase. What's your bottom line?"

Stefan was making little progress. "My government suggests that we gradually move towards qualified elections over a period of twenty-five years. Blacks that achieve a minimum education standard and a pre-agreed wealth threshold will be allowed to vote with the whites at that time. In return for that the United States guarantees the external and internal security of South Africa."

"You're in fucking cloud cuckoo land," was the response. "Try something like release all political prisoners immediately and hold universal election within a year. We'll bring the ANC along and guarantee the safety of the whites."

"There would be a revolution in my country on such terms. The Government would fall and be replaced by an extremist regime."

Gene reflected for a moment. "You're most probably right on that one. Indications are your Government is tottering now."

"All the more reason for a quick settlement. What about releasing all non-violent political prisoners and twenty years to universal elections?"

"Won't work unless Mandela walks free. He's their leader when all's said and done. That's not negotiable."

"Release Mandela in two years and universal elections in ten years."

"Mandela walks now and five years to elections."

"Mandela is freed on condition he renounces violence, election in five years followed by a Government of National Unity where there's a white in joint charge but only so long as there are political guarantees from the United States and the British Government agrees to stop the flight of capital from my country."

"Better," replied Gene. "The President will go along with something like that; I'm sure the Brits will too. I'll get the Canadian monitors who visit Mandela to make a pitch to the ANC. Are you sure your guys will go along with it?"

"The Government will and most of the people can be persuaded. Our problem will be with the hard-line whites. It will be a struggle controlling the fanatics. There is also a related problem we need to discuss."

"I can guess what you are going to say?"

"What's that?"

"Your nuclear weapons stockpile. You don't want it to fall into the hands of an unknown and untested black leader. I can tell you we're with you on that one."

"Well officially we don't have nuclear weapons," replied Stefan.

"Yeah right. We will insist that South Africa is free of nuclear weapons and has signed the Nuclear Non-Proliferation Pact before there can be universal elections. That will be a non negotiable condition imposed on the ANC."

"A radical black leader with nuclear weapons is not the only worry. Any radical, black or white group poses a threat if they get their hands on such weapons," added Stefan."

"You're right," replied Gene. "The sooner we get a rap on this deal the better. I also think once we're agreed, you hand your weapons over to us immediately."

"That might not be acceptable – handing them over to you that is."

"What about the United Nations?"

"Possibly."

"And if the United States provides the UN troops on the ground?"

"The South African Government could most probably live with that."

Drakensberg
Wednesday 24th January 1990

"You have done well on the first two operations. Now a more imposing task lies ahead of us." Peter van Stardan briefed his men in the great cavern in the Drakensberg.

"Our Government is weakened. It is bending under international pressure. For most of my life I have worked to give our Government a tool that will allow them to negotiate from a position of power. They have proved incapable of gaining advantage from what has been presented to them. Therefore we must take control ourselves. We must be strong where the Government has proved weak. You are the only people that now stand ready to protect our folk culture, our way of life and perhaps even our very existence. Are you ready for this challenge?"

Van Stardan was surprised at the intensity of the fanatical response to his words.

"Now I will hand over to Lieutenant Colonel Okra who will go over the plan with you in detail once more. I will not wish you luck because we do not need luck when God is with us."

Victor Verster Prison, Paarl, South Africa
Thursday 1st February 1990

Even Nelson Mandela was beginning to believe the unbelievable. It was not just the improvement in his prison living conditions and the changed attitude of the prison warders. Now there were frequent visitors. In addition to the Scandinavian and Canadian prison monitors, there were people, white people, coming to sound out his views and opinions, virtually negotiating with him although they never actually used that word. Contact with the free leadership of the ANC although still technically illegal was becoming much easier.

Mandela was bemused at what his visitors considered a major sticking point but to him, and the leadership of the ANC, was a non-issue. Despite all his assurances they kept coming back and asking the same question.

"Please just read our constitution and manifesto," he consistently pleaded. "The ANC has been and remains committed to a world free of nuclear weapons. Not only will a democratic South Africa not have nuclear weapons of its own but it will also campaign on the world stage for the abandonment of nuclear weapons by all nations. We are unequivocal on this matter."

Only now, as he lay on his bed, in the relative comfort of his prison cell, listening to the BBC World Service News on his recently acquired radio, did he dare to believe the message.

"Reports are coming in from the AP News Service that Nelson Mandela, the leader of South Africa's African National Congress, is being considered for release from prison," announced the news reader. *"We now go over by phone to our correspondent in South Africa."*

"For the past twelve hours I have been trying unsuccessfully to get a statement from the Ministry of Justice here in Pretoria. However unofficial sources confirm that the release of Mandela is being seriously considered. If the rumours turn out to be true and Mandela is to be released it can only be for one of two reasons.

The Apartheid regime might release him on humanitarian grounds. In the recent past Nelson Mandela has been suffering from health problems necessitating hospital treatment. Some supporters believe that the Apartheid Government will release Mandela if his condition is diagnosed as terminal. Clearly they do not want to suffer the international condemnation and consequential internal unrest that is likely to follow should he die whilst in their custody.

On the other hand if Mandela is to be released and it is not on humanitarian grounds, this would signify a major change of policy by the Apartheid Government and might be seen as the prelude to universal democratic elections and majority rule. Commentators, as well as watching the Government, will be keenly watching the leadership of the

ANC to see if moves are made towards declaring a ceasefire in their long running guerrilla war."

Nelson Mandela switched the radio off, rolled over in his bed and closed his eyes ready to dream the dream that had been his life's work.

Meadow Vale Hotel, Pretoria
Wednesday 7th February 1990

Sunshine bathed the glistening pool terrace as black faced, white coated waiters pandered to the needs of guests. Duncan sat alone in the gloomy hotel bar sipping the dregs of a beer that he didn't really want and that had long since passed the stage of being refreshing. A youthful and enthusiastic white bar manager tried to chat but sensing his customer's irritability discreetly withdrew, leaving a sullen Duncan to wallow in his own thoughts.

Stuart had asked him to come back to Pretoria. He'd come but for a week he'd had nothing to do but hang around and Elizabeth had crept back into his mind to occupy the empty space, dragging his mood down. Stuart was too busy to notice Duncan's increasing moroseness. Each morning he'd trotted off to the British Embassy, where he spent his time sifting through piles of communiqués. Jane, often at his side, sought out the hidden innuendo in the text. Together they tried to fathom the true sincerity and intent of the South African Government. Their efforts were not limited to analysing the written word. They needed to get inside the mindset of the decision makers and they could only do this by socialising. There were lunches, cocktail parties, receptions and informal diplomatic parties. They went where they could and listened to anybody who spoke. They rejected American 'up-front' confrontational methods, relying instead on the gleaning of discarded and indiscreet comment, the gathering of careless words and telling facial expression. The physical and intellectual strain made Stuart oblivious to Duncan's needs whilst Jane, deep inside, still struggled to come to terms with the events at Hoedspruit.

Duncan should have gone to his room long ago, he needed to sleep, but sleep eluded him and his mind relentlessly turned back to Elizabeth. He found it better to sit at the bar and it was in the bar that the hotel's bell boy had found him.

"Mr Murdoch, your friends are looking for you. They'd like you to join them on the terrace."

Without haste he wandered towards the terrace where the lowering sun shone into his eyes and blinded him.

"Duncan!"

He raised his hand to form a visor over his eyes.

He still couldn't see the expression on Stuart's shadowy face but the tone of the single word was enough to indicate that Stuart's mood was little better than his own.

"Come and join us."

The table at the edge of the terrace was overhung by a leafy palm whose foliage wafted gently in the evening breeze. Jane was already sitting there. Duncan thought her face had changed somewhat, had taken on a more serious aura. Some of the youthful twinkle in her eyes had gone. He wondered if her introduction to his life, a life where violent tragedy so often intervened was dragging her down too.

Stuart ordered three beers without consulting his companions.

"I'm sorry to have ignored you for so long. There was so much to do, but the news is actually promising. I suppose I should feel more enthusiastic. It might be a bit premature but I think we have what could be termed as the promise of a result. I think the South Africans, the senior politicians at least, are sincere in their intentions. Apartheid may be coming to an end."

Jane didn't raise her head and Duncan's expression remained blank.

Stuart continued undaunted ignoring the lack of response. "In the next few days you should see some news that will attract worldwide attention and I think we can proudly claim to have made a not insignificant contribution. Nelson Mandela is to be released from prison." Stuart paused for dramatic effect.

"That's good news," replied Duncan forcing a smile.

"Of course that piece of information must remain strictly confidential for now. The South Africans will make the announcement themselves. They don't want to appear to be bowing to international pressure."

"They don't have to worry about foreign governments claiming credit for ending Apartheid," said Jane. "The people who will be crowing most about 'victory' will be the loony left and the anti-apartheid activists around the world."

Stuart nodded. "That's normal, when something good happens there's never any shortage of people ready to claim credit."

"Our real victory however will attract a little less attention. Whilst the cameras are focusing on Nelson Mandela walking to freedom, the Americans will be taking charge of the South African nuclear stock pile. They won't be called Americans though- they'll be working under the flag of the United Nations and in the name of the International Atomic Energy Authority."

"How international will it be?" asked Duncan, the question escaping from his mouth involuntarily.

"There will be a few international observers in the advance party, but it'll be Americans in the lead for sure. Eventually the stockpile will be destroyed. The technical stuff and reports will be done by the IAEA, but that will come much later. The most important issue is that the weapons will be made secure immediately. That's got to be good."

"I suppose it is," replied Duncan.

"Your enthusiasm is overwhelming," said Stuart disappointed at the response. "It is a win."

"It might be a win in your eyes but in means little to me. The truth is we came here on a hair brained unauthorised operation, made a complete bags of it, let the Americans take all the glory and are now about to pack our bags and go home. I don't see that much to celebrate."

Stuart was taken aback. "Come on Duncan. You have been instrumental in the whole operation. If you hadn't been suspicious over the death of Jomo in the first place and if Jane hadn't, rather unconventionally, brought the Russians into the equation, the result could have been very different. Give yourself some credit."

"You're quite right I did make a big contribution," responded Duncan. "If I hadn't been suspicious over the death of Jomo then Elizabeth would be alive right now! I'd let the South Africans have their bombs if I could have Elizabeth back."

"The South Africans were coming for Morgan and Tembo no matter what happened. They were the ones in the killing business, you're not responsible for their ineptitude."

"I didn't come here with you to save the world. I didn't come here for the money. I think, deep down, I came here to get the bastards who killed Elizabeth and in that I've failed."

A wave of silent sympathy swept over Stuart and Jane. For a while nobody spoke.

Stuart's mind went back to the beginning of their relationship, the war in Aden. Duncan, the youthful private soldier that had been unjustly convicted of murder had remained stoic, never wavered, never cracked, never suffered from self-pity and Stuart knew it was not self-pity that affected his friend now. It was pity for Elizabeth, the African Princess that had given him love. He was not angry for himself, he was angry for her. She had deserved better.

Jane spoke, her voice barely above a whisper.

"You saved my life Duncan, I will be eternally grateful for that. It seems unfair that you were able to do for me what you could not do for your own wife. I suppose if there was natural justice Elizabeth would have lived and I'd have died. Elizabeth did nothing wrong, made no mistakes, but I was a fool. I can't feel what you feel but I don't think you will be able to put the matter to rest until you are satisfied that you have done what you can for Elizabeth. I promise that I will support you for as long as you want."

Stuart continued. "I'm sorry for being insensitive to the depth of your pain. I don't know how I would have behaved in your position. I'm with Jane on this we should seek justice for Elizabeth. I'm not sure how we'll do it but we'll work together to get those responsible for what happened at Stirling Farm."

"I appreciate the words," replied Duncan, "and I believe you mean what you say but the truth is that what has happened has happened and it's probably better if I go back to my kids. In reality nothing can be done. "

"I'm not sure that is true. I do believe there are good people, white and black, but they have been too afraid to come forward. Things are about to change, the unthinkable is about to happen. The people who did bad things in the past will have to answer for their actions. The truth is nobody knows how it will pan out but we may find the authorities and the law working in our favour."

"That's pie in the sky," replied Duncan.

"I understand you wanting to get back to your kids but I think you need to do something first. The people who controlled Vastrap are responsible for Elizabeth's death, hers and a lot more. The Americans will be there soon. They haven't got a clue what they are going to find. They don't even know what they are looking for.

Go there, I'll arrange it. Take Tembo and Morgan with you, they know the place. Gather what evidence you can before it is lost forever. Keep it safe until the time is right to use it."

"I don't know," replied Duncan.

"Stay here for a while. Speak to Tembo and Morgan on the phone. Tell them to get ready. Let's see what we can do."

They heard a hand bell ringing and looked up. The Bell Boy circled the pool area carrying the sign and shouting, "Phone call for Mr Cameron, phone call for Mr Cameron."

Stuart stood up. "Just don't you leave this hotel, okay?"

Stuart took the phone call at the hotel's reception desk. To any casual listener it would have sounded very much a one-way conversation. The caller spoke unknown words and Stuart answered with monosyllables, just yes's and okay's. The call was short, without any pleasantries. Stuart hung up the receiver and thanked the receptionist before crossing the lobby and heading out onto the street his eyes darting around, watchful for the incongruous. Darkness had fallen and the street was bathed in the yellow glow of sodium street lights. He waited a few moments for his eyes to adjust knowing that he'd have to be sharp. He turned left and walked to the first crossroads and waited for the green man to appear before crossing to the other side of the road. He then double-backed up the street, passing the hotel on the other side, stopping for a moment to look into a jeweller's window, not seeing the trays of diamonds but looking at the reflection in the glass for evidence that he was not being followed. Satisfied he continued his journey for two blocks, till he reached the McDonalds on the corner. He joined the queue and got a coffee before choosing a seat, facing the plate glass window, in a booth close to the washroom door, as he'd been instructed. The coffee was too hot to drink. He sat and waited and watched.

The washroom door opened. A young woman pushed hard against the door's self-closing mechanism to get a child in a pushchair through, not helped by the fact that the pushchair was overburdened with shopping bags hanging from the handles. Stuart stood and held the door. As the woman nodded and came through the pushchair overbalanced and began to tip backwards. Stuart shot forward to steady the pushchair and there was an awkward moment in which the woman and Stuart struggled in the tight space. In a second the woman had regained control and with a brief nod of thanks continued on her way to the main entrance. Stuart retook his seat. On the bench alongside him was a plastic Burberry shopping bag. He didn't react. He sat for five minutes and got through half his coffee before leaving with the bag in his hand and making his way back to the hotel. He took the lift to the fourteenth floor where he got out alone. He walked along the corridor to the exit and used the stairs to walk down to the twelfth floor, where his room was located. He spent the next three hours reading the content of the file he'd found in the Burberry bag.

Washington D.C.
Thursday 8th February 1990

It took Burt Zimmerman about twenty five minutes to drive over to his partner's place on Dunaway Drive. Jack Carter's wife opened the door before he had a chance to ring.

"Saw you coming," she said. "Come in, he's not quite ready yet. Want some coffee?"

"Hi Betts, I'll skip the coffee if you don't mind. Is that Jack's bag? I'll drop it in the trunk if it's ready."

"Yep, it's ready to go. Come through when you're done."

Burt put Jack's bag alongside his own in the trunk and returned to the house. Jack was in the kitchen downing a glass of fresh orange juice and munching a piece of toast.

"Be with you right now," he mumbled in between bites and gulps.

A few minutes later Burt walked ahead as Jack said goodbye to his wife. "You all be careful now," he heard her say as she gave him a final kiss and hug.

"See you in a couple of weeks and don't worry, we're taking an army with us."

The run from Dunaway Drive to the car pool at the CIA Headquarters at Langley was only a few minutes but today they weren't going to their offices. Instead Burt steered the car towards Washington DC and made his way to a building on the corner of 21st and H, a building that housed the CIA's public affairs office. The briefing room was small and sparse, just a table and a couple of plastic chairs. They'd just sat down when the briefing officer arrived, a po faced middle aged woman with close cropped wiry hair and thin lips that rarely saw lipstick. With an air of super efficiency she launched into the briefing.

"No official press statement will be issued. If the media pick up the mission the story is that it's part of a UN operation and the United States is merely providing logistical support and security. That's what you say off the record. On the record you say nothing. We don't expect to see your faces on any TV screens."

Both men nodded. "It'll be difficult to say it's an international mission if it's only Americans there," Burt chipped in.

"When you refuel at Ascension Island there will be some passengers to pick up. The Brits have been co-operating well with us. In addition to letting us use Ascension they've whistled up a few neutrals for you to take along; a couple of Swedish engineers, a Swiss physicist or something and an Irish guy."

"What does the Irish guy do?" asked Jack.

"The Brits were a bit vague about that. They said although he's highly qualified you'd most probably find him useful because he'd keep the Swedes and the Swiss entertained and out of your hair. They also said it would be advisable if the grunts weren't allowed to attend his parties. Make of that what you will. Any questions?"

"Are the Brits pissed because we get to do the glory stuff?"

"Doesn't appear so. As I said they have been helpful. We did get a request from them though. One of their field guys, a Stuart Cameron, says a man of his has some unfinished personal business and would like to be involved in the operation."

"We met this Cameron at Victoria Falls. He's an okay guy but I'm not sure about having someone with a personal agenda hanging around."

"We thought that too," replied the Briefing Officer, "however he will be bringing a couple of African assistants with him, men who worked on the site and are familiar with the layout and operations. We thought that might be useful to you and so have agreed to his request. Help them where you can without jeopardising the operation. Any other questions?"

"No that's it," said Jack.

"Good luck." The Briefing Officer left the room.

When she'd gone the two men looked at each other. "I'd rather face a hundred ranting guerrilla fighters than meet her on a dark night. Wadda you think?" asked Jack.

"Didn't like her aftershave!"

The drive from 21st and H took them on to Independence Avenue. They passed the White House on the left and headed down the wide dual carriageways of Pennsylvania Avenue. They followed Pennsylvania all the way, crossing the Sousa Bridge and eventually picked up the signs for Andrew's Airforce Base.

The Lockheed C5A Galaxy aircraft were long in the tooth but still ranked highly as one of the world's best and biggest military transport planes. They didn't look that impressive in the distance but when you got close up the size became obvious and when you got to look inside the space was truly awesome. Three C5's stood, side by side on the expanse of the cargo loading apron.

"You're assigned 'Alpha', the lead plane" said the supervising Major. It's carrying an advance guard with light vehicles and enough support to set up a perimeter and hold it. 'Bravo' will carry the bulk of the men and vehicles and will land as soon as given clearance by 'Alpha'. 'Charlie' will carry the logistical support supplies and the Neutrals that join at Ascension."

"Okay," said Jack. "How long before go?"

"The Cargo Masters are just about done and signed off. We're embarking the troops right now. Then it's a go. You can get straight on. There'll be no disembarking at Ascension so expect to be on board for twenty hours minimum."

"And what's the in-flight service like?" asked Burt with a grin.

"Hot coffee when they can manage it, cold sandwiches or ration packs, your choice. Don't drink too much you'll need to book the can!"

"What no in-flight movie?" smirked Burt.

The Major gave a one-fingered salute and turned away.

"An officer wouldn't do that in my day," said Jack but the Major was already out of ear- shot. "Come on let's go."

The General Electric TF 39 high by-pass engines needed all their immense power to raise the 381 tonnes of C5 off the ground. The take-off roll was long; the plane required over two and half kilometres of runway to build up enough speed to get sufficient lift under the wings. Several hours later when it landed at Ascension Island it was nearly one hundred and seventy five tonnes lighter; that was how much fuel it had burnt on the trip.

Jack Carter and Burt Zimmerman would have liked to have got off and had a stroll but the rules were the same for them as they were for the grunts in the back. Everybody stayed put whilst the engineers from RAF Ascension Island checked over the plane and added another one hundred and seventy five tonnes of fuel. The RAF guys were good. They wanted to get flight 'Alpha' off the ground before flight 'Bravo' landed. Not that there wasn't enough space at the airfield. Quite the opposite, RAF Ascension had the proud distinction of being the busiest airport in the world for a short time during the build up to the Falkland's War, handling more take-offs and landings than London's Heathrow. But for this operation there was a tight schedule. The space between the aircraft had been carefully timed. 'Alpha' had to land at Upington Airport and secure it for the following planes quickly. 'Bravo' and 'Charlie' would be running short of fuel by the time they arrived and wouldn't be able to circle for very long. There was no alternate landing place.

Philip Avery was twenty three. Two years ago he'd dropped out of university after a string of rotten marks left him demoralised and depressed. It took him twelve months of counselling to get over the blow to his inflated ego. The therapist felt that Philip's problem lay routed in his family's wealth that had helped make him spoilt, self centred and used to getting his own way without having to apply too much effort. Fortunately the family's wealth stretched far enough to pay the therapist's bills. Now Philip wanted to be an air traffic controller. His father's influence and contacts managed to get him started. He was however finding it exceedingly frustrating being confined to a darkened room one floor down from the glass observation gallery that enjoyed spectacular views of Upington Airport and the longest paved runway in the world.

His current job was to sort out the incoming fax and telex messages; to deliver weather and situation reports to the qualified controllers and other general duties. In fact he was performing the function of a clerical assistant. He still maintained hopes of progressing to the glass tower; unfortunately his superiors felt he'd most probably reached the limit of his capabilities but that disappointment was for another day.

Despite his poor level of achievement, Philip enjoyed his father's support and that was because Philip did whatever his father told him to do. He had the redeeming feature of knowing which side his bread was buttered. When he'd got the job his father had told him that if he ever heard of anything interesting or out of the ordinary he should let him know. Now Philip held a faxed letter that had just come in. He didn't understand anything other than that it was out of the ordinary. Incoming flight information normally came via the computer network but the fax he read came from the South African Ministry of Aviation and just said that three large American military planes would be arriving within hours and that they were to be given permission to land. They were to be directed to a 'remote' part of the airport and allowed to get on with their duties without interference. Even Philip knew that this was out of the ordinary. He picked up the phone and dialled home. His mother answered the phone; she immediately wanted to chat and only reluctantly passed the receiver to his father. His father was less gushing. Philip told him the content of the fax message.

"Well done Philip," was his father's curt response before hanging up.

Immediately Philip's father picked up the receiver again and dialled a number that he knew by heart. He too knew what side his bread was buttered. His building business was only successful because of the string of official contracts he received due to the high standing he enjoyed within the Brotherhood. At the last meeting of his lodge, members were reminded that it was their duty to pass on any interesting or out of the ordinary information. Philip's father thought letting planes from a foreign power land in South Africa and operate without restriction might be classified as out of the ordinary. Within an hour the information was being received by the communication section in the cavern below the Drakensberg.

Peter van Stardan was instantly alarmed. Upington Airport was the nearest major airport to Vastrap. Matters would have to be brought forward. He cursed the Americans for spoiling his well ordered plan. He'd have to move quicker than he wanted to .They'd have to start moving straight away. Fortunately the men were positioned.

Puma Game Reserve, Kruger National Park
Thursday 8th February 1990

Stuart drove quickly. He was serious.

"I really don't understand this," said Jane. "One minute we're sitting in the hotel hanging about waiting for the Americans to give the word and the next you want us to dash halfway across the country. Was it something I said?"

"Yes," replied Stuart.

Mark Plumly was having trouble working his way through the pile of paperwork that was strewn across his desk. At any time the endless stream of official forms and questionnaires were an anathema to him but today his concentration was more challenged than normal. His mind kept drifting to the cryptic phone call he'd received from the strange woman who'd stayed at the Reserve before and had caused so much trouble. When he heard the car approaching in the distance, it was the only trigger he needed to get to his feet and abandon the task in hand. He was in the courtyard as the sleek Nissan Bluebird came to a halt.

Jane Ashton got out of the passenger side and approached, followed by the driver, a stranger, not the man who was with her last time.

"I didn't expect to see you again," said Mark extending his hand, "at least not so soon."

"I didn't expect to be back either," replied Jane. "Can I introduce you to Stuart Cameron? He's the one who wants to speak with you."

"You're Jane's fiancé?" asked Mark offering his hand.

Stuart and Jane looked at each other. "Yeah, you could say that," she responded hesitatingly. "It's complicated."

"Better not ask any more," said Mark. "You wanted to see me about something else? Come to the veranda, we can sit in the shade. I've already dug out the visitor's register that you asked about. You can look at it while I organise some drinks."

The pages of the hard-back register were yellowed with age and the cover was faded and scuffed at the edges but inside the writing was pristine and clear. A scrap of paper acted as a book mark. Jane ran her finger down the column stopping near the bottom of the page.

"Here's the name you were looking for, Alfred Smidt. He signed in with two other guests, a Peter van Stardan and a Matthew Bowdler on the 20th March 1963."

"Any other guests that day?" asked Stuart.

"No just the three of them. No comments or remarks."

Mark returned with a jug of orange juice and glasses balanced on a tray. "Missed my vocation," he said with a smile. "Find what you want?"

He sat down with them at the table.

"Yes I think so," said Stuart. "I take it, it was Matthew Bowdler who got shot?"

"That's right."

"Can you remember anything of the incident?"

"No, not really, I was very young. There was a lot of fuss for a while and my parents were very upset. What I do remember though is that that day changed my father forever. He was never the same after the shooting. In fact as he got older he got worse. It almost became an obsession with him."

"You told Duncan, the chap that was here with Jane before, that your father thought it was murder and not an accident. As far as you know did he tell the police that at the time?" asked Stuart.

"I don't think so. It was always referred to as '*the accident*'. He was just very quiet for a long time, protective, less carefree. It was years later that he started saying it was murder. To tell the truth we thought he was losing his marbles a bit – not about everything, just on that subject."

"Did he report it to the police then?"

"No. He said the police were in on it. He had this conspiracy theory, said if he went to the police it would be worse for us, we'd lose everything. The truth could only come out after his death. That's why he went to a lawyer and had all the details recorded in a legal fashion. He spent more money on that than we could afford in truth. We humoured him."

"Who are the lawyers? Can we get access to the papers he left behind?" asked Jane.

"They're a firm of lawyers in Johannesburg. The papers are in a safe deposit box and the lawyers have the key. That's the way he wanted it."

"Do you think there is anything in what he said?" asked Stuart.

"I think you're asking me if he was mad. I don't think so, especially now. He said that one day somebody would come and ask. And here you are!"

"How do we get access to the papers?" asked Jane.

"You need this." Mark produced a sheet of paper from his breast pocket. "It's a release letter. I'm his sole executor, it only needs my signature."

"If you don't mind my saying you're very easy with that. Aren't you curious about what's going on?" asked Stuart.

"My father in his heart was a good man, a thoughtful man. He loved the peace and beauty of nature, he loved this place. But something during that incident all those years ago troubled him greatly and he went uneasily to his grave. I don't think his soul will rest till the matter is resolved. Before he died he told me to have confidence in my own judgement. I'm taking that advice. I'm letting you have access to his papers. All I ask is that you don't use the information to damage us. We have precious little as it is."

"Are you going to tell me what that was all about?" asked Jane as they drove away.

"I will, in the hotel tonight," replied Stuart.

Vastrap Nuclear Test Site, Kalahari Desert
Sunday 10th February 1990

David Liebermann was both confused and indignant. He looked with disdain at the two unfamiliar armed guards that stood solidly silent and erect, barring his way to the door of the tiny underground office that was now his prison.

"When van Stardan hears of this you'll be finished," he protested neither expecting nor receiving a response.

They'd arrived late in the afternoon. That was unusual in itself. Convoys usually travelled overnight to avoid detection. This one had travelled in broad daylight. It wasn't big, just a half dozen vehicles: a Nissan Patrol staff car, four SAMIL 50 transport trucks and an articulated self loading forty foot container transporter pulled by a MAN heavy duty all terrain tractor unit. The convoy's arrival at the main gate coincided with the landing of a light plane on the runway.

Jan Kutz was a messy eater. He barely had time to mop his plate clean and wipe the residue from his lips and chin before dashing off to personally meet the unscheduled plane. Normally David Liebermann would have been there too, to greet his boss, but he hadn't been informed of his impending arrival.

Peter van Stardan walked the short distance from the plane to the reception at speed. Jan Kutz' short legs struggled to keep up with the purposeful strides of van Stardan. In the hall, chatting in small groups, were the off duty security staff. Although an eclectic looking group they had similar backgrounds: firstly and foremost they were Afrikaners that had been selected from various units of the South African Army and been chosen for the characteristics of overt nationalism and loyalty. When Vastrap was conceived it was always intended that security would be independent of the army that was diluted and contaminated by the presence of non-Afrikana's. The selection process had been vigorous and, in Peter van Stardan's opinion, there had only been one recruitment mistake, but it was a bad one; Jan Kutz. The Head of Security had let his unit's proficiency slide at an inversely proportional rate to that at which his waist had expanded. He'd started well enough but over the years had developed slovenly habits that had trickled down to his staff. Despite this slipping of standards Peter van Stardan was confident that the bulk of the men remained loyal and true to the South African Republic. But as a precaution he'd insisted that they attended the meeting unarmed.

When van Stardan entered the room the men began to shuffle into some kind of order and the chatter gradually fell away. In those few minutes of disorganisation they were all unaware that nearly forty men of van Stardan's armed elite fanatics had spilled from the trucks that had entered the camp. Before van Stardan raised his arms in a gesture to call the meeting to order, the main gate, the radio room, the tower and the armoury were under the control of men taking their orders from Daniel Okra. Jan Kutz had effectively been made redundant in less than four minutes although he was unaware of it at the time, just as he was unaware that the facility commander, David Liebermann, was at that moment being escorted by armed guard to the tiny office in the underground bomb assembly hall.

Liebermann's belief in his own ability was countered by his lack of confidence in others. First and foremost an engineer he believed that no other could match his achievements and that is why he'd jealously guarded his dictatorial control over the detail of the project. As the years passed the project and his own persona had become synonymous. A challenge to him, no matter the source, was a challenge to the project.

Now on the cusp of success, at this most vulnerable moment, his authority had been inexplicably usurped and no immediate plan came to mind to help him cope with the situation. Logically the only way he could prove his superiority and vindicate his position was to complete the project. Now as a prisoner sitting in the windowless office his mind turned to finding a solution to the conundrum.

Outside the office Daniel Okra's men were busy in the assembly plant. Unseen by Liebermann they hurried to complete their designated tasks. There was urgency in the very sounds that filtered through to Liebermann. He needed to see what was going on.

"Diesel machinery should not be used inside the hall," shouted Liebermann. "It is a clean area. The delicate electronics could be damaged. Only electric hoists should be used. The ventilation system is not designed to handle the particles and fumes. If you let me out I will help you do things properly."

The guards neither understood nor cared what Liebermann was shouting.

Liebermann's clumsy attempt at talking his way out was frustrated. He concentrated his gaze on the wall clock, eyes fixed on the predictable sweep of the red second hand. More than sixty revolutions of the hand were completed before the door of the office opened and Lieutenant Colonel Daniel Okra stepped into the room. The meeting in the assembly hall had been completed and the objective achieved.

Liebermann jumped to his feet. His first words were not on his own behalf but in defence of the project. "I need to protest. Your men are most probably doing irreparable damage. You must let me supervise them. I demand you stop and contact my controller, Peter van Stardan, he knows the nature of this project."

"If you wish to report any matter to Peter van Stardan I suggest you do it in person," said Okra.

Van Stardan followed Okra into the room and shut the door behind him.

"Mr van Stardan!" said Liebermann jumping to his feet. "Thank God you are here. Help me stop these people jeopardising our dreams."

"They know what they're doing," said van Stardan. "They're obeying orders. The situation has changed. Kutz has been relieved of his security responsibilities. He is no longer able to do what is required."

"That is no bad thing," responded Liebermann.

"I thought that would be your response. I'm sorry that it was necessary to lock you up for a short time but when I explain the situation you will understand. The South African Government has surrendered our Nation. As we speak Americans are on their way to take over this facility."

Liebermann got to his feet. "No that is not possible. I will not allow it."

"It is true and you have no choice. I am here to salvage what I can. As we speak men are loading what they can to take away. When that task is done I want to destroy what is left. Is it possible for you to detonate one of the bombs?"

"Not without the fuses?"

"I have the fuses."

Liebermann's eyes lit up. "Then yes I can arm one of the bombs in a couple of hours."

"Good. I want you to set it on a timer. Then you will come with me. We will escape and carry on our work in secret!"

Liebermann needed little time to think. "No I will not do that. I will not come with you. Having control of Vastrap is of no concern to me. What is of concern is the project. This project is my life, when the project ends so does my life. I will not leave this place. I would rather perish with my bomb."

"But I will need you later," replied van Stardan.

"No you won't. There is enough information for you to continue without me. Even a simpleton could carry on from this stage. I will ensure you have everything you need. Take me to the weapons."

The three men, van Stardan, Liebermann and Okra entered what had been the ultra clean test laboratory. Even before they had got to the brightly polished stainless steel assembly table Liebermann recognised the devices that rested there. His eyes brightened and he smiled. "At last, the final missing pieces, the Electronic Bridgewire Detonators."

His hands caressed the device as if it was loved and cherished. "You have the others too," he asked without raising his eyes.

"I do, but not here. I thought that two was enough for our present needs."

Convincing a fanatic to do what they are programmed to do is not difficult. The discussion over, Liebermann stayed in the laboratory and began the final part of his task. Two armed guards remained with him. Okra and van Stardan walked up the service ramp into the night air. The compound was not in its usual quiet darkness. Arc lights flooded the area with light so bright van Stardan and Okra had to momentarily shield their eyes from the glare. They walked with purpose and quickly squeezed past the two containers that were resting close to the entrance to the ramp. They watched a fork lift truck spewing black smoke as it struggled to lift its heavy load into the back of one them.

They marched across the compound towards the aircraft hanger, the place where the camp personnel had been herded. A series of small explosions cracked in the night air. Van Stardan looked towards Okra.

"That's the communication aerials, radar dishes and ILS neutralised. Vastrap in now truly isolated from the outside world. We have full control. But it is only a matter of time before people realise what we have done."

"We will achieve our objective," replied van Stardan. "The men here are true and will do their duty. We must see the truck leave and then we can go ourselves. Soon the eyes of the world will be upon us."

St Lucia, Blyde River Canyon
17.00hrs Friday 9th February 1990

They didn't even try to make the drive from the Puma Game Park to Pretoria in one go. Stuart suggested they stop at St Lucia, a small town close to Blyde River Canyon.

"It's a fantastic spot," he'd told Jane. "Really beautiful with loads of wildlife."

"You getting soft?" she replied.

It wasn't so much a hotel as a cross between a very posh guest house and a motel. By the time they'd booked into their separate chalets the sun was already low in the western sky. They both showered before walking the short distance to what passed for Main Street in the little town and found themselves an almost deserted Italian restaurant.

"So come on Stuart," began Jane, "you've got something to tell."

"I have," he replied, "And after our trip it's beginning to look promising. Firstly our round of cocktail parties and receptions looks like they are paying off. Remember a few days ago I got a phone call at the hotel? Well it seems like we've got ourselves a mole high up in the South African Government."

"Wow, that's great," replied Jane, "Who is it?"

"That I don't know. He wants to remain anonymous."

"Ah, that's not so good. How do you know our mole is what he says he is and how do you know it's a he?"

"He or she I don't know for sure. The courier was female but there are few females high enough in the South African Government to have access to the information that got passed on so I'm assuming it's a he. I collected a paper drop at a McDonald's. Stack of information. Whoever the mole is, he has access to Cabinet papers. Some of the information he gave me we know and checks out easily. Some of the stuff was revealing, gives an insight into the Government's thinking at the moment."

"Are you sure it's not a set-up?"

"No. I'm not sure of that at all. You can read the stuff yourself though and form your own opinion. I think it's genuine."

"What's his motive? Is he after money?"

"No. Says it's his conscience, says he wants what's best for the people of South Africa, all the people."

"Difficult to control people who are motivated by conscience. They think for themselves and don't like orders that go against their beliefs. I prefer the mercenary type, the ones in it for the money. They do as they're told as long as they get paid."

"I didn't get to choose," replied Stuart.

"So go on. What did you get?"

"It's mainly good news and much as we thought," continued Stuart. "The South African Cabinet has accepted the basic plan. Give up nuclear weapons, release Mandela, five years to universal elections followed by five years shared government and then an ongoing guarantee for the whites."

"That's great. Job done, we can go home."

"Not just yet," he continued. "There are a couple of flies in the ointment. Since the Nationalists took power in 1948 they have consistently told the whites that they will never give into the black nationalists, there will never be a black President of South Africa. Now they have landed themselves the job of convincing the people that put them into power that it's best to surrender without a fight. That's a big ask, doing an about face on public opinion like that."

"So are they saying they can't deliver?" asked Jane.

"From the documents that were passed to me it appears the Cabinet believe that the majority of whites are more or less open minded. They could be persuaded to go along with the deal. On the other hand if opposition coalesced and a strong ultra-nationalist leader emerged, they might be persuaded to resist change and opt for war. Of course without US backing they'd lose in the end but there would be an awful lot of casualties in between."

"Well there's no ultra-nationalist candidate and the Government more or less have control over the media don't they?"

"True about the leader but they don't have that much control over the media and there's the unknown. How will the Brotherhood respond?"

"Well if they don't know who does," said Jane. "They're all members aren't they?"

"They are all members, that's true but the Brotherhood is more complex than that and it's got the Cabinet worried."

"Explain," said Jane.

"There is strong evidence that a splinter group within the Brotherhood is reacting. The Cabinet is absolutely sure that the assassination of Andrew de Kluge was actually carried out by a faction of the Brotherhood."

"So who's the leader of this faction? Do they know?"

"Well it used to be a chap called Alfred Smidt."

"Oh my God. I'm beginning to see. That's the connection, that's why you wanted me to take you back to the Puma Game Reserve. Alfred Smidt was at the Reserve when the shooting took place. But Alfred Smidt is dead, how can that help?"

"Well it won't help me exactly but it might help the South African Government and it might also help Duncan get some justice. That's why I didn't want you to say anything to him until I was sure, false hope and all that stuff!"

"Okay."

"Alfred Smidt was one of the original 'old guard' of the Brotherhood. Not only did he control the most secret parts of the Brotherhood, it also appears that he controlled South Africa's nuclear programme. It was he that carried out the original negotiations with the Israelis and ran the programme."

"Are you saying he had executive authority?"

"Yes, himself and a small organisation of fanatics. That's how they managed to keep it so quiet. It never was a Government run programme."

"So who's in charge now he's dead?" asked Jane.

"Well they don't exactly publicise what they're doing but the clever money is on a chap called Peter van Stardan."

"As in the Peter van Stardan that the Plumly chap said committed the murder at the Puma Game Reserve?"

"I'm sure there is more than one Peter van Stardan in South Africa, it's a fairly common name, but I'd say it's too close to be a coincidence. But there's more. The general consensus is that this van Stardan has been deeply involved with the nuclear programme since its inception."

"So this van Stardan might be the one who's behind the attack on Stirling Farm and the killing of Elizabeth?"

"The evidence is beyond suggestive," said Stuart.

"So where do we go from here?"

Stuart didn't get a chance to answer. A waiter walked over to the table.

"We're not quite finished yet. Perhaps you can bring us some more coffee."

"I'm sorry sir," said the waiter, "but are you Mr Cameron? There's a phone call for you."

"That's not possible," responded Stuart, "Nobody knows we're here."

"Mr Stuart Cameron," persisted the waiter who looked around the otherwise empty restaurant. "There's nobody else here of that name. The phone is over by the bar."

Stuart returned a few moments later. "I've paid. Get your bag, we're going. We'll pick up our things. We're driving back to Pretoria tonight."

"Why? What's happened?" exclaimed Jane.

"I'll explain on the way."

They grabbed their things at the guest house. Stuart stopped only long enough to make one phone call. Thirty minutes later they were on their way, leaving behind a bewildered guest house keeper who'd been aroused from his sleep to take payment.

Stuart drove.

"Now will you tell me what's going on?" asked Jane.

"It's started. The Americans are on their way to Upington Airport, near Vastrap. There is no South African Army security at Vastrap and they're not putting any there. They don't want any kind of incident. The facility is in the hands of its own internal security and there's been some kind of incident there. It's not clear what it is yet but it appears the Americans are going to have the devil's own job getting there. On top of that Vastrap has had its communications cut with the outside world. Nobody knows what's going on there and somebody is jamming the South African military communications network. It looks like the beginning of a coordinated operation."

"Who told you all this?"

"My new contact."

"How did he know where we were?"

"I didn't ask. We must have been followed and they must be good. I didn't notice anything. Did you?"

Victor Verster Prison, Paarl, Cape Province
21.00 hrs Saturday 10th February 1990

Nelson Mandela felt trepidation. This would be his last full day in prison and he would enter the unknown soon. The clothes he'd wear as he left prison had already arrived and hung on a mirrored stand that had suddenly appeared in his cell. The clothes were not of his choice; he'd wanted to wear traditional African clothes but had been persuaded otherwise. The world would be watching and the image he portrayed that day would be the enduring image. The first time the world would see Nelson Mandela in twenty-five years he'd be in a tailored grey suit, white shirt and red tie.

And the world would see him. His impending release was not just the lead story with SABC. Every serious news organisation in the world would be watching. Outside the prison gates media from around the globe were already congregating.

For twenty-five years he had been 'safe' in the hands of his enemy. Imprisonment, not action, had raised him to the world stage. He'd grown in stature to such an extent that his captors dared not harm him. He knew that in prison he had to do nothing more than exist for his power to increase. But freedom would change that. He was re-entering a world where he would be measured by his own actions, where he would have to make choices and people would judge those choices. After so many years, freedom was a daunting prospect. In the dark recesses of his mind lurked the fear that he would not be strong enough to carry his nation to freedom, but he would try. He grappled with these thoughts, completely oblivious to the existence of his enemies who would do their utmost to wrestle this day of victory away from him.

Upington Airport
22.30 hrs. Saturday 10th February 1990

Upington Airport closed to commercial flights at 2200 hrs each evening and didn't reopen until 0600 hrs the next morning. Usually there was maintenance going on overnight and a single Air Traffic Controller manned the tower in case of emergencies. But tonight it was going to be different.

Eugene Forester was listed as Third Secretary to the US Embassy in Pretoria. He had two roles; Cultural Attaché was his public persona. His other role was as the State Department's main representative in South Africa. This was not so well publicised. He pulled up outside the closed chain link gates that were the main service entrance to the airfield. He passed his diplomatic accreditation out the window of his Buick Century Sedan to a sour faced South African Army guard. The guard took it without a word and retreated into the guard house. Eugene waited impatiently. Only the steady throb of the Buick's engine broke the night silence. He looked through the windshield at the stars and wondered how far away the first Galaxy Transport was. He'd received no information since the plane had taken off from Ascension Island. He tapped his fingers on the steering wheel impatiently.

The guard returned holding on to Eugene's Pass. "What business does the American Cultural Attaché have at this airport in the dead of night?"

"Nice try bud," replied Eugene. "Not your concern, you got clearances from your Air Ministry, let's just get a move on here."

The rebuke elicited a downward curl of the guard's lip. "Park your car over there." He pointed to a parking lot fifty yards back up the approach road. "Your escort will meet you there."

"No way, the car is going in with me. It's covered by the pass. Look again."

The guard stared insolently.

"Get out. I need to search the car before it clears security."

"Check out the licence plates. There's a big fat CD there. That's '*Core Diplomatic'* to you and means you don't get to search this vehicle."

"This is a high risk area. Pass or no pass the car needs to be fitted with a spark arrestor before it's allowed airside. Those are safety rules," the guard smirked. "Does your car have a spark arrestor fitted?"

"Listen carefully arsehole, the only threat to safety at the moment is that you're in danger of getting a big fat lip if you don't open that gate pretty quickly."

The guard took a step back and put a hand on the rifle that was hanging loosely from his shoulder. "Are you threatening me?"

"No I'm not threatening you. I got a job to do and you're stopping me doing it. Open the God damn gate will you!"

Eugene saw the approaching lights of a Jeep crossing the airport apron at speed heading towards the gate. "I think your boss is coming. Now open the gates."

The guard looked up. "Wait," he ordered. "I'll be back."

Two minutes later he returned accompanied by the driver of the Jeep, a lieutenant of the South African Defence Force.

"At last, somebody with a bit of gumption I hope," said Eugene. "This monkey here of yours has shit for brains and is holding up the show."

With a flash of anger the guard pulled his gun to the horizontal.

Just as quickly the lieutenant put his hand on the barrel of the rifle and pushed it downwards. "No need for that, go back to the guard house," the lieutenant's voice was calm and measured. The guard turned and walked away.

"No so fast," shouted Eugene. "I want my pass back."

The guard gave the pass to the lieutenant who handed it to Eugene. "You need to choose your words more carefully in South Africa. It's not good to call a white man a monkey, it has bad connotations."

"Yeah, right. Okay to call a black man a monkey though? Shit like that doesn't wash with me or my country."

"We'll you're not in America now. This is South Africa and we have our way of doing things and from what I understand the record of the United States is not exactly exemplary in matters of race so we won't be taking lectures from you. But I'm not here to discuss politics. I have orders and I will follow them. When the gates open you will follow me closely and I will take you to your allocated area."

"It better be out the way, that's all I'm telling you."

Fifteen minutes later Eugene stood alone on rough ground at the far north of the airport, as far away from the terminal as it was possible to be. He watched the tail lights of the Jeep disappear into the darkness. He looked around, before popping the lid of the trunk and pulling out a solid black transport case which he placed on the ground, clear of the car. With practiced hands he quickly opened the clasps and extended the antenna before switching on the unit which immediately started transmitting a pre- set five digit code that would be picked up by the pilot of the first Galaxy. He didn't stop. Within five minutes he'd set up a solid aluminium tripod with extending telescopic legs and fastened a bulky set of night vision binoculars to the protruding spigot with a snap clamp and began a slow scan of the surrounding area. He expected that there would be prying eyes and in that he was not wrong.

Over his head-phones the pilot heard the Electronics Officer confirm that the local transponder was on-air and transmitting. He looked towards the First Officer who had already begun the descent towards Upington. The pilot threw a switch on the radio console by his side and spoke on the plane's intercom, "Touchdown forty minutes."

US Rangers in the back of the plane began making their final preparations before buckling in for the landing; it was a well practiced routine, one that they'd gone through many times before. Landing and securing a perimeter at an alien airport was standard procedure. What was to follow was not.

Vastrap
01.00hrs Saturday 11th February 1990

A Captain hurried towards Lt Col Okra.

"Sir we've received a message. The Americans have been given permission to land at Upington. The airport has been shut to all other traffic. They will be landing within the hour. The staff will do what they can to slow them down."

"That's the advance guard," said Okra. "The main body will be following close behind. It will take them some time to get the full force assembled but it won't take them long after that to get a patrol on the road. You will be ready for them." It was not a question.

"We are ready," confirmed the Captain.

"The transport truck and its escort have left. There is nothing more for me to do here. You are in charge now." Okra saluted, turned and walked towards the light plane that was already on the runway with its engine running. He joined van Stardan in the passenger cabin.

Upington Airport
02.00hrs Saturday 11th February

Though low on fuel the Galaxy was a heavy plane not susceptible to buffeting even when flying through the unpredictable desert thermals that were prevalent on the final approach to Upington. The ride was smooth but still the tension built. The cockpit chatter stopped and the pilot concentrated on keeping the nose tight onto the centre line of the glide scope for his 'instrument only' approach. As they got closer and descended below six thousand feet the co-pilot got busy. He began calling out the height at five hundred feet intervals. He put his hand on the levers but didn't drop the undercarriage until two thousand feet. The huge wheels, hitting the air, increased the plane's drag dramatically, and the frame shuddered and slowed perceptibly. Without reference to the captain he added five percent power to compensate, just enough to keep the plane above stall speed. At five hundred feet he began shouting the height at fifty foot intervals, "950, 900, 850, 800...... 100, 50' and finally "Flare."

Only then did the pilot lift his head and go onto visual. Within a minute he landed the plane, deftly using the rudder and foot brakes to keep the aircraft centre line on the runway as it dramatically slowed to a manageable ground speed.

The pilot's orders were not to take instructions from the airport Ground Controller. Instead he used the plane's ground direction finder to hone in on Eugene Forester's transponder. It gave him a heading and distance. He eased off the brakes and continued the roll, letting the plane run on to the turning area at the end of the runway before bringing the plane through a one hundred and eighty degrees turn, so it was facing north and going back up the runway.

As soon as he'd heard the plane land Eugene had placed a flashing strobe light on the roof of the Buick. It couldn't be missed in the darkness.

The pilot raced the plane towards the strobe lights as the co-pilot switched the tyre air pressure control to manual and partly deflated the tyres, ready for rough terrain.

In the cargo bay, handlers loosened the restraining straps on the two Hummers. Rangers, armed and helmeted, lined the sides of the hold, crouched and ready for rapid deployment.

The Cargo Master got into position and donned his headphones so he could listen to the cockpit. He lifted the metal protective cover on the hydraulic control unit and flipped the locking mechanism to disarm before pulling on the lever. Slowly the rear cargo door began its descent and the waiting Rangers got their first glimpse of an African night sky through the rear of the plane. The Cargo Master raised an arm in the air as he heard the pilot's command "stand-by" over his head-phones. The plane juddered to a halt and the command "deploy" came through. He pulled the hydraulic lever fully down and the rear ramp dropped the final couple of feet. Simultaneously he brought his raised arm down and shouted "Go! Go! Go!"

The unit had only been equipped with the vehicle for a year or so and they loved it. The first live deployment had been for the invasion of Grenada and it had performed well above expectations. Its full name was the High Mobility Multipurpose Wheeled Vehicle but that was too much of a mouthful so the grunts started calling it the Humvee and then later, as affection grew, the Hummer.

There were three on the Galaxy. Almost before the plane had come to a halt the first two were moving. Each with a driver and five troops, they drove off the plane's tail ramp. One went left, the other right. Within two minutes the Hummers had deployed their men in a circle that had a one hundred and fifty yard radius from the plane, the outer security cordon. As the Hummers finished their job other Rangers ran down the ramp and made a second circle surrounding the plane, an inner cordon at about a seventy five yard radius. The grunts on grass furiously began digging fox holes. Those on solid ground lay flat and pointed their guns outward. Eight minutes after landing the inner and outer cordons were established complete with medium machine guns and light mortar protection. The area was declared secure and the third Hummer, a command and control vehicle, rolled down the ramp less hurriedly. It was followed by the bulk of the Rangers. Cargo handlers hurriedly unloaded the rest of the equipment.

There wasn't much for Burt Zimmerman and Jack Carter to do at this point. They moved to the cockpit. The pilot, co-pilot, flight engineer and electronics officer were still strapped in and the cockpit display was still lit up, powered by the auxiliary gas turbine engine embedded in the tail section of the aircraft.

The pilot looked over his shoulder as Burt and Jack entered.

"How's it going?" asked Jack.

"The pilot nodded. "So, so. We have to stay on stand-by for now, just in case a quick exit becomes necessary. Expect the unexpected. Bravo's right behind us, it'll be landing soon and Charlie's thirty minutes behind that. You want me to call the Major see if you can get off now?"

That'd be good," replied Jack.

The pilot pushed a button and mumbled a few words into his face mask.

"Okay. You can go, use the rear ramp.

Jack and Burt found it unexpectedly cold as they stepped into the African night air. A skid mounted diesel generator started, spluttering for a second, before racing away and settling into a steady regular throb. Almost as soon as the generator had settled a string of pole mounted halogen lights came on and flooded the area, which was now in effect a brightly lit base. The command and control Hummer was ahead of them and a large tent had been set up slightly to the left. They walked to the Command Hummer, the Major greeted them with a smile.

"We're set, secure and ready for Bravo. It's all yours now!"

"That was slick," acknowledged Burt. "What's with the big tent over there?"

"Field kitchen and PX. I reckon you'll be sending the guys off to Vastrap soon, thought it'd be nice to give them a hot meal and some coffee before they go. It's just about open for business. Go grab yourself some coffee and chow before the rush."

The last words were drowned out by the roar of jet engines on full throttle in reverse thrust. They saw the ghostly shadow of the second blacked out Galaxy as it touched down on the runway.

"That'll be Tex," said the Major as the din diminished with the plane rolling into the distance and disappearing into the darkness along the runway. "He's got a reputation for being a bit of a Maverick. Treats the Galaxy like a hand-glider, approaches high, puts his engines into idle and brings the plane in on a very fast very steep glide. It's an almost silent approach. Only problem is that by the time he's at the end of the runway he's going too fast to stop. So, because it takes the engines six seconds to get from idle to full power, he engages reverse thrust whilst he's still in the air – that's against regulations and a bit hairy. No room for error and no aborted landings with Tex, but as he says "They don't know I'm coming but they sure as hell know when I've arrived."

The three men looked down the runway into the darkness and waited for the plane to complete its turn and make its way back to them. They saw the flash and heard the explosion a second or two later. By the time the boom hit them the sky was lit with a mushrooming ball of flame climbing into the night sky.

Upington Airport
05.00 Sunday 11th February 1990

All three Galaxies had landed and disgorged nearly a thousand tonnes of men and equipment. They were now ready to leave just as the dawn light was arriving. The explosion in the darkness as Galaxy Bravo landed was not connected with the plane, not directly. The information was that one of the airport's fuel tanks had exploded. There was an adrenalin rush for those who witnessed the explosion and an atmosphere of nervous expectation now pervaded the camp.

Jack Carter was in control and trying to keep things calm. Specifically he was concentrating his attention on Eugene Forester who was becoming purple with rage and worrying Jack. Eugene was being encouraged in his excess by Tex, the pilot of Galaxy Bravo who'd have been more at home in the wild west and, at this point in time, most probably thought he was in the wild west.

Carter's voice was measured. "This is not an invasion, we are friends of the South Africans. They have invited us here. We are their guests and it is very rude to point guns at your host and even worse to shoot at them. So let's just come down a few thousand feet to a less hostile altitude."

Eugene tried to speak calmly but it was difficult for him. "Since I arrived at the gates those bastards have been nothing but arseholes. There has been no co-operation only obstruction and now that we're established, they're deploying a line that threatens us. I say we take it out before they become a real threat."

Eugene was referring to a unit that the South African Army had deployed on the far side of the runway no more than five hundred yards from what had by now effectively become a US base within the Airport perimeter.

"They're not threatening us," replied Jack Carter. "They are merely countering us. If they were threatening us they'd have closed the airport to commercial traffic. They haven't. Now we haven't been able to talk to them on the radio, God knows what frequencies they're using. So I think we ask Burt here to take a stroll over and have a word and then he can tell us what's happening." Jack Carter turned to Burt Zimmerman, "You okay with that Burt?"

"So long as I can get across the runway, no problem."

"That's another thing," raged Eugene, "Even the frigging control tower won't answer us and we know their frequency but they'll talk to every God damn plane in the sky."

"We'll test that," replied Jack. "I think it's time we let one of the transports go. Tell Galaxy Charlie to ask for permission to taxi to the main apron for refuelling. If they're agreeable tank up, file a flight plan and head it back to Ascension Island."

Burt had pulled on his flak jacket and donned a helmet and was about to set off when Jack turned to him. "Burt, if it pans out and they're friendly, see if you can get some fuel out of them for the Hummers. I'm guessing that tank of fuel going up was the fuel intended for us and we need it now. We're already an hour late getting started for Vastrap."

Burt walked off. "See what I can do Jack," he shouted over his shoulder.

Jack turned, "Eugene, if we don't get the gas from the South Africans we might as well not be here. So just be a little bit nice."

"In my experience being nice doesn't pay," said Tex. "People need to know who's boss!"

"You just get on your God damn plane, keep your fat mouth buttoned and get ready to leave. You're next to go, as soon as Charlie gets away. And who invited you to this meeting anyway? Now I'm going to get some breakfast."

Meadow Vale Hotel Car Park
02.30 hrs Sunday 11th February 1990

Stuart made Jane drive most of the way whilst he tried to sleep. Jane had protested about driving in the dark on unfamiliar roads when she was tired. The response was curt. "Not that long ago you were demanding to drive. You should be careful what you wish for," said Stuart as he reclined his seat and closed his eyes, discussion over.

Stuart woke just as Jane pulled into the car park of the Meadow Vale Hotel.

"Over there," he said pointing to a long wheel base Toyota Land Cruiser parked in the far corner of the lot. As Jane approached, the driver's door of the Toyota opened and Duncan stepped out. But not the Duncan she'd last seen. He looked different, more square and erect, masculine and serious, ready for business. "What happened to him?" she asked.

"Trained men put their personal feelings to one side when there's work to be done," replied Stuart. "That's the difference between men and women."

"You chauvinist bastard," shot back Jane. "Where are we going?"

"You're staying here, Duncan and I are going to Vastrap."

"What's suddenly wrong with me?"

"You're not trained for this type of thing. It's best if we all stick to our specialities. Besides I need you to visit a lawyer and read an affidavit and gather what information you can on this van Stardan chap."

Jane didn't argue, just pursed her lips like a chastised child. She pulled up alongside the Land Cruiser. Stuart got out of the car and grabbed his bag from the trunk. The two men exchanged a few words and got into the Land Cruiser.

Duncan got into the driver's seat and quickly left the car park. "She didn't look too happy. Engagement's off then I suppose?"

"Looks like it," replied Stuart.

Both men laughed.

"So what are we up to? You going to brief me?" asked Duncan.

"I am, but first did you do what I asked?"

"I did."

Twenty Miles North of Maun, Okavango, Botswana
10.00hrs Saturday 10th February 1990

Everybody knew of Gus but nobody knew about Gus. He never spoke about himself, he never spoke about anything much. There had been rumours over the years, mostly untrue. He'd become a cross between an enigma and a legend. Some said he was a tramp, others a hermit but he didn't quite fit into either category. Nobody disputed he was old but nobody knew his exact age and that was becoming problematic for some.

Gus still stood at six foot one despite having a stoop due to curvature of the spine. Lathe thin, his long grey hair hung almost to his shoulders and his face was masked by a full beard that hadn't been trimmed for a couple of years. He never wore anything but scruffy bush shorts and cheap stained shirts that were never tucked in. The shirts were unusual in that they were all long sleeved with just the cuffs cut off. Any skin that was exposed was brown, cracked and weather beaten. Only piercing bright blue eyes gave evidence to what once had been. Gus lived in a remote area. He owned a small plot of flat raised land, land that rarely flooded even in the wet season. It wasn't large enough to farm, but was just big enough for his improvised landing strip. Gus had a plane, not a very good plane, but a plane. He'd done some home modifications to it. The twin engine, six seater Piper had its rear seats ripped out. He'd squeezed a couple of large polypropylene tanks into the space where the seats had been and, with total disregard for manufacturer's recommendations and good engineering practice, plumbed in some pipes and ran them out along the wings. The plane was the basis of his one man business spraying the Okavango for mosquitoes. It wasn't that foolish an adventure. The Botswana Government did have a mosquito eradication programme but like most Government programmes it was both ineffective and costly. That's why many of the larger safari lodges that dotted the Okavango were willing to pay Gus to spray around their camps every couple of weeks. The safari lodges were happy because it kept the customers comfortable and they didn't get malaria. What they didn't know was that Gus would regularly 'overrun' the designated spray areas and 'inadvertently' spray around native African villages. No elder of an African village ever complained, they just looked up as he flew over and silently thanked him.

Gus didn't have any enemies, but he did have demons. He'd been born Gustav Frode in Gjerdrum, a suburb of Oslo, capital city of Norway during the winter of 1920. His father Georg had worked as a senior clerk in the Customs House. Although relatively wealthy his father and mother Gerda had declined the use of a nanny to care for their only child, preferring to bring up Gustav themselves. But theirs was not a warm loving home. Gustav's memories were of formality, austerity and discipline. Excellence in academic studies was expected and emphasis was placed on the qualities of loyalty and obedience. Physical punishment for failure was the rule, not the exception.

Georg and Gerda were of one mind and that mind was drawn instinctively to the rising fascist movements in Italy and Germany. Georg became an activist in the fledgling fascist party that was developing in Oslo and when war finally broke out in 1939 he celebrated. In 1940 when Britain and France tried to occupy Norway but were beaten back by the Germans they rejoiced and were further elated when Quisling was appointed ruler of their country, under German tutelage.

Georg, unable to maintain his conservative ways, could not resist the temptation to get involved. He left his job in the Customs House and joined the recently established Norwegian SS Division. Thought of as too old for active service, he'd been appointed to an administrative position and although surprised, was not disappointed to receive his first overseas posting. One chilly day with flurries of snow blowing down the street, his father had left their home after formally kissing his wife on the cheek and shaking Gustav's hand. Gustav watched as his father walked cheerily down the street. He never saw him again.

Gustav's confidence grew when he was alone with his mother and he finally felt able to express his own views. They were not well received. Gustav dreams were of a world community where people helped each other not because of compulsion but rather through desire, a place where the strongest helped the weakest and harmony was the goal.

Letters flowed between Georg and Gerda and from afar his father applied pressure on Gustav to join the German Army. He refused point blank and even evaded conscription into the Norwegian Army by getting a student deferment to attend university. Throughout his studies he was kept on the fringe of poverty by his reluctant parents. The situation culminated when his parents refused to pay for his final year unless Gustav agreed to join the Waffan SS on graduation. As Gustav would have to join the Norwegian Army on graduation anyway, he naively saw little difference in deferring to his parents request.

In January 1944 Gustav found himself making the short sea trip from Oslo to Flensburg on the German / Danish border to begin his training. By that time the tide of war had turned against the Germans and it was clear to all that the end was near. But none who valued their life dared to utter those thoughts aloud. Gustav knew he had to throw himself into his training and just hope the war would finish before he received a posting. At Flensburg he'd volunteered to become a pilot/spotter for an artillery regiment. He'd learnt to fly in a single engine Frieseler Storch. In the air, in that flimsy aircraft, he'd felt a sense of freedom, a freedom he'd never felt before. Alone in the sky he was happy.

By the middle of April the Americans and Russians had met at the River Elba and split Germany in two and the British were progressing along the North of Germany and even threatening his own training camp. The end came suddenly. Grand Admiral Donitz moved his Headquarters to Flensburg and the next day Hitler committed suicide naming the Grand Admiral his successor. Donitz held on for a few days, trying to negotiate with the Allies. On the 7th May he met with British Field Marshall Montgomery and surrendered.

Gustav was made a prisoner of war. He spent more than a year behind wire uncertain of his future. Finally it was decided to release him and the other trainees in his unit but because they'd been members of the SS they were forced to undergo a denazification process. Gustav had thought that denazification would be a series of lectures saying that fascism was bad and democracy was good. But it wasn't like that. Denazification changed Gustav. The British had surprisingly let the young SS trainees express their feelings openly. There wasn't any compulsion but there was a lot of exposure to the practicalities of fascism. There were endless newsreels and films about death camps, forced labour and civilian casualties. The trainees were allowed to discuss what they'd seen. Some didn't believe and thought the British had manufactured the evidence, but Gustav believed and knew that the thoughts he'd harboured earlier in his life were good thoughts, that he'd been right all along. Gustav wrote to his mother. She was unrepentant and sent a letter back saying that she was ashamed that he hadn't sacrificed his life for the Fuehrer. He tried to trace his father through the Commission for Displaced Persons. He'd received a short and curt letter from the Commission stating that his father had been executed by the Russians for 'Loathsome and Despicable Crimes against Humanity'. Gustav thought the Russians had most probably done the right thing.

On his release, disillusioned with life, he made his way to Africa because it wasn't Scandinavia. But he couldn't escape completely. Each morning as he washed he was reminded of his past and what he'd nearly become. In the mirror he would see the tiny tattoo on the underside of his left arm. The Gothic letters 'AB'; his blood group. All Waffan SS soldiers had such a tattoo. It was a constant reminder of his shameful family history. That is why his shirt sleeves were longer than most, to hide his shame.

It was almost midday, the shadows were at their shortest and the heat was intense. Gustav slipped out the back door of the wooden house that was not much more than a shack and dashed for the cover of the bush. The engine of the approaching car had roused him from his afternoon sleep. It wasn't the past catching up with him that made him hide, it was the future. Gustav's life was the patch of land and his decrepit aeroplane. To fly his plane, even in this remote part of Botswana, he needed a licence. Gustav knew that when he was seventy years old that licence would automatically be withdrawn and life as he knew it would come to an end and he was not prepared for that. Now every time he heard somebody approaching he was afraid it was the Civil Aviation Authority.

Gingerly Gus circled the little clearing in front of his cabin making sure to remain concealed by foliage. As soon as he saw the vehicle he knew he was in no danger. The battered Nissan Cherry stopped and two men got out. He knew them, not well, but enough to know that they were not bad men. He walked forward and let the men see him. They smiled but he didn't return the gesture, he merely emitted his customary grunt. For more than an hour the visitors spoke in the open sun. Gustav listened. The meeting ended without pleasantries. The men in the Nissan Cherry left knowing they would return before daylight next day and Gustav would be ready for them.

Route 14, Northern Cape Province
0500hrs Sunday 11th February 1990

The Orange is the longest river in South Africa and although mostly un-navigable it is still of immense economic importance providing both hydro-electric power and irrigation water all year round. Its source lies in the mountains, not far from the Indian Ocean. Despite many twists and turns the river runs westward until it finally reaches the Atlantic Ocean somewhere between Cape Town and Windhoek. The final third of its course is the most tortuous as the waters slice through the Southern Kalahari Desert leaving a fertile narrow ribbon on either bank. Route 14, the major highway that runs south west from Pretoria, kisses the banks of the Orange River over a hundred kilometres shy of Upington. Duncan and Stuart looked for somewhere to stop. They took a dirt track on the left and drove down to the river's bank. They got out of the vehicle and looked down at the rapids as they stamped their feet, struggling to get the circulation back into their legs after the epic overnight drive. With feeling restored they drove to the remote petrol station. It was early morning but they still managed to get food. After they'd eaten Stuart made a call from the pay phone, Duncan tanked up the vehicle and checked the jerry cans in the rear, two with water and four with petrol.

In truth they needed to get some rest but that wasn't going to happen. The part of the journey they'd just completed was the easy bit. Soon they'd be leaving the tarmac highway to cross the hostile desert on unmade roads and tracks, to a destination where the welcome was uncertain. There was no time for sleep; they'd continue their journey without respite, each man grabbing what rest he could as the other drove.

Upington Airport
06.00hrs Sunday 11th February 1990

Burt Zimmerman was with the South Africans for more than forty-five minutes. Jack Carter had finished his breakfast and was watching as his friend walked back across the runway, urgency in his stride.

"Okay Burt, what have you got?" Jack asked not giving him any time to regain his breath.

"First the good news," he began. "They're at Company strength, about ninety men with a young lieutenant in charge. He's friendly but a bit out of his depth I think. The last order he got was to let the Americans, that's us, get on with things but if we made contact he was to give no material assistance."

"So what's the bad news then?"

Before Burt had a chance to answer Eugene Forester appeared. "We got a problem with direct comms to the US. There's no geo-stationary satellite coverage for this area and we're not locking in to the orbiting satellite but I did just get a call from the Embassy in Pretoria."

"So what did they say?" asked Jack.

"The Foreign Office in South Africa is telling the State Department that they no longer have control of Vastrap and that there is the possibility we may get a hostile reception. They recommend we proceed with extreme caution."

"Okay, so what is the State Department recommending?"

"Get to Vastrap a.s.a.p. and secure the nuclear devices at any cost!"

"Got anything to add to that Burt?"

"Ties in with what I heard from the South Africans. The lieutenant says the reason we couldn't make radio contact was that their entire ComNet system is down, jammed. ComNet is their main military communications system. They're trying to fix it. At first they thought it was a technical fault but now they think it might be sabotage. The only communications the Lieutenant has with his headquarters is by civilian landline from the airport main building and what he's getting from there is confused! One thing he could tell me was that Vastrap lost all communications even before the radio network went down, landline and all. There's no way of contacting them. They thought they'd send a plane to take a look but decided against that in case we got the wrong message."

"What about gas Burt?"

"The lieutenant isn't supposed to co-operate with us but I persuaded him that it would be a good idea if he shared what fuel he had with us. He agreed!"

"Right, that's great, let's get the vehicles fuelled up and get the show on the road, we're going to Vastrap."

"Any other news?" asked Jack.

"Not sure. There might be," chipped in Eugene. "The last part of the message said that the Brits were on their way to assist."

"That's something, what kind of strength?"

"Two."

"Two what?"

"Two men."

Jack raised his eyes to the sky and shook his head, "Great." His sigh was drowned out by the roar of the SAA Jumbo jet as it landed hard on the threshold of the runway.

"What's that?"

"No problem," said Eugene. "That's most probably direct from London. SAA planes don't have over fly rights from any of the black states. So SAA long haul is almost all over the ocean. Takes a Jumbo to the limits of its range. It's normal for long haul flights to stop here for fuel. It's the first long runway in South Africa."

"Just as long as there are no surprises on it for us."

When Duncan and Stuart had driven out of the Meadow Vale hotel car park Jane hadn't gone to her hotel room. She'd waited till the Land Cruiser was out of sight before re-starting the car's engine for the short journey to the British Embassy where she ensconced herself in a secure communications room.

As Stuart had slept and she'd driven she'd taken his advice and done what she did best. She'd analysed the known facts in her mind and tried to project into the future. By the time she sat in front of the telex keyboard her mind was clear and it didn't take long to commit her thoughts to the machine. In twenty minutes she'd finished typing and struck the send key. She addressed the communication to the Foreign and Commonwealth Office in London and signed the message *Tulip*.

The South African Lieutenant had been as good as his word. He'd helped as much as he could even going so far as to deprive his own unit of fuel reserves to ensure that the American convoy would have enough to reach Vastrap. South African sappers had also cut a hole in the airport perimeter fence for them. Now the Americans would only have to drive a couple of hundred yards to get onto the Vastrap road, escaping the necessity of using the main airport exit and avoiding prying eyes.

Jack Carter was getting close to moving out when his mobile radio crackled.

"Sierra One to Juliet Charlie. We got something strange coming towards us. Over." Sierra one was an outer perimeter guard.

"What now?" said Jack Carter frustrated by the disturbance. He lifted his radio set to mouth level, pressed the transmit button and answered, "Okay Sierra one, what you got? Out."

"Juliet Charlie, some dude in a business suit and carrying a briefcase is walking down the edge of one of the taxiway towards us. Looks like an insurance salesman to me. Unarmed and unsupported as far as I can see. Sierra one, over."

"Okay Sierra One. When he gets to you find out what he wants."

"Could be a long time speed he's going at. We're looking at him through glasses."

"Okay. Send a Hummer out and see what he wants."

"Gotcha skip. Sierra one, out."

Fifteen minutes later Jack Carter, Burt Zimmerman and Eugene Forester were at the command vehicle; in front of them was the visitor. The observer wasn't exaggerating. Standing awkwardly, the young man was clean cut and freshly shaven. He wore a tailored grey suit complete with white shirt and a tie with diagonal red and blue stripes. The tie meant little to the Americans. The visitor didn't look as if he'd broken sweat on his long walk in the open sun. Only the dust on his black lace up shoes spoiled his perfect appearance.

Despite his appearance the visitor was unsure of himself. Before this trip his previous travel experience was limited to summer holidays on the French Rivera and winter skiing breaks at Davos, Switzerland. Less than twenty-four hours ago Africa was little more than an abstract concept. Now suddenly transported to the southern fringe of the Kalahari Desert he stood square shouldered concealing his bewilderment. Even though his first words were clear and precise it wouldn't take the Americans long to realise that the young man was empowered only by the confidence of naivety.

"My name is Ralph Foulkes. I work for the British Foreign and Commonwealth Office. I have been sent here to deliver a personal message to the commanding officer of this unit."

Eugene Forester was the first to respond. "You see that," he said pointing to the miniature Stars and Stripes flag stitched on to the jacket of a passing Ranger. "We've been taking our instructions from Washington for quite a time now. You guys are out of the loop."

Undaunted Ralph continued. "I realise the relationship is different from pre 1776 but I also think that we have recovered the situation somewhat and that we would now consider ourselves allies."

"Yeah that's right bud. We crossed the pond a couple of times to pull your coals out of the fire. There are proper channels if your Government wants to tell my Government something. Why don't you walk back and use them?"

"I'm perfectly familiar with proper channels. However the imperative of the situation, in the view of the Foreign and Commonwealth Office, warrants this unusual approach. Furthermore it is my understanding that you are expecting British assistance."

Eugene laughed. "You must be fifty percent of the force the Brits are committing to the operation!"

"No, I am in addition to our other commitments."

Burt Zimmerman struggled to suppress his smile. "Okay, listen here Ralph we're very busy. You got a couple of minutes to say your piece, that's it."

Ralph began the speech he'd practiced on the overnight flight. "I am sure you are aware of some of this. Nelson Mandela will be released later today. However not all people in South Africa will share in the joy of the occasion. In fact we are certain that there are elements, armed elements, with considerable influence who are planning a dramatic event hoping to overshadow what is planned. As well meaning as they may be, we believe that the South African Government does not have full control of events."

"I know it's your language," butted in Jack Carter, "But can you give me that in a simpler form of English."

Ralph smiled. "You already know that Vastrap is in the hands of dissident elements. You are most probably unaware however that the dissident elements plan to set off a nuclear weapon to coincide with the inauguration. You need to get there quickly. Is that simple enough?"

"Yeh, we know somebody has taken control of Vastrap and they have bombs but we're also quite sure they don't have the means to set them off," replied Jack.

"They do have the means," countered Ralph opening his brief case and withdrawing a buff cardboard file with a broad red strip running diagonally across the front and the words 'Top Secret' printed in bold lettering. "Some days ago a plane from Israel landed at a military airbase in the northern Limpopo province. We believe that its cargo was nuclear detonators. The consignment has disappeared. We believe some of the detonators are already at Vastrap."

"What's your source for this information?" asked Burt Zimmerman.

"I'm not really at liberty to divulge that other than to say it came from our own asset that has an impeccable reputation."

"You'll have to do better than that," retorted Eugene. "Burgess and Maclean were impeccable British assets!"

Ralph thought for a while. "All I can tell you is that the source has the code name 'Tulip' and I am even now exceeding my authority."

Eugene was about to respond but was stopped by Jack Carter's hand on his shoulder. "Do you know a guy called Cameron?"

"If you're referring to Lieutenant Colonel Stuart Cameron, yes I am acquainted with that gentleman and it is also my understanding that he is on his way here as we speak."

"I'm Jack Carter," he said extending his hand. "You just might have got yourself a ticket to the ball game. But just tell me one thing first will you?"

"If I can I will," responded Ralph.

"What are you doing dressed like that?"

Ralph's shoulders sagged a little with relief and he smiled sheepishly. "Well it was 4.30 yesterday afternoon and I was just about to leave the office. I was scheduled to go to a dinner party in Cricklewood. Before I could leave Sir Basil told me he had a special errand for me to run. We got into a waiting car and he briefed me on the way to Heathrow. Before you know it I was on a plane coming out here. I actually think they delayed the take off until I was on board. And there you have it."

"You don't have a bag or anything?"

"No," Ralph smiled. "I am as I am."

"You guys are crazy sometimes! But then again so are we. We're still heading for Vastrap. You can come with us but not till I've fixed you up with some fatigues. You in?"

"If by fatigues you mean more appropriate clothing that would be very welcome. I've been in these clothes for more than thirty hours."

"Do you shoot? What's your weapon?"

Ralph was a little taken aback and confused at the change in subject. "I do shoot. Actually my father says I'm a very good shot. My personal preference is for a Purdey, double barrelled 12 bore, preferably an over and under. I find them better balanced than a side by side, much easier to get a brace of pheasants in one I think."

"I'm not sure what you are talking about kid," responded Jack. "I think you're saying you use a shotgun. All we got is Remington pump actions, I'll get you one. Now is there anything else you need to tell us before we set off?"

"Not a definite," replied Ralph, "But our people are doing all they can to get a couple of chaps down here that are familiar with the layout of Vastrap. We thought they might prove useful to you."

Route 14, Northern Cape Province
07.00hrs Sunday 11th February 1990

Back on the road Duncan drove slowly along the R14 carefully watching for the unmarked turn. There wasn't a road sign, not because of municipal negligence but more because the sign maker was at a loss as to what he should write other than '*Desert*'. Stuart held the map and counted off the mile pegs. It was the only sure way of knowing they'd found the right road and not some track that led to a remote homestead or abandoned mine.

"Should be before the next peg," said Stuart, transferring his gaze from the map to the right-hand side of the road. It had been the first words spoken for half an hour, both men concentrating on what was to come.

The dusty turning appeared. Duncan stopped the car. "Are we sure?"

"Yep, this is it. Decision time. The options are going on to Upington and joining up with the Americans. With them we'd just be two 'hangers on'. Or we take this route and have the possibility of closing the back door."

"The downside is we're only two and we're hardly armed. If we do encounter anything that's hostile we're not likely to be able to do much about it," countered Duncan.

"Observe and report. That's mostly what we do best in any case."

"Here goes then, three hundred and fifty klicks." Duncan turned the car onto the gravel track. The driving conditions changed immediately. The track alternated between stretches of rutting that made it difficult to steer as the vehicle wheels locked into the parallel depressions like a tram following rails. When the ruts disappeared there were long sections of corrugations; ripples in the compacted gravel's surface, like the tiny undulations found in beach sand when the tide retreats. Unlike beach sand though they were unyielding. Duncan couldn't make up his mind which was worse, the inability to steer or the teeth chattering judder of the corrugations. Whatever the surface he never managed to get above thirty miles per hour and even then left behind a huge cloud of dust. They settled down for a long monotonous journey.

The land on either side was almost featureless, endless stony sand, occasional undulations and scattered scrub consisting of nothing more than a few thorny bushes and cacti, randomly dotted around, hanging on to a parched and meagre existence. Occasionally the scene was interrupted by the presence of an isolated giant erratic rock, weathered round and smooth, like a ball, rocks that had stoically resisted the forces of nature for millennia.

Another corrugated section changed to rutting. "Well some kind of wheeled vehicles have used the track," said Stuart.

"Yes, but not that recently. The ruts are real enough but there are no fresh tyre marks."

It was more than two hours before they saw any signs of civilisation. The track suddenly split in two, one fork veering sharply to the left. Duncan stopped and both men got out. Through the shimmering heat haze less than a mile from the main track they thought they could see a small cluster of buildings, white walled with what appeared to be red corrugated iron roofs. There was a tall wooden tower supporting a rudimentary wind vane that was motionless.

"A bore hole. I wonder how far down the water table is here?" pondered Stuart.

"Too far down to produce much water judging by the lack of greenery," replied Duncan. "It's not on the map but doesn't look abandoned."

They continued the journey, Stuart taking a turn at driving. The track became fainter and fainter. At times it almost disappeared and they had to strain their eyes to follow the route. It was another hour before Duncan spoke. For a long time his gaze had been fixed on the horizon. At first he thought it was a tiny rain cloud but quickly dismissed that prospect, then he thought of smoke from a fire and finally he considered the distant swirl to be from one of the mini tornadoes that occasionally erupt in the desert air. But now he was sure it was none of those things.

"There's something coming in our direction," he said.

Stuart's eyes had been occupied closer to home, concentrating on the next couple of hundred yards of track.

"Can't tell how many vehicles," continued Duncan, "The dust trail is quite big though."

"Not likely to be the milkman," said Stuart slowing to a crawl to lessen the dust cloud they were producing. "We need to make a quick decision. We're exposed here. Do we carry on, do we turn and run or do we go off road and try to conceal ourselves?"

"The latter I think," replied Duncan. "We can't confront them without proper weapons and I don't fancy going back. There's an erratic over there," he said pointing to a giant boulder standing off track to the right about six hundred yards into the desert. "Let's try to get behind that and hope they haven't spotted us yet."

Stuart didn't reply. He stopped the vehicle and manipulated the levers next to the gear stick, selecting four-wheel drive. As the Toyota crept forward they felt the tyres sink into the un-compacted gravel and struggle for traction. They moved forward at not much more than walking pace. Duncan kept a watch on the approaching dust cloud. For fifteen minutes Stuart steered the Land Cruiser on a zigzag course, always seeking firm ground while heading in the general direction of the boulder. Soon a black spot was visible at the base of the approaching dust cloud.

"You'll have to do better than this," said Duncan. "They'll be on us when we're still in the open.

In response Stuart pressed harder on the accelerator. The wheels slipped and a larger dust cloud billowed out behind them as the vehicle lurched forward. The sun was climbing into the sky so the rock, four times the height of the Land Cruiser, cast little shadow.

They'd reached the rock and were as hidden as they were going to be. Both men were out of the vehicle. Stuart used binoculars to look at the approaching cloud whilst Duncan drank from a water bottle. "One lousy Webley revolver that should be in a museum and six rounds of more or less similar vintage hardly make us a credible force," moaned Duncan. "The gun is from WW1. It even has the lanyard fixing in case it got dropped in the trenches."

Stuart ignored Duncan's words and kept the binoculars to his eyes. "There are at least two vehicles possibly three; a jeep of some kind followed a good way behind by a big lorry. Can't see properly if there's anything behind the lorry. I reckon they'll pass in less than ten minutes. What's the situation with the radio?"

"The best I could get was an old mains HF\VHF set, 110 volt DC. Came out of the cellar in the embassy. Don't know what they used it for. I'm hoping the main circuit board is 12 volt so that I can bridge out the transformer and hard wire it to the car battery direct. If I can get it going we might pick up the Yanks on one of the emergency frequencies."

"You want to give it a try?"

"I'm on it." Working on the tailgate of the truck Duncan already had the back off the beige Motorola unit and was twisting a bit of twin core to the output side of the black plastic transformer that was now exposed.

"I can see it now, the lorry. It's a military tractor unit pulling a container unit. It's a big beasty!"

The tension began to build. The Jeep came close to the spot where Stuart had left the road. It stopped and a uniformed soldier got out and searched till he found the tyre tracks. He stood up and stared in the direction of their hiding place. Stuart pulled back, involuntarily holding his breath. The lorry came to a halt a few hundred yards behind the Jeep.

Duncan edged a look. "They're on to us," he said.

The Jeep lurched forward, turning off the road, following the trail that Duncan and Stuart had left behind.

"Forget the radio for now," said Stuart. "We'll go deeper into the desert and hope they don't have too much time to waste following us."

Duncan abandoned the radio, just lifting the tailgate and letting the bits fall on to the truck floor. As Stuart made for the driver's door, Duncan intercepted him. "No, let me drive."

Stuart didn't object. Duncan fired the engine and pulled away. At first he drove slowly keeping obscured from the Jeep by using his mirrors to keep the rock between them and the Jeep. "Pull your belt as tight as you can, it's most probably going to get bumpy. Watch out behind and tell me when you think they have seen us."

It wasn't long. Duncan caught sight of the Jeep at the same time as Stuart spoke. "Game on. They're speeding up."

Duncan turned slightly to the right bumping along the stony ground choosing which bits of parched vegetation to avoid and which to ignore. He ran over the soft succulents. They gave way without resistance. But he avoided the black thorn knowing that their tough barbs would puncture tyres as easily as a pin popping a balloon. The ground was gently undulating, small ridges were interspaced with troughs running north to south. Duncan steered for the top of one of the ridges. He stopped the vehicle, got out and jumped on to the bonnet. Shielding his eyes with the flat of his hand, he quickly surveyed the surrounding landscape. Inside Stuart had got the gun from the glove compartment and checked it was loaded. In a second Duncan was back inside and the Land Cruiser was jolting again.

The Jeep that was following was visibly bouncing all over the place in pursuit, indicating the occupant's determination. There was no doubt now that they had seen something they were not supposed to. Duncan went down one trough and climbed to the peak of the next ridge before swinging the Land Cruiser to the north and following the crest in full view of their pursuers. They were now running parallel to the road, such as it was.

"Fuck," exclaimed Stuart. "There's a third vehicle, a good bit behind the lorry. Looks like a small APC. It must have been obscured by the dust cloud."

"Wheeled or tracked?" shouted Duncan with urgency in his voice.

"Wheeled, but it's got a turret. Maybe a medium machine gun or possibly small cannon I'd guess."

"It won't be able to shoot with any accuracy on the move. Tell me if it stops." Duncan pushed the vehicle harder and it became more difficult to maintain control as he tried to follow the ridge line. The Jeep was closing in on them, it had gained ground by turning to the north early and following the parallel ridge to their left.

"That's good," said Duncan. "About five hundred yards and we'll make our move."

Before he'd finished speaking Stuart cut in, "APC stopped." Even with all the jolting Stuart could see the turret rotating in their direction.

"He's taking aim. Get off the ridge line."

"Not yet, it's too steep, we'll roll," replied Duncan. "Let's hope he's not too good at moving targets."

"*INCOMING!*" shouted Stuart in response to the muzzle flash he'd witnessed from the turret of the APC. *"Cannon fire."*

They didn't see it but the cannon shell passed from left to right about a hundred yards in front of them before hitting stony ground and exploding on impact.

"Light armour piercing," said Stuart eyes now back on the APC. "Could have been a warning or ranging shot."

If it was a warning Duncan took little notice. He had his own plan. The sharp drop to the right became less severe, just a slope for a couple of hundred yards. It was what he'd been waiting for. Duncan steered off the ridge line, the Land Cruiser lurched to the right and slid on the loose surface so that Duncan was forced to point the bonnet at an upward angle and make the Land Cruiser crab along the length of the slope keeping below the ridge line and out of sight of the Jeep. After a few hundred yards the slope increased in intensity again, another hundred yards and the slope became a sheer drop of twenty feet, a mini cliff. Carefully he judged the distance, taking his mark from a lone thorn bush that survived improbably near the top of the slope. As soon as he was abreast of the thorn bush he pointed the Land Cruiser straight up towards the crest and stopped. His eyes were now fixed on the ridge line where he hoped the Jeep would appear. He wasn't wrong and didn't have to wait long.

Once the driver of the Jeep lost sight of the Land Cruiser he had to make a decision. The only logical one was to get on the same ridge as the Land Cruiser. He descended one side of the trough and blindly accelerated up the slope to the crest of the next ridge hoping to arrive at the crest close to his target. He saw too late the sheer drop on the far side of the ridge and braked too late to stop the Jeep toppling over the drop. Two men were quick enough to jump out of the Jeep before it fell off the edge, the other two were not and accompanied the vehicle on its short vertical drop to the exposed bedrock of the cliff. Duncan didn't wait. He pulled away up the slope, the four wheels spinning wildly seeking traction. Over the crest he descended into the trough and swung right, following the valley knowing the APC would not be agile or fast enough to follow him. He merely had to keep out of sight. Half a mile later Duncan steered towards where he thought the road was and approached the crest at a slight angle. Stuart strained his neck to get a view.

"Road's a couple of hundred yards to the left, the lorry's still stopped five hundred yards to our rear. No sign of the APC. Expect they're looking for their mates. I think we're clear. But what was all that about?"

"I'd like to know for sure what's on that truck. I can hazard a guess. But I don't fancy going up against that APC," added Duncan. "I'm going to have another go at that radio and see if the Yanks can do anything."

Twenty Miles North of Maun, Okavango, Botswana
06.00hrs Sunday 11th February 1990

The sun was barely a red tip on the horizon as Gus pulled his single engine Piper from the rudimentary home-made hanger. The mornings used to be the best time for him. He'd be up and about early, sharp as a razor but now all he felt in the morning was the pain in his joints, aches which gradually subsided with the soothing heat of the sun. And it was even worse today, because he hadn't had much sleep; he'd worked late into the night making the necessary modifications to the plane's fuel system.

Now from fifty gallon oil drums he manually pumped fuel into both the wing fuel tanks and then, when that was done, began filling the internal tanks, the ones that he'd put in the cabin himself and usually carried pesticide. His arms were weakening with every stroke of the pump handle. By the time the two men in the Datsun Cherry arrived he was exhausted. Tembo was the first to get to his side.

"Come old man, let me do that. My arms are younger and stronger."

Gus gave way without resistance, something pride would have stopped him doing not so long ago. "Just make sure the tank is full to the brim, we will need all the fuel we can carry for the journey."

Morgan opened the boot of the Datsun and gathered the weapons that they'd recovered yesterday from the hiding places. They too had worked all night, cleaning and oiling the weapons, getting them into pristine working condition. He carried the two AK47's to the plane together with a dozen magazines and a small wooden crate containing one thousand rounds of loose ammunition.

"You can bring the guns and the spare magazines but not that box of ammunition," said Gus. "It's too heavy."

Fifteen minutes later the three men were cramped into what remained of the tiny cockpit, Gus in the pilot's seat, Morgan alongside on the left. Tembo was squeezed in the back, hunched around the tank and guns but somehow still able to operate the *Gusher* diaphragm hand pump that he would use to transfer the fuel from the pesticide tank to the wing tanks as the level fell during flight.

Gus taxied the plane to the very end of the dried mud runway and slowly pushed the throttle lever forward. The engine began to growl, as if anxious to start its work. The propeller bit into the air; the plane strained to move forward and began to vibrate alarmingly. Gus pushed hard on the brakes, holding the plane back until the throttle was fully open. Then he let go the brakes and the plane moved forward gathering speed. Gus' eyes were fixed on the air speed indicator. Normally the plane needed sixty-five miles per hour for takeoff but he reckoned it would need an extra five mile per hour with all the extra weight inside now. His calculation was not generous. As the needle crawled to sixty-five he pulled back on the yolk and the nose of the plane lifted almost hesitatingly. For a while the main wheels remained stubbornly fixed on the ground. Morgan felt a flutter of panic and the colour drained from his black face turning him ashen grey. Tembo didn't look out of the windows keeping his gaze firmly fixed on his own feet. At last they felt the final bump from the undercarriage as the wings took the full weight and lifted the aircraft into the air. Gus pulled a little harder on the yolk and the plane lumbered on slowly, a hair's breadth from stall speed and disaster. They just cleared the vegetation at the end of the runway. Eventually Gus leaned back into his seat and looked at Morgan with a big grin on his face.

"Relax, we're over the first problem." Gus was always happier in the air, a different person. He banked the plane to a due-south heading and gradually gained altitude, levelling out at ten thousand feet, as high as he dare go in an unpressurised cabin. He fixed the throttle to fifty-five percent which gave him an indicated air speed of exactly one-ninety-six knots. That was as good as it was going to get. All the figures were in his head. At last he turned to look at Tembo in the back.

"You can start pumping now, and don't stop till I tell you or the tank is empty. We've already used a lot of the fuel in the wing tanks. I don't want to walk across the Kalahari so keep pushing that lever back and forth."

Before he settled down to the cruise Gus switched on the radio and tuned to 121.5 megahertz. He turned the volume down. Old habits die hard.

Morgan had regained his natural colour, was breathing more or less normally and the thumping in his chest had subsided.

Vastrap
07.00hrs Sunday 11th February 1990

There was enough water for everyone, the problem was containers to carry it. The white support staff were the first to leave. They'd taken all the available vehicles and a lot of the water containers. The only motorised transport that remained at Vastrap was reserved for the guards to make the final dash. The black labourers had been told little but knew something bad was going to happen and that they had to leave and leave quickly and cross the desert on foot. They'd been warned they needed to be twenty miles away and that they should run all the way. The dilemma was whether to stay and look for water bottles or run immediately. Most took the latter course of action. Even so within the hour everybody had gone.

The underground assembly hall was eerily silent. David Liebermann had finished his work and now sat looking at his creation, his mind brimming with pride. He had done it. His skill and determination had made this moment possible and he was drawing a kind of perverse happiness in the knowledge that soon he would go with his creation to eternity. To him this creation was more than an engineering feat. It embodied life itself. It was a being. Just as engineers referred to their ships as 'she' implying more than just an ordered collection of metallic components, so David Liebermann saw the bomb as his creation, the culmination of all his efforts and he was prepared to stay with his beloved creation to the end, just like a mother who would not desert her child. In a way Liebermann had lost his mind, he was impatient for the end but knew he had to wait; he had to keep his word. It would be at one pm exactly that the world would first know of his success. Liebermann knew that there would be no greater thing that he could achieve, that all that faced him after climbing to this pinnacle was a decline into oblivion. It was how he rationalised to himself the decision to stay.

One other had no choice. In the locked windowless room Jan Kutz stood sweating and trembling, praying to the God that he'd scorned for so long, promising his very soul in exchange for escape. As minutes passed his fear turned to panic and he resorted to banging and screaming at the door, alternating between demanding and then pleading for release. But van Stardan's instructions had been clear. It was not because Jan Kutz was useless at his job or that he knew too much. It was because his loyalty was in doubt and there was only one punishment for those who were disloyal.

There were six people in the Hummer, the second vehicle in the convoy. Jack Carter sat beside the Ranger driver. Eugene Forester, Burt Zimmerman and Ralph Foulkes were squeezed in the back together with the Comms Officer and his radio set. Three hours behind schedule, they'd set off from Upington. They were short of vehicles, short of fuel and short of men. The only thing not in short supply was flags; flags depicting in white, a map of the world clasped in laurel leaves on a blue background. It was the flag of the United Nations that fluttered from each of the vehicles, the symbol that gave them authority to carry out this mission.

They'd bumped along the road for hours, each man lost in his own thoughts when the driver received a message on his headphones from the convoy's lead vehicle.

"It's the point Sir, they have unidentified oncoming traffic. Several vehicles."

"They might be hostile, better deploy and set a road block," responded Jack Carter without hesitation.

"Sir," replied the Comms Officer who instantly began chattering into his mouth piece.

It was a well practiced routine. Vehicles went right and left into the desert sands setting up lines of cross fire that converged just in front of the truck that would form the roadblock, the obstruction in the way of the oncoming traffic.

Jack Carter got out of the Hummer, taking his weapon with him. He'd barely taken five steps when the Comms Office shouted. "Sir. Message relayed via Upington Base. Washington wants to know if we've secured Vastrap yet."

Carter took a three-sixty degree scan of the blank desert horizon before looking at the Comms Officer. "What do you think soldier?"

"Think I got that Sir."

The motley collection of vehicles drove right up to the road block and stopped. The Rangers made everyone disembark and carried out a search. The only problem came when the white driver of the rear truck objected to being frisked by one of the black Rangers. The white driver relented when he was informed he could go back to Vastrap on foot if he didn't like his treatment.

Jack Carter and Burt Zimmerman walked to one side, out of earshot, to discuss the situation.

"It looks like that Ralph guy the British sent might be right," said Burt. "In fact it might be worse than he said. Everybody we've spoken to wants to get the hell out of here pretty damn quick. They say the place is going up any minute! Those people are not armed but they're not stopping either. Looks like we're heading to some place we'd rather not be."

"Admittedly it doesn't look good but there's a lot riding on this. The State Department are trying to patch through to our radio direct"

Eugene Forester stepped forward, he'd been listening. "I'm the representative of the State Department here and this is the State

Department show. It's not part of our orders to get killed. We must return to Upington immediately. I'm ordering it."

"You're not in charge here," replied Jack Carter.

"You have to abort the mission," demanded Forester.

"For fuck sake try and get us a radio hook up," demanded Jack Carter.

The White House, Washington DC
04.00hrs (EST) Sunday 11th February 1990

Most insiders considered the term Presidential Personal Aide a euphemism for Presidential Punch bag. This President was no different than others before him. He didn't believe in shooting the messenger but he was not averse to giving him a good verbal kicking from time to time.

The Aide walked quickly and led the way from the Oval Office towards the Situation Room, the President following despondently.

"It's always bad news when I make this journey," said the President. "It was supposed to be a good day today. What's going on? Who's raining on my parade? I want to be up to speed before I face those Generals. You got sixty seconds Wilbur, shoot."

The Aide took a deep breath. "The sequence of events was clearly laid out in the Protocol. The South Africans hand over their nuclear weapons. We approve the secret protocols of the Treaty guaranteeing South Africa's future. Mandela gets released. You hold a press conference congratulating Mandela and revoke sanctions against South Africa. We brief the media so you get the credit in the US for liberating all the blacks in South Africa and with the gratitude of all our black voters you win a second term."

"I already had that Wilbur. What's going wrong?"

"It appears that the South African Government is going along with the deal and our guys are on the ground and all fired up. But someone has hijacked the South African nuclear arsenal before we could get to it."

"The whole fucking arsenal?"

"Yes Sir, the whole arsenal."

"Well let's just get it back then Wilbur."

"Not that simple Sir. The Brits informed us a couple of hours ago that they believe whoever's controlling the arsenal are preparing to let one off, just as Mandela gets released."

"A nuke!"

"Yep."

"Who gets the blame for that?"

"Possibly us for not securing the arsenal."

"Jesus Christ. I'm supposed to be taking my part of the credit for solving the South Africa problem today not presiding over a fuck up. The press that aren't in South Africa will be in the Rose Garden in a couple of hours. Better hold the notes on the press briefing."

"The press are already gathering. The event is planned as the lead story for the morning news. We gave them the press briefing note so they can organise their schedules."

The President stopped in his tracks. "Fuck I'm going to look like an idiot. You better have a cat to pull out of the bag Wilbur, I'm warning you. How did you let a situation like this develop?"

"We've been struggling with communications up until now but we have got a solution. We got one of our AWACS planes that should be over the Kalahari about now."

"So we've got a handle on this?"

"Just about."

"The answer is yes or no, not 'just about'. Is it yes or is it no?"

"One of our AWACS planes is on station but it's got a British crew onboard."

"Observers?" asked the President.

"No. They're flying the plane. There are no Americans on board," replied the Aide

"Are you frigging kidding," the President exploded. "Since when have the Brits been running our Air Force?"

"The Brits wanted to buy some of our AWACS but we couldn't deliver to their timescale so we loaned them a couple of ours in the interim. They just happened to be on a long range training mission in the area so we refuelled them from a KC9 tanker and they agreed to do air control on our behalf."

"Are you saying we gave them the plane and the gas? Are you going to tell me they're on the payroll too?"

"No Sir, we're not paying them."

"Wilbur there better be a solution. I'm not supporting any black nationalist leader of South Africa that has the bomb in his hands. You tell those Generals in the Situation Room to send a message to the South Africans to hand over their nuclear arsenal or I'll send a carrier task force down there and blockade every South African port. I'll starve the bastards out. Now I'm going back to my office. Don't come to me unless you have good news. What time's my press briefing due?"

"Four hours Sir, eighteen hundred Eastern Standard Time, to coincide with the release of Mr Mandela at 1pm South African local time."

"So what are you doing standing here Wilbur? You need to move your arse." The President turned and walked away.

The English oak panelling in the Ambassador's office had been salvaged from the state room of a passenger liner that was being wrecked on Clydebank. It was of the classic linen-fold design and rumour had it that the cost of its reclamation, restoration, transport and installation had been double that of building new panelling utilising South African timber. But cost had not been an inhibiting factor, image had been a higher consideration. Hanging over the cocktail cabinet and its Waterford cut glass crystal decanter and glasses was the *'piece de resistance'*, an oil by Constable.

Jane Ashton was sitting on one of the armed regency chairs looking down, her focus on the intricate pattern of the Persian carpet that covered practically all of the room. The Ambassador paced the floor in silence, his hands behind his back as if in deep contemplation as they waited for the secure line on the telephone on his desk to ring.

When Jane had presented her thoughts to the Ambassador he politely rejected them as being the product of her youthful and fertile imagination. Undeterred Jane had composed her telex and sent it off directly to the Foreign Office in London where it had received more detailed consideration resulting in the Ambassador receiving the diplomatic equivalent of a reprimand. This accounted for the stony silent wait. The Ambassador would now fulfil his duty in an exemplary manner, to the letter, but without good grace.

Both jumped with surprise when the phone rang. The Ambassador motioned for Jane to pick up the receiver and respond to the expected call from GCHQ in Cheltenham.

Over Kalahari Desert
08.30hrs Sunday 11th February 1990

The visor was down and Gustav wore sunglasses but still his eyes hurt from the sunlight penetrating the windscreen of the Piper. Hours passed and he wanted to let his eyelids close. He hadn't undertaken such a long flight for many years and in a strange way he knew he was fighting to maintain his concentration but couldn't rouse himself. Now he wished he'd had the auto pilot fixed but at the time he'd never envisaged doing anything else but a bit of local low level flying. For the first time it crossed his mind that the men from the Aviation Department were right. Perhaps his flying days were drawing to a close. He became aware of a change in the tone of the engine, immediately followed by jogging from his left. Morgan was shaking his shoulder, trying to rouse him. The plane had entered a shallow dive as Gustav's mind had been drifting.

"How much further?" asked Morgan hoping that conversation would help Gustav stay awake a little longer.

"As we don't know where we're actually going how am I supposed to answer that? I can tell you we're less than an hour from Vastrap by my dead reckoning but I don't think it would be advisable to land at that runway just now. We don't know who's in charge. What's happened to your friends? We should have heard from them by now."

Duncan had tried to get the radio working as Stuart drove but the jolting made it impossible. Meeting with the container lorry had lost them a couple of hours all told. They had a long way to go but they urgently needed to find out what was going on. Nobody even knew where they were. They had to stop and give Duncan a chance to fix the radio.

They didn't pull off the road. Stuart just climbed on to the roof of the Toyota and kept watch for the tell tale dust whirls of approaching vehicles as Duncan started where he'd left off on the dropped tail gate.

"In the heat of the moment when the Jeep headed towards us I just threw the lot in the back," said Duncan. "I think I've broken the internal antenna but there's a telescopic radio aerial on the front wing of the truck. I'll run a lead but I haven't got a clue if it'll work."

Duncan found the tool kit that Mr Toyota had kindly supplied with the vehicle. It was neatly rolled up in a cloth pouch with the spare tyre. It had never been opened. With a screwdriver he forced the radio out of the dash-board and disconnected the aerial lead. Under the bonnet he found where the lead came through the bulkhead and wound its way towards the near-side wing. He gently pulled the cable through the bulkhead and loosened it from the retaining clips that held it in place on its circuitous route. It was just long enough to reach the front passenger seat. Then he stripped a couple of cable lengths that he hoped were only for the side lights. One of the pieces of cable he fastened to a bolt on a front suspension strut to act as 'earth', the other to the plus terminal on the battery under the driver's seat. All he had to do was connect the other ends to the output side of the radio transformer. He paused holding the two loose cables. He was lacking one piece of information.

"Problem Stuart," he shouted. "Don't know the polarity of the radio set. If I get it right the radio might work, if I'm wrong it'll burn out the circuit board and we're bolloxed."

"Hobson's choice," replied Stuart. "Do what you think is best."

Duncan shrugged, connected each of the cables to a terminal, turned on the radio and waited for some kind of life in the set. There was nothing. "Doesn't look good," said Duncan.

Stuart jumped off the Toyota roof and went to the driver's door. Leaning in he turned on the car ignition. The radio panel immediately lit up and the small liquid crystal display of the radio set read 000.0. "I've always learnt it helps to turn the power on," said Stuart with a smile.

"Our best chance is picking up something in the air, a plane. I'll try the civilian distress frequency on 125.5." Duncan turned the dial and watched the display numerals wind up to 125.5. He picked up the hand set, pressed the transmit button and spoke. "Golf Oscar Oscar Zulu. Test transmission. Anybody reply please. Over."

The two men waited but there wasn't even a crackle on the speaker. They tried again.

"Try the military emergency frequency, 243.0." said Stuart.

Duncan readjusted the dial and tried again. Still no response. "I'll give it five minutes, alternating frequencies. I've done the best I can. All we can do is head for Vastrap if there's no response."

John Devlin had stopped growing when he reached five foot four inches. He was fifteen. As a child he'd always assumed he would work in the shipyards of South Shields when he left school. He expected to become a plater like his father. Unfortunately his small stature, fragile frame and boyish looks wouldn't get him entrance to the shipyards. Undaunted, resourceful and enthusiastic he'd looked elsewhere. Salvation came from a strange source. The fifty-eight year old, arthritic sports teacher at his Secondary Modern school, who doubled as the career's advisor, had an uncharacteristic flash of inspiration when he suggested that John might consider becoming a ship's radio officer. In his deliberations the teacher hadn't considered that John would require five good 'O' levels to stand a chance of gaining one of the coveted training places with the Marconi Company and that this school did not actually offer 'O' levels to its pupils, in fact it offered no education beyond the age of fifteen. An alternative route was to join the Services, get trained and then convert to the Merchant Navy. He'd picked the Royal Air Force because they had more opportunities for radio operators and he only needed to sign up for three years. But when the three years were up he didn't leave, he signed for another twenty-two years. He loved the Royal Air Force – and they loved him.

He never expected to fly. His aspirations didn't extend beyond humble ground crew. But he was good. After basic training he was sent to RAF Kinloss and became an Electronics Operator on anti-submarine Shackletons, that distant descendant of the Lancaster bomber that provided Maritime surveillance over the Norwegian Sea during the Cold War. Later he was posted to 8 Squadron at Waddington, south of Lincoln. The unit was to be allocated the first of the new variant British Nimrod early warning planes. He'd been deflated when the project was cancelled. But the dejection didn't last long. The Squadron was told it was going to be equipped with the latest Boeing E3D Sentry Airborne Early Warning planes. What the Americans called AWACS. And it was in a US loaned AWACS plane he now sat; at his own console.

They'd set off from RAF Waddington on an endurance training mission. The flight plan called for them to head South, refuel over the Atlantic from a Victor tanker and then head on to the Falkland's. Then there would be another mid–air refuel before heading north for Bermuda where they'd land for a bit of R&R. They had done the first leg and were well on their way to the Falklands when the signal had come through. The pilots had turned the plane around and met the American KC9 air-refuel tanker plane and topped up their tanks before heading towards South Africa.

John Devlin, with the benefit of youth, was not feeling tired despite the hours he'd already spent at his console. His sophisticated equipment was capable of multi-channel operation. He saw the first flashing icon at the bottom left of his main screen. He tapped in 121.5 megahertz and listened to the ground transmission. He immediately responded but it was soon apparent that whilst he could hear the sender they could not hear him. The transmissions stopped but then restarted on 243.0 megahertz. Again they clearly couldn't hear his response even on the emergency military frequency. He'd have been justified in just logging the incident had he not recognised the call sign Golf Oscar Oscar Zulu. All call signs suffixed Zulu were Cold War Intelligence signals. He immediately patched in the Mission Tactical Director and a few seconds later the Duty Officer in the Control Room at GCHQ in Cheltenham England was receiving information on the contact. In the meantime John was passing on the transmission to the Surveillance Officer and requesting a ground fix on the transmission and picture if possible.

The Surveillance Officer came back immediately, "Will do John."

John didn't have time to answer. A Flash message appeared on his main screen, the type of message you don't want to see except in training. *'Red Alert. Possible Nuclear Event'*. The same message appeared on the pilot's screen. His response was calm. He spoke on the intercom, but the crew already knew. "Buckle up tight everybody. Set for instrument flight. The co-pilot pressed a couple of buttons on the centre console and dark screens came down to cover the windshields. The flight deck darkened. If the pilots were unfortunate enough to be looking in the direction of a nuclear explosion the bright flash could be intense enough to destroy the retina of their eyes, blinding them instantly. After the flash would come the shockwave. The damage they could expect was a function of power and distance.

John pulled the straps of his harness tighter and got straight on to contacting the unidentified plane.

The operator had kept Jane hanging for what felt like an age, the situation not helped by the Ambassador's impatient pacing up and down the room. Eventually the Duty Officer at GCHQ spoke. "Sorry Jane it's hell here at the moment. I can't talk for long. I've got to trace an unidentified call sign we just picked up from the Kalahari."

"What call sign?"

"It's an old one, out of use. Golf Oscar Oscar Zulu."

"Stop your search. It's Duncan Murdoch one of our former Rhodesian Operatives."

"How do you know that?"

"I read his file recently. I was with him a few days ago. He's active again and friendly. He's most probably with my operational partner. Where are they exactly?"

"Not sure precisely but in the vicinity of a nuclear threat as far as we can determine."

"Is he aware of the situation, have you been able to warn him?"

"All I've been able to do is let the AWACS know. I'm not sure if they're able to pass the message on."

"You need to do something to let him know, it's important. I'm going to keep this line free. Keep me up to date. In the meantime I have to get on with something else. "

Morgan was running out of things to say. Gus was not communicative at the best of times. But he persisted. He started to ask questions about the plane.

"What's this wheel for?" he asked pointing to a solid wheel that was between the seats of pilot and co-pilot.

It's to trim the plane. Keep it in level flight."

"What's that?" asked Morgan pointing to a flashing green light on the centre console.

"It's the radio," responded Gus irritated at the way his thoughts were being interrupted.

"Why is it flashing?"

"It's flashing because somebody is transmitting on that frequency."

"Why can't we hear it then?"

"Because I got the set turned down. Now leave me alone."

Morgan reached over and turned the radio on. "I still can't hear it."

"You have to wear the headphones!" Gus pointed to a set of headphones.

Morgan put the headphones on. "Isn't this the radio that Duncan is supposed to contact us on?"

Gus looked blankly at Morgan.

For a few seconds Morgan was still, his gaze fixed ahead. "I can't understand what's going on. The voice seems urgent."

Gus abandoning his reverie put his own headphones on. Tembo, in the rear leaned forward. "What is happening?"

Eventually Gus spoke. "Somebody is making a low power ground transmission I think. It's too weak for us to hear. They're using emergency frequencies."

"Who is the voice speaking?" asked Morgan.

"That's not clear. It's not South African Air Traffic Control for sure. But there is a problem with the communications. Whoever he's talking to can hear him but he cannot hear the reply. There's most probably a technical problem."

"What should we do?" asked Tembo.

Gus clicked the radio to transmit. It could be your friends."

John Devlin raised his eyebrows as another icon on his main screen began to flash. But it was not just John that was alerted in the AWACS plane. The Tactical Director saw the flash on his screen also. He spoke on the intercom, addressing the Surveillance Operator. "What's that, why didn't we pick that up? There's something else there."

The Surveillance Operator was defensive. "I've got the ground radar fixed on a small area; I'm trying to get an exact location for the first transmission. The new one's outside the radar footprint and its transponder is turned off. It's not swalking."

"Radio, make contact."

"I'm on it," replied John Devlin. "Unidentified transmitting on 121.5. Respond. Airborne Sentry One, over."

Gus pressed to transmit. "We are Piper One. Are you American? Over."

"Piper One. No, we are British Military. Please turn on your transponder. Sentry One."

"Negative. Not functioning. Piper One."

"Piper One. You are in a designated no-fly zone and are in danger. You must leave the restricted area immediately. What is your destination? Over."

"Piper One. We are out of Maun, Botswana. I have two passengers wanting to link with a US ground force. Can you assist?"

"Piper One. Hold."

John Devlin thought quickly and pressed the intercom. "Surveillance. Have you got a fix on transmissions yet?"

"Better than that. I have a visual on the ground transmission."

The Surveillance Operator had located the ground transmission and fixed the high resolution ultra violet camera on to the reference. He flicked a switch and a picture appeared on the secondary console in front of John Devlin. The picture was grainy but was clearly a four wheel drive vehicle somewhere out in the desert.

"How's that?"

"Great. Now can you give me vector and distance for Piper One to intercept the ground transmission?"

"No problem. Give me a second." The Surveillance Operator punched commands into his keyboard. "Are you ready? Vector 239 South, about eighty miles."

John Devlin was not afraid to use his initiative. He didn't seek authority. "Piper One. Turn heading 239 South. Descend to 1500 feet. In about twenty five minutes you will see a four-wheel drive in front of you. I need you to get a message to them. You must tell them to travel away from Vastrap as fast as they can. You might have to write a note and drop it from the plane. Tie it to something heavy. Do you understand? Sentry One. Over."

"Sentry One. We have little fuel for low level flying. Over."

"Piper One. Do what I ask and I will then try and vector you directly to the Americans but you must give me more identification. The Americans might treat you as hostile. Over."

Gus looked towards Morgan. "What shall I tell them?"

"Tell them we are friends of Stuart Cameron and Jane Ashton."

Vastrap
08.30hrs Sunday 11th February 1990

David Liebermann was very calm, almost in a catatonic state. He wandered around the assembly hall his mind savouring his achievement. The logical end of his endeavours was approaching; there could be nothing beyond this pinnacle for him. In his distorted mind the belief that he should perish with the product of his own endeavours felt quite natural.

Operating on a lower intellectual plain, Jan Kutz felt differently. His instinctive response was primitive, based only on the primeval desire to survive under any circumstance. There could be no esoteric satisfaction in death for him. Success would only be measured in terms of survival. He'd broken a metal leg from one of the chairs and had flattened the end to make a kind of pick that he used to chip away at the wooden door frame around the door handle. The force he was able to exert did not diminish as his arms tired, instead it grew in line with his desperate anxiety.

First of all the architrave gave way and Jan was able to wedge his bar under a loose piece and lever the wood away which exposed the door frame proper. As he worked on it each blow brought away a few more splinters till eventually the wood started to split. He forced the point of the metal leg into the crack and twisted. The split grew wider and he was able to prise it open far enough to get his fingers into the gap. With slight purchase but much determination he pulled away a long sliver of the frame. The receiver was now exposed. After a final onslaught of blows it came away, the door finally surrendered and swung easily on its hinges. He left the room, his mind unclear, a frenzied jumble as he rushed around.

The security guards that he had so recently commanded had departed with the rest of the staff in a panic, heading towards the Americans, but not to fight, only to escape. They had hurriedly abandoned their weapons and it was an abandoned Beretta pistol that Kutz now picked up from a bench. He made his way towards the exit ramp past the clear glass wall of the assembly room seeing to his horror the device that he feared. He also saw the white coated figure that he had viewed with antipathy for so long. David Liebermann had his back to the glass panel and rocked gently back and forward like a man demented. In truth Kutz was not capable of understanding the intellectual thoughts that now passed through Liebermann's mind and that had pushed him over the brink. Liebermann, in his madness, was only just beginning to understand himself. Now he knew, at the end, what had driven him so passionately.

Rejected from the Jewish faith, Liebermann had been declared a non-person for his behaviour in the Nazi era. Because of that rejection he'd spent his life spitefully trying to defy the God that had rejected him and now, at the climax of his work, he would use science to prove the impotency of that God, perhaps even to challenge His existence. All Kutz saw was an opportunity. Not astute enough to realise that Liebermann accepted, even sought death, Kutz believed, in his blind panic, he could make the man in front of him disarm the bomb at the point of a gun. Kutz stood at the open door to the clean room.

"Liebermann," he shouted. "Stand up you buffoon. You will disarm the bomb now or I will shoot you."

Kutz did not lose just the intellectual argument. Liebermann was after all a man of great practicality. His reaction was calm and deliberate. Slowly he rose to his feet and turned. To his horror Kutz saw in his adversary's hands the familiar black shape of an Ingram MAC 10 machine pistol. He also saw the muzzle flashes as Liebermann fired the weapon in a sweeping arc in his direction. Only his acute sense of self preservation saved him. Disappearing behind the door jamb he fell to the floor. The spray of bullets passed harmlessly above his head. He scrambled to his feet, ran towards the ramp that led to the outside and didn't stop running till his breath could no longer provide the oxygen to supply his legs. He collapsed on the floor, gasping, his mind still racing, seeking a solution.

"Don't direct them this way bud. We got enough problems of our own. We need orders. Unless you can get us connected to Washington quickly we're getting out of here as fast as we can. We'll withdraw back to Upington. Now I ain't got time to jabber." Jack Carter threw the hand piece into the back of the truck. He had too much on his mind. John Devlin was doing what he'd promised, trying to get the light plane to the US force. At least now he had a ground fix.

Jack Carter was not interested. He drew breath and took stock. Looking down the road he saw the assembled white workers, huddled in the shade of their vehicles.

He made his mind up. "Get them loaded up and send them on their way," he said talking about the whites that had come from Vastrap. "We're headed back to Upington ourselves."

The black staff-sergeant didn't move, just stayed at attention.

"Something wrong with that?"

"Sir, those white dudes took all the motorised transport and left the non-whites to walk. We can't leave them out there in the desert. They'll either go in the explosion or die from thirst. Wadda you say we take the transport from the white dudes and let them continue on foot. Then we send the trucks back to fetch the black workers. At least everybody gets a fighting chance that way."

Jack looked at Burt Zimmerman. He shrugged. "Sounds fair but I can't order men to drive towards a nuclear explosion."

"I volunteer," said the black staff sergeant without hesitation.
"Are you sure you know what you're volunteering for?" asked Jack.

Staff Sergeant David Evans had been born in an old brownstone on 103rd and Broadway. His father was absent for the birth and for the rest of his life thereafter. That part of upper Manhattan that was his world was a transitional neighbourhood where midtown gave way to Harlem over a couple of blocks. It was a grey place in more than one sense. It was where black and white shared an uneasy co-existence, split by colour but united in poverty. It had been a tough place to grow up for an unprotected Negro child. His playground had been the streets, a place where he'd learnt that to earn respect a person, even a child, had to be willing to stand their ground and keep their wits razor sharp. Before his tenth birthday he'd seen that being part of a gang gave security and a sense of belonging but also raised antagonisms and fears in others that it was tempting to exploit. Had it not been for his mother the descent into an unrighteous life would likely have been swift. But she'd saved him.

She worked downtown in the stock room of Bloomingdale's, a prized position which despite its lowly nature was not just the sole source of income but also the lifebuoy that kept their heads above water. An only child, he'd been the centre of his mother's life and he had repaid his mother's devotion with uncompromising love. It was not out of any religious conviction but for love of her that he continued to attend the Baptist Church on West Milledgeville Street. It was there that he'd learnt about the differences between right and wrong and black and white.

It was the Baptist Church that had been her main support when she'd gone down with breast cancer. It was the church that was there when she'd got to the advanced stage when she could no longer work and support herself or her son. She'd received medical treatment but it wasn't the best and it was no surprise when, after a few painful months, one frozen Sunday night, she'd passed on, in her own bed, with David and the Preacher at her side.

David was just seventeen. With her usual foresight one of his mother's last tasks was to sign the parental consent form that would allow her son to enlist in the US Army, the only place that would take care of him now. It was the sum total of his inheritance from her. He was grateful and made good use of it. He'd shone from the beginning. It was not long before he'd got a transfer from the Infantry to an elite Ranger Battalion. There he'd progressed to Staff Sergeant. It was not an easy journey and that was as far as he could go without Officer training, which he hoped that one day the Army would give him. In the meantime he would do his duty - and a bit extra.

"I know what I'm volunteering for," replied David Evans stepping forward.
"Okay, we need more."

Three more men stepped forward, one was Ralph Foulkes.

Burt Zimmerman intervened. "This is a US operation and city types like you can't drive this type of vehicle."

Ralph squared his shoulders. "Excuse me, those flags fluttering on your trucks are blue I believe. That makes this a United Nation's operation and the United Kingdom is a member of the United Nations. Furthermore I have driven Land Rovers across fields in the past, often pulling a loaded horse box. Gymkhanas can be very rough in an English summer I assure you."

"What the fuck's a gymkhana?" asked Jack looking at Burt.

"Beats me, but if the kid's that keen let him go."

Three more Rangers stepped forward and made up the complement of volunteers.

It took fifteen minutes and a lot of prodding to get the whites to move away from their vehicles; it took a while for them to realise that no was not an option. But once that fact had sunk in they didn't need much encouragement to start running in the direction of Upington.

Jack gave his final instructions to the Staff Sergeant David Evans. "You have command. Go down that road as fast as you dare, pick up all you can then high tail it out of there. Remember the objective is to save other lives not lose your own. We're going to withdraw in the direction of Upington and wait till we get clarification or fresh orders. Good luck."

Victor Verster Prison, Paarl
09.00hrs Sunday 11th February 1990

"What do I tell the press? They're pushing me for confirmation and the waiting crowd are getting very anxious too. I don't want another Sharpeville on my hands, not today." The police Inspector in charge of public order was in the prison Governor's office.

The Governor shrugged. "I can't release Mr Mandela until I get the say so from Pretoria. I have not received that permission yet. As far as I am concerned he's still a prisoner. But there's still time, Mandela is not due to be released till 1pm. He's sitting in his cell ready to go."

"What's the hold up?"

"You didn't hear it from me but I understand that the release of Mandela is part of a wider deal which includes the Americans. As it is, the Americans are not fully satisfied. They are hung up on some technical issue or other. A lot of people are working on it. All I can advise is that you tell the waiting press that everything is on schedule and Mr Mandela's release is being timed for the early morning news in the US and midday news in Europe. I'm as anxious as you to get him out of here, but I'm bound by duty."

Over Kalahari Desert
09.30hrs Sunday 11th February 1990

Morgan was the first to see the sun's reflection bouncing off the Land Cruiser's windscreen. He tapped Gus on the arm and pointed. As they got closer they could see the dust cloud left by the moving vehicle. Gus made a tight circle, dropped to five hundred feet and made a low pass in front of it. The Toyota stopped and two men got out. Tembo in the back of the plane was the first to see through one of the side windows. He let out a wild whoop and shouted.

"It's Duncan and Mr Cameron!"

"Can you land?" pleaded Morgan.

"The road's very narrow and the surface is rough but I suppose I've landed on worse. It looks like there's a straight bit clear of vegetation ahead."

Gus brought the Piper to a halt about a hundred yards shy of the Toyota. Even before he'd stopped Morgan was unstrapped and opening the door. He jumped clear of the plane, dropping off the back of the wing, not heeding Gus's warning, "Watch the prop!"

It was a good moment, the smiles real, the hugs prolonged.

"My God, Morgan, Tembo how did you get here? How did you find us?"

Tembo laughed in response. "You said come as quickly as we can and that is what we did." Tembo paused to look around the barren desert, "Although I am not quite sure where 'here' is."

"It was Mary Scobie who had the idea," added Morgan. "She knew a little about Gus and told us that even old men had ideals at one time and that, in the right circumstances, these ideals could be resurrected. So we spoke to Gus. Mary had got it right."

"Okay that's the plane but how did you locate us in the desert?"

"There is a plane in the sky; a spy plane Gus called it. They could hear you but you could not hear them. They directed us to you."

Stuart broke in. "Is the plane in the sky still there, do you have contact with it?"

John Devlin picked up the flashing icon immediately. "Sentry One to Piper One. Go to 107.3. Over." He directed them to a quiet frequency, one where not everybody could listen into the conversation.

Stuart sat in the pilot's seat with Duncan next to him. The others gathered around the open doors of the plane, the reception turned to loudspeakers.

"Sentry One to Piper One. We got you on the ground. What happened? Over."

"This is Lieutenant Colonel Stuart Cameron," Stuart began formally. "I understand you are British. I'm not sure how you got here but I need you to get a flash message to GCHQ. Can you do this? Over."

"Piper One. They've been looking for you. They want to talk. I'm going to patch you through if you give me a moment. Sentry One. Over."

The Duty Officer at GCHQ told his assistant to get through to the Embassy in Pretoria as soon as he picked up the incoming call from Sentry One and identified Stuart Cameron. "Somebody needs to speak to you urgently," he told Stuart.

Jane was talking on the Ambassador's open line when his secure phone began to ring. She broke off the call.

The Ambassador protested, "You were talking to a South African Government Minister, you cannot put the phone down on him like that."

"This is more important," she replied picking up the secure phone. The patch through was instantaneous.

"Hello, hello."

Stuart recognised her voice immediately. "Good to hear your voice Jane."

"Thank God you're safe. What about Duncan?"

"He's okay, he's here with me. He can hear you."

"Thank God. But I need to warn you that I believe you're in great danger. Listen for a moment. The South African Government no longer controls Vastrap. The Americans have not reached there either. The installation is in what we have to assume are hostile hands."

Stuart broke in. "I think we can confirm that. We had an encounter a while ago with some of them."

Jane continued. "They are most probably part of the group that Peter van Stardan controls. We are presuming he is not willing to surrender his brainchild. But it's more than that. This van Stardan fellow is showing distinct fanatical tendencies. He appears to have lost the plot. He is becoming unpredictable and he is most probably the one who is responsible for the events at Stirling Farm. Did you get that Duncan? Do you understand what I am saying?" She didn't wait for a reply. "I'm putting a plan together to nail him from here but I can't do anything about the situation at Vastrap. I believe that his intention is to either steal or explode a nuclear device on site. They spent several hours there with technical staff and we understand, from the Americans, they might have now left. My gut feeling is that martyrdom is not in their manifesto. If they do let one off you are in the blast area. I've made the Americans aware of the situation and I understand they may be withdrawing back to Upington as we speak."

"Okay. Do you have any idea when they plan to detonate?"

"There is no firm evidence on that but it is my belief detonation will be around 1300 hrs local."

"What do you base that on?"

"That's the time Mandela is due to be released?" replied Jane. "They want to overshadow the event."

Stuart didn't reply to Jane. "Sentry One. Are you listening? Over."

"Roger on that Piper One. How can I help?"

"Can you give me a vector to Vastrap and estimated flying time in this crate?"

"Hold Piper One."

Another light began to flash on John Devlin's screen. He ignored it, instead passing on the request for a vector and ETA to the Surveillance Operator. The response came in ten seconds. "Two seven three degrees west, 25 minutes."

Before John Devlin could pass the information to Piper One he felt a hand on his shoulder. The Tactical Director had unbuckled and walked over to Devlin's position. "That flashing light you are ignoring is the President of the United States wanting to speak to his ground troops. Answer it."

Devlin looked up at his boss and shook his head, "No, this is more important."

The Tactical Director thought for a second and came down on the side of his subordinate. "As soon as you can then, I'll tell him you're busy."

The discussion in the desert didn't last long. Stuart spoke.

"It's about an hour and fifteen minutes before Jane thinks the detonation will take place. We can get there in thirty minutes with this plane. Do we make an attempt to stop the detonation or do we make a run for safety? Gus it's your plane. You first."

"We are tight on fuel but I can get you there. Well no more than three of you. That's all there's room for."

"Duncan?"

"Get me to the device and I'll disarm it in less than five minutes."

Morgan chipped in. "I know my way around the camp. The bombs will most probably be in the assembly hall. I can get you there if there is no resistance."

"I go if Morgan goes," responded Tembo without compromise in his voice. "I know the place too."

"Gus can take Morgan, Tembo and me. You head back to Upington in the Toyota," said Duncan to Stuart. "Forget the captain of the ship malarkey. You have nothing to add to the operation. All agreed?"

"Get the Toyota off the road," said Gus, "I need a clear run."

Duncan and Tembo squashed into the back of the plane, Morgan sat alongside Gus. He would direct him to the Assembly Hall entrance once they'd landed. Gus opened up the throttle even before the Land Cruiser was clear of the road.

Once the plane was up Stuart drove the Land Cruiser back on to the track. He stopped for a moment and watched the plane climb away before starting to drive, not to safety but in the direction of Vastrap. He'd already made the mental calculation that he'd be just over halfway there before the bomb went off, that is if Jane's hunch was right.

Zodiac House, Pretoria
11.30hrs Sunday 11th February 1990

Peter van Stardan checked the time on his wrist watch before looking at the clock on the wall. The minutes were dragging and he was agitated. His feet sank into the deep pile carpet as he walked over to the window of what used to be Alfred Smidt's office but was now his. In Peter's mind Alfred Smidt's presence would always be here and he knew that Alfred would be happy with what was about to happen. From the top floor of Zodiac Buildings he scanned the city skyline taking in the solid visual evidence of his nation's achievement; a capital city that could stand alongside any capital city in the world. In the distance, blocked from view by the skyscrapers, was another source of his country's wealth, the mines of the Rand, mines that had gold reserves that added up to more than the total gold reserves held by all the major banks of the world combined. And all they had to do was dig it up. And beyond the mines lay the rich farming land, land that was capable of feeding the whole continent of Africa and more.

They had it, his people had it, all they needed was the political will to keep it. His heart told him that if the white people of South Africa had a strong leader, a new Smuts or Kruger they would follow him. History had proved that a nation's political will stems from strong individuals, leaders that had stepped forward. Somebody had to step forward now in South Africa, in this time of crisis, and he was going to be that person. He knew exactly how he was going to achieve it. The people would always coalesce around one of their own that they thought was being persecuted. It was the British that had given Smuts and Kruger their power by opposing and threatening them. Even Mandela's greatest achievement was just to sit in a prison cell for twenty five years. He didn't actually do anything and now, without raising a finger, he posed the biggest danger to the Republic in its history. Peter van Stardan clenched his fist in determination. Soon people would see him locked up for the love of his country and they would rally around and rise up and he would in the end be victorious. The time was coming quickly when he would announce his arrival to the world and the world would take notice and remember the name of Peter van Stardan.

There was just an hour to go. Everybody was preparing to listen to Nelson Mandela. But instead they would actually witness the resurgence of The Nationalist Afrikaner. Not since April 1642 when Jan van Riebeek landed at the Cape would such a momentous event have taken place. All the descendents of the Voortrekkers would rise and follow him, Peter van Stardan, in claiming their birth right. For a moment he wondered as he looked down into Church Square, "In a hundred years will there be a statute of me there, will tourists take photographs of me as they do today of Paul Kruger?"

He gathered up the sheets of paper from his desk and tucked them into the breast pocket of his suit before making his last farewells to this office. There would be national pandemonium for a while as everybody tried to work out what had happened. He would use that time to make his way to Cape Town. Once there he would call a press conference and would read aloud the words that were written on the sheets of paper. He would claim credit for the nuclear explosion and call on all the white people of South Africa to stand resolutely and defiantly face world opinion. He knew he would be arrested but he also knew that the democracies were too weak to take decisive decisions. They would put him on trial where again he would have a world stage to expound the true way forward.

He made his way towards the lifts.

Vastrap
11.30hrs 11th February 1990

Gus called the tower on the radio, just in case. As expected there was no response. He circled the airport low to see through the tower windows. Nobody was there. He wasn't used to the luxury of a paved runway and he found the experience of space disorientating. He'd got used to tight landings with trees and rocks as visual references and only ever paying cursory attention to his instrumentation. He misjudged the height. The plane hit the ground hard and yawed from side to side for a moment, until it had lost some speed. He didn't stop when he regained control, just continued his taxi, taking instructions from Morgan's pointing finger.

The signs of a hasty evacuation were clear. Tugs, fork lift trucks, crates, even bits of abandoned uniform littered the apron area close to the entrance to the underground facility. They came within fifty yards of the open ramp.

"Here is good," said Morgan. "It is open, we can go down on foot."

Gus stopped the plane and immediately turned the engine off.

"The dial is indicating that there is no fuel left but there might be a few dregs in the tanks," said Gus. "If you fail to defuse the bomb get back here and I will take us as far as I can, until the fuel runs out."

Duncan, Morgan and Tembo began to run towards the ramp. They'd hardly started the descent down the slope when Jan Kutz stepped out from behind a stanchion pointing his gun at the three men. They stopped dead. Nobody spoke for a moment. Kutz' gaze darted from Tembo to Morgan and back again. Somewhere in his mind a flicker of recognition was prompting his memory. At last it came back to him.

"You two darkies, I know you. You are the ones that ran away from here and took the sick one with you. I have photographs. You should be dead. I sent people to kill you. You caused me a lot of trouble. I don't think you are going to be so lucky now."

"Who is he?" asked Duncan, "Is he the one that killed Elizabeth?"

"Shut up kaffir lover. I will tell you when to speak."

Morgan ignored the command. "I don't know if he killed her but he is the head of security and was surely involved in what happened at Stirling Farm."

Duncan felt his rage begin to build. His immediate instinct was to run at Kutz and tear him apart with his bare hands. Seeing Duncan's complexion changing Tembo spoke slowly and calmly.

"Do not attack him. You are the only one who can save the situation here."

A glint came into Kutz's eyes, his mind keen and focused. "You can stop the bomb! That is good. Come down the ramp, slowly. You will save me."

A voice came from behind. "Duncan don't step forward." It was Gus.

"Who are you old man? Join your friends here," Kutz motioned with the pistol.

Gus's voice was calm. "I will not come down there, but you will come up here and you will let my friends pass."

"Why would I do that?" laughed Kutz.

"I have an aeroplane. I can fly you away from here now, to safety, but only if you let my friends go."

"You can't you don't have enough fu….."

Gus cut into Morgan's words before he had a chance to finish the sentence "Be quick, you don't have much time. We will all be dead if you take too long."

Kutz hesitated, struggling to make the obvious decision, the cogs in his mind slowly chewing up the words. Eventually he got there. He motioned Duncan, Morgan and Tembo to move to one side as he sidled past them, never lowering the gun. Once he had passed, the three men ran down the ramp. Kutz aimed his gun at Gus. "You better not be tricking me old man."

The once busy hall was now silent and the running footsteps of the three men echoed through the rooms. Liebermann awoke from his day dreams still cradling the Ingram machine pistol in his arms. He turned just in time to see the three men arrive at the door. He raised the gun and pulled the trigger. Nothing happened. He had not reloaded since shooting at Kutz. The failure caused an adrenaline rush. He glanced at the wall clock. Still fifteen minutes to go. He could not wait; the only option was to detonate the bomb now. He turned and dashed towards the device but Morgan was quicker. He moved forward and pounced. The two men fell to the floor. Liebermann struggled to break free but the matter was settled an instant later when Tembo landed on top of both of them.

Duncan stepped towards the bomb. He walked around quickly taking in what he saw.

"Exploding bridge wire fuses," he muttered to himself. He found the cross head screwdriver he needed on an adjacent bench. He'd never worked on a nuclear device before but his hands were sure and swift. The years in prison and all the reading he'd done on the subject served him well. He thanked the Lord that the guards at Cheltenham Military Prison were too stupid to realise the type of text books he was requesting and had supplied them without question.

In moments the retaining rings at both ends of the bomb had been removed. He turned the metal sleeve at one end to the left and, when he felt it coming free, pulled the well lubricated canister out. He gently placed the unit that contained the priming TNT charge and detonator on the bench before turning his attention to the other side of the bomb and repeating the process.

Tembo and Morgan were now on their feet, holding their prisoner tightly. They looked at Duncan silently. When he'd removed the second canister Duncan stood straight and looked towards his companions with a smile.

"Is it okay?" Tembo's question was tentative.

"It's okay. There won't be a nuclear explosion now," replied Duncan. "I have removed the priming charges. There can be no chain reaction.

The relief was palpable in Morgan's voice. "So we are safe?"

"Not quite," said Duncan. "The priming charges are still set to go off at the same time. There are enough conventional explosives to do a lot of damage to this building."

"But they won't go off will they?" asked Morgan now a little less sure.

"They're timed to go off," Duncan looked towards the clock, "in three minutes."

"Stop talking. Do it," there was panic in Tembo's voice.

Duncan smiled and turned his attention back towards the devices. He worked on the left hand one first. It was old hat to him. Three snips of the coloured wire and Duncan eased the capacitor from the top of the fuse, the capacitor that held enough stored electrical power to set off the detonator and TNT.

He stepped sideways along the bench towards the second unit. Tembo and Morgan had relaxed their grip and Liebermann had somehow found some hitherto unknown reserve of strength. He was free of his captors in an instant and bounding the few feet towards Duncan and the single remaining live detonator. Duncan had his back towards them and didn't see him coming. With a powerful shove from Liebermann his head went forward involuntarily and banged on the steel rim of the bomb casing, his nose split wide open, blood spurted from a ruptured blood vessel in his nose and a pain like lightening shot up his forehead, hurting his eyes and blurring his vision.

Suddenly Liebermann had the live detonator in his hands and was moving quickly around the bench, putting it between him and his captors. Duncan struggled to get to his feet and regain his senses. He looked to the wall clock. There was less than a minute and a half to go. Not enough time to retrieve the device and defuse it.

"Run! Get the fuck out of here," he screamed as he moved towards the entrance, pushing Tembo and Morgan ahead of him. The three raced across the workshop floor and gained the bottom of the ramp. It seemed as if they moved in slow motion, each upward step leaden and laboured. They'd nearly gained the summit when the TNT detonated. Duncan had feared that Liebermann would follow them in a ghoulish attempt to take as many people with him as he could. But that thought never crossed Liebermann's mind. He simply stepped forward, clutching the TNT close to his chest and lay on top of the nuclear bomb. He would never see the fruits of his work, but at least he would die with it.

Five kilograms of highly oxidized and purified TNT is enough to do a lot of damage. The blast was clean and crisp because of the purity of the explosive and the resultant shock was magnified in strength by the speed of the explosion.

Minister of Homeland's Office, Pretoria
11.30hrs Sunday 11th February 1990

"He doesn't have to see you, you're not accredited. If he does consent please be careful and observe the niceties. It's important." The Ambassador used the mirror discreetly provided in the anti-room to ensure his dress was correct. "And I do wish you'd worn something more appropriate."

"Party dresses have not been at the forefront of my mind for the last day or two," replied Jane Ashton rolling her eyes towards the ceiling.

"That comment and the manner in which it is made is exactly the type of thing that bothers me. It can cause a lot of upset in these circles."

"Not as much as a nuclear explosion I bet."

"Stop it Miss Ashton or I won't press your case."

The Minister's Secretary came into the anti-room. "The Minister is ready to see you now but I am instructed to tell you that today is extremely busy and he can only spare you a few minutes. Come please."

The Minister had his back to them; he was looking at a television that was normally concealed in a large mahogany cabinet. He was watching a live SABC broadcast from outside Victor Verster Prison trying to pick up the mood of the waiting crowd.

The Secretary announced their arrival. "The Ambassador for the United Kingdom and his assistant."

The Minister turned to face them, stepping forward to shake hands. The greeting was mannerly but not friendly. Jane thought it was due to the Minister's pre-occupation with events rather than any innate hostility.

"I would have preferred it if you had directed your enquiries through normal channels at the Foreign Affairs' Office," began the Minister. "Today is one of the biggest days in South African history and I do not need to be distracted. Things could go very wrong."

The British Ambassador introduced Jane. "Miss Ashton is one of our foremost analysts," he began. "Her work has on several occasions been used to adjust British Government policy."

"Very good. You do well for one so young," replied the Minister. "Most of our advisors only achieve such status when they have more years under their belt. We value experience here. But please go on, time is pressing."

Jane stood to leave as soon as her conversation with the Minister was finished. He extended his hand and smiled warmly at her. "The conversation was very interesting and informative and will be useful to my Government." He hesitated for a moment. "But only if we get over the next few hours I suspect."

Jane placed the folder of documents she'd been carrying on the Minister's desk. "I think everything you need is in here."

The crowd was swelling outside Victor Verster Prison. The Governor was becoming more anxious. If the planned release got aborted at this late stage not only would there be problems outside the prison but he was sure that the inmates would riot inside. The Chief Warder came into his office without knocking.

"How is the prisoner?" asked the Governor.

"Mr Mandela is fine, quite calm. He says he is not going to worry about a situation he cannot influence. The problem is his entourage, which includes his wife Winnie. As instructed we let them in so that they could be with him to help prepare. But they have not stopped screaming at us since they stepped foot inside the buildings. If anything goes wrong they will whip up the crowd. They say if Nelson is not released as promised that they will get the crowd outside to break in and fetch him. I believe they could do that."

"We can only prepare for the worst," replied the Governor. "I cannot release the prisoner without permission of the Ministry and they know the situation down here. They only have to watch the television."

Vastrap
11.45hrs Sunday 11th February 1990

Kutz kept his gun pointing at Gus, suspicious of a trick. The two men got into the plane. Gus had long given up the habit of carrying out a formal pre-flight check. He just had a cursory look around and relied on gut instinct. However this time he did concentrate on one instrument with interest, the fuel gauge. No matter how hard he looked it still read zero. He reached to a handle below his seat, checking that the reserve tank cock was in the fully open position. It was.

Gus pressed the engine start button. The engine gave a little splutter before settling down, as it normally did. But this time the splutter made Gus's heart skip a beat. He didn't bother with taxiing to the end of the runway. He just checked the windsock near the tower. It hung limply on its post. Any direction would do, the plane didn't need much space. He pointed it in a clear direction and opened the throttle. They were airborne before they'd got halfway across the apron. Gently he pulled on the yolk and banked the plane due East climbing slowly to three thousand feet.

"I'll follow the road towards Upington," he said.

"Take me to Cape Town," instructed Kutz, allowing a slight curl of a smile to appear on his lips. Only now was he daring to believe he was escaping and could make plans for the future.

"I don't think I have enough fuel," replied Gus honestly. "We need to get as far away from here as possible, following the road would be the best option."

"I don't believe you. Head for Cape Town."

Before Gus had a chance to reply the engine began to sputter. Within a few seconds the engine had stopped completely. Gus quickly feathered the propeller and pushed the yolk forward a little putting the plane into a shallow dive.

"What trick is this?" Kutz raised the gun.

"No trick, we're out of fuel. I'd put the gun down if I were you and check your seat belt is fastened properly whilst I look for a spot to land.

"I'll kill you for this. You knew there was not enough fuel."

"You'll kill me when we land?" laughed Gus. "Well I suppose there's no point in me making the effort then. Might as well go down in a blaze of glory." He pushed the column forward and the plane's nose suddenly dropped.

"No, no. Land the plane. I won't kill you. I promise. Just get us down on the ground safely."

Gus levelled the plane. "Now why would I believe that? Perhaps it would help if you passed me that gun."

It took Kutz a second or two to realise he had no option. He turned the gun around and offered it butt first to Gus who opened the pilot's sliding window and threw the gun out. Without the noise of the engine they heard it clatter down the wing and off the edge. Gus now concentrated on finding a landing spot within gliding distance.

Staff Sergeant David Evans was struggling to keep the Hummer on the dirt road. He drove fast, leaving the slower rag-tag collection of South African vehicles behind. There was no air conditioning in the Hummer and the sweat was rolling down his forehead, trickling into his eyes, the salt irritating and blurring his vision. He constantly had to wipe his brow with the flat of his hand.

It was more than an hour before he saw the first of the black workers walking towards him. Even before he reached them he could see that they were worn out, their strength sapped from the sweltering desert walk. He came to a halt in front of the lead man and got out of the vehicle.

He didn't see it coming. The small plane was gliding, no engine, no noise just the whoosh of air passing over the aircraft's wings. The undercarriage cleared the top of the Hummer by feet and the plane touched down on the track just a few yards behind the vehicle. It looked good for a moment then the front wheel of the plane hit a solitary rock causing the aircraft to veer to one side. Gus reacted immediately as the plane slewed to the left but he overcompensated and the plane swung violently to the right and left the road. On the rock strewn roadside the pilot lost control; he didn't have a chance, the plane tipped and a wing dug into the ground causing it to cartwheel. The wing broke off and the plane ended up nose down in the ground.

David Evans ran towards the wreck. There was no fire but he knew the situation might change quickly. He yanked at the cabin door; it was twisted and resisted his efforts. He put a foot up against the fuselage and held the handle as he pushed with his leg. The door yielded. Inside were two men, the younger man was conscious but struggling with his harness, the older man, underneath, was out cold. Evans reached in and released Kutz's harness. Kutz found purchase with his legs and heaved himself out of the mangled cockpit pushing Evans out of the way as he passed. Evans climbed into the cabin and released the old man from his harness. He looked around for help, the old man was a dead weight, but Kutz was gone. He struggled alone finally heaving the old man out of the cabin and dragging him clear of the wreckage. Looking around he spotted Kutz near the Hummer, opening the door.

"Hey bud, what are you doing?" shouted Evans running towards the Hummer.

Kutz was already climbing into the driver's seat by the time the Sergeant got back to the vehicle.

"Not so fast there," shouted Evans grabbing Kutz by the arm and dragging him back out of the vehicle. Kutz could not resist the strong arms of the Ranger but managed to grab the assault rifle that was lying on the passenger seat. The Ranger let Kutz fall to the ground and watched him roll. He could see the man bringing the gun up and moved quickly. Crouching and stepping to one side he pulled his side-arm from its canvass holster and in a single sweeping move brought the gun around, flicked off the safety and cocked the gun. Kutz didn't stand a chance. Relentless and repetitive Ranger training meant the result was inevitable. The double tap at close range put two slugs into Kutz's chest. Death was instantaneous. It was a clean kill, he didn't bleed much.

Experience had taught the escaping Africans what to do when they heard gunshots; they fell to the ground in unison. It took half a minute before the lead African raised his head to look and tentatively get to his feet. Slowly he walked towards the Ranger.

"We are escaping from Vastrap. We think there is danger. You should not go on."

"I know that replied Evans. We came to look for you, to help you. I didn't expect that," he nodded towards the prostrate corpse.

"I know this man," said the African. "He was the Head of Security at Vastrap. He was not a good man. We will not mourn his departure. He had the blood of many on his hands."

"Stay here," replied Evans. "I need to check the man over by the plane."

A hazy light was returning to Gus's eyes and the fuzz in his brain was clearing leaving a residual throb in his temple where he'd banged it during the crash landing. As focus returned he saw the Ranger standing over him, gun hanging loosely from his right hand.

"Don't try anything old fella. Your friend tried that and he won't be trying anything again."

"Americans! Thank God. He's no friend of mine. He forced me to fly him away from Vastrap." Gus pushed himself up into a sitting position and looked around. "It's dangerous to go on to Vastrap, there might be a big explosion. You need to turn around."

"We're ahead of you on that Chief, but how do I know who you are?"

"There is an AWACS somewhere above. Can you contact them?" Gus didn't wait for a reply. "Tell them the Piper has crash landed near you and that my passengers are at Vastrap doing what they can."

"There are still people at Vastrap?"

"Behind you," Gus pointed down the road. "There are more vehicles coming."

The Ranger gave a quick glance. "That's the transport for the black workers. Can you walk?"

Ralph was driving the lead truck, quite at home in his new environment. It didn't take long to get the trucks turned around and the African workers loaded.

Ralph spoke to Staff Sergeant Evans. "There's more than enough room in the trucks for the workers. I want to go on to Vastrap. Will you let me take one of the vehicles?"

"The whole idea is to get everyone away from Vastrap. What do you want to go up there for?"

"The pilot of the plane told us that Mr Murdoch is at Vastrap. He is an expert in these matters. Now that he is there I think the danger is significantly reduced but I think they might benefit from my assistance. You should let me take that," he said pointing to the Hummer.

"No way that's US Army property."

"I think that the Hummer has a radio and can communicate with the AWACS. If I get there I will be able to let people know what is going on. That may solve a lot of problems for a lot of people."

"Oh, I don't know bud."

"Well the way I see it," continued Ralph, "is that I'm willing to commit my life to the effort whilst the United States is only committing itself to a single vehicle at worst. I think you Americans would normally consider that to be quite a good deal. Am I right?"

"We get into trouble for not looking after US property. I think it's better if I take you in the Hummer with the radio."

"Don't you want to ask permission from your commanding officer first?"

"I know what the answer will be and my Mom always used to say don't ask a question if you know what the answer is going to be and you don't like it. I'll take her advice on this one. Come on let's go."

Church Square, Pretoria
12.15hrs Sunday 11th February, 1990

The sun was shining but the parks and greens that would normally have been busy with tourists and office workers were uneerily quiet. Nobody was taking advantage of the sun during their lunch break. The momentous release of Nelson Mandela had captured the attention of virtually the whole population. Everybody who didn't have more pressing business and could get to a television set had done so.

But Peter van Stardan was not going to watch on a television. He was going to spend the last fateful minutes in the presence of the memorial statue of Paul Kruger, founder of the South African state. He thought it was a prophetic gesture as he walked to an empty bench, noting with approval the *'Whites Only'* plaque. He sat and took in the moment not noticing the Peugeot 405's pulling into two empty parking bays. Nor had he noticed the strange men that were entering the square. He had not even noticed the man that had followed him during the short walk from his office. All Peter van Stardan wanted to do was have a last chat with his hero on the plinth.

When they got back to the Ambassador's office in the British Embassy the Ambassador had remarked how full his diary was and how inconvenient the re-scheduling was going to be. He'd hoped that Jane would take her leave and go but Jane was unreceptive to the hint and the Ambassador, following his ticking off from the Foreign Office, was unwilling to press the matter further. Succumbing to the inevitable he pushed a button on the intercom and ordered tea from his receptionist.

"Earl Grey good for you?" he asked Jane who'd plonked herself back into the Regency chair close to the secure phone.

She didn't have time to answer before the phone rang, not the secure line but the normal one. The Ambassador lifted the receiver. There followed a few Oh's and Yeses', even a nod or two, before he hung up.

"Suppose you could say saved by the bell. That was the Ministry of the Interior calling in respect of our recent visit. It's quite extraordinary really. It appears they have decided to act upon your suggestions and you are invited to be a witness. A car will be waiting for you outside the Embassy in a few minutes. I have never known the South African Government act with such haste previously. I of course accepted on your behalf. "

"Accepted what?"

To a casual observer it must have appeared strange, several men suddenly moving simultaneously and converging on the bench that was occupied by Peter van Stardan. By the time he'd realised what was happening it was too late. He attempted to stand but strong hands rested on his shoulders and pushed him back into the sitting position. One of the men spoke.

"Peter van Stardan I am Detective Sergeant Kevin Druik of SAP and I am arresting you."

Peter van Stardan took it in his stride. "I did not expect to be arrested so soon, I would have preferred Cape Town, but no matter it will not affect my plans. It only confirms that my plan is working."

"You will be handcuffed and taken to Pretorius Street where you will be charged."

"There is no need for handcuffs I will come willingly."

"Handcuff him," the Officer repeated ignoring van Stardan's offer.

Vastrap
12.50hrs Sunday 11th February 1990

"It's all destroyed, it's no good," said Tembo.

Morgan nodded in agreement struggling to get his breath back after the run to the top of the air traffic tower and back.

"There must be some way of letting people know. You can't give up now," said Duncan scrunching his face with the pain.

"It's more important we take care of you," said Morgan kneeling down beside Duncan who was still lying where he'd fallen on the ramp after the blast. Morgan gently lifted the gauze dressing that he'd applied to the burns on Duncan's back. Duncan winced in pain.

"We need to get you to hospital. How is the leg?"

"It's gone numb now. I think it might be broken."

Morgan and Tembo laughed. "You don't say boss. I suppose the bone sticking out of the side is a clue. You're lucky it's not bleeding. Morgan will stay with you and I will go and search the other buildings for a radio."

Tembo had run halfway across the apron towards the isolated administration block when he heard the revving engine. He turned to see an unfamiliar military vehicle heading towards him. Caught out in the open, his eyes darted around looking for cover. There was nowhere. He had no choice but to stand and face the threat. Only when it was near did he recognise the blue pennant fluttering from the aerial.

Tembo smiled as the vehicle drew up alongside him and an American soldier got out.

"Staff Sergeant David Evans, United States Rangers."

Tembo was surprised at the accent. He'd never met anybody that had skin as black as his own but spoke like an American.

Ralph joined the men feeling that he too should introduce himself. Straightening his torso into a position that he thought resembled attention but actually only made the oversized fatigues look ridiculous on him, he announced,

"Ralph Foulkes of Her Majesty's Foreign and Commonwealth Office."

The two blacks hid their smiles as Ralph continued. "We are looking for Mr Stuart Cameron and Mr Duncan Murdoch. Furthermore we understand that there is some danger here at the moment. Can you advise us?"

"He means are you with the two Brits and is the bomb defused?" clarified David.

"The nuclear bomb is defused but there has been an accident and Duncan is injured. He needs medical attention. I was trying to find radio equipment. There are no telephone lines or working radio equipment here; it's all been sabotaged. Stuart Cameron is in the desert somewhere, driving a truck."

"We have a radio. Take us to the injured man." David climbed back into the driver's seat.

John Devlin and an AWACS was a good combination. He took the call from the Hummer and immediately knew what to do. He scrolled down the incoming call log and pressed the connect icon when he'd found what he wanted.

In the White House Situation Room everybody was quiet. They could only act on information and they weren't getting any information –not till the comms room speaker came to life.

"Got an incoming message from the AWACS. Message for the President."

Wilbur Rice sat at the conference table in the Situation Room. He pressed his speaker 'on' button. "Who's calling the President?"

"Guy called Devlin, says he flying around the Kalahari Desert and is returning the President's personal call."

"Patch me through."

The line went dead for a moment.

"Says he'll only speak to the President."

Wilbur pushed another button. The President, sitting at his desk in the Oval Office answered.

"Got something Chief. The AWACS wants to speak with you directly."

"Okay," said the President, "but leave the line open so you in the Situation Room can hear."

"This is the President of the United States. Who am I speaking to?"

"Just a radio operator you tried to call today Sir. I'm returning your call and I also have somebody on line that may have good news for you."

"I could do with some good news. Put em through."

The Hummer had been moved up to the ramp. Ralph, recalling his first aid training as a Boy Scout Leader was attempting to put a splint on Duncan's leg. Staff Sergeant David Evans was standing by the Hummer wearing the radio headset.

A green receive light flicked on the radio console. "Who's that?" he asked.

"I'm the President who are you and where are you?"

Evans came to attention even though his commander in chief could not see him. "Staff Sergeant David Evans, US Rangers SIR! Currently at South African Airbase Vastrap in the Kalahari Desert. SIR!"

"Do you have control of the South African nuclear arsenal?"

"Can you hold a moment SIR?"

David Evans looked down the ramp. "Hey you guys, do I have control of the nukes?"

Duncan looked up smiled and nodded. "You do!"

Evans pushed the transmit button. "I do Sir. I'm a little short handed here at the moment but the Brits tell me reinforcements are on the way."

"Well done Sergeant. Where you from."

"Harlem Sir."

"That's good Sergeant your Mama's going to proud of you today."

He didn't say it with intent, it just slipped out. "She's passed Sir."

"That's really sad. Tell you what, I want you to come and see me when you get back stateside cos I'm proud of you. And by the way you're not a Sergeant anymore!"

The line went dead.

When the Situation Room heard the arsenal was secure they started sending the prepared secure message to the President of South Africa confirming the ratification of the bi-lateral treaty between the two countries.

Victor Verster Prison
13.00hrs Sunday 11th February 1990

The slow and dignified walk that Nelson Mandela made, at exactly 1 pm local time, holding the hand of his wife Winnie, from the prison gates towards the waiting crowds and throng of press gave no indication of the drama that had preceded the event. He'd been dressed and ready sitting calmly although even he had begun to have doubts as time pressed on.

Pictures were beamed live all over the world news networks. Blacks in South Africa erupted in euphoric joy, leaders of nations queued to broadcast their congratulations and anti-apartheid activists in pubs and bars downed self-congratulatory drinks to celebrate '*their achievement*'.

Few were aware of the true events. Inside the prison the Governor sat, slumped in his chair, exhausted by the tension; staff in the South African Prime Minister's Office were relieved that an immediate civil uprising had been averted but looked with some trepidation to the uncertainty black rule would bring; in the US the President was pleased that he'd neutralised a potential nuclear threat and simultaneously enhanced his credibility with Afro-American voters thus virtually securing for himself a second term of office. In London Sir Basil Parker Smythe smiled with satisfaction, assured that his holidays at the Stellenbosch family vineyard would continue for some time to come. The British Chancellor of the Exchequer leaned back in his chair, smiling as he watched the green screen that showed share prices in South African listed companies rise as investors expressed their new found confidence in South Africa's economic prospects.

Jack Carter and Burt Zimmerman, still in the desert, had to about face the convoy once again on hearing the news. It took them two and a half hours at breakneck speed to get to Vastrap, arriving just before Stuart Cameron trundled through the gate in his Toyota Land Cruiser. By that time the jamming of the South African military network had stopped and a medi-vac helicopter had been arranged for Duncan.

Pretorius Street Police Station, Pretoria
13.30hrs Sunday 11th February 1990

It's a sad fact that joy is generally not universal. In a stark and bare interview room Peter van Stardan sat on one side of a plain table, Detective Sergeant Kevin Druik on the other. Behind Druik was another police detective with Jane Ashton at his side. On the table were the possessions van Stardan had with him when he was arrested.

"What is the news?" asked van Stardan for the fourth time.

"The same as when you asked before," replied Druik. "Mandela has walked to freedom."

"What other news?"

"There is no other news."

"There must be by now."

"No there is no other news. What has you so concerned?"

"You will know when it comes."

Jane took a step forward. "I know the news that he is waiting for. May I tell him?"

Druik nodded.

"The news is that there will be no news from Vastrap."

"I don't believe you. It's a trick."

"No trick. Vastrap is now controlled by the UNAEA. It's over."

Druik broke in. "Do you know why you have been arrested?"

Peter van Stardan smiled. "I have been arrested because I love my country and I will be the martyr that will halt the madness of our Government."

"No. You have been arrested for murder and I am now about to charge you for that murder."

"What are you talking about," protested van Stardan. "Look here is my statement. I want this given to the press so that they can know the truth."

Druik picked up the thin sheaf of papers and gave them a cursory glance before passing them over to Jane who browsed through their content before tearing the sheafs first into halves and then quarters."

"My statement!" shouted van Stardan.

"What statement?" replied Jane.

"Peter van Stardan you are charged that on or about the 23rd March 1963 you did kill, by shooting, one Matthew Bowdler in the vicinity of the Puma Game Reserve, Kruger Park. You do not have to say anything but anything you do……."

Druik didn't finish his caution before van Stardan vaulted the table and was upon him. The Detective at the rear of the room hit the panic strip that ran around the perimeter of the room as he moved forward to assist Druik. Jane joined in the milieu by holding on to van Stardan's legs. Within seconds the door flew open and other officers rushed in to help.

"I am a political prisoner," screamed van Stardan struggling hopelessly, against five men. Jane had released her hold and stepped back against the wall.

"No you are a common criminal."

The comment prompted van Stardan to renewed efforts. The reaction was just as she'd predicted and wanted.

A few minutes later when van Stardan had been subdued, handcuffed and held tightly by three officers Druik continued his caution with an added rider.

"That was abnormal behaviour," said Druik.

"Do you think I'm mad or something? I'm as sane as you and I will not let this happen."

"Sane as me? I don't think so. Take him away."

The restraining officers dragged the struggling van Stardan from the room as he continued to protest about his status as a political prisoner. Druik and Jane remained alone in the room.

"It was as you said it would be Madam."

"Yes. I'm sure that a mental evaluation could take quite some considerable time. I think that is one fly that has been removed from the ointment. Now I have to leave. One of my colleagues has been injured and I must see how he is."

Vastrap
18.00hrs Sunday 11th February 1990

They'd set up headquarters in one of the smaller rooms in the admin block. Services were back on including air conditioning and telephones. The US technicians had worked quickly and well. Coffee and doughnuts were on the table.

"Just like home, help yourself," said Burt Zimmerman.

"What's the news on Duncan?" asked Jack Carter. "He did an amazing job, real risky. It's a shame he got hurt."

"Compound fracture of the left femur and burns on his back. He's in the hospital at Upington. They won't let Tembo visit," replied Stuart. "Apparently somebody at the hospital doesn't like black visitors to a white only ward."

"It's that kind of shit that tells you what this is all about. We'll send someone around from the base at the airport to see he's got what he needs and we'll look after those twins as well, they're a pair of characters. They seem to be quite a hit with the men. None of them have met guerrilla fighters before."

"Former guerrilla fighters," corrected Stuart. "I appreciate that but there are more important things we need to discuss. I'm worried about a couple of issues"

"Let's get Eugene over. He's the liaison with the UN technical staff."

Eugene sat down with a polystyrene cup of coffee already in his hand. He picked a doughnut up with his free hand and took a bite. "God I miss these," he spluttered between chews. "So wadda you want to know?"

"How about a status report," asked Jack.

"What in front of this fella here. He's not one of us." Eugene pointed but did not look at Stuart.

"There wouldn't have been anything to count if it wasn't for 'that fella there'," replied Burt not disguising his sarcasm.

"Okay, just checking. The assembly hall's a mess, the Swiss and Scandinavian guys are working their way through it with our help. We identified five bombs in their cradles. They're pretty much intact, the outer casing protected them. There's a sixth that's pretty badly damaged on the test bed but again the core casing protected it and there's no radiation leak. Pretty lucky I suppose. It's a bit gory in there, blood and bits of body. I already let Washington know that I got it all buttoned down."

"You did what?" asked Carter.

"I told Washington I got it buttoned down."

"Listen bud I'm in charge of this operation and communications with Washington go through me!"

Eugene sat back in his chair and took another bite of his doughnut and exaggerated his chewing. "Yeah well you might be in charge of the Rangers but I ain't a Ranger. I work for the State Department, so I don't report to you. You just don't like the idea of me getting any credit do you."

"You son of a bitch." Carter started to stand but was stopped by Stuart's palm on his forearm.

"I have the inventory here, supplied by the South African Government," said Stuart. "Your inventory is wrong. There should be seven complete bombs. You only accounted for six. Where is the other?"

"Yes," said Carter, "Perhaps you'd like to contact Washington and tell them you lost one."

Eugene stopped chewing. "What do you mean?"

"We came here by the back route," continued Stuart. "On our way we encountered some vehicles, including a heavy container coming in the opposite direction. They didn't stop and they were very hostile. I think there's a good chance the container contained the last bomb."

"Bullshit, we only got your word for that."

"Burt Zimmerman cut in. "Unless you got a better explanation I'm inclined to go along with Stuart here."

Eugene got to his feet tipping his chair backwards onto the floor. "I'll find that frigging bomb if it exists."

"You do just that," shot in Carter, "Or start writing your explanation to Washington.

Eugene stormed off. Jack looked towards Stuart. "Sorry that kid has got a bad attitude."

"Actually," corrected Burt, "if there is a seventh bomb we've all got a problem."

Hillbrow District Court, Pretoria
Monday 12th February 1990

Peter van Stardan's Advocate didn't even get the opportunity to contest the first point. The Judge, as soon as he entered the chambers, declared that the proceedings should be held *'in camera'* and ordered the public gallery cleared *'in the interests of National Security'* thus depriving van Stardan of the publicity he craved.

The Court Clerk went on to read out the charge of murder. No sooner had he finished than the Prosecuting Counsel stood and sought permission to make a special submission.

"Your Honour, we the prosecution believe the defendant to be guilty of the charge brought against him. However we also feel that, based on the defendant's recent behaviour, he may not be fit to plead. Therefore, in the interest of justice, we ask that the Court seeks a full and comprehensive psychiatric evaluation before asking the Defendant to plead."

Van Stardan's enraged Advocate was on his feet in a flash. "This is highly irregular. It is not the duty of the Prosecution to seek psychiatric evaluation. Their only concern should be getting a conviction. I object most strongly."

The Judge avoided eye contact with van Stardan's lawyer.

"It is true that the normal practice is for the Defence team to plead 'insanity' if they feel their client is unfit to plead. However that is only custom and practice. I see no reason in law why the Prosecution cannot request psychiatric evaluation. In the circumstances, particularly with regards to the reports in my possession concerning the defendant's behaviour during questioning, I am minded to grant the Prosecution's request whilst noting the objections of the Defence Counsel.

Now to the question of jurisdiction."

The Judge had already read the papers in his Chambers and his mind was set.

"The law is quite clear. A defendant will normally be tried in the Province where he is charged. The exception is that if the crime was committed outside the province in which he was charged he should be tried by the issuing authorities. The papers I have in front of me were issued by the Cape Province Public Prosecutor. I have no option but to order the defendant's removal from this jurisdiction to Cape Town." The judge's voice was calm and dispassionate.

"This is a travesty," protested van Stardan's Advocate. "This is a crude political attempt to silence my client and get him as far away from his support as possible. Its legality is dubious and it is definitely against the spirit of the law. I request that his trial be conducted here in Pretoria as the alleged crime did not occur in Cape Town."

"Neither did the alleged crime occur in Pretoria. It occurred in Limpopo Province as I understand it. I have therefore taken into account your objection but am still minded to discount the Defence request on the basis that the best forensic psychiatric facility in the country is located in Cape Town and the defendant would undoubtedly benefit from the expertise available in that facility. Cape Town it is."

Peter van Stardan sat next to his Advocate his blood boiling. Instinct told him to interject but the firm hand of the Advocate on his shoulder kept him in his seat.

"You can make your protest to the Judge in Cape Town," continued the Judge. "If he sends your client back then I will reconsider the position at that time but not before."

"This is an absolute outrage, a disgrace." The Advocate was pushing the boundaries as far as he could.

The Judge nodded to the chief Usher who stepped forward and stood directly in front of the Advocate, a silent threat.

"If I order you removed from the court you will have to appear before the Bar Committee and answer for your actions," added the Judge. "If you wish to continue representing your client or any other client in the future for that matter, I suggest you sit down and respect the Court."

The Advocate tried another tack. "Then may I request that the transfer of my client be delayed for fourteen days so that I may have time to consult with him?" The Advocate knew that fourteen days would give him enough time to formulate a strategy and lodge an appeal with a higher Court.

"You can consult with your client for as long as you like," conceded the Judge, "So long as it is in Cape Town. I order the prisoner removed by the most expedient method, tonight if possible."

The Advocate persisted. "The suggestion is my client is insane. My Lord I ask you to look at him. He is as sane as you or I. He does not need to be sent to the far ends of the country for assessment for something so absurdly incorrect. This is just a cynical attempt by agents of the Government to stifle political dissent."

"I suggest you limit your comments to your own sphere of expertise and leave others better qualified to pronounce on your client's sanity. Take the prisoner down." The Judge stood and left the Court Room.

Drakensberg
Thursday 1st March 1990

Uniformed men stood at ease in a double line facing their commanding officer. In the valley the setting sun cast gloomy shadows. To increase his diminutive stature Daniel Okra stood on an upturned packing case. Uncharacteristically he was contemplating his words before he spoke. Okra had been left in charge by Peter van Stardan, now a prisoner of the State. Okra felt the burden pressing down on his shoulders. He would try to draw on Afrikaner folklore for his inspiration.

"Men it is a difficult time. We are betrayed from within by our political leaders. Weak men have given way and everything that we and our forefathers have achieved is threatened. The leaders that we once trusted are preparing to hand over the reins of power to our enemies without even a fight. They have been taken in by the Western mantra of 'one man one vote'.

We have stood strong and have not left the path that our forefathers pointed out for us and you, all of you, have proved your loyalty. It is true however that in the last few days we have suffered setbacks. Our plan to lead an uprising was thwarted at the final minute and our leader is now a prisoner. But it is not the end. Our nation has faced difficult times in the past and has come through victorious. In my heart I know that this will be the case again. We need only stand firm in our beliefs until the time is right to strike.

Until that time comes we must remain concealed but ready. So today I will ask you to take off your uniforms, return to your homes and wait until the call comes, as surely it will. I ask you to do this for the sake not only of our country but also for our children who should not be denied their inheritance because of the actions of weak men."

In disciplined unity the men, their thoughts fixed on the uncertain future, listened as the National Anthem was played on a tape recorder.

British Ambassador's Residence, Pretoria
Thursday 1st March 1990

An Embassy car took Duncan to the airport. His leg was still in plaster. The de-briefing had taken place at the Ambassador's residence just outside Pretoria. It had taken two days, much longer than expected. Duncan was anxious to get away; he wanted to get back to Stirling Farm and his family. He'd only been persuaded to stay on by the promise of a private plane to take him back to Paarl Airport and the Okavango.

Ralph Foulkes, almost purring like a cat, had been given the honour of writing up the final report. Stuart and Duncan had sunk a few Castle beers. Jane was there but a little quiet, inclined to watch more than participate. Duncan sensed sadness in her demeanour. The parting hug was a little tighter than it might have been, the embrace longer than expected and, as their eyes locked for a while he thought he saw the trace of a tear.

"Good luck," Duncan had said to her. "You'll be glad to get back to Cheltenham."

"Not so sure about that," she'd replied. "I'll miss being out here."

"Well maybe it's not all over yet. Might see you again, you never know, it's a funny old world. You'll always be welcome at Stirling Farm! Keep in touch won't you?"

"I promise I will."

For a fleeting moment Duncan felt warmth inside that was quickly followed by a wave of guilt. Nobody would ever replace Elizabeth. He turned to Stuart and offered his hand. The handshake turned into a clasp.

"I'll bet my bottom dollar that we haven't heard the last of this lot. It's in the hands of the United Nations and that's a guarantee of a cock-up."

Duncan wanted his return to be a new start. They were all waiting for him when he arrived. James and Maggie stood in front, behind was Mary Scobie and beside her a freshly shaved Gus smiled.

James and Maggie ran forward and hugged their father. Coming back had rekindled old thoughts. Stoically James and Maggie had taken their loss but for long enough they'd lived under a pall of gloom. He'd not concluded his business in South Africa. Elizabeth had been partially avenged but for now there was nothing more he could do. Duncan knew as a family they had to move on. He hoped they would never forget their mother but they had to put the past where it belonged and get on with living. Duncan struggled to express his hopes in words. He needn't have worried.

The thought had hardly settled in his mind when he was presented with the unlikely apparition of Morgan and Tembo pushing a handmade cart of some kind around the house. Gus walked forward and jumped into the driver's seat.

"What on earth is that?" laughed Duncan, unable to believe his eyes as Gus over steered in a bend and the cart tipped to one side spilling him on to the sandy ground.

"It's a mini hovercraft," shouted Tembo, Morgan, Gus, Mary and the children in unison.

"Or a model of it in any case," corrected Mary, "And we have been waiting for you so we can get the project on the road!"

"What project?"

Everybody gathered around shouting together.

"Please, please," said Duncan. "Just one of you talk."

Mary pushed to the front. "Gus here," she said pointing to the old man now sitting cross legged in the dust grinning, "Gus here has lost his plane, his licence and his job as well. He used to make a living spraying for mosquitoes around the game reserves but the crash in the Kalahari put paid to it all."

"I know," replied Duncan. "Perhaps if I had had a word with the British or even the Americans they might have helped him out."

"No good," said Mary. "He's too old to go back flying." She pointed to him, "He's hardly safe on the ground anymore! He should have stopped flying years ago."

"We've got a better plan," said James. "I read about a little hovercraft being used in the swamps of South America. We reckon if we build one here and put a tank of insecticide on it, Gus can still spray around the swamps and charge the people in the game reserves just the same."

"What makes you think firstly that it will work and secondly that the customers will still pay?" asked Duncan.

"We asked them," replied Morgan displaying his broadest white smile. "We already have some contracts for next season."

"What do you mean you have contracts, you don't have a hovercraft yet?"

"We thought you'd help out with that," said Tembo displaying embarrassing amounts of childish enthusiasm.

"I don't even know what one looks like," protested Duncan.

"I have some plans," chipped in Gus. "Bought them from a UK company called Ferranti."

"If we can get this going it will solve the cash problem on the farm and we should also be able to spray around the native villages free of charge. Think of the lives that will save. All we need is you to make it work," said Tembo.

"Oh, I don't know. I'm really tired, I just want to rest."

Everybody stood and looked at Duncan in silence. It was a question of who would break first.

Duncan gently closed his eyes and shook his head from side to side. "I'll take a look in the morning," he sighed.

The group erupted.

Valkenberg Psychiatric Hospital, Cape Town
Wednesday 14th February 1990

Valkenberg had been receiving psychiatric patients of all races since it opened in 1891 but they'd always been segregated: Whites and Blacks. Valkenberg was also part of the Cape Town Medical School, teaching doctors of all races. The system was cumbersome under Apartheid. White medical students could attend the autopsy of a black woman but it was considered to be immoral, even disgusting in some people's eyes, for a black medical student to attend the autopsy of a white woman. Black doctors were not allowed to see naked Whites, not even dead ones.

While racial segregation of patients and medical staff remained for sane patients it quickly disappeared for the mentally impaired. The abandonment of Apartheid in mental healthcare was in the vanguard.

When Peter van Stardan arrived at Valkenberg he was not aware that Apartheid was disintegrating in the State psychiatric system. The transitional period was difficult for staff and patients as they struggled to understand. It was a time when traditional values and practices that had been inoculated since birth were being jettisoned without any clarity as to what would replace them.

It felt like an eternity but it was actually only for the first two days he was kept in a solitary cell on Ward 20. The square windowless room was bright, its walls freshly painted, the floor covered with thick linoleum. There was no furniture other than a mattress on the floor that acted as his bed and two large lidded plastic buckets, for him to carry out his ablutions. The heavy door was fitted with a large opening grill and a spy hole. There was always electric light, mostly it was bright but sometimes it was dull. Peter thought it must be night time when it was dull. Often he fancied that he caught sight of a prying eye in the spy hole. A black orderly brought food regularly. It was always delivered in plastic crockery with a wooden spoon and passed through the opening grill; there was always water. The orderly wouldn't pass the food over unless Peter handed back the used utensils through the hatch. Peter didn't know what frequency he got fed, they'd taken his watch, but he never felt hungry.

On the second day he heard the keys rattle in the lock. The door opened slightly and a foot slid empty fresh sanitary buckets into the cell. Peter passed out the used ones and the door quickly slammed shut.

A little while later a white male nurse came into the cell. Two other white male nurses stood by the open door, watching but not participating as Peter had observations taken: temperature and blood pressure. He couldn't understand why; he thought perhaps they needed to do it to convince themselves that this was a hospital. He didn't fight, he tried to remain calm, he knew he needed time to come to terms with the situation.

Peter thought he would have gone mad if he couldn't hear the voice of Alfred Smidt. Alfred told him he needed to make a plan and so long as the voice came Peter knew he could manage. Alfred had warned Peter that he wasn't to tell anybody about his visits under any circumstances.

On the third day the light had only just changed from dull to bright when the door opened. Van Stardan expected the nurse but instead there was a white coated doctor. "Stand," he'd said. "My name is Dr Richardson. I am part of the team assessing you."

Peter got to his feet slowly.

"Today you will be allowed to walk around the ward. You will take your meals with the others at the main table and you may associate with other patients on the ward till 9pm. Then you will be returned to this room for the night. This is a privilege. If you misbehave at any time you will be returned to this room immediately. Is this clear to you?"

Peter nodded.

"This is a mixed ward, all the wards are in this hospital; it may take some getting used to for a man of your background."

"I am used to women," replied Peter.

"I mean racially mixed not gender mixed."

Peter made no attempt to disguise his feelings. "There are Kaffirs here? I do not mix with Kaffirs!"

"Firstly you don't have any choice in the matter and secondly we don't use that word in this hospital. It's forbidden."

"And if I use it what will you do? Lock me up," Peter laughed. "Kaffirs are Kaffirs."

Dr. Richardson remained calm. "If you use it I will still do my best to look after you but you will not be making my job easy and it will affect the type of medication I prescribe for you. Furthermore your attitude will be mentioned in the final report to the Court. My honest advice is that it would be better for you if you tried to fit in."

The Doctor continued, not waiting for Peter's response. "You will be under close observation. A nurse will accompany you constantly when you are free on the ward; we call this one to one observation. If you make life difficult for your allocated nurse you will be returned to this cell immediately. Is that clear to you?"

Peter stood in silent insolence for as long as he could, pushing the Doctor to his limit before finally conceding with a nod.

"Good," said Richardson. "This is your nurse for the day."

Richardson turned and motioned to somebody, outside the cell, to step forward. "This is Nurse Eunice Hagan. She is a graduate nurse, trained in the United Kingdom. We are very fortunate to have her here. She is a very popular member of staff and is part of the team carrying out your evaluation."

"She's black!"

"Strictly speaking she's coloured. Her mother is black and her father white, but such distinctions are less important than her ability as far as I am concerned. Now, you stay with her for the day or I lock you in the cell for a while longer. Your choice."

Eunice Hagan was born Eunice Bott in Rhodesia in 1955. She was now thirty-five years old and a mother of three, a boy and two girls. When she was eleven she'd gone to the United Kingdom with her mother, father and younger sister. They'd been granted political asylum. Eunice was never quite clear what the grounds for the asylum were. The family had lived in a council house in Hackney. She did okay at school and managed to get onto a nursing course based at Chelsea and Westminster Hospital in London. After eighteen months she'd decided that general nursing was not for her, she wanted to specialise in mental health. She got a transfer to St George's Hospital in Tooting. Because she was an exile from renegade Rhodesia she was eligible for extra help with her education. On completion of her basic nursing course she obtained a bursary from the British Council to attend Nottingham University Hospital to 'upgrade' her basic nursing qualification to degree level. By that time she'd been allocated a subsidised council flat of her own in Putney. When she went to Nottingham she lived in university halls but didn't hand the keys back to the Council flat in Putney; instead she sub-let the flat at a full commercial rent and pocketed the difference for herself.

She met Paul Hagan when she was on night shift on the acute psychiatric admission's ward at Nottingham Hospital. He was a patient. She suspected him of something immediately. He was just a little bit too sharp, a little bit too aware. She watched him from a distance. It wasn't long before she found out but she bided her time for a day or two before confronting him, waiting until she caught him red-handed.

Paul had done the deal. He was just making the delivery when she struck. As he came out of the lavatory she was waiting.

"Ah, Paul," she'd said. "Come with me will you."

"Will it wait a bit?" he asked smiling, trying to bypass her.

She blocked his way. "No it won't wait!" She leaned forward and spoke quietly to him. "If you don't come I'll ring the panic bell and there'll be half a dozen people on top of you in no time. And don't think about dropping the package either. I'll shop you."

"What package?" protested Paul.

"Don't even think about it. I've been watching you for days!"

Paul had quite a lucrative little scam going on. The idea had come to him after he read that over sixty per cent of admissions to mental hospitals were drug related. He'd learnt how to project the symptoms of manic depression perfectly. He could convince any doctor that he was suicidal and a risk to himself. It was always good to get a few days in an acute ward where he'd get to work selling his goods and his goods were any illegal drug his customers wanted – as long as they could pay the going rate plus a 'hospital premium'.

Paul and Eunice became a great team, she, the perfect nurse, always willing and smiling, passing on information on the particular addictions of individual patients and he fulfilling the requirements. They did quite well for some time. Eventually she gave up her full time job and became a 'bank' nurse, getting temporary assignments in mental hospitals around North London and the Home Counties. Finally the inevitable happened. Paul was caught by an alert security guard and a remote CCTV. By feigning imminent suicide he'd managed to confuse them just long enough to make his escape. But the "game" was up. It didn't take them long to find out about all Paul's hospital admissions and it was only a matter of time before Eunice was implicated. For the quick witted pair it was time to quit the UK. Paul had a South African passport. All he had to do was marry Eunice and they were on their way to the Cape Province. Before long they were back in business at Valkenberg Psychiatric Hospital.

Of course there was no way Peter van Stardan could have known about the smiling nurse that followed him around all day, the nurse that he demeaned and insulted with every word he spoke. Eunice, like a true professional bit her tongue, she never admonished nor threatened her patient. She even smiled and bid Peter good night when she locked him back in his cell at 9pm.

It didn't take long for Paul to organise things once Eunice had told him how van Stardan treated her. Just before midnight somebody stopped at the door of Peter's cell, silently slid the key into the lock and twisted it anti-clockwise. Peter never heard a thing. He didn't wake till he felt the full weight of a man on his back and strong arms holding him. He was still disorientated when the gag was tied and the pillow case pulled over his head. Four pairs of hands picked him up and carried him out of his cell down the corridor and into the soundproofed padded cell at the end of the corridor. Inside was a four legged table, thirty-six inches by thirty-six inches, ready and waiting. The men knew what they were doing. They'd done it before to others. They forced Peter to stand facing the table. He felt his feet being pulled apart and could hear the gaffer tape being peeled off the role as his ankles were taped to the bottom of the table legs. Then he was pushed over, his face resting on the table, wrists pulled tight and taped to the other two table legs. His hospital pyjamas were ripped from him. He couldn't move, fully exposed stretched over the table. A hand came up between his legs and grabbed his genitals and squeezed. He wanted to scream but couldn't. It was as if he'd been kicked in the solar plexus. He knew what was coming and tried to wriggle free but it was useless. The first man came from behind and penetrated him. There were no words spoken but Peter, in his mind, smelt Kaffir. He vomited into the pillow case. He thought he was going to choke. He arched his neck backward and fought for breath. The second man came into him and pumped hard. The pain was not so bad when the third man entered. By the time he'd finished Peter was beginning to stir.

Peter didn't understand the anatomy of a man that well. He didn't realise the prostate gland was located very close to the anus and that it was possible to stimulate the prostate by penetration. He didn't understand why by the time the fourth man had finished he was completely hard. That man had put his hand between Peter's legs and grasped his penis. Peter couldn't help himself, it took only a few strokes and there was an involuntary eruption of sperm. The humiliation, the violation, was complete. The men laughed.

"If you speak of this you will receive the same again. Keep your mouth shut. Understand?" All Peter could do was nod before he passed out.

A soft hand shook him, gently rocking, trying to wake him. "Peter, come now it is time to get up, you have been asleep for hours."

He opened his eyes to see the smiling face of Eunice. "Is anything wrong Peter, you don't appear to be very well?"

For a while he tried to decide if it was just a nightmare but quickly realised it was not. The pain was real, so real. What had happened was real. He wanted to scream. He wanted to tell somebody. He looked at Eunice.

She cut him off. "Peter, I think it better if you stay here for today. Rest, get your strength back. You should not speak, not to anybody; it would do more harm than good. Do you understand that Peter?"

"I do," he muttered.

"I hope you do Peter, I hope you do."

The next day there was a smell of hashish around Ward 20. The day after that came Peter's case review. It took place in the doctor's meeting room, Peter was not there. Dr Richardson addressed the team. He had no good news to report.

"According to the case notes the patient is a paranoid schizophrenic. Unfortunately I have been unable to engage with him, he has cut himself off altogether. There is a total absence of cognitive behaviour and social interaction. Under such circumstances it is impossible to form a professional opinion. I think we have no option but to report this to the Court and seek an indefinite amount of time to carry out the review."

Eunice smiled and nodded in affirmation at Dr Richardson's words. "I have to agree," she said. "I have been unable to communicate at even the most basic level with Mr van Stardan."

Peter's lawyer had visited and told him the outcome of the review. Peter was not surprised. He gave in to the inevitable, what logic he retained telling him that resistance was futile. To observers he appeared disconnected, not interested in his surroundings. But in his own mind he was obeying instructions; watching, listening, planning. Alone in his room at night he would have long discussions with Alfred Smidt. Peter believed it was these talks that kept him sane. His only comfort came when he was with Alfred Smidt. Alfred always told him the truth even if it was bad news and Peter always felt better for it. It was time to use the weapon of Armageddon, just like it said in the bible. Once he understood the message he felt better, knowing there was a purpose to his life. He knew he must play his part, he must take the lead, he still had work to do and he would not let Alfred down. He would do what was necessary and that made his present life bearable.

BOOK FOUR
Downtown Manhattan
Three Years Later
Monday 6th September 1993

Most people in the know considered the Rib Eye served at the Rodeo Steak House to be the best in town, which was good even if the accolade did fall somewhat short of the claim on the immodest banner, printed at the head of the oversized menu, proclaiming them to be the best in the world. Still it was a good place to bring people if you wanted to impress or intimidate.

Eugene Forester was exhausted and irritable. He'd put in a full day's work in the White House before slipping away and catching the NY express. It was dark when he'd arrived at Penn Station and he'd only had time to book into his hotel and freshen up before setting off for the restaurant. It was only two blocks so he walked. There was an unusual sharpness to the air, a chill not normally associated with September in New York. He pushed open the restaurant door and a blast of warm air hit him, laden with odours of onions and smoke.

The maître d' greeted him and after taking his coat lead him towards the back of the restaurant, weaving through a labyrinth of tightly packed tables. Eugene had wanted a private room but the restaurant couldn't accommodate; the best they could do was a booth tucked away at the rear of the dining room. His guest had already arrived and was sitting on one of the booth's dark stained bench seats. The combination of dark wood, dull red leatherette upholstery, subdued lighting and air that was heavy with smoke raised images of illegal speakeasies from the twenties. It was an appropriate venue.

His guest stood and offered his hand. Eugene shook it without enthusiasm or a smile.

"A waiter will be along shortly to take your order," said the maître d'.

"Just get me a large beer and a twelve ounce rib eye, well done, with a side of fries, responded Eugene.

The maitre d' looked to his guest.

Taken by surprise he responded in a heavily accented voice, unmistakably Germanic. "The same for me please." Eugene's guest barely concealed his disappointment, he'd been looking forward to a leisurely stroll through the menu.

"I have a copy of the final draft of the report with me if you want to see it," said the guest quickly recovering his composure.

Eugene took the papers and read through them quickly. Ten minutes passed in silence. "This is the same as the President's copy I read this afternoon."

"Was he happy with it?" asked the stranger smiling, flattered by the thought that his report might have been read so promptly by the most important man in the world.

"No, because I didn't pass it on to him."

"Why? Was there something wrong?"

Eugene, although able to kowtow with the best when necessary, never minced his words when talking to those he considered to be his inferiors. "It's taken you, and the rest of the International Atomic Energy Authority, nearly four years to produce a document that could have been written in three days and even then you have come up with the wrong conclusion. That's why the US has no respect for what goes on in that UN building on the East Side. You've got to do better than that."

"We have merely written the facts," defended the stranger.

"And interpreted them wrongly. You conclude that only six South African nuclear weapons were dismantled."

"That is true, but we clearly state that there were sufficient components to manufacture another weapon."

"Your report leaves open the possibility that there might be another weapon in existence. That is politically unacceptable."

"But we can only draw on the facts."

"Listen bud, I was there. I know what the facts are. We got all the bombs. You have got to write that in the final report."

"I need some evidence to corroborate that statement before I can persuade the committee to draw that conclusion."

Eugene drew a few folded sheets of paper from his inside pocket. "I've done the work that you should have done." He passed the papers to his guest.

The waiter arrived, placing their meals and drinks on the table."

"Read that," said Eugene, "That gives you enough supporting evidence." Eugene cut into his steak and ate while his guest read the document.

"The tabulations on the back support the text and conclusions," said Eugene between mouthfuls. "I had our best men carry out the work. It is totally reliable."

Ten minutes later the guest lifted his head from the document. "I need more time to study the contents."

"Take as long as you want, so long as your report is ready for full distribution with the right conclusions on the 9th September, that's three days from now. You can say the South Africans had seven atomic devices but you also have to say you have accounted for them all. What's more you will say you have analysed the production of all South African highly enriched uranium and this tallies with what you found in the field. No ambiguity. You have to do that or the whole South African peace process will fall apart and you will get the blame. Do you want that?"

The guest shook his head, "No."

"So that's settled then, you'll make the corrections to your report." It was a statement not a question.

"I will do what I can and I apologise for disappointing you. I hope this won't affect our arrangement. Your support is essential for my new appointment."

Eugene wouldn't and couldn't say what he was thinking. He would never tell anybody that his meteoric rise from Third Secretary in the South African Embassy to Principle Advisor in the White House, with direct access to the President, was primarily due to the credit he had claimed for neutralising South Africa's nuclear weapons. If it emerged that he'd given false assurances to the Nation's Chief Executive his decline would be more rapid than his rise. For Eugene's sake the IAEA's report could have only one finding; the entire South African nuclear arsenal was accounted for. Eugene was not going to stand idly by as some anonymous technical bureaucrat held the balance of his career in his hand. He had a plan and was secretly pleased with his own astuteness. Keeping close to the issue he discovered that the man commissioned to write the report was an ambitious Swiss German who sought to become the next head of the IAEA's, the highest and most prestigious position for a physicist in the world and who recognised that obtaining the patronage of the United States would do him no harm. It was a natural, if uneasy, trade off.

"If the report is satisfactory I don't see any reason for me to change my point of view." With this less than conclusive reassurance Eugene stood.

"I'll have to leave you to finish your meal alone. I have pressing matters to attend to." He threw four twenty dollar bills on the table. "That should cover everything. Be sure to let me see the report before it goes out."

Valkenberg Psychiatric Hospital, Cape Town
Wednesday 9th October 1993

It wasn't every night, it wasn't every week but it did happen again and again and there was a pattern. Alfred Smidt had been right, Hell on Earth had arrived; for him at least. Peter had got used to the actual act, he could manage that now. If he didn't resist it was over quickly. It was always the same male nurses. They weren't rough anymore and they didn't bother to hide their faces. They were certain Peter was too terrified and too far gone to talk. They believed Peter's mind had left for a different place and it wasn't coming back. They were wrong.

On the third Wednesday of each month Peter received a visit. He was still a criminal, albeit an insane one, awaiting trial and was allowed access to a lawyer. Peter's lawyer travelled a long way to see him, all the way from Ladysmith and the meetings were always held in private.

Knowing what was going to happen in advance helped him to devise a plan and he was able to pass on the plan piecemeal on the third Wednesday of each month.

The solution was in the staff rotas. The nursing shifts were worked out four weeks in advance and were posted on a notice board at the nurse's station. From the communal area it was possible for patients to see through the glass observation window into the nurses' station and view the lists. Eunice Hagan organised the staff rota lists and regularly put herself on the unpopular night shift. It would normally be a weekend. The support staff on nights with her were always the same four male nurses.

On the first of her night shifts Eunice would let her husband Paul on to the ward. He came to collect the amphetamines that had been stolen from the pharmacy and to take orders – for the inmate's recreational drugs. The second night was always quiet. On the third night Paul would return. He always brought hash and whisky for the 'staff' party. That was when Peter was taken to the padded cell.

Daniel Okra couldn't get everything into place until the 1st April. It had been difficult, he didn't have contacts in Cape Town and it was too dangerous to use contacts from the Brotherhood. It took a lot of quiet observation before he found a way.

Getting into the hospital was easy; the hospital security wasn't great. The flaw was in goods being delivered. The kitchen received its food from a network of suppliers. Fresh vegetables were delivered by Golden Cape Fruit & Veg. They used a covered Hino truck for the deliveries; it was such a frequent visitor to the hospital that the guards just waved it through, never giving much thought to what it might contain. "Who would want to break into a mental hospital after all?" they joked. Okra found it would be easy to get men onto the grounds.

Getting on to Peter's ward was more complex. Hot meals were delivered to all the wards in insulated trolleys, directly from the central kitchen. It was one of these trolleys that two strange men pushed towards Ward 20 that night. The food trolley was aluminium. It stood over five feet tall, was four feet deep and five feet wide with double doors on the front. The wheels were rubberised making it an easy push for the two men.

It was just after 7pm when Eunice heard the bell at the service door ring. She'd only taken charge of the Ward minutes before and was still sitting in the control room. On the security monitor she could see the two men with the trolley waiting at the entrance.

She pushed the intercom button. "What do you want?"

"Got the food for Ward 20."

"It's already been delivered. Everybody's eaten hours ago."

"It's got Ward 20 written on the paper work."

"The patients on this ward eat at 6pm. They let us know if they don't get their food on time."

"Well it belongs to somebody. They never make too much in the kitchen. Can you do us a favour and give the kitchen a call and ask where we should take the food to? Bet somebody is getting hungry."

Eunice sighed. "Okay, hold on."

She picked up the phone and dialled the extension for the kitchen. It rang and rang without reply.

"Nobody's answering," she said her finger on the intercom button again.

"We'll have to go back and see what's going on. They're most probably chilling out in the rest room. Can we leave this trolley with you, in the hall, save us pushing it all the way back? We'll find out where it's supposed to go and come back for it."

Eunice shook her head and pushed the lock release for the first door. The men pushed the trolley through the first set of double doors and stopped in the vestibule whilst the first doors closed and automatically locked. Eunice then pressed the release for the inner doors and the men pushed the trolley through to the inner hall.

"Just push it up against the wall."

"Thanks for that," said one of the men as they exited the way they had come in. "We'll see you later."

"Yeah, right," replied Eunice turning away, taking little notice.

By 9 pm Eunice had completed her rounds, all the medication had been doled out and the patients were locked in their rooms. None of the inmates complained or probably even noticed that their doses had been bumped up for the evening. Eunice wanted a quiet night and the 'chemical cosh' was pretty useful in providing that. By prior arrangement she was back at the service door by 10pm to let in Paul. He was never late. She pushed the button for the outer doors. Paul stepped out of the shadows and into the intermediate hall and then into the building proper unaware that he was being watched by the men that had delivered the food trolley earlier. One of the men pulled out a hand radio. He pushed the button, two short, two long, two short. Inside the food trolley Daniel Okra held his radio close to his face. The sound was muted. But he saw the light flash and knew what it meant.

Van Stardan was locked in his room, waiting. He'd calculated they'd come for him tonight. He prayed as he waited. He asked God that it be tonight that Okra led the attack that would bring about his release from prison. The seconds passed slowly. He guessed it was gone eleven thirty when he heard the sound of footsteps coming down the corridor. His heart began to beat faster. Normally only two came to fetch him. The footsteps stopped outside his cell. He got ready. The observation hatch opened and a shaft of bright light pierced the darkened room.

"He's standing there ready," said a voice. "I told you he's gagging for it now."

"Yeah well he's going to be disappointed tonight," said the second voice. "There's fresher meat down the corridor. Why have mutton when lamb's available?"

It hadn't occurred to Peter that there might be another to take his place. It wasn't part of the plan. He had to be the chosen one, he had to give the signal to those who waited outside, the signal that would start the plan.

The men moved away from his door. Peter began to panic at the implications. Even if Okra was there he would not attack without the signal. "Take me," he shouted after the men. "I am ready. Take me."

Peter could hear laughter in the corridor.

"I told you he really wanted it. The dirty bugger enjoys it. He should be paying us."

"Never thought about that," said the second voice. "Perhaps we could charge him. That would be really funny." The laughter faded as the men moved further down the corridor.

Peter listened helplessly. He heard a hurried shuffle, and then a suppressed shout. There was a scuffle outside his cell. He could hear it clearly.

"Fuck, the bastard's bitten me," said a voice. "Eunice, give him another injection to calm him down, he's too lively."

Peter heard Eunice grunt. There was a pause.

Eunice spoke. "I'm ready, hold him down."

"Not too much now Eunice. We want him alive. Necrophilia isn't one of my fantasies."

If it wasn't for the closed door Peter would have seen a young man on the floor being held down by the two male nurses. Eunice was holding a hypodermic needle.

Their victim was very troubled, he'd truly earned his place in the psychiatric unit. But the doctors had missed one of his conditions.

Tryparophopia was its proper name. Most people just call it fear of needles. When he saw Eunice coming at him with the hypodermic his reaction was immediate. With an incredible surge of physical strength the victim broke free of the restraining arms and in a moment was on his feet. He hesitated only for a moment, eyes darting, seeking an avenue of escape. The second delay was too long. The two men were back on their feet and now joined by two more male nurses. The struggle was short and violent. Eunice stabbed the needle into the young man's thigh and pushed the plunger, giving him the full dose.

During the struggle nobody in the corridor noticed that the venetian blinds of the window had become dislodged. Outside, in the shrubbery, Okra's men saw the light flooding out and mistook it for the signal from Peter van Stardan they'd been waiting for, the signal to initiate the operation.

In the food trolley Daniel Okra waited patiently. When the light flashed again his heart fluttered. He slipped the mask over his head and released the trolley doors. Out of the trolley he screwed the silencer on to the Ingram and made his way to the nurse's station. He knew that nobody would be there; all the staff would be upstairs. He pressed the electronic door release. The two men slid into the building. Inside they didn't talk, but went straight to the food trolley, collected their own weapons and one extra they were to carry upstairs for van Stardan.

The three men knew the way; the Advocate had drawn a map for them. He'd also made sure they knew where van Stardan's room was. Their sneakers were silent on the linoleum floor. They took the stairs two at a time. Okra led, hurrying down the corridor counting the doors. He stopped suddenly. The door to van Stardan's cell was locked. It should have been open.

Inside Peter van Stardan heard the door being tried. He guessed who it was and whispered. "Go to the padded cell, they have the keys."

Okra and the men moved. They had just come to the turning for the padded cell when, almost from nowhere, she walked into them, directly into the arms of Okra. His reaction was instinctive, without hesitation. He grabbed her, forcing her surprised body to the ground whilst stifling her scream with the flat of his hand. He knew who she was from the Advocate's description.

"Open van Stardan's cell," he demanded without releasing his grip.

She nodded, terror clear in her eyes.

Her hand shook as she slid the key into the lock and opened the door. Van Stardan stepped through the opening. Okra made a half attempt at a salute.

"No time for that," he said. "You have my weapon?"

The Ingram was passed to him. He immediately flipped the safety and raised the barrel to Eunice's head and pulled the trigger. There was no loud crack, hardly even a pop, more like a sudden release of air, the silencer ensured that. Eunice stood motionless for a short while, her eyes wide open. The neat red dot in the middle of her forehead had a narrow black halo caused by powder residue. Behind her, on the magnolia painted wall was an Andy Warhol burst of white bone, grey matter and red flesh, splattered in a grotesque death pattern. At some point her legs crumpled and she went down in a straight line collapsing on to the floor. Even van Stardan's rescuers were shocked by what they'd witnessed, but there was no time to think about it.

"Wait here," said van Stardan.

He strode off down the corridor in the direction of the padded cell. A few moments later he returned. Without a word he walked past the men on his way to the exit, the only evidence of what he'd done a curl of smoke coming from the Ingram's barrel and the acrid smell of cordite in the corridor.

In was not until the morning when the day shift arrived that the alarm was raised. They found the security doors wide open but not a soul in sight. They called Central Security and waited. The search revealed that most of the patients were still locked in their cells but a female nurse, four male nurses and one patient had been murdered - executed by single shots to the head.

The authorities tried to keep a lid on things but it didn't take long for a young reporter from the Cape Argos to pick up the story. Because the authorities wouldn't co-operate he got it a bit wrong. It was presented in his newspaper as a drugs related massacre. There was no mention in the article that a patient had escaped. That suited the authorities.

Foreign and Commonwealth Office, London
Friday 5th November 1993

Stuart walked across Westminster Bridge from the South Embankment, a walk he'd taken many times before over the years. He felt a few drops of drizzle on his face. He lengthened his stride hoping to get to his destination in Whitehall before the few drops of rain turned into a downpour. He knew that rain was forecast yet he'd still decided to risk it on foot. He increasingly bemoaned his sedentary position and even a little walk was becoming a welcome break from the tedium of the office.

It had become a force of habit. Despite the threat of rain, halfway across the bridge he paused to look down on the empty riverside terrace of the House of Commons. The contempt he held for the members of the House had not diminished over the years and he was still glad he'd chosen a military career. There was an irony though. Now that he'd achieved 'seniority', the prospect of a Peerage in respect of his long and faithful service to the Crown was of concern to him. If he accepted the offer when it came it would mean he'd acquiesced and joined 'them'. If he refused he would be rejecting the gratitude of the Crown that he'd served and sacrificed so much for over the years.

He pressed on. Crossing Parliament Square he realised he'd beaten the rain but he didn't slacken his pace for the last couple of hundred yards. He was looking forward to the meeting.

Stuart thought all was not well with Sir Basil Parker Smythe. He was thinner, his skin had taken on a grey pallor and his cheeks were beginning to look a little sunken. But the welcoming smile was genuine.

"Stuart, so good to see you. Come through, the others are here already. Sir Basil led the way through the carved double doors to the meeting. Ralph Foulkes stood with his back to them giving Jane Ashton a history lesson.

"This building and this room are of great historical significance to the United Kingdom. Some of the history is depicted by the pictures that hang on the walls. There are three pictures in honour of Nelson," said Ralph pointing to each in turn. "The Battle of the Nile, The Battle of Copenhagen and of course Trafalgar. Wellington is honoured by only one picture however." He pointed at the giant oil painting of the field at the culmination of the Battle of Waterloo. "But what a picture!"

Ralph continued with infectious enthusiasm. "Most people don't realise that although Nelson and Wellington were contemporaries they actually only met once and that was in the anti-room that you just came through. Apparently their conversation was limited to grunted good mornings and half-hearted salutes. That is what happens, I'm told, when one prima donna meets another."

"Very good," interrupted Sir Basil, "but I really think we should be getting on."

Ralph turned around to face his chief and Stuart. "I'm sorry I didn't realise that you'd arrived." Ralph offered his hand to Stuart who shook it warmly.

"Ralph has been acting Under Secretary in this Department for some time. His position is to be confirmed shortly."

"Congratulations," said Stuart.

"I always knew he had it in him," added Sir Basil. "Never a doubt in my mind."

Both Stuart and Ralph knew the truth and as their smiling eyes met they shared a twinkle of bemusement and a raised eyebrow.

Stuart turned his attention to Jane. "Jane, good to see you again." The greeting was warm and genuine. Initially there was a little hesitation as they stepped towards each other and shook hands.

"Good to see you again too," she replied. "It's been a long time."

"Shall we begin?" asked Sir Basil taking his seat at the head of the table. "I'll start with the customary warning. This meeting is unofficial. It is the result of a communication by Miss Ashton in her role as '*Tulip*'. The report she produced has been studied at the highest level and I have been asked to decide if there is merit in what is written and if so what should be done about it. I will hand over to Miss Ashton so that she can bring you up to speed Mr Cameron. Ralph and I are already familiar with the contents of the report."

Jane smiled and looked directly at Stuart. "I've been keeping an eye on the situation in South Africa. The basic protocol as agreed between the US, the UK and South Africa is being adhered to. Nelson Mandela remains free and no longer encourages terrorism, De Klerk, president of South Africa has lifted the ban on the ANC and generally speaking the progress towards democracy is on track. In fact we have the rather bizarre situation of a former convicted terrorist, Nelson Mandela and the leader of a renegade racist state, Mr De Klerk being nominated to receive the joint Nobel peace prize. To be truthful that is a bit of a side issue and of no major consequence. Of more significance is another issue. In April Chris Hani an important figure in the ANC was assassinated by a 'rogue' white South African. This incident had the potential to derail the whole peace process and demonstrate the fragility of the current situation. Only the intervention of Nelson Mandela himself stopped the black South Africans going on the rampage. The country is actually on a knife edge."

"Okay, but the incident has passed?" asked Stuart.

"Yes, but there's potentially a more serious one on the horizon. Our old friend Peter van Stardan has escaped custody and is on the loose and it looks like he's not too happy. In fact for a while we thought that it was him behind the Chris Hani assassination. But it wasn't."

"I never heard about van Stardan's escape. What happened?"

"He was being held in a psychiatric unit in Cape Town. There was an organised break out and several of van Stardan's jailers were executed in a rather cold bloodied manner."

"Why didn't I hear about it?"

"The South African's weren't exactly shouting about it from the roof tops and the whole incident was clouded in a drugs and illicit sex scandal. I only came across it by accident."

"So van Stardan's on the loose and he has some kind of support group behind him?"

"He might have more than that," replied Jane, "He might still have control of a nuclear weapon – if there's a stray one still about."

"What do you mean if there's one still about? The IAEA should have taken care of that surely?"

"Their report came out on 9th September this year. It says there isn't a problem, that they have recovered six bombs and parts for a seventh. Case closed. They're quite emphatic, everything has been accounted for. And the truth is that conclusion suits a lot of people."

"Did they find that truck Duncan and I saw?"

"Not even mentioned in the report."

"Did they take into account Duncan's statement; he was first at Vastrap with Tembo and Morgan?"

"Not mentioned."

"Have you taken it up with the Americans? We were dealing with a couple of good guys in the CIA."

"The Americans aren't talking about the issue; somebody has put a block on it. And apparently it's not coming from Langley, it's coming from the White House."

"So why are we getting involved?" Stuart shifted in his chair.

"Mrs T at No 10 read my report and she's worried. Jane pulled a sheaf of papers from her briefcase.

"Let me summarise my thoughts.

Peter van Stardan has declared that he's not going to let South Africa fall into black African hands. Taking that simple statement at face value I applied basic criminal investigation techniques to work out various scenarios. All crimes must have motivation, means and opportunity.

Van Stardan is highly motivated, there is no doubting that. Secondly he has the means, he definitely has a trained and armed support group and, as far as I'm concerned, taking everything into account in all probability he also has a nuclear weapon. More than that, he has previously demonstrated his willingness to use a nuclear weapon."

"Okay, I go along with that," said Stuart. "Where is his opportunity?"

"Well it is conjecture but a great opportunity would be the Presidential inauguration. Setting a nuclear bomb off in Pretoria at that time would take out the entire new black leadership and what van Stardan believes to be the traitorous whites who surrendered the country. And before you ask I have no evidence."

"So without any evidence why does the PM want us involved?"

Sir Basil cut in. "Two reasons, firstly she has a high regard for reports that come from 'Tulip' and secondly she's got an invitation to the inauguration! That leaves her with a dilemma."

"Ah! Got you. The PM doesn't attend and that's a snub for the new president and black government, a diplomatic disaster. She does go and it's possibly her last public engagement! Interesting. What's expected of us?"

Sir Basil continued. "Firstly the Parliamentary Committee has to be appraised of the situation to ensure that if anything goes wrong we are in the clear."

"Cover our backsides before we start I think you mean."

Sir Basil smiled. "Then the best thing would be if you went off and found Peter van Stardan or his bomb, either would do.

I have set the wheels in motion to advise the parliamentary Committee. They will see us in camera. You will be a witness. I take it you have no objection? Duncan Murdoch would also be a good witness if you could drag him in. I understand he was the first and only 'expert' to reach Vastrap before it was damaged by an explosion."

"That could be problematic."

"You don't think he'll come? He is on our side isn't he?" interjected Sir Basil.

"I suppose so but I don't know why."

Sir Basil stiffened with surprise. "Of course he's on our side. He's been fighting for Queen and Country for God knows how many years."

"No, he hasn't. He's been doing what we forced him to do and then only if his conscience will allow it."

"Explain that to me," asked Sir Basil.

"The Queen and Country you talk about did him no favours; they locked him up for life for a genuine mistake because it was politically expedient for you lot in this Department. Strictly speaking he is in breach of his parole conditions and he should be arrested when he sets foot on British soil."

"It's the first I've heard of it. And what was his crime?"

"Murder. He machine gunned the son of an Egyptian diplomat in Aden. He was seeking revenge for the death of a close friend but he shot the wrong man."

Sir Basil's face went from pale to ashen. "You are telling me that a murderer, escaped from custody, has been working for this office, for me? The press would have a field day. That would be the end of my knighthood, my pension, everything. How could this have happened?"

"Don't panic," said Jane. "I know the chap. He's very nice."

"I rather like him too," added Ralph.

"And the bare facts sound worse than they are in reality" said Stuart

Sir Basil despairingly covered his face with his hands. "The world's gone mad," he muttered. "He can't be a witness."

Stirling Farm, Okavango
Saturday 15th January 1994

It was an unusual way to make a living, but they were managing to make a success of it.

The female of the Anopheles Genus of mosquitoes feeds on blood and it is this mosquito that passes on malaria. It lays its eggs in stagnant water, suspended from a thin thread just below the surface. The surface tension of the water stops the thread from becoming detached thus ensuring the eggs don't sink to the bottom of the water. About two weeks after being laid the eggs hatch, the tiny mosquitoes climb up the thread and escape into the atmosphere to start their destructive work. It has been long known that one way of controlling mosquitoes is to spray the surface of stagnant water every couple of weeks with a detergent that breaks the surface tension of that water causing the eggs to drop to the bottom, effectively drowning the mosquito. The life cycle is broken and the population of mosquitoes in the sprayed area begins to fall rapidly. The trouble has always been dispersing the detergent over large areas. Sometimes planes sprayed from the air but it was a costly process, particularly for small plots.

Now they had a few seasons under their belt and things couldn't have been much better. Duncan was astounded at how such an improbable idea had developed into a commercial venture. But it was not without effort, ingenuity and some luck. The team was just as improbable. Gus was the brains, or at least that's what he liked to think and nobody was going to argue with him. Tembo and Morgan carried out the spraying contracts. James, now 15, had been the surprise contributor and Duncan had made things happen and struck the deals.

The plans for the first hovercraft had come from England. It was a simple design, two engines; one driving a lift fan which filled the skirt with air and raised the hovercraft eighteen inches off the ground and a second, driving a propeller enclosed in safety mesh for forward movement. Steering was achieved by vectoring the draught from the propeller by means of a joystick in the tiny one man cockpit. In trials, the hovercraft had manoeuvred well on water but the skirt had worn quickly when travelling over reeds and elephant grass. The edges of the reeds and blades of grass sliced into the rubber skirt, slicing it to threads after a few hours. Duncan tried a few different materials and, at the insistence of James, ended up substituting the rubber skirt for one made from some old conveyor canvas they'd found lying around in an abandoned mine. It did the trick.

The original idea had been to disperse the insecticide by means of a long pipe with holes in it that stretched out either side of the hovercraft. The problem with this was that the pole stuck out so far the hovercraft became impossible to steer anywhere near the vicinity of vegetation. It had been James again that came up with the solution. He'd suggested using a nozzle to pump the insecticide into the draught made by the propeller and let that do the distribution, allowing them to dispense with using the pipe altogether. Once more it worked a treat and the added bonus was that the whole machine was small enough to transport on a trailer, from customer to customer.

They'd actually made a profit in the first season. Now they were planning two more hovercraft. Their first customers had been safari lodges, then a hospital had approached asking if they'd spray the water around the grounds, then came a few other municipal buildings and even a couple of the larger farms. They struggled to keep up with demand. For the first time Stirling farm was in profit. They had money in the bank and it was possible to make plans. Duncan wanted to give electricity to the kraal huts. In his opinion even if the tribe did want to live in traditional buildings there was no reason why they shouldn't have some modern comforts and electric lights would be a good start. They did the work in the dry season themselves.

They'd converted one of the outhouses into accommodation and Gus had become a more or less a permanent feature around Stirling Farm, living there most of the time, rarely visiting his own place unless it was to collect some special tools or materials. Before the crash he'd been thought of as a miserable recluse by most people; that Gus had gone. He laughed now, as did everybody else. Duncan had observed him with Mary. They were about the same age. Duncan thought there might have been a bit of late onset romance but there was never any indication that things would progress beyond friendship.

This season, although it was now January, rains hadn't fallen on the delta itself but had fallen in abundance further north. The Okavango River was in full flood. The swamps of the delta were full of stagnant water that slowly seeped into the sub-soil and porous bedrock. Lush greenery and prolific colourful flowers were sprouting everywhere, and as if by magic game and wild animals were appearing in greater numbers than had been seen for years. Word had spread, bookings in the safari lodges were at record levels and tourists were flocking in. But with the heat and still water came the unwelcome but ubiquitous mosquito – and the business orders.

Life at Stirling Farm had settled down. There were of course all the day to day problems that had to be faced and overcome, but it was fair to say that happiness, for so long absent, was now a more frequent visitor. It had been a long process and, even now, it was a rare day when Elizabeth was not a visitor to somebody's mind.

Duncan used to spend his evenings sitting alone on the stoop. For a long time nobody wanted to disturb him believing he was in spirit with Elizabeth. Only Maggie would come and sit with her father, at first in compassionate silence. But that silence didn't last long. She began to talk, and then talk a little more and eventually her chatter became incessant. She spoke about everything and anything. Duncan was forced to pay attention. Every so often Maggie would throw in a question and low and behold Duncan if he nodded when he should have shook his head or shook his head when he should have nodded! It developed into a game with Duncan getting caught out more often than he would have liked. James and Mary, not wishing to miss out on the fun began to join in. Long statements were followed by quick fire questions. They didn't quite know what they were doing but it was effective. Duncan could no longer divide his thinking between two worlds, he had to stay sharp in the present. Nobody could say when it actually happened but at some point they all realised that despair and despondency was receding. Duncan was learning to leave Elizabeth where she was and re-enter the world occupied by the living.

The telegram was not a surprise when it came and Duncan was looking forward to the visit. It would be good to see Stuart and Jane again. He knew the reason for the visit must be important and it concerned him slightly. He hoped their presence wouldn't disturb his newly found peace and tranquillity.

"Can we forget about work till the morning," Jane had asked on their arrival at Stirling. "Let's just enjoy the rest of the day."

They'd arrived in the afternoon; they'd flown in to Maun and driven over in a hire car. It didn't take long for them to settle. They ate early; Duncan, Stuart, Jane, Mary, James and Maggie. It was a long time since Mary had had so many people around her table but she'd risen to the challenge. After food, as darkness was falling, they all moved to the stoop. Not long after Tembo and Morgan emerged from the gloom and shortly after they spotted the beam of a torchlight approaching and Gus turned up.

"Quite a party," said Stewart. "It feels like family."

"It is family and you're part of it," responded Mary. "Jane, what do you think of Africa?"

"This is so incredible but I don't know if I'd manage it – all the time."

"It couldn't be more different than the Gorbals in Glasgow, that's where I come from, but I'm not going back."

"I just love the sounds."

"We can be quiet for a while and listen. I'm sure the men can manage that," replied Mary, raising her voice for emphasis.

They all sat and listened to the night sounds of Africa: incessant insects, the distant cackle of scavenging hyena and even the occasional roar of a far off lion. There was no moon so they couldn't see animals making their way down to the now full watering hole but they could imagine the scene that was in front of them. Suddenly, close by came an insidious high pitched scream.

Jane jumped involuntarily in her wickerwork chair. "What was that?"

"A frog," replied Duncan laughing.

"I never heard a frog make a sound like that."

"They don't do it often. In fact a frog only does it once."

"Why only once?"

"It's the death croak," he continued. "Some species of frog hold a bag of air in their throat. When they die the air is released suddenly giving rise to that horrible screech. That's why we used to say that when somebody died they'd 'croaked', that's where we got the expression – from the frogs!"

"Wow, so does that mean a frog just died. How did it die?"

"I think it most probably was a snake that killed it. That's what gets most frogs around here."

Jane didn't reply at first, she just got up and walked to the edge of the stoop and peered into the darkness. After a few seconds she took the two steps down on to the gravel path. "Are there a lot of snakes around here?" she asked as she stepped forward into the darkness no more than three paces.

"Yes," replied Duncan, "And I wouldn't be walking further than that without a torch."

The snake that had taken the frog was by this time some distance away already in the process of swallowing his meal.

Unfortunately it was not the only snake in the vicinity. To Jane, wearing only flip flops, it felt like she'd stepped in a soft cowpat and she wasn't immediately alarmed, not until she felt it move. Instinctively she flicked her foot, trying to throw whatever it was away. Then she felt the bite. The fangs were small and it was more like a sting. She screamed and nobody could mistake the terror in her voice.

Duncan got to her first, jumping the two steps. Jane was already lying on the ground clutching her ankle. Gus was next, holding his torch. "Take her inside," he said.

Duncan picked up Jane's petite frame, carried her into his own bedroom and laid her on the bed. All the others, except Gus, followed.

The pain was intense; already tears were flowing down Jane's cheeks. Duncan examined the wound.

"It was small but that means nothing out here."

"Do you have anti-venom in the house?" asked Stuart.

"No. We need to get medical help quickly."

"What's quickest?"

"There's a doctor not far away but I bet he'll be in the back of the bottle store right now.. He's fond of his drink in the evening. Tembo go and fetch him."

"I'll take him in my car, it'll be quicker," said Stuart.

"I'll do what I can here," said Duncan turning his attention to Jane.

Already the flesh on her ankle around the bite was puffed up and red. She gripped the bedclothes with clenched fists in a vain attempt to ease the pain.

"Duncan," she gasped, "Will I be alright?"

Duncan didn't answer, just smiled gently at her. "Mary get me a damp towel, she's starting to burn."

Beads of sweat were forming on her forehead and her temperature was rising.

Mary came back with a bowl of water and flannel. Duncan mopped her brow. Then he loosened the top buttons on her blouse and saw how her chest was heaving. Her eyes, once crystal clear, were beginning to glaze over and dilate. Jane loosened her grip on the bedclothes and began holding her neck. Her breathing started to come in gasps. Duncan thought he could see her throat beginning to swell. As her head began to loll from side to side she tried to speak, her voice hardly above a whisper. Duncan put his head near her lips.

"I need to go home now?" her voice was barely audible and words slurred. "I'll be late I must hurry," she gasped.

"She's starting to hallucinate with the fever," said Duncan. "I'll have to try and keep her awake."

Duncan began shouting and shaking her with little effect. Her eyes rolled upwards, so all that was visible were the whites.

It seemed like an eternity before they heard the car skid to a stop outside. "Thank God," said Duncan.

Stuart and Tembo pushed the doctor into the room. "Don't worry I can do it," he said, "I have serum with me." The doctor was fighting the effects of several hours of alcohol abuse. He didn't examine her or ask any questions, just rummaged in his bag eventually finding what he wanted. With shaking hands he managed to fill a hypodermic syringe with liquid from a small vile. "Hold an arm still for me, I need to find a vein."

For a moment the doctor hesitated as he tried to focus on the white open arm, looking for the tell tale blue line of a blood vessel.

"I wouldn't let him stick that needle in her," said a voice from behind.

Duncan and Stuart turned. Gus stood in the doorway. Hanging from his hand was a dead snake about eighteen inches long.

"This is the snake that bit her," said Gus. "I saw it slither away and go back into its hole. I had to dig it up. I know this type of snake. She shouldn't have serum. It will make her worse. It might even kill her."

Duncan grabbed the doctor's wrist stopping him plunge the needle into her arm. "What do you mean?"

"It's a Bilbron's Asp. The serum will react with the venom from the snake."

"So what do we do?" asked Stuart.

"Nothing," replied Gus. "Leave her alone."

"Look at the state of her. We have to do something."

"The Bilbron is quite rare around here. It only injects a small amount of venom. It might be enough to kill an infant or somebody old I suppose but it won't do her any harm. It's just not going to be nice for her for the next forty-eight hours and she'll most probably need a couple of weeks to recover after that. But there are no recorded deaths from a Bilbron Asp."

"I don't know," said Stuart to Duncan. "She looks pretty bad to me."

Duncan looked Gus in the eye. "Are you sure?"

Gus nodded. "No doubt."

Duncan took a moment to make his decision. Once made, he spoke calmly and with clarity. "Leave her alone."

Duncan took the lead, making Jane as comfortable as he could. For the first couple of hours she tossed and turned, sometimes slipping into a sleep then suddenly awakening and rambling, talking nonsense, tossing about and visibly sweating. Eventually she quietened down and her ranting became mumbled murmurings as her mind drifted in and out of that hazy place between consciousness and unconsciousness.

Duncan and Stuart pulled chairs into the bedroom and settled down for a long night. Whenever she appeared to be rousing Duncan would raise her head and hold a glass of water to her mouth to get her to take liquid. Occasionally he'd see her lips move, almost imperceptibly, taking a tiny sip. Stuart could not help but notice the tenderness and gentleness of Duncan's touch.

You do know we've kept in touch for the past four years?" said Duncan eventually.

"What do you mean in touch?" asked Stuart. "About work?"

"Not about work. Privately. She's been helping with the children's education. There are no good schools around here. Most kids have to go to boarding school but I couldn't face sending them away, not after what happened to their mother. Jane's been organising correspondence courses. I don't know what I'd have done without her help. She's never let me down. She says it's the least she could do after Hoedspruit. That incident shook her to the core."

"I didn't have a clue, she never said anything. Not that we are in constant communication or anything."

"It started with cards for Christmas and birthdays, then letters." Duncan smiled. "She even sends presents, things we can't get out here. Recently it went ultra modern. She encouraged me to get a computer. To be honest I'm not very good on the technology, the kids are better than me. But it's an IBM compatible 286 – whatever that means. I have an account with a company called CompuServe and we use a thing called e-mail. Have you heard about it?"

Stuart smiled, "Yes I know about it. Very useful but it does have its shortcomings. Not that reliable and there are security issues. We can't use it in the office, the Ministry are Luddites when it comes to progress. I suppose it's the way forward for informal and social things. I'm surprised you have it out here."

"James is doing six O levels this year thanks to Jane."

"That's wonderful. So you had advance warning we were coming out here?"

"Well, not exactly. I didn't know why you were coming but I got the drift from Jane I'd be seeing her soon, and I guessed you'd be with her. And I'm sure I know what it's about. It was hardly likely that you would be making a social visit.

Stuart shook his head and smiled. "Is that why it was quiet on the stoop tonight. Are you worried what this visit is about? Are you worried it is going to rekindle old memories?"

"I suppose so, but I think it's time you told me why you are here?"

Stuart nodded. "We've a potential problem. Van Stardan has escaped from his mental hospital, mad as a hatter, killed a stack of people on his way out. On top of that the International Atomic Energy Authority has put out its report on Vastrap. For some reason there's been a whitewash. They've said that all South Africa's bombs are accounted for. You and I both know that is incorrect. And finally we have Mandela's inauguration coming up, with Mrs T in attendance. Somebody from the Royal family will be there too not to mention half the world's leaders. It doesn't take Einstein to work out the potential danger."

"Is he mad enough to do something like that? It would be quite a risk for Thatcher and the Queen. I don't have a lot of regard for the Royal family really but I wouldn't like to see the Queen harmed."

"Don't worry about that. Mrs T says it's too dangerous for Her Majesty to attend. She is insisting Prince Charles goes in the Queen's place."

"Thank God for that."

"The problem we have is that the Americans that matter aren't taking the threat seriously. We've decided to take it to the top political level. But before the PM does that she wants all her ducks in a row. What this means is that I will most probably have to testify before the US/UK Joint Security Committee and I need a supporting statement from you. We both saw something being driven away from Vastrap but you alone saw the inside of the assembly plant before it was damaged. We've stopped off here to ask you to attend and then Jane and I are going on to South Africa to see if there is anything else we can glean. That's it in a nutshell. What do you think?"

"I'm a convicted murderer. What good is my word?"

"I have to be honest, the Foreign and Commonwealth Office are on to that. They say the Americans will think it detracts from your credibility."

"So what's the point of me giving a statement then?"

"You're all we've got."

Jane stirred and rolled over, nearly falling out of the bed. Duncan lifted her back to the middle of the bed and mopped her brow.

"Listen there's no point in two of us sitting here. You go to bed and I'll look after Jane. I'll think about it."

Stuart left and Duncan settled down. He spent the rest of the night looking at her pained and restless face. He couldn't help his feelings but always lingering in the back of his mind was Elizabeth.

Just after the sun rose Mary peeped through the door. She re-appeared a few minutes later with tea for Duncan. "Go now and I'll take over for a while."

"I'll stay," is all he said.

Twice Jane stirred and twice he tried to give her a drink. Duncan dozed in his chair. Later Maggie came in with flowers she'd picked from the garden. The curtains were closed but Duncan knew the sun was high in the sky because of the way it tried to break into the room.

Eventually Stuart returned. "That computer of yours isn't so bad," he said. "Managed to send an e-mail to the Liverpool School of Tropical Medicine, the office said they were the best in the country to advise. They came back quickly. If Gus is right about the snake, if it is a Bilbron's Asp, then what we are doing is correct. She just needs time."

When the message had time to sink in Duncan came away and let Mary take over. He slept in Maggie's bed.

Vijoen Street, Arcadia, Pretoria
Friday 21st January 1994

"You finish shovelling the rubbish on to the back of the truck then give the yard a brush and a hose down. Make sure it's spotless. I'm going to see the Gaffer. I want him to square up today."

Lenny stopped shovelling. "Ed, I'm glad this one's over. It's a fucking stupid job and the guy's a nutter. I hope he fucking pays us."

"It's okay by me if he's not 'all there' and I don't care what he asks us to build so long as he pays us and he has so far. Everything I've asked for he's doled out. He's just a lonely guy on his own."

"Lonely guy on his own my arse. I thought there were two of them. He's always talking to his mate Alfred. You never see Alfred though! What about the work? This garage was crazy. It's big enough to take a bus. What the fuck does he want that for? For Christ's sake he doesn't even have a car. He doesn't even go out!" said Lenny. "And why was he on our backs every five minutes to make sure we'd made the door big enough?"

Ed laughed. "He can do what the hell he likes with it, it's not our problem."

"And what was that thing with the fence at the bottom of the garden? He had perfectly good concrete panels that we had to rip out and replace with a woven wickerwork job. It doesn't make sense. He paid us two thousand rand to downgrade the bloody thing."

"Two thousand three hundred actually," corrected Ed. "I don't know, perhaps he prefers the rustic look. I don't care. You just clean up and I'll collect the money!"

Ed put the final hand-written invoice on the kitchen table. A pale wrinkled hand picked it up. The man looked at it for a moment, nodded and without comment began writing out the cheque. He signed the name slowly and deliberately, Edward Purvis, for that was the name Peter van Stardan had been using since he'd moved into the house twelve months earlier.

"We've cleaned up; do you want to have a look around before we go?"

The man that Ed knew as Mr Purvis just shook his head.

Okra's plan had got van Stardan out of the psychiatric hospital and as far as the Drakensberg. He hadn't thought any further than that. But that was okay for van Stardan. He'd stayed in the cavern for three weeks, planning and arranging. He knew there would only be one opportunity to fulfil Alfred Smidt's wishes. The plan was complex and had several component parts. By mid- November each part was indelibly etched on van Stardan's mind and on the mind of his first lieutenant, Daniel Okra.

Okra's first job had been to find a house in the right place in Pretoria. He'd done it well. The house on Vijoen Street was in exactly the right place. It had been up for sale for nearly a year. He offered the full asking price and the vendor nearly snapped his hand off and promised to rush the paperwork through within a couple of months. Okra had balked at the time scale, demanding immediate occupation. The lawyers wouldn't budge on the time scale so Okra had done a deal with the vendor. He'd rent it immediately and keep paying the rent till the purchase had gone through. Okra had laughed to himself at the deal. If the lawyers went slowly enough he wouldn't have to buy the house at all.

Van Stardan had moved in immediately. He had little trouble fixing him up with a false identity, Edward Purvis was a fine enough alias. Van Stardan as Edward Purvis had started his work straight away. From the classifieds in the Argos he found Arcadia Builders (Pvt). Ed, the jobbing builder, had come around straight away and found his customer Mr Purvis easy to deal with. There was little discussion about money, but Mr Purvis had exacting requirements that were not negotiable. That was okay with Ed and his brother Lenny, the only two employees of Arcadia Builders (Pvt).

With the work finished in the house Edward Purvis prepared for his trip to Durban.

Stirling Farm
Thursday 27th January 1994

Gus hadn't exaggerated; the first two days were bad. It was not until the third morning that she'd woken up and started to speak. Duncan was there when she opened her eyes and smiled. She was pale and had lost weight that she could ill afford to lose. Mary prepared food as only a mother could and Duncan had fed her. Propped up in bed and cleaned up they'd all come to see her, James, Maggie and Mary. Tembo and Morgan had come together and even Gus stuck his head in. Nobody but Duncan stayed too long.

Stuart spoke longest with her. He explained he couldn't wait for her full recovery and asked her to stay on the farm until her strength had come back. He told her he was going on to South Africa and she could catch up with him when she felt well enough. She was too weak to argue.

It was another week before she ventured on to the stoop and sat in a chair and another few days before she ventured a little walk, her arm supported by Duncan. The warmth in Jane's eyes when she looked at Duncan was obvious to everybody, except Duncan. Although kind and caring it was clear that he was afraid to give in to his feelings.

He'd taken to slipping away in the late afternoons. He'd walk up the kopje, up the path to where Elizabeth was laid to rest and there he would stand with her. Then one day he was followed.

"It's okay you know Dad," said Maggie.

Duncan turned to see Maggie and James behind him.

"Mum wouldn't want you to be unhappy all your life," said James. "She'd want what was good for you."

Duncan, unable to face his children, turned back towards the grave.

"Sometimes you are very quiet and it is difficult to talk to you," said Maggie, "so if I have questions that I know you can't answer I come up here and ask Mum. And you know Dad, I never hear her voice but she always speaks to me and I always feel better and come away with an answer. You could do the same.

Jane is a really nice person. Why don't you bring her up here too, introduce her to Mum. I think she'll like her like we do."

Duncan turned to his children, tears running down his face. James and Maggie stepped forward and embraced their father, the shadows of the trio falling softly on Elizabeth's grave.

James whispered, " it's okay Dad, Mum will let you go."

The next morning Jane made her own way to the stoop. Mafuti, Mary's friend from the Kraal, had arrived with a calabash of soup.

"This is good medicine. It will make you strong like a man," she declared loudly putting the calabash on the table in front on Jane. Jane tried the concoction. She winced and screwed up her face at the taste of the pungent liquid and pushed the calabash away.

"No thanks Mafuti. It's very kind of you but I think I'd rather remain a woman!"

It was the first time everybody laughed, including Duncan. He put his hand on hers. "It's good to have you back."

By mid-afternoon Jane's natural enthusiasm for life was returning and they started talking about business.

"What were you and Stuart going to do in South Africa?" asked Duncan.

"It was a bit of a long shot really. If we could trace the missing bomb it would be great. We know a container left Vastrap, you and Stuart saw it. We're pretty sure it contained the last of the South African bombs. If we could somehow trace where it went it might give us a lead. It may have gone by road but as there's a container terminal at the railway station in Upington we thought it might be worth seeing if there's anything in the records there. The line leads right into the main rail network, though, so I suppose it could have gone anywhere in South Africa."

"Why into South Africa, why not the other way?"

"The line that passes through Upington links South Africa with Windhoek in Namibia. I don't think anybody would have been likely to send a bomb into a foreign country, do you?"

"Well I wouldn't have known this except for what's in the papers. Firstly the line doesn't stop at Windhoek, it continues on to Walvis Bay," said Duncan

"So?"

"Walvis Bay isn't in Namibia. It's a South African enclave, or at least it will be till 28th February. Then the South Africans are handing it over to the Namibians. Walvis Bay is known to be a hotbed for white South African diehards and, according to what I read, there's a huge panic to get all kinds of stuff out of Walvis Bay that shouldn't be there. Apparently the port was used a lot when there were sanctions against South Africa. It wouldn't have been such a stupid place to send a container in 1990."

"That's more of a long shot than ours," replied Jane.

"Well if Stuart's checking the stuff going into South Africa he might as well check the stuff going the other way whilst he's there. It's not going to cost anything."

Walvis Bay Container Depot
Thursday 3rd February 1994

"We won't even be able to blame this on Mandela," said the stevedore with the pick.

"What, that the grass and weeds have grown so much," replied the one with the shovel.

"No you stupid sod. It's our glorious leader that's given up Walvis Bay, not the black one. That's our real problem."

"They guaranteed our jobs didn't they?"

"We'll see how long that lasts. Mark my words it won't be a couple of weeks before the first 'blackie' stevedore arrives. They won't be bothering with training and union membership. It'll be all their brothers and cousins here in no time. Our days are numbered. I'm going back to the Cape to see what is happening. We should be okay there for a couple of years at least."

"If you don't start moving that pick you'll be going back to the Cape today. We got six hours to finish this job. There are a lot of ships leaving here and it won't be appreciated if they're delayed because of you gassing. How long has this stuff been parked in the corner of the yard anyway? Bloody weeds have grown everywhere."

"Years I'd guess."

"Don't they move them on after a while?"

"Not if somebody's paying the demurrage."

"What's demurrage?"

"The fine for not removing a consignment on time. It's a bloody fortune but somebody must have been paying it or management would have disposed of the goods ages ago."

"Maybe we got something valuable here."

"More likely some clerk in a shipping office has forgotten about the consignments and they just keep paying the bills."

"Well somebody wants the stuff now. Get a move on so we can get finished."

South African Railways & Harbours HQ Johannesburg
Monday 7th February 1994

Stuart didn't like travelling on the train, which was ironic as he was going to the Headquarters of South African Railways. He drove from Pretoria instead; it had taken him less than two hours, hotel to office.

Getting permission to sift through the archives had taken longer than he'd expected and hadn't been easy. The Head Archivist had required a letter from Lloyds of London stating that Stuart was a bona fide insurance investigator checking up on a potential historic fraud. Fortunately Stuart had a contact that could supply the letter. Once in the offices of the National Railway though he found them quite accommodating. Trish was the name of the young girl assigned to him; she was excited at the thought of being involved in uncovering an international crime. She'd have been more excited had she known what she was really looking for.

"So what is it you actually want to see?" asked Trish.

"The consignment we're trying to trace would have been loaded at Upington on 11th of February 1990 or say in any of the ten following days. I'm not sure of the destination but somewhere in the Republic. There's no chance of finding the actual consignment I'm sure but if I could trace the name of the consignee that would be a great start."

"That should be fairly simple. We have consignment notes for every load. It will just take a bit of running around. If you sit here, at this desk I'll rummage around the shelves and bring you the appropriate files."

As it turned out Trish was a little gem. The consignment notes were filed for the entire train: every consignment that had joined or left every train on the full length of its journey and there were up to eight trains per day. Stuart settled in for the long haul. He took Trish out for a quick sandwich lunch, for which she was very grateful. By four o' clock he'd finished trawling through the sheaves of paper. He gathered the names of over twenty consignees for the relevant route and dates. None of them looked promising.

Exhausted and bleary eyed Stuart finally closed the last file. "I know it's a bit late in the day but I was going to ask you…" Stuart began.

She cut in. "Is there anything going the other way. I thought you might ask that. I've got the files ready, they're much smaller thankfully."

"You're too good for this place," Stuart flattered.

He opened the first file: Route 4668. Rand to Walvis Bay, stopping at Upington; Date 11th February 1990 16.45 hrs. One consignment had been loaded on to a wagon. There was just a single sheet of paper filed for the load. It was a despatch note, all on its own. No details of consignee listed.

"That's interesting but it's not much good. There's only the one piece of paper."

"That's very unusual," said Trish. "The paper work should have arrived here by now and it's unusual for us to misfile. Let me have a look," she said taking the file and thumbing a few pages backwards and forwards. "I don't know, that's strange. The file couldn't possibly still be live?"

"What do you mean?"

"We're only supposed to receive complete and closed files. If a file is still live it should be in accounts."

"So how could you check that?"

"Oh, that's not easy, there's no computer and we'd have to go to the Central Accounts Department."

"Where's that?" asked Stuart.

"Two floors up."

Half an hour later Trish and Stuart were sitting at the desk of an elderly male clerk. "That one. It's the Department joke, it's been standing in the depot for years accruing demurrage and it just keeps on getting paid."

"What's been standing?"

"The consignment, in the yard at Walvis Bay. You'd think they'd have the gumption to warehouse it. It would be a fraction of the cost."

"So that actual consignment is still in your possession?"

"Hold on a second." The Clerk pulled a file from the shelves behind his desk and opened it to the front. "Yes it is, or at least it was four days ago, that's when we got the last return. We will invoice it again tomorrow. But we are about to hand that facility over to Namib Ports and Harbours soon. I am not sure what will happen to it then."

"You have an address as well?"

"I do."

Trish walked with Stuart to the door. "You've been a great help, thank you very much."

"It's pretty boring working in an archive," replied Trish. "That's the most exciting thing I've done since I've been here. If there's anything else I can do will you let me know?"

"Of course I will."

"And could I ask you a little favour? If you catch the crooks will you let me know? It would be so nice to think I'd done something really useful."

"I will indeed."

Trish produced a scrap of paper. "I'd hoped you'd say that. Here's my phone number, office and home."

Meadow Vale Hotel, Pretoria
Tuesday 8th February 1994

Stuart hadn't gone to the Embassy that morning. If he had, he would have received the message earlier. Instead he'd gone to the central library to do some research. He was at the doors when the library opened at 9.15. He'd have been there the previous night if he hadn't been so late getting back from Johannesburg. It had been an agonising night of waiting for him.

The wait was worth it. He spent several hours in the reference section of the library going through all the business directories, even the Yellow Pages. Then he'd looked in the Official Business Register before turning his attention to the Register of Corporate Tax Payers. There was no reference anywhere to the company *'Natal Agricultural Machinery Pvt.'* When he had exhausted the directories he went through endless microfiches trying to find a reference to the company in back copies of newspapers. In the end all he had for his efforts was the copy of the note he'd got the previous day from the Accounts Department at National Railways giving the name of the company and a PO Box in Ladysmith. Surprisingly he left the library elated. That somebody had gone to so much trouble, creating a fictional company and paying high storage costs for years, suggested that something was amiss with that consignment. There was only one way left to trace the individuals behind the cover up. The bank account that the payments had come from should lead him in the right direction. But Stuart didn't have access to that information. He'd have to see what the Trade Section at the Embassy could dig up.

The Ambassador had allocated Stuart a small non-descript office on the second floor at the rear of the building. The only outward indication of the nature of Stuart's work was the high security electronic entry system that had been fitted to the door. Inside, the office was sparsely furnished, but that didn't matter, he wouldn't be entertaining guests there. When he got inside the light on his phone was flashing indicating that there was a message waiting for him. He picked up the receiver and dialled '0' for the operator. He immediately dialled the international number that the operator had given him. The phone rang for a long time. Eventually it was picked up. He recognised Duncan's "Hello" on the other end but all he said was "*B – bravo 1500*."

Duncan listened as Stuart repeated the message and then hung up. He looked at his watch. He had an hour to think, and then he'd have to head off for the restaurant.

Duncan watched as Jane withdrew a slip of paper from her purse. On it was a list of four hand written phone numbers prefixed a, b, c and d.

"We have to call this one at 2pm," she said.

"He said 1500," corrected Duncan.

"Stuart sticks an hour on the time he wants me to call as an extra precaution. He must have found something. Is there somewhere we can go to make the call?"

"The bottle store has a payphone."

Stuart walked the three blocks to the little Italian Restaurant. Inside he was immediately greeted by the owner.

"Hey, Mr Cameron, good to see you again."

"Hello Luigi. It's been a long time. You got a special table for me?"

"No problem, anything for you Mr Cameron. And how about a bowl of bolognaise and a beer?"

"Sounds good to me."

Luigi led Stuart to a small round table covered in a red gingham table cloth, at the back of the restaurant, a table close to a phone jack.

He sipped the beer and ate the bolognaise as he waited. He had to admit to himself it was pretty good. He pushed the empty plate away and checked his watch. Exactly two o' clock and on cue Luigi came over with a phone in hand. He plugged the cable into the jack and handed the set to Stuart, "Your call."

"Hello."

"How's Pretoria?"

"Good. You feeling better?"

"Much. We've been talking and think it would be good if you checked out transport going in the opposite direction."

"I'm way ahead of you on that one, but good thinking in any case."

"Anything?"

"Absolutely. Only one consignment on the day going the wrong way. Consignee doesn't exist and, wait for this, the consignment is sitting on the docks at Windhoek."

"You mean it's there now?"

"Yes. It was confirmed there five days ago. It's thrown a spanner in the works. I was going to follow the financial trail which means a trip to Ladysmith but now I also need to go to Walvis Bay to check out what exactly is there."

"Perhaps we can do Walvis Bay," said Jane immediately.

"You're too sick and it's not your type of work."

"I'm not sick now and Duncan will come with me."

Stuart thought for a moment before he spoke. "Okay, check out how you would get there but don't move till we talk again. I need to check something out here first. I'm going to a reception this evening so we'll speak in the morning. Is 11am okay on C for Charlie."

"C for Charlie, that's fine. How come you have time for socialising?"

"It's not socialising."

Stuart checked his bow tie as he waited for the electric gates of the American Ambassador's residence to open. Fortunately he was a standard fit and was able to wear one of the small stock of dinner jackets that the British Embassy kept 'for emergencies'. A lot of the diplomatic receptions were formal dress although formal meant different things to different nationalities. Stuart, being British, could only have worn a black tie. American tuxedoes came in many colours with flamboyant flourishes. At one US reception a new French diplomat actually thought he'd got the dress code wrong and he should have been in fancy dress! No such surprises for Stuart, the US Ambassador was in black tie as were his senior adjutants. Only junior staff, the uninitiated and visitors would don more garish garb.

Burt Zimmermann and Jack Carter fell into the visitor's category. Once inside Stuart didn't have to waste much time singling them out; Burt wearing large black and white check and Jack powder blue. They saw Stuart walking over to them drink in hand. Their broad smiles were irrepressible and genuine.

"How you doing buddy? Good to see you," was Burt's greeting. Jack was hardly less effusive. The handshakes were big, firm and long. Stuart could not help but feel pleased to see them, even though his mind was on other matters.

The pleasantries and jokes lasted long enough. Eventually Stuart broke in. "I need to talk business with you. Can we walk in the gardens?"

"No problem, let's go."

Once away from the crowd Jack got straight to the point. "So what's on your mind?"

"Not to put too fine a point on it I was surprised at the conclusions of the Atomic Energy Authority's report on Vastrap. It left little scope for there to be a rogue bomb about. Word around the UN is that the Chairman was leaned on by someone on your side. I thought we were of the same opinion; that there was every possibility of another bomb. Why did you change your minds?"

Burt and Jack looked at one another as if deciding who was going to speak first. Jack took the plunge.

"You clean? No wire?"

Stuart opened his jacket to show his pressed shirt. "Not my style to be wired up, not with friends."

"Yeah, sorry about that. Strictly off the record?"

Stuart nodded.

Jack continued. "All's not well in our camp. Do you remember Eugene, Eugene Forester; he was at Vastrap?"

"I think I do. He was a little rude if my recollection is correct."

"You British are so polite. The man's a total arsehole."

Stuart smiled. "You said it, not me."

"He took full credit for the 'success' of Vastrap and, when we got back, wasted no time in milking the situation. Now he's in the White House, a Presidential Aide. That's quite a leap for a man from his background. The President believes that Eugene won him the black vote and another term in office. But that's based on him having got rid of the South African nuclear stockpile. However the President isn't that dumb. If it turns out that there's a bomb knocking about then Eugene's next posting will be in North Alaska! We think he put the pressure on the AEA and we're pretty pissed about it."

"I'm sure you know that van Stardan's on the loose" said Stuart "and it's not too long until Mandela's inauguration. Half the Heads of State in the world are going to be there. Van Stardan is mad; he's not going to pass on that opportunity."

"Why do you think we're here?" replied Burt.

"So there are people in the US who believe there's a danger then?"

"Only us I'm afraid," replied Jack. "We had to exert a lot of pressure just to be allowed come on this trip. Every effort was made to try to block us. As it is, our remit is so tight we almost have to check with Langley if we want a crap."

"That tight?"

"That tight. Our brief is to check for major dangers at the airport, hotel, venue and transport links between. That's it. I don't think we're even allowed out of the city."

"That's a shame."

"Why you got something?" asked Burt.

"Might have, but it means a trip to Walvis Bay."

"Where the frig's that?"

"Namibia."

"Count us out on that one. But tell us what you got."

Stuart filled them in.

"It's not solid enough. We can break the rules once. If it's a false alarm we're on the next plane to Washington. We'll assist but it has to be really solid. That's the best we can do. Expect no help through official channels."

"If there's going to be an attack it will take place on inauguration day I'd guess," continued Stuart. "That's when everybody is going to be together. I suppose all you can do is concentrate on that area."

"That's what we'll do," replied Burt. "But keep us in the loop good Buddy. Why don't we exchange cell phone numbers?"

"We're not allowed cell phones, or as we call them mobile phones," replied Stuart.

"Wow you Brits are in the dark ages."

"We used to have them but some of our Royals were a bit indiscreet about their love life when using them and now it's been decided they're not safe to use."

"Yeah I remember that. Didn't that Prince Charlie fella of yours let loose about tampons and his girlfriend or something?" asked Burt. "We had a laugh over that."

"He did," replied Stuart. "Put the security services back ten years. I'll take your numbers in any case."

Port of Durban
Thursday 10th February 1994

The coaster MV Mazowe was barely twelve hundred tonnes. It was the oldest of three vessels owned by Cape Shipping. The other two vessels weren't in the best of condition, the MV Mazowe was worse. The engineer from the insurance company who had carried out the last inspection had left three pages of remedial actions to be carried out before the next renewal period. None of them had been actioned.

The vessel was powered by an undersized and worn out twelve cylinder Mann diesel engine. It created a lot of smoke, even in cruise mode. When it picked up its cargo in Walvis Bay, contract engineers had come aboard and tried to adjust the injectors to improve the situation. They were there for several hours but for all their efforts the Chief Engineer could detect no improvement. The engine room was his worst nightmare. The Chief Engineer was never to know that the same contract engineers had left a small incendiary device in the hut that the stevedores at Walvis Bay used to sort out their paperwork. In the dead of night the device had gone off and burnt the hut to the ground together with all the paperwork generated in the previous twenty four hours.

It would not have been the vessel of choice to carry a delicate load from Walvis Bay to Durban but then again not many people knew what it was carrying. As far as Mr Purvis was concerned Natal Shipping had a couple of things going for it. Firstly the owners had a relaxed view towards rules and regulations and secondly the Master of the Mazowe had a pilot's licence for Durban which did away with the necessity of picking one up at the outer buoys to the harbour. This gave the Master a free hand inside the harbour.

Van Stardan aka Edward Purvis sat in his car, tucked away in the shadows between two buildings. It was ten pm. In truth there was no reason for him to be there. Okra had advised against it. But Alfred Smidt had reminded van Stardan how important it was for him to oversee the mission personally and he would never let Alfred down. He could not risk entering the main port facilities using false papers and he didn't want the container to be subject to a search by customs. So he'd arranged for the MV Mazowe to 'stop off' at Fisherman's Wharf, a small dock tucked away in a secluded corner of Durban harbour. A special mobile crane was waiting as the ship tied up. The shore party moved quickly; the container had been lifted from the deck even before the crew had got the spring lines properly in place. The Captain of the Mazowe, having fulfilled his duty, signalled cast off and slow ahead on the engines. The MV Mazowe moved away slowly, heading towards it's official berth at the container depot.

The two men with the lorry worked quickly securing the twenty foot container to the lorry as the operator stowed the jib of his crane.

Edward Purvis, now out of the car, lurked in the shadows watching. He saw him first, the security guard.

The guard had been in his hut, settling down for the night looking forward to some sleep. He wasn't supposed to be on-duty, he'd already worked a day shift on another dock, but the Supervisor had twisted his arm. The guard that was rostered had phoned in sick. It was going to be a doddle for double time, he thought. Nothing was due to dock that night at Fisherman's Wharf.

The lights of the MV Mazowe had alerted him; he'd left the hut and crept forward. He watched for a long time deciding what to do. It wasn't unknown for a bit of contraband to be shipped through the port but he'd never been in on any deals. Now he had to decide should he radio the ship's unscheduled movement or should he approach the men at the lorry in the hope of picking up a tidy backhander for keeping his mouth shut. In the end he'd decided that discretion was the better part of valour and picked up his radio to call it in to control. He never got a chance to press the transmit button. The bullet was a bit off target but still hit the guard in the lower back, severing his spinal cord. He collapsed to the ground unconscious. Edward Purvis looked around for witnesses; there were none but his own men who were climbing into the lorry's cab. There wasn't time for a final shot to finish off the guard. . He quickly unscrewed the silencer from the pistol and got back to his car.

The lorry left the wharf turning on to Canal Road. Within a short time it was on to Highway 3 and a straight overnight run, all the way to Ladysmith. Edward Purvis was to follow as soon as he carried out his final task.

The lorry and the container were well on their way as the MV Mazowe edged into the container berth allocated to it. The ship's engineer was cursing with all the movements being signalled from the bridge. He prayed the engine would hold out, his only solace being that as soon as they were alongside he could leave his dirty hot hole and get a few cool beers. That was not to happen. The plastic charges that had been planted underneath the engine room plates, directly onto the hull by the contract engineers were military grade, set off by a radio activated detonator when Edward Purvis pushed the button – which he did.

As planned the charges ripped through the ship's plating and broke it's back at the same time. In an instant the bulkhead separating the engine room and cargo hold was ruptured. Water rushed into the engine room. But the engineer wouldn't drown; he'd been killed outright by the initial explosion. The ship began to sink stern first. The water hadn't reached the bulwarks before the Mazowe began to list alarmingly; in a few seconds it had turned turtle and all that stuck out of the water was the upturned hull.

Okra had two of his best men in the cab, one of them a professional driver during the day, but still they had trouble negotiating the tracks to the Drakensberg cavern. The lorry was built for standard roads and without all wheel drive, low gears and a differential lock the tyres slipped and struggled for grip. Adding to the difficulty, no large vehicle had used the track for a long time and the foliage had grown over the road; it was like driving through a green tunnel for much of the time. It was 9.30 am by the time they arrived at the cavern entrance. The lorry had a hydraulic self- discharge facility so it didn't take long to get the container on to the waiting dollies. By 10am the lorry was on its way back down the mountain and the dollies, supporting the container, were being pulled by a Beaver military field FLT down the tunnel and into the cavern. Also in the cavern, waiting was a Mamba Mk1. Now they had everything. Edward Purvis could disappear for now and Peter van Stardan could re-emerge to oversee the work. Okra and van Stardan made sure they were alone to savour the moment when they opened the container that had come from Vastrap and had stood for so long in Walvis Bay.

When the Cubans arrived in Angola in 1975, the South Africans got a shock. They were no longer fighting a rabble of unorganised rebels but faced a disciplined and well equipped modern army. Things didn't go their way. One of the areas where they were lacking was troop mobility. This resulted in a crash programme of development. South African companies, in co-operation with British companies rushed to find rough terrain armoured personnel carriers. One of their early efforts was the Mamba. To save time they decided to use the chassis and engine of the German Unimog, a vehicle initially developed for farmers. The Mark 1 was a bit of a hotchpotch and came in several variants. The great thing about the Unimog chassis was that it would go anywhere.

The one in the cavern was longer than most. It had a specially lengthened wheel-base. Angled armoured plates had been fitted over the wheels to deflect mine damage and the steel plating of the body would resist small arm's fire if not a rocket propelled grenade. Because of its weight it was underpowered and difficult to drive but it was fit for purpose. It had arrived in the cavern three years earlier. It had come from a recovery regiment and had been marked off the Army's inventory as 'damaged beyond repair' having run over a land mine on the Namibian / Angola border. When driven on the open road it had a tendency to crab and so was unsuitable for long journeys but as it was not going to have to travel very far that didn't matter too much.

Meadow Vale Hotel, Pretoria
Wednesday 16th February 1994

Stuart and Duncan had been sitting on the hotel's sun patio for an hour waiting. Duncan was first to see Jane approaching. He saw her with different eyes now. He dared to see the woman that walked past the pool bar towards him as not only beautiful but also desirable.

A couple of days ago, when it was time for her to leave Stirling Farm he'd suggested he should accompany her. She'd fully recovered and it really wasn't necessary but he'd taken heart when she hadn't discouraged him. Tembo and Morgan had seen right through him when he asked "Do you think you could manage to run the business for a few days while I take her to Pretoria?"

They both laughed. "Who do you think has been running the business for the past weeks? It certainly was not you, your mind has been elsewhere for a long time. You go with our blessing and do what you must. We are all happy for you."

"It's quite like old times," said Stuart to Duncan as Jane got near. "I didn't expect you to come but I'm glad you did. And as you're here you might as well be useful."

Jane arrived at the table and sat opposite the two men. The softness she'd shown when she was alone with Duncan was gone.

"So what have we got?" she asked.

Stuart was taken aback at the abruptness. "Jane you haven't even unpacked your bags properly yet. Relax a little. I think the steam's gone out of the situation."

"No I haven't unpacked, I've been to the embassy to check my communications."

"Is there a problem?" asked Stuart.

"You go first. Give me a run down."

"Okay. Before I sent you two hightailing it off to Walvis Bay I made a couple of phone calls. Apparently our consignment was shipped out on the 3rd February. That's why I didn't send you there in the end.

Walvis Bay is pretty busy at the moment. Actually two ships left that day, one for Spain and the MV Mazowe, for Durban. It has to be the Mazowe we'd be interested in. The MV Mazowe is a plodder, it makes hardly any speed. It was only due into Durban on the 10th. That's when things went wrong. As it was approaching the berth there was an engine room fire and explosion and the ship quickly capsized and sank in the harbour.

Through our embassy the South African Government was immediately warned about our suspicions. We don't know how seriously they're taking the warning. I suppose they don't want to cause alarm so there's nothing in the papers. Fortunately the ship is in shallow water so they are, as we speak, recovering all the cargo, container by container. It's going to take some time. All we can do is watch and wait."

"Aren't they panicked about the possibility of a nuclear bomb being in their harbour?" asked Jane.

Stuart butted in. "It's not a serious problem. The bomb is unlikely to go off."

"Unlikely? That's very reassuring," continued Jane, "But not good enough. I've just got a reminder that the Foreign and Commonwealth Office are waiting for my opinion on security during the inauguration."

"Okay, we'll keep digging," said Stuart.

"That's fine but I'm giving them an interim report in the meantime."

"What are you going to say?"

As Stuart, Jane and Duncan sat in their hotel, not far away, at Jan Smuts Airport, Edward Purvis and Daniel Okra settled into their business class seats on their Iberian Airways flight.

"It gall's me to travel on one of these," said Edward Purvis as he tucked the false British passport into his top pocket, "Even if it is for a good reason."

Foreign and Commonwealth Office, London
Monday 21st February 1994

Ralph Foulkes was enjoying the renaissance in his relationship with Sir Basil Parker Smythe. Confidently he leaned back in the chair with his hands clasped nonchalantly behind his head and waited for his boss to kick off the meeting. Sir Basil finished fumbling through the pile of papers on his desk and eventually found the card he was looking for.

"So Ralph, what do think?" Sir Basil had begun to value Ralph's input and was even beginning to think the youngster had a keener sharper mind than his own, but he was not yet ready to admit that openly.

"The Americans want to know what we're doing about the inauguration. I'm going to have to talk with the State Department later this afternoon. In fact the PM is having a meeting tomorrow and she wants an opinion and recommendations before then. The issue is becoming pressing." Sir Basil laid down the invitation card from the South African Embassy on his desk.

"There's no doubt in my mind," said Ralph confidently, "the security situation is uncertain. The PM should not attend."

"But what happens if the US President attends Mandela's inauguration and Mrs T doesn't. The South Africans will see it as a snub. That's a real possibility. As I understand it, the Americans don't perceive the risk to be as great as we do."

"I think the Americans are underestimating the security risks for political reasons. Mrs T should not travel to South Africa at the present time."

"But what shall we tell the South Africans and who will go in her place, we need to be represented."

"We just tell the South Africans this is their day, that Mr Mandela should be at the forefront of world attention and we don't want Mrs T's attendance to distract from this in any way. As for who should attend I'm sure there are any number of Cabinet Members that Mrs T wouldn't mind losing."

"Ralph! You can't say things like that."

"I'll bet she'd be tempted though," Ralph laughed.

"What about the Queen? She's invited as head of the Commonwealth."

"She's far too important to risk. Recommend Charles attends in her place."

Sir Basil shook his head in mock despair. "I'm glad this is a private conversation." Then he smiled. "Thank you Ralph. I think that might work, particularly if I can persuade the Americans not to send their President."

The lights were off in the Oval office. Bright sunlight from a clear blue sky was streaming through the window behind the President. Four men sat on overstuffed couches facing the Commander- in- Chief. It was hard for them to see his facial expression but the President could see theirs and of all the men in the room Eugene Forester looked the most worried.

The President began. “So Mr Secretary of State, what's your take?”

“I think it would be good for both the US and your own personal standing if you were to attend Mr Mandela's inauguration. He's about the most famous and popular black man on the planet at the present time and it would do no harm for the world to see you standing next to him.”

“What do Security think?” asked the President.

“We think we can assure you of the normal level of close personal security. We can cover for assassination attempts etc. We're less confident about a general threat. There's going to be a lot of tempting targets all gathered in close proximity and the loyalty of the South African security services is untested. Many of their top people are unhappy at the idea of working for a black South African President. And always in the background we have the British sending messages about a possible nuclear threat.”

Eugene Forester broke in a little too hastily. “The United Nations report says there is no nuclear threat.”

“And you were there Eugene weren't you, when their nuclear arsenal was secured?” asked the President. “You gave me your personal assurance that all the South African weapons had been accounted for didn't you? Want to change your mind?”

“No Sir,” was Eugene's response.

The President was not convinced but he didn't challenge Eugene further.

“What are the British doing?”

The Secretary spoke again. “Maggie isn't going; they're sending a scaled down delegation.”

“What's the excuse?”

“They say they don't want to up-stage Mandela.”

“Okay. I don't think Maggie is stupid. We'll send the vice-President and give the same reasons.”

The Leader of the House spoke for the first time. “I don't care if you don't go but you need to get in on the act somehow, even if it's just for home consumption. The black voters in this country need to see you supporting black freedom.”

“What do you suggest?”

The Secretary of State cut in. “I have an idea that might work.”

“Shoot!” said the President.

“Remember when we had that shitty twenty-four hours grabbing the South African weapons? In the end a sergeant from the Rangers came good for us, a black guy. You spoke with him on the phone yourself. I think you actually promoted him.”

The President smiled. “Yeah, I remember him. Sounded like a nice guy.”

"What if we give him a medal or something on the day of the inauguration? Make him the hero that made the elections in South Africa possible. Get the domestic press in. That would go down well with the voters."

"I think the guy comes from Harlem. Why don't you present the medal in Harlem," chipped in The Leader of the House.

"I think I said I'd like to meet him at the time," said the President. "Yeah that sounds good. We'll go with that." As an afterthought the President looked to his security advisor. "I presume I'm safe in Harlem?"

The security advisor took a deep breath but decided not to say anything.

Drakensberg
Friday 15th April 1994

"So it is finished Daniel?"

Van Stardan had started to call Daniel Okra by his Christian name for the first time. Daniel liked it, he saw it as a sign of the esteem in which his chief held him.

"It is finished, all I have to do is drive it down the track and meet the transporter before we start on the final leg of our long journey."

Van Stardan had one last look around the place. He knew he would never return but there was no feeling of nostalgia. He looked at his desk, at the scraps of paper, bits of receipts and bank statements but made no effort to clean them away. He just walked emotionless out of the office, not even bothering to lock the door. A few moments later he was driving down the track, following Daniel who was ahead in the freshly painted dark blue Mamba armoured personnel carrier.

Once the Mamba had been reversed onto the transporter, at the bottom of the track, just outside of Ladysmith, Peter van Stardan had gone on, driven ahead so he could make preparations before Daniel and his load arrived.

Vijoen Street was normally very quiet during the day, in the early hours of the morning it was deadly. It was the kind of street where people kept themselves to themselves at least that was what Peter van Stardan was counting on. It was quarter to five in the morning when Daniel arrived and reversed the transporter into the driveway of the house. It took them only a few minutes to pull back the canvas cover and drive the Mamba off the transporter into the garage. Van Stardan's concern had been unfounded; the garage door was tall enough, the garage itself was big enough. The Mamba fitted in perfectly. By five fifteen everything was locked away from prying eyes, the transporter gone and van Stardan leaving in his car. The riskiest part of the mission had been accomplished without a hitch.

Union Building, Pretoria
9am Monday 18th April 1994

The Union Buildings in Pretoria constitute a National Monument and central tourist attraction. They were built to celebrate the creation of the Union of South Africa. The designer was Sir Herbert Baker and they were completed in 1930 although the land and other buildings had been owned by the Government since 1856. Sir Herbert wanted them to be big enough to hold the entire administration for the whole country. In that task he totally failed although the buildings remain the office of the President of South Africa. Sir Herbert chose the Meintjieskop as the site not only because it was the highest available site in Pretoria but because it also reminded him of the Acropolis in Greece from where he drew some inspiration.

The buildings made use of the natural shape of the land including some old quarry workings. Two wings were built, the left to commemorate the Afrikaner language and the right wing to celebrate the English language. The two wings were joined together by a semi-circular colonnade in the Greek style, which formed a back-drop for an amphitheatre which would be the stage for important ceremonial state occasions. Unfortunately Sir Herbert lost the 'classical' plot and the buildings ended up incorporating design features from just about every major school of architecture that existed in history. The result was a patchwork design with no original or innovative features. The finished building was however visually imposing and for a considerable period it remained the largest building in the Southern Hemisphere. It would be from a specially constructed dais in front of the colonnade that Nelson Mandela would be sworn in as the first black President of South Africa. He would have an imposing view himself as the ground fell away from the buildings revealing formal gardens featuring thousands of carefully tended indigenous plants and trees. Normally public access to these gardens was strictly controlled, but for inauguration day the open spaces would be crammed full of people of all races who wanted to witness the momentous and historic event that was about to occur. Representatives from over one hundred and forty countries were expected to attend. The occasion would be the biggest international political event ever hosted by any country in sub-Saharan Africa.

With twenty days to go preparations were well on the way. This morning would be the first time that security representatives from the visiting delegations were to be allowed to inspect the security put in place by the South Africans.

"We tossed for it," said Burt Zimmermann. "I won, I get to stay, Jack has to go back."

"So when do you go?" asked Stuart.

"Got to be in New York for the 25th at the latest. I have to write up the citation and all that guff first. Ceremony's on the 10th, to coincide with this shindig I guess. I feel sorry for David Evans. He was a good chap, got on with his job as staff-sergeant in the Rangers. That's not a bad achievement in itself. Now he's going to be a Major and a hero and paraded in front of the public. He might not be cut out for that."

"Well give him my regards," said Duncan. "I spoke to him at Vastrap. He's a real sharp guy, interested in everything."

"Say where is that girl of yours, Jane?"

"She's off doing her own thing. You just got Duncan and me today," replied Stuart. "I think the four of us should be enough to assess the lay of the land. Shall we walk?"

Three hours later the four men had finished their walk around and were heading down Volk Street. "There's a nice looking French Bistro over there," said Stuart.

"Begging your pardon," cut in Burt, "I've already experienced your idea of food. There's a pretty good steak house around the corner. The kind of place they give you meat."

"Don't come between Burt and his food," advised Jack with a laugh.

"Steak house sounds good to me," said Duncan.

The girl took their orders and delivered beer to the table.

"So what do think?" asked Stuart looking at Burt.

"Well for a regular event with regular risks, it's not too bad. They've got all the necessary checks and precautions set up. They've even been shaking the place down regularly for the past couple of weeks. Now I am assuming that there are no nukes in the equation. That's a different ball game. The way we got it figured, maybe you guys were wrong and there never was a rogue nuke or, if you were right, there is a nuke but it's at the bottom of Durban harbour. Am I right?"

"Possibly," began Stuart. "But just for now indulge us. We're assuming, just for good form, that there is a nuclear bomb around. How would that change things? Duncan give us your assessment first."

"Well if there is a bomb about we know quite a lot about it now. We got that from the IAEA report. It would be a fairly primitive low yield device but it would still be big enough to cause devastation if it goes off in a city."

"If you were going to set it off where would you hide it?" asked Jack Carter.

"Well pretty much anywhere within a mile or two radius but definitely above ground. My first choice would be in front of the amphitheatre to get the best effect. That would take out Mandela and all the dignitaries. There wouldn't be any state funerals for sure, everybody would be vaporised, including the entire crowd. My least favourite position would be on the far side of the hill, at the back of Union Buildings. There'd be a chance that not everybody would be vaporised because they'd be protected by the hill itself. The shock wave would be deflected upwards but they'd still die"

"That's a pretty big ruck of land. The only people with enough resources to check out that kind of area are the South African security forces and they're not even considering the possibility. As far as the lot up here are concerned this is a nuclear free area. Period. So what's this about? You got some new information?"

"No not really," answered Stuart, "But Jane isn't convinced. She's poking about. I always feel a little uneasy when Jane isn't comfortable."

"A woman's hunch isn't much to go on," said Burt. "If I acted on all the hunches' my wife had I'd be bankrupt and probably in a lunatic asylum."

"I wouldn't say that in front of Jane," suggested Duncan wincing.

" And Jane's hunches have been on the money for years. That's why she's held in such high regard," added Stuart.

"Okay," said Jack. "There's not much we can do now. Will you keep Burt here in the loop whilst I'm away?"

Meadow Vale Hotel
28th April 1994

Jane was tense. “They have already recovered over sixty containers from the bottom of Durban harbour and not found the one we’re looking for and there’s not that many more to lift. I’m beginning to believe our container was not on board the *‘Mazowe’* when it sank.”

“Where does that leave us?” asked Duncan.

“I’ve uncovered bits of circumstantial evidence. A hut containing paperwork mysteriously burnt down when the ‘*Mazowe*’ left Walvis Bay preventing me getting information about all the containers that were on board. Also the night the ‘*Mazowe’* sank a guard was shot in a berth not that far away, and there’s no motive. Is that a coincidence or is it connected? I don’t know. What else have we got?”

Stuart spoke. “I finally got the bank and postal details for whoever was paying for the container all this time. Again I can’t say if it will just end up as a wild goose chase.”

“I want to go to Durban,” said Jane with finality. “I want to look around.”

“You’re not going off alone!” replied Stuart. “Twelve days to the inauguration; it’s getting a little late in the day for me to go swanning off. I need to be around here in Pretoria for the run up to the inauguration.”

“I can handle anything up here,” interjected Duncan. “If a bomb does turn up here I’m most probably the best one to handle it after all. At least I’ve done one before and I could advise them. You could go with Jane to Durban and stop off at Ladysmith and check out your own lead at the same time. It’s better than all this sitting around.”

Stuart nodded and smiled. “I suppose you could buddy up with Burt. I bet he’s lonely since his mate went back to the States.”

Eglin Air Force Base, Florida USA
Monday 2nd May 1994

David Evans walked smartly into the room, stamped his feet to attention and executed a perfect salute. Jack Carter was surprised at the performance and the immaculately presented staff-sergeant's uniform.

"Hey bud, you don't have to do that for me. I'm not in the Army. Sit down relax. I've only come to go over a few things with you."

"Sir." David Evans went to 'at ease' and tentatively moved to take up the seat opposite Jack Carter's desk.

"I had to come a long way to see you. How come they shipped you here and how come you're still in a sergeant's uniform? By my reckoning and according to the bits of paper in front of me you're a major now."

"Sir."

"Just call me Jack and I'm gonna call you David, if that's okay and you can drop the Army speak when you're with me."

"They shipped me here, took me away from my unit, when the President said he wanted to decorate me. This is a grunt's training base, I guess they just didn't know what to do with me. I got nothing to do here but kick my heels. As for the uniform they said I could put on the Major's uniform but then I had to move out of the barracks with the men. So I just stuck with the sergeant's uniform – at least till I get my officer's training."

"What does your CO say about that."

"I guess because the President's interested in me he's scared to say anything. I can do just about anything I want."

"Sounds like a whole heap of a mess to me. Let's park that, I'm here to write up your citation. It's up to me to suggest the award too. I'm putting you forward for the Defence Distinguished Service Medal. That's the highest non-combat award around. My write up will say you rescued a whole bunch of civilians without regard for your own safety. I'm not going to mention anything about a nuclear arsenal though. You okay with that? You do need to agree. That's why I'm here and by the way you don't look too happy."

"Excuse me if I don't seem grateful for all the effort you're making but the way I see it is that this is more for the President than for me. If I was a white guy I don't think they'd be making such a fuss."

Jack Carter looked David Evans straight in the eye. "I guess you're right, the President is using you but that is most probably what the pricks that advised him have suggested and secondly that doesn't mean you don't deserve a medal. I'm not lying on the citation. You did what you did. I saw it. I was there. The sad thing is not that you're getting the medal, it's that a white guy doing the same might not have in these circumstances. And the hullaballoo in Harlem might be a political stunt but it might just inspire one or two of the guys there, give them a bit of hope. That's not a bad thing is it?"

"I guess not."

"So down to business. You have to sign off on this citation so let's talk about what happened in South Africa.

Vijoen Street, Pretoria
Thursday 5th May 1994

The two men sat in the sparsely furnished living room. A single sixty-watt bulb hung from the ceiling rose casting a dull light. There was no lamp shade. They had just eaten their evening meal, an improvised pork stew. The bowls were chipped and the spoons odd. They ate in silence. The atmosphere was hardly celebratory.

Peter placed the spoon in the empty bowl and leaned back in his chair. "So, it is all but over, there in nothing left for us to do, the wheels are in motion. It is time for you to think about leaving, you have done your duty well. Our forefathers will be proud of you."

Daniel Okra had not expected this moment; he had not planned for it. His mind had been consumed with the tasks he had been given, his future had never entered his thoughts. "But where am I to go? What am I to do? My place is here with you?" His expression was that of a loyal dog being abandoned by his master, and in truth he had become little more than that.

"The events we have set in train will probably end in my death. You have no need to accompany me along that path. You can go and make a new life, somewhere far away."

"I can't leave you alone at this time."

"I won't be alone, I am never alone."

Daniel Okra looked perplexed, he had no idea that Peter van Stardan was referring to his constant companion, Alfred Smidt, who lived on inside his mind, his confidante and master.

"I will stay till the end," Okra said.

Before van Stardan could answer there was a knock on the door. The men sat motionless. The knock was repeated and this time accompanied by a loud "Police, come to the door."

"I will get the weapons," whispered van Stardan, "you go to the door. I will be right behind you, out of sight."

Daniel tentatively opened the front door.

"Good evening." The uniformed officer was smiling. "You're aware of what is happening in Union Buildings, on the other side of the kopje on Tuesday?"

"I think everybody in South Africa is aware," responded Okra with remarkable calmness.

"We are checking the area. It is important that if you see anything suspicious in the next few days you contact us. This card has the number to ring." The officer thrust a business card towards Okra.

"Thank you I will keep it safe."

"Good night," said the police officer.

Durban
Friday 6th May 1994

They'd driven directly from Pretoria. Stuart had resurrected his guise as an insurance investigator but the army guard at the container terminal was having none of it.

"Nobody is allowed in."

"Some of the containers are insured by my company. I have the right to see if anything is salvageable and make an assessment of the damage."

The guard was adamant. "This half of the container terminal is out of bounds to everyone. The army with their heavy lift gear are in charge of the salvage operation. When they hand the area back to the dock authorities I'm sure they'll let you in."

"We've driven from Pretoria," Jane tried.

"Tough."

They retreated, booked into a hotel and spent the evening in the bar putting a plan together. Stuart was going to approach the Harbour Master's office to try and find out more about the containers; Jane was going to respond to a little niggle that wouldn't go away; she'd investigate the shooting across the harbour. After breakfast they went their separate ways, agreeing to meet back in the hotel that evening.

Stuart took the car while Jane made her way on foot to the offices of the Mercury, Durban's main newspaper. The young reporter who'd written up the story was initially eager to meet Jane, hopeful he'd pick up a tit-bit for another story. His enthusiasm quickly faded when he discovered that Jane had nothing for him. She had to use all her skills to stop him walking away.

"It's only a couple of quick questions."

"Nothing much to say, it's all in the article."

"Is there anything you might have missed? You did get to the scene just after it happened."

"It was just a shooting. There are a lot of shootings in this city. Listen I'm trying to find a scoop, I haven't got time to talk about a non-story, unless you've got something for me that is. I got to go."

"Why do you think somebody would murder a security guard like that?"

"Listen lady you didn't even read the story properly. The guard wasn't murdered, he was shot, he didn't die."

"What? Where is he?"

"I don't know. Last I heard he was in a coma in Addington. That's a hospital in case you don't know. Bye."

"Wait, what was the guard's name?"

"Read the fucking article lady!"

Jane took a taxi, first to the hotel to retrieve the newspaper cutting, then on to Addington. She bought a bunch of flowers from the stand outside the hospital entrance and joined the queue for the help-desk. The line moved quickly.

"I've come to see Henry Velt, what ward is he in?"

The grey haired voluntary worker smiled as she looked through her lists. Ah, Mr Velt is in acute care on the sixth floor. Unless you are immediate family you cannot visit. You are not immediate family are you?"

"Yes I'm his sister."

"His sister!" the receptionist appeared surprised.

"Half sister really." There was a slight pause. "We have the same father."

"Oh. Then I suppose it is alright." The receptionist's demeanour had changed dramatically for the worse. "The lifts are behind you. Next."

Jane made her way to the nurses' station on the acute care ward and waited whilst the nurse on the station finished filling out a patient record form. Eventually she looked up. "Sorry, the records are important, we can't make a mistake?"

Jane gave her best understanding smile. "No problem at all. It only surprises me how many people don't appreciate how much you nurses have to do."

The nurse returned the smile. "It's nice when somebody appreciates us. How can I help you?"

"I've come to see Henry, Henry Velt. The kind lady at the reception desk sent me up."

"She shouldn't have done that. Henry's still very ill. He's only just regained consciousness. We're not encouraging visitors at the moment."

"I've only brought some flowers to cheer him up. I won't stay long. I'm a friend."

"A few minutes will most probably do him no harm. It's the third door on the left down the corridor."

Henry was in a private room. The blinds on the window were closed. He was propped up in his bed. Even in the dull light Jane could see the reason for the surprise and disdain of the lady on the help desk. Older people often didn't approve of mixed race relationships and Henry wasn't white, coloured guessed Jane, the result of a mixed marriage. He half opened his eyes as Jane came into the room.

"Hello Henry," said Jane. "You don't know me but I am a friend. I just want to ask you a few questions about your accident. Do you feel up to it?"

"Are you the police?" he spoke in a hoarse voice.

"No, Henry. The police don't bring flowers." Jane pulled up a chair and sat beside the patient. "Just tell me what happened."

"I was just patrolling the dock and somebody shot me from behind. They say I'll never walk again and I'm lucky to be alive." Tears came to Henry's eyes. "I was only doing an extra shift to earn a few Rand for the family. And now I'm no good to them at all"

"I know it's tough Henry. Help me get the person who did this to you. Give me a bit more detail."

"I saw a ship on the wharf that shouldn't have been there. I was just calling it in. That's it."

"Do you remember the name of the ship?"

"I'll never forget it, it was the MV Mazowe."

"What else?"

"It was discharging a twenty foot container on to a truck. It didn't seem right."

"Why's that Henry?"

"A mobile crane was lifting the container from the ship to the truck. They normally use a dock's and harbour crane for all discharging. This one was different. I could see the sign written on it clearly '*Kutz Plant Hire: Ladysmith*'. They never use private cranes on the dock, never mind ones from Ladysmith. That's all I know."

"You've been very helpful Henry." Jane said as she took her leave.

"Slow down Stuart, we don't want to be pulled up by the police."

"Jesus Jane a spot fine is nothing compared to what's at stake now. For the first time I'm getting really scared."

When Jane had got back to the hotel in Durban she had to wait for Stuart to return. She made good use of her time by contacting Duncan. Luckily he'd been in the hotel. Ignoring phone security protocol she'd told him of the MV Mazowe's unscheduled stop. The implications were immediately clear to Duncan. "It's going to be like looking for a needle in a haystack against the clock," he'd responded. "I'll do what I can. Leave messages for me at the embassy and I'll ring in every couple of hours. Do whatever you can to give me a clue will you."

"You can be sure of it; we'll be on our way to Ladysmith as soon as I get hold of Stuart."

Jane's second call had been to the British Ambassador. She'd tried to drum in to him the importance of the information and the need to get the South Africans involved. "I won't be flustered," he said. "I'll use the proper channels to reinforce your message but I'm sure that the authorities are already taking all the necessary precautions here in Pretoria."

Instead of goodbye Jane had parted with a "Damn your arrogance," before slamming down the handset.

The Manager at Standard Chartered Bank in Ladysmith didn't keep them waiting long. He took Stuart and Jane into a side office.

"Please sit down. What can I do for you?"

"We're trying to track down an individual that has an account in this branch," began Stuart. "It's a long standing account."

"Who are you trying to find? Do you have an account number?"

Stuart produced the copy invoice he got from the National Railways Archive. The Manager looked at it and scribbled down the payee account details.

"Wait a few moments please."

The Manager left the office but returned quickly. "I'm sure you appreciate that as a bank we have to maintain professional standards and a big part of that is client confidentiality. I'm afraid I cannot divulge the information you have requested."

"This is very important," said Jane. "It may even be a case of life and death."

"Then I suggest that you obtain a Court Order. If a judge will grant you one I will be obliged to disclose the information you have requested within fourteen days. That is the best I can do."

"Please," said Jane. "It is very important."

"I have told you the situation."

"Come on Jane," said Stuart. "We're wasting valuable time."

The Manager waited till Stuart and Jane had left the office before picking up the phone and dialling a number he knew by heart. He let it ring for a long time but nobody picked up. He'd try again later.

Jane and Stuart walked the fifty yards to their next destination. The Post Office was one of the oldest buildings in Ladysmith. They went straight into the Post Room where banks of neat boxes with lockable doors lined the walls. All the boxes had a number on them and some also had sticky labels with the names of the owners.

Jane and Stuart started looking at the individual doors, trying to locate the box they were looking for. From behind the counter a young girl emerged, a Post Office employee badge on the lapel of her blouse.

"Can I help you," her manner was sweet and unthreatening.

"We've got a PO Box number and we're trying to find the person who owns it," said Jane honestly.

"The idea of a PO Box is not only convenience but also confidentiality. We are not supposed to divulge the actual addresses of the people who use PO Boxes." The girl was almost apologetic.

Jane smiled at the girl and said "Please, it's important."

Sometimes, even with a stranger, there is an instant rapport, an unexplained chemistry. Jane's luck was in. This was one of those occasions. Stuart recognised the situation and quietly withdrew.

"I cannot tell you the name and address officially," said the girl as she took the couple of steps back to her desk. She didn't speak, just scribbled a few words on a post-it slip and slid the paper towards Jane, who picked it up.

"Thank you very much," said Jane and left. Outside she'd read the handwritten note. On it were just two words, a name and a road. "Right Stuart, let's get a move on."

They drove up and down Piet Retief Drive several times before finding the dusty road that led eastwards to Starkies Lane. There were only half a dozen plots on the lane. In Britain they'd be known as small-holdings, in South Africa they were just houses with very big gardens; two or three acres each.

In the absence of a house number or name Stuart picked a house at random, one with an open gate, and drove up the drive. Together they walked up on to the stoop. Stuart knocked. A petite woman, mid-thirties, smiling wearing a happy floral print dress answered, and spoke to them through the closed fly screen.

"Good morning."

Jane pushed Stuart to one side. "What's a girl from Manchester doing here?" Jane had immediately recognised the broad Lancashire accent.

"I'm from Salford actually. Is my accent that bad?"

"No," said Jane, it's wonderful. It makes me homesick."

The woman thought for a moment. "Can I detect a bit of Scouser in your voice?"

"No not Liverpool, I'm from the Wirral actually."

"Ah!" said the woman, "A posh Scouser. Come in, I'll put the kettle on. But don't you go stealing anything!"

Both women laughed at the reference to the light fingered reputation of Liverpuddlians. She took them straight into the kitchen. They sat at the table as the woman made a pot of tea.

"It's only Yorkshire Tea I'm afraid. It's all they sell in the local store."

"It'll be fine. I'm Jane by the way and this is my friend Stuart."

"I'm Susan."

"What are you doing here?"

"My husband's an engineer with BICC in Beldon. They make telephone cables. He's on secondment over here for three years. We're about halfway through the contract."

"Bit different from home?"

"It's much better than I thought it would be. The people are really friendly and the life style is so different. I've two boys, seven and eleven, they love it. All the sports, they never got outside in Salford. My husband's with them now at rugby practice."

"The weather helps."

"The weather has its moments. It can get cold enough here in winter and when it rains it rains."

Jane was about to say something else when Stuart cut in. "We're rather pushed for time actually."

"Sorry," said Jane. "We're hoping you can help us. Do you know where a Mr Okra lives?"

The reaction was spontaneous. "That old goat."

"You don't like him then?"

"You had to pick the exception that proves the rule. He's rude and bad mannered. No wonder he lives alone, no woman would have him. He hates the British only slightly less than he hates the blacks. He's the only person that's given us a hard time. With the likes of him there's no hope for this country. Thankfully he's not around all that much. He lives in the next house up the track, on the right."

"That's great, thanks," said Stuart. "Do you know if he's around now?"

"Haven't seen him for days."

Stuart finished his tea in a single gulp. "We have to go Jane."

"Well, if you're passing please call in again. I'd love to chat," said Susan.

"I will," replied Jane.

"Oh, but don't come in the next couple of days. We're going to Pretoria. We're taking the children to see Mandela being sworn in. Not often you get the chance to see such an historic event. We think it will be great for the country."

Before Jane had a chance to respond, Stuart put his hand on her shoulder. "Come on."

"We should have told her not to go," said Jane.

Stuart didn't reply, he just pulled the car into the gravel driveway of Okra's house, stopping outside the front door. There were no other cars and the house had an abandoned feel. After knocking and receiving no response they walked around the back of the house and shouted out Okra's name a few times.

"What now?" asked Jane.

Stuart tried the handle of the back door. It was locked. He gave it a heave with his shoulder; it gave easily. "We'll have a little look around I think."

Inside was dark and dingy. It smelt stale. The walls, which hadn't seen fresh paint or paper for years, were hung with old pictures and drawings from South African history; men, at the turn of the century, in bush hats holding long rifles; covered wagons being drawn by long trains of oxen over virgin bushveld. All the pictures had a similar theme.

"God, this is a dirty shrine," said Jane as she poked around the living room.

Stuart went off to search the bedrooms. He wasn't gone long before he called out. "Jane, come here."

Jane went through. Stuart was standing by an open wardrobe filled with crisply pressed military uniforms. "It's the only thing that appears to have been cared for here."

"I recognise the uniform," said Jane. "It's the same one the men who tried to shoot me were wearing. I think we've found the right place!

There's a stack of papers and maps on the table, we should go through them."

"I don't think we should hang around here for too long," replied Stuart. "Gather up what you want and we'll take them with us."

Twenty minutes later they were back in their car with two large plastic bags in the boot, filled with papers. "Let's find somewhere we can go over these papers properly," said Stuart.

Pretoria
Saturday 7th May 1994

"Do we tell him or keep him in the dark?"

"Like it or not he's going to be our boss in a couple of day's time. Tell him and let him decide."

Nelson Mandela never hesitated when the Head of Security asked to see him. In truth Mandela had no option but to trust him. He always said he had every faith in the Security Service and that he felt sure that if they did their job diligently then everything would be alright.

Even when the British warning was passed on he only said that he did not entirely trust the old colonial powers. He'd said whilst there were many good people in Britain that had worked to bring about the momentous changes in South Africa, there still remained reactionary influences in places of power that would do what they could to rob the South Africans of this victory. He would not let that happen.

"My people have waited for this day all their lives and they have made many sacrifices. Whilst the ceremony will not right the wrongs of the past it will offer some hope for the future. If it costs my life I will go ahead."

"The vice-President's personal bodyguards have arrived in Pretoria," said Burt Zimmermann to Duncan, "but I don't think they're going to be of much use. They're supposed to take care of close protection and they don't stray much from their mission. Besides they always eye us Spooks from Langley with a bit of suspicion."

"Pretty much the same with the Royal Guard I'm afraid to say, not that they'd take any notice of me. I've got a blot on my copybook, it's only Stuart that uses me as the occasion arises."

"Bit of an unusual situation that. What's the story?"

"Oh, I'll tell you one day," replied Duncan brushing off the question.

"We've gone through the building twice. Why don't we take a walk around the hill, take a look at the back and see what we think?"

"Fine, but it'll take us a couple of hours."

Duncan and Burt were at Union Buildings. The podium where Mandela would take his oath of office was already in place and the various marquees were just about all up. A few technicians were rushing about installing and testing the PA system. All Duncan and Burt could do was to keep their eyes peeled for anything suspicious and hope that Jane and Stuart came up with something.

Behind the main buildings and columns that looked down on the amphitheatre there was a service road and parking lot. But there was little room for cars now, the space had been taken up with a mobile control centre for the police and several outside broadcast trucks. A narrow concrete road led off from the car park and wound its way around the perimeter fence, right round the top of the kopje, like a sweat band on a tennis player's head. The top of the hill, the crown, was more or less in its natural state, indigenous trees, bushes and shrubs all growing wild, even a few small antelope were rumoured to live there. The top was a park and normally open to the public but was now closed until after the inauguration. Security patrols were supposed to take place regularly with the guards travelling the perimeter in buggies. Unfortunately the outside broadcast vehicles had trailed communications cables everywhere and getting to and from the perimeter road had become all but impossible. Because of the blockages only occasional foot patrols were being sent out. It was not a popular assignment, particularly in the heat of the day. Duncan and Burt found themselves walking alone around the kopje.

The crown of the kopje was elongated, a bit like a fat cigar. As they rounded the end of the hill, the suburb of Arcadia came into full view, a sprawling stretch of mixed residential and commercial developments, vanishing into the distance. They stood near the top, the ground fell away sharply and there was light vegetation and rocky outcrops. At the bottom of the hill, the ground suddenly flattened out. Houses were built right up to the spot where the kopje began.

"Pretty steep incline," said Burt. "Access would be difficult from this side of the hill."

"Yes," replied Duncan. "You'd need a tracked vehicle or a pretty good off-roader to get up here. Anybody coming on foot would be knackered before they got to the top."

In the end it was the President's personal protection unit that had had the final say on the venue. Not everybody in Harlem liked the President so the PPU advised that Thomas Jefferson High School on 96th and 1st Ave Manhattan would be the most appropriate place. It had a big sports hall that could take the President, the crowd and most importantly the press and it was only a block from the river front. Granted it was barely in Harlem but they'd bus in plenty of black kids from the projects. The cameras would see what the President wanted them to see.

Ladysmith
3pm GMT Monday 9th May 1994

They'd worked late into the previous evening in Jane's hotel room, papers strewn all over the floor. They'd sifted out the irrelevant from the relevant. They'd found enough of a paper trail, invoices and bank statements, to convince themselves they were on the right track with Daniel Okra, but precious little to tell them what they should do going forward.

During the first sifting process Stuart had set aside the military ordinance map they'd found lying on the table in Okra's house. It was only after breakfast, when they'd each gone to their rooms that Jane had picked up the map from the floor and spread it on her bed. It was not a new map, faded yellow at the edges from exposure to the sun with lots of faint hand written notes and arrows scrawled throughout. In two areas the markings were fresh. A blue biro had been used to circle a heavily contoured area on the map. The other fresh marking was in the top left hand corner, in the same blue biro. It read "*Kutz Plant Hire- Return when finished*". She walked around to Stuart's room and knocked.

"It's a detailed map of the Drakensberg," said Stuart, when she had shown it to him.

"It looks as if it has been used recently," she replied, pointing out the circled area. "*Kutz Plant Hire* was the name mentioned by the security guard who got shot in Durban. Do you think it's worth taking a look?"

"It's a bit remote and remember we're not really equipped for that sort of field trip."

"What equipment would we need?"

"Personal protection equipment. What if we come across people who wouldn't like us to be there? We'd be exposed, out on a limb."

"I've gone through the papers. We've confirmed we're on the right track. It's got to be worth just having a look. We'll be careful."

Stuart drove up the main road till he found the unmarked track on the right that appeared to be heading into the hills. He stopped at the '*No Entry*' and '*Warning*' signs and shrugged his shoulders before making the turn. Steadily he guided the car upwards through the narrow winding gorge.

"This track's been used recently" he said and a little later, "this vehicle isn't made for this type of road." Still they proceeded, the car slipping from side to side on the muddy ground. The overhanging canopy of foliage made travelling eerie. When they entered the section between the steep sided cliffs Jane opened a window; the smell was of rotting vegetation. Eventually they could see sunshine in the distance and Stuart stopped the car.

"Stay here, I'm going ahead on foot to take a look."

He returned in twenty minutes.

"Well?" she asked.

"There's a valley ahead, open flat bottomed. Nice meadow, very pretty."

"Sounds great, let's take a look."

"I'm nervous," replied Stuart. "Once we're out in the open we are easily spotted and easy targets."

"If somebody sees us we can turn around, head back down the track," said Jane. "We know it's clear behind us."

"Well I suppose. To me it doesn't look like there has been anything up here for a few days."

"How do you know that?"

"Last vehicle here was a heavy vehicle, its tyres pressed into the grass. The grass is already springing up straight again."

"Let's go and look."

When they broke through in to the valley floor he speeded up and followed the newest tyre marks.

Jane was the first to spot it. "What's that over there?" she asked pointing to a dark patch on the approaching rock face."

"Beginning of an old mine working I'd guess. We'll find out soon enough, that's where the tracks are leading us."

Stuart kept his eyes peeled in all directions but it did nothing to diminish his feeling of apprehension. He stopped the car two hundred yards short of the tunnel entrance, behind a large isolated bush.

"We'll walk the rest of the way."

They walked slowly, keeping close to the rock face to minimise their exposure. As they got closer they could see that the dark patch was actually large steel doors, closing off the tunnel entrance.

"They normally block off old mine workings for safety," said Stuart.

"This isn't old though," replied Jane. "The brass padlock is still shiny."

"You're right and there's plenty of evidence of activity around the entrance. Jane pulled on the padlock that was hooked through a hasp. It fell away in her hand. She stepped back startled. "It's not locked."

Stuart pulled carefully at one of the steel doors, opening it just enough for him to see in. Then he pulled it wide open.

"There's nobody inside, not unless they can see in the dark."

Jane opened the second door; it moved easily revealing a dark tunnel, daylight penetrating a few feet only.

"It doesn't smell mouldy," said Stuart. "Actually I think I can smell lubricating oil or something. This place had been used and not that long ago."

"Wish we had a torch," said Jane.

Stuart hesitated, all his instincts telling him they should turn back.

"Look" said Jane pointing to a green steel cabinet on the wall. On the cabinet's door, painted in black lettering, was the word *'generator'.* Stuart breathed a sigh of relief knowing that if the generator was turned off the place was most likely deserted.

He opened the cabinet door. There were instructions on the back, written in both Afrikaner and English. He pulled down an electrical breaker, set a dial to auto and pressed the start button. In the distance they heard a rumble.

"What's that," asked Jane.

"Diesel generator" replied Stuart.

The rumble settled down to a low throb and as if by magic lights along the tunnel came on, flooding the place with light. Tentatively they walked forward down the tunnel and towards the cavern.

"Holy Christ," said an astounded Stuart as they entered the vastness. "It's a full blown military installation, and what an installation! Let's have a look around. There's an empty container there for starters.

"Could it be the one we're looking for?"

"I don't think so," replied Stuart. "I know it was a long time ago and we only saw it in the distance but I think the one we're looking for is forty foot long, that's a twenty foot container."

"Oh, you never said that before," said a surprised Jane. "The one that came off the Mazowe was definitely a twenty foot container."

"Fuck, are we barking up the wrong tree?"

"Could they have swopped the containers around. Everything else points to this being the right place with the right people involved."

"Let's just park that question for a while and see what we've got here."

They separated, Jane working her way around to the left and Stuart to the right. It was more than an hour before they came together in the middle of the cavern.

"Find anything interesting?" asked Stuart.

"I think I found the 'office'," replied Jane. "There are a lot of papers in there. I've been sifting through them. How about you?"

" Look at this by the container. There's been a vehicle here of some description and somebody's been painting it and there are some used stencils over there."

"What do the stencils say?"

"POLICE in eight inch high letters."

"What type of vehicle was it?"

"I can't say exactly but they did drive through some wet paint and left tyre tracks. The markings are pretty chunky. I'd say they belong to an off-roader of some kind."

"Like a Land Rover?"

"Bigger. And there's more, come over here." Stuart led Jane over to some work benches, at the side of which were cardboard boxes stuffed full of documents. "Look at these." He picked a file at random from the top of one of the boxes and handed it to Jane.

"Wow. That's it then. No question we're in the right place. This is some kind of manual for the nuclear weapons."

"Yes, and drawings and all kinds of other stuff as well. I wonder if they've abandoned this place?"

"I think it's pretty obvious," replied Jane. "They could have stuffed the bomb into a truck or something that's been disguised as a police vehicle and taken it to Pretoria with the intention of detonating it at the inauguration. And to answer the last part of your question, I don't think they're coming back."

"We need to let Duncan know what he's looking for pretty quickly. Let's get back to Ladysmith and a telephone."

"Just give me a few minutes," said Jane. "The papers on one of the desks are personal and recent. I'll scoop them up. You never know, it might help."

Light was fading as they left. The final part of the drive was treacherous and in complete darkness.

"Can't you go faster?" Jane prompted.

"I can hardly steer, the road's badly rutted, the car's all over the place."

"With what we've got now, the South Africans will have to believe us."

"They might," replied Stuart, "if we can get to the right people. It's most probably too late though. The Inauguration is tomorrow. I expect Pretoria is stuffed full of people with more arriving all the time. I know every hotel room is jam packed; people are even sleeping rough just to be there. They could never evacuate the place in time. The only chance is to neutralise the threat."

Once off the track they followed the road back towards Ladysmith and stopped at the first hotel they came to. There was a payphone in the bar. They rang Duncan first; he wasn't in his hotel room. Jane left a message with reception, then phoned the British Embassy and spoke with the young duty officer. He took down a note of what she was saying without any display of emotion, indeed almost as if he were merely taking a routine report. When she'd finished she'd wondered if he'd understood the implications of the message.

"You do understand what I'm saying don't you?" Jane asked.

"Perfectly," came the reply. "Leave it with me to contact Mr Murdoch and set the wheels in motion at the Embassy and with the South Africans."

Jane hung up. "He didn't fill me with any confidence!"

"Come on, we're heading to Pretoria," said Stuart moving swiftly towards the door.

Meadow Vale Hotel Pretoria
1am Tuesday 10th May 1994

The night porter knew Duncan well enough and spotted him as he came through the revolving door into the hotel's lobby. "Mr Murdoch, a couple of people have being trying to get hold of you, they've left several messages. I think there is some urgency."

Duncan took the numbers and went to his room to phone the embassy. He got straight through to the duty officer who was still unruffled. "Mr Cameron and Miss Ashton are on their way to Pretoria. They will go directly to Union Buildings. In the meantime they say you should concentrate on finding a large police vehicle painted blue, most probably with off- road capabilities. The Ambassador is taking the matter seriously and is currently on his way to talk directly with the Minister for the Interior. I have informed the duty officers at friendly embassies that there is an imminent and credible threat. I have also arranged for non-essential staff and families from this embassy to leave the capital. Lastly a Burt Zimmerman from the US embassy..."

A red light started to flash on Duncan's phone indicating an incoming call.

Duncan cut off the embassy, pressing the change caller button and hoped it was Stuart and Jane. It wasn't.

"Hiya bud," was the greeting with a strong American drawl. "What's up?"

"Literally just got your messages," replied Duncan. "It appears that my colleagues have found some information that confirms the threat to the Inauguration. I haven't spoken to them myself but they've given me an idea what we're looking for. I'm going back to Union Buildings. Stuart and Jane are heading directly there."

"Gotcha. Just going to pick up a few things and then I'll be with you."

The phone clicked and the line went dead.

It was 4am when the knock on Nelson Mandela's bedroom door woke him. Without waiting for a response his personal aide entered the room and turned on a table lamp that stood on the bureau.

Mandela turned over and sat up in bed. "Is it time already?"

"No it is not time to get ready but there is an important matter. You need to speak to the Minister for the Interior. He is here waiting."

Mandela got up, put his feet into slippers and pulled on his dressing gown in the warm room. The comfort he now enjoyed constantly reminded him of the years of deprivation he'd suffered in prison and the hardship that the majority of black South Africans still endured.

The Minister was in the living room, unshaven and without a tie and clearly shaken.

"What is it?" asked Mandela.

"We have received a warning from the British about a security threat to today's proceedings."

"I will not be the President for a few hours. Why aren't you at the bedroom door of the man who is currently in charge?"

"Mr de Klerk says that the political ramifications for him, a white man, cancelling the inauguration of the first black President would be unacceptable. He says it is up to you what happens."

Mandela nodded. "That is true. But is this the same issue that the British made us aware of previously?"

"It is. But they are more convinced than ever now."

"I thought we had already had this discussion. Let us try another way. Answer me this," said Mandela, "When I am President will I have to call Downing Street, or possibly Washington, every morning to find out what is going on in my own country? Are not my own services capable of ensuring the safety of the state – and me?"

"They are both capable and willing to do their duty Sir."

"Are the British more capable of gathering information in South Africa than your people?"

"They are not Sir. I - we have control of the situation."

"So based on the information in your possession are you willing to call off the Inauguration? Please bear in mind that the whole country waits and the rest of the world watches. This is no easy decision."

The Minister shifted from foot to foot his discomfort clearly visible. The Minister like the majority of politicians had spent his entire life contriving to grab hold of the reins of power and when they were finally in his grasp he was terrified to exercise that power or take responsibility.

The Minister remained silent.

"I am going back to bed," Mandela eventually said. "I may get another hour or so sleep. In the meantime go away and make your decision – whatever it may be. And it should be the right decision. I need to have faith in my Ministers."

Union House, Pretoria
6am Tuesday 10th May 1994

Duncan stood next to the dais where, in a few hours, Nelson Mandela would be sworn in as President of South Africa. As daybreak came the crowds that had gathered and camped out overnight to get a good position spread out in front of him.

The Minister for the Interior had made his decision. He had sent a police captain, Conrad Skelly, to liaise with the British and Americans. The Minister would make further decisions based on the reports of the captain. At a minimum the Minister would have somebody to blame for any bad decision.

Burt Zimmerman gave a two fingered whistle from the back of the podium area. Duncan turned to see the American standing next to Captain Skelly. He walked over.

Skelly began. "To answer your question; I have done what I can. Because of the magnitude of this event the Pretoria police have had to draw from resources from many other police forces. Policemen have been drafted in from all the major cities and brought with them vehicles of all descriptions, from patrol cars to armoured personnel carriers. However, as far as I can ascertain there are definitely no tracked vehicles and no rough terrain vehicles deployed on the streets of Pretoria. All police and security staff have been told to keep a lookout for such vehicles and report them in immediately. That is as much as I can do for now."

"That's more than anybody else has done so far. You will call us immediately you find anything? This guy here," said Burt pointing to Duncan, "he's already defused one of those there bombs. He only needs a few minutes - right Duncan?"

"It's not quite that simple but get me there," replied Duncan.

Stuart and Jane were in a small temporary cabin that had been erected behind one of the outside broadcast vehicles in the car park at the rear of Union Buildings. It was the only place that Captain Skelly had been able to arrange. Other than a large table and a few odd plastic chairs the cabin was unfurnished. Burt, not satisfied with the facilities had, within thirty minutes, managed to get a fridge full of cold Coke and a coffee machine, that he placed on top of the fridge. A little later Skelly had turned up with a couple of hand held radio sets.

"They're simple enough. Three dials on the top: volume and squelch as normal and a channel selector. Channel two is being used by the police for this operation. You can select that when you want to listen in. Channel eight is free. I suggest you use that for private communications between yourselves."

Burt was the last to arrive. He struggled carrying a wooden crate that he placed on the floor, in a corner, before pouring a strong black coffee into a plastic cup. "Not quite home but it'll do."

"The coffee's very welcome," said Jane the black rings under her eyes evidence of her recent lack of sleep.

"Situation report!" said Stuart in a slightly raised voice to get everyone's attention. "To say the least it's not looking good. If we're right, the device, if there is one, will go off during the inauguration. In that event we and everybody within a radius of a couple of miles of the point of detonation will die immediately and many more at a greater distance will die in the following days, months and years."

"At least it'll be quick for us" said Burt, his humour failing to raise a laugh.

"The South Africans are looking for suspicious vehicles now and have agreed that if they find anything, as well as alerting their own bomb disposal teams they will call Duncan immediately."

"I've been thinking," said Duncan. "We had a look around the far side of this hill the other day. We thought it would be less effective to set the bomb off there and that the hill was pretty much impregnable. But what if this van Stardan has a 'go anywhere' vehicle? If he's got a sense for the dramatic he might like to get to the top of the kopje and detonate there."

"Do you and Burt want to go and take a look?" asked Stuart. "See if anything catches your eye. But don't wander too far. Jane and I collected a load of paper in Ladysmith. Somewhere in the pile there might be some clues. We'll sift through them as fast as we can."

There was a knock on the cabin door. Burt opened it. A South African PTC technician stood there. "I was told to give you a couple of emergency land lines," he said walking in holding two telephones and trailing some cable. "They're already connected. You just have to dial. No time to lay the cables properly," he said as he left the cabin in a hurry.

"They can get things done when they want to," said Duncan.

Jane spoke. "So far we've got a few pieces of information that don't make sense. Firstly we have a false British passport in the name of Edward Purvis with a photograph that looks suspiciously like Peter van Stardan. It appears he made a trip to Madrid a few weeks ago. He was only gone a few days. What was that about? Also from bank statements we know that 'Mr Purvis' made some payments to an estate agent in Pretoria. We've asked Conrad Skelly to try and trace the estate agent but he's not that hopeful as it's just about a public holiday here, nobody's working that doesn't have to. We also got some correspondence from an Italian diplomat that we don't understand and then there's the consignment note as well."

"What's a consignment note exactly?" asked Duncan.

"It's a container to you and me," replied Stuart.

"Then why don't they call it a container?"

Jane put the palm of her hand into the air to stop people talking as she concentrated, an obvious pained expression on her face.

"That may not be such a stupid question. A horrible thought has just hit me. Is a consignment the same as a container?"

Stuart pulled his wallet out of his back pocket and searched for the scrap of paper. "I might just be able to sort this out, if the phone works that is."

He dialled and waited, the phone rang five times before she picked up. "Hi, is that Trish, from National Railways?"

"Yes," she replied her voice wary of the stranger on the line.

"I don't know if you remember me? I'm Stuart and you helped me with an insurance matter a few weeks ago!"

Her voice immediately lightened. "Oh yes I do remember you. Did you catch the crooks?"

"Not yet, but we're close. I was just wondering if you could clear a matter up for me. I'm a little bit confused. It's just terminology. Why do you always use the word consignment and not container in your documentation?"

"That's easy. A consignment could be a single container or a number of containers. Say somebody was sending ten containers from one destination to another there would only be one consignment note but ten containers."

"That's not very clear from the consignment note you gave me."

"Yes but you only have a photocopy of the front of the consignment note. It's a two sided forms. The number of containers and their description is written on the reverse side."

"So there could be more than one container in the consignment I was looking for."

"Oh yes."

"Thanks for that I get the drift."

"Did it help?"

"Possibly."

"I have to go now. I'm going to the inauguration. Isn't it exciting?"

"It's exciting for different people in different ways," replied Stuart truthfully and hung up leaving Trish wondering what he meant.

"Did you get that Jane?"

"I did. That could explain what we found at Ladysmith. The container we found was a twenty foot one, right?"

Stuart nodded.

"But you and Duncan said that what you saw coming from Vastrap the day you were attacked was a forty foot container?"

"It was at a good distance," replied Duncan, "but I'm sure that's what it looked like."

"I've seen those container trucks on the road. I think sometimes they have one very long container on them or sometimes two smaller one's – I guess one forty foot one or two twenty foot ones. Am I right?"

She didn't wait for an answer. "Is it possible that there are two containers and two bombs?"

"There could be two containers," replied Duncan, "but I'm absolutely sure that there couldn't be two missing bombs. I physically inspected Vastrap and checked the paper work."

"So what are you saying," asked Burt, struggling to follow.

"We wanted some information from Walvis Bay container depot. They couldn't give it to us because they'd had a mysterious fire that had destroyed a lot of the paper work. It's possible that somebody was trying to hide something isn't it."

"Perhaps the other container was on the MV Mazowe and is now on the bottom of Durban harbour," suggested Duncan.

"All those containers have now been recovered. I'd guess the container went elsewhere."

Jane picked up one of her files, flicking through pages of notes until she'd found what she wanted. "That's a possibility. One other ship left Walvis Bay the same day as the Mazowe; it was headed for Cadiz. The second container could have been on that vessel."

"I'm still confused," said Burt. "Cadiz. Why?"

"We need to see what else is in that pile of paper," said Jane.

"It won't even be of academic interest if the bomb goes off here," said Stuart.

"How about me and you go check out the perimeter," said Burt to Duncan.

"I'm not sure if I should be out of touch."

"Got one of these things," said Burt pulling back the left side of his jacket revealing something that resembled a brick wrapped in a leather case hanging from his belt. "It's a cell phone, they can call us, I'll leave the number."

It was incidental that Burt was looking straight at Jane when he next spoke. "You carrying?"

Jane looked shocked. "Not as far as I know?" Her words were hesitant wondering if she'd heard Burt correctly.

"Miss Ashton is single," said Stuart, trying to avert the embarrassment.

Burt screwed his nose up. "Are you guys carrying guns? I know you Brits don't carry them all the time," he looked toward Duncan, "I thought they might be appropriate if we're going walk about. I brought a couple of spares from our embassy. They're in the box."

The laughter went over Burt's head. Duncan took a Smith and Wesson revolver and tucked it into the belt of his pants, hidden by his jacket.

By the time Duncan and Burt left, taking one of Skelly's radios with them, Jane was busily sifting through the papers. Stuart quickly joined her.

Vijoen Street, Pretoria
8am Tuesday 10th May 1994

Daniel Okra only had a mattress on the floor and a couple of old blankets for a bed in his room but he didn't mind, the conditions were little worse than he endured in his own house. As he lay there he could hear van Stardan speaking, as if in conversation. Daniel had asked Peter about it the first night. Peter had replied that he was saying his prayers, having a conversation with God. It was not that far from what he believed in reality. He was actually talking with Alfred Smidt who in his mind was in heaven with God. When the talking had stopped Okra got up from his mattress and went to the kitchen and made coffee for them both.

Peter came through. He was smiling. It was rare for him to smile. It made Okra happy.

"Today will be a good day for me whatever happens. Either our actions will re-ignite the Afrikaner people to rise up and wrestle back control or I will go to a better place and join my friends in union with God."

"And I will be with you," replied Okra. "I will be with you and your friends."

The smile left van Stardan's face. "I gave you the opportunity to leave. If you go now you can still get away."

"Don't you want me to join you and your friends?"

"I did not expect to see you there," replied van Stardan immediately initiating a disappointment in Okra. "But if it is God's will then I will accept it."

The reluctant endorsement was accepted by Okra. Who was he after all to go against the will of God? "I will go out to the garage and test the engine of the Mamba."

"No. You must not go outside. Look," van Stardan pointed through the kitchen window to the crest of the hill behind the house. "There are men looking, watching for anything suspicious. They must not see us before the time is right."

"What part will I play," asked Okra?"

"I planned no part for you."

"But somebody must drive the Mamba up the hill. I am used to such vehicles. Would it not be good if I drove and sat next to you?"

Peter van Stardan thought for a moment. "Yes, you can do that."

Duncan and Burt stood at the side of the track below the crest of the hill. They'd used a police buggy to get there, the only one that was stuck on the right side of the trailing cables. Burt stood looking through binoculars that he'd whisked out of his box scanning the streets at the bottom of the slope.

"I can pick out the individual streets now. To the right is Mann Street, the one at right angles is Hadley Street and further to the left is Vijoen Street. But there's no movement. Quiet as a graveyard."

"What about vehicles, parked or moving?" asked Duncan.

"Nothing, not even in the driveways. I can see right into the gardens. There are some tidy houses down there. I suppose some of them have money. I can pick out bits of new fencing and even a newish building."

"We'll I hope the owner hasn't wasted his money."

"What do you mean?"

"If it all goes wrong he'll have wasted his money won't he?"

"Suppose so. There's nothing here. Let's get back to the cabin and see if they have made any progress."

Manhattan New York City
6am (EST) Tuesday 10th May 1994

The President was in foul humour. Even the luxurious beds of the Waldorf Astoria had done nothing to placate him. Last evening he dined in a private room with Party Grandees and had been less successful than he'd hoped in raising funds. The people with the money were blunt, they could be; they were the paymasters.

"You have to be in the running to win if you want money from us," they'd said. "Improve your popularity and we promise to see what we can do."

The President preferred to give promises rather than receive them; that's what politicians are good at.

"Why are you getting me up at this God forsaken hour?"

"South Africa is seven hours ahead of us," replied Eugene Forester. "Mandela's inauguration is taking place three pm their time, that's eight am our time, right in the middle of US peak morning viewing. We need to get you in front of the cameras so that the networks have something to show."

"I got a headache already."

"We'll just get you to the school. All you have to do is stand there when the kids do their flag raising and swearing allegiance thing. Then you go into the hall. You'll give out certificates until the Networks are ready. Don't worry we got a big stock of kids on stand-by. Once the Networks say, you're going live coast to coast, make your speech about how Mandela was only elected because of the US and then present the medal to that hero guy. We'll have you out of there and helicoptered back to the White House for lunch."

"You got a helicopter on stand-by?"

"As always. It'll be in Central Park, ready and waiting."

"Good. This is your show, it better go smoothly Eugene."

Jack Carter and David Evans were already at Thomas Jefferson High School. David Evans looked pristine in his major's uniform.

"You look the part," said Jack.

"I hope so; the bastards made me pay for this out of my own pocket," replied David.

"Privilege of being an officer," laughed Jack. "Sure you got it right? Want another rehearsal or are you ready to go?"

"I'm ready to go and get some breakfast."

"Sorry bud. You don't get so much as a cup of coffee until after you've seen the President. I am not risking a mark on those nice clothes before you're done with the cameras."

"You shitting me?"

A man in a white baseball cap hurried over to where Jack and Eugene were standing. He spoke quickly, the words rattling out of his mouth. "I'm the producer. This hall's a bit small for us all so the Networks are going to share a single camera. They'll all put on their own commentary live. Inside is going to be easy, but once you get outside it's going to be a bit of a free for all. As well as the Networks there will be some local TV companies jostling for a picture. Sometimes they throw funny questions. Be careful what you say, the whole country will be listening. Got that?"

"I'm not sure if I can do that, talk to the cameras," replied David.

"Listen the President does it every day and I'm not joking if he can do it so can you. See that guy over there with the clipboard? He is organising everything inside, just take your instructions from him. He'll tell you where to wait. By the way any of you got a cell phone?" The producer didn't wait for an answer. "Turn it off now."

Union House, Pretoria
1.45 pm Tuesday 10th May 1994

The band was playing and the activity outside the cabin was frantic, making it hard for Jane to concentrate on the papers she was searching through. The door of the cabin opened and Conrad Skelly walked in. They all looked around expectantly.

"Nothing," he said, "Except that Mandela's arrived. He's on the platform listening to the entertainment. What about you?"

Nobody spoke, the answer was self-evident.

"Everybody for the VIP area is seated now."

Duncan picked up another piece of paper and was about to discard it when something caught his eye. He took a second look. "Burt, remember when you were looking through the binoculars, you mentioned some street names?"

"Yeah, so what?"

"What were they?"

"Now you're asking; Headly or something, Mann Street and something beginning with a V."

"Vijoen Street?"

"Yeah that's the one. Why what have you got?"

All eyes turned to Duncan. "A receipt for a rental deposit on a house in Vijoen Street!"

"Holy fuck, that's it," exclaimed Burt.

Conrad Skelly stepped forward and took the slip of paper out of Duncan's hand. Quickly he spoke into his hand-held radio. When he'd signed off he looked up. "Everything we have got is heading that way now."

"I think we need to get there too," said Stuart.

"You won't be able to drive, all the roads are impassable. It's the crowds. They're not listening to any instruction."

"We can get to the top of the hill," said Duncan. "We could try and run down from there."

"Mount up, the buggy's outside. You might want a gun too," said Burt to Stuart. "They're in the box."

Stuart picked a pistol, "Jane, you better stay here. It is vital to find out if there is anything else of significance in the paperwork."

Peter van Stardan had insisted that the back wall of the new garage be built from a single skin of cinder block stuck together with a weak cement mix. He told the builders he planned to extend the garage down the garden at a later date and didn't want too much trouble knocking through. It was plausible and they believed him.

The Mamba was parked in front of that wall, the bull bars just three feet away. There was more than an hour and a half to go but van Stardan had insisted they move from the house to the garage. They'd carefully looked out of both back and front windows of the house to ensure the coast was clear before taking the few steps in the open. Okra had climbed into the driver's seat whilst van Stardan had gone to the back of the truck and opened the doors, laughing at what he saw before firmly closing up the hatch.

He slipped down the narrow space between the side of the vehicle and the garage wall until he was opposite Okra's window. "Have you checked everything, are you sure that the correct gears have been selected?"

Although he'd already done it several times, Okra went through the motion of checking the various gear selectors again, this time speaking aloud. "Four wheel drive selected; wheel lock on; low range selected. All is as it should be."

It was then that they heard the first siren. It sounded distant. Soon others followed and they appeared to be getting closer. Van Stardan's heart missed a beat as if it knew the time had finally come. He climbed into the seat beside Okra.

"Be ready but do not start the engine until I tell you."

Okra felt for the key in the ignition. It was there. The sound of the sirens intensified. By now van Stardan was sure. It would not be exactly to plan. He'd disguised the Mamba as a police vehicle in the hope of getting close by stealth. Now he'd have to force his way through. But he was more worried about the timing. He wanted it to happen when the world was watching and that would not be until Mandela was actually taking the oath.

The first police vehicle to arrive in Vijoen Street was a Nissan Bluebird. The two uniformed officers got out of the car, weapons at the ready, one with a hand pistol and the other with a shotgun. They waited for backup. It arrived in seconds. The officers had hardly got out of the second vehicle before the first two officers moved forward. Exposed and out in the open they ran up the short drive separated and weaving, until they got to the shelter of the front of the house. They looked in the front window. Nothing.

The second two officers were coming forward now as more police vehicles arrived. They passed their colleagues and made their way between house and garage to check the rear. Even before they'd made the garden an officer was banging on the front door and shouting "POLICE OPEN THE DOOR."

In the garage van Stardan looked to Okra and nodded. "You know what to do!"

Okra turned the key in the ignition and the dashboard lit up. The orange glow plug light was on. They waited for it to go out, indicating that the cylinders in the Mercedes engine were warm enough to start. It felt like an eternity to both men. Behind them a police officer was rattling the garage doors. At last the orange light disappeared and Okra turned the ignition key to the next position. The hefty six cylinder engine barked into life, its power apparent.

Taken by surprise the police officers backed off and prepared for what they expected would be the emergence of some kind of vehicle through the garage doors.

Okra selected first gear and let out the clutch. The ratio was so low in the gear box that even at full revs, the engine in the Mamba would travel at no more than ten miles per hour, but at that speed nothing much would stop it. The Mamba moved forward and the bull bars came into contact with the rear gable wall; it crumbled away without even straining the engine. The Mamba rolled forward down the garden.

The speed of the vehicle was so slow the police officers were able to run and catch up with it. A young policeman, pistol in hand managed to get alongside the cab. Through the toughened Perspex window he could see an impassive Peter van Stardan looking back at him.

The officer yelled "Stop." The occupants took no notice of him. He yelled again. The instructions over the radio had been clear. "Apprehend the people at the house at any costs." He knew what that meant. On the run he raised his pistol and began firing at the side window. He was wasting his time and his ammunition.

The six millimetre bullets were never going to penetrate the toughened windows – that's what they'd been designed to resist. The vehicle reached the new fence at the bottom of the garden and crushed it as if it was not there. It began to rise up the slope. On the steep incline the policemen could not keep pace. Formed into an impromptu line they followed and fired at the back of the vehicle, chipping the paint, but otherwise to no effect.

Inside van Stardan and Okra felt the cab begin to lurch as the huge wheels encountered loose boulders. As some strain came on to the engine the tone deepened and the noise inside the cab increased, but the vehicle didn't slow.

Van Stardan shouted, "Follow the route I have shown you. It will lead to the track. Then we will be clear. Van Stardan pulled an M16 rifle from its rack. He held it with one hand and used the other to hold on to the hand grip that stopped him being thrown about.

It had been a mistake to take the buggy. The security track snaked around the contour of the hill. Duncan realised they probably could have run across the top of the hill in less time. But they were there now.

They saw the Mamba coming. The police officers had stopped shooting. Some, the younger ones, had holstered their weapons and were, almost hopelessly, trying to climb the hill, following the Mamba.

Duncan, Stuart and Burt watched as the vehicle lumbered over the rough ground, slowly but surely heading towards them and the track.

"What's his intention?" asked Burt, thinking aloud more than anything else.

"Perhaps he's trying to get to the top of the hill before he detonates the bomb?"

"That doesn't make sense. Why risk getting caught? Why not detonate now? He'll still kill everyone," said Stuart.

"There's no bomb in that vehicle," said Duncan.

"Why do you say that?" asked Stuart.

"No time to explain now. Trust me. But there's still a danger. I'll take one of the hand-guns, follow me down Stuart. Burt use the radio, tell Jane the bomb's not here."

"You got it," replied Burt, "But you can't stop that thing with a hand-gun."

Duncan ignored him and shouted at Stuart. "Just shoot into the grille, as many shots as you can."

Duncan jumped down a few feet from the edge of the track. A gun slit opened up on the front of the Mamba. A barrel poked out. They saw the muzzle flashes.

"He's shooting wild," shouted Stuart, following Duncan over the edge. "He can't take aim with that thing lurching about."

Duncan was the first to shoot at thirty yards, a difficult enough shot. The bullet ricocheted off the armour. He moved closer and shot again. This time he hit the grille. Stuart joined in.

The engine air intake on the front of the Mamba consisted of four louvered steel bars. Behind the louvers was the radiator; the unseen target. Stuart was doubtful but had nothing better to suggest. He knew that even if they did get a deflection and damage the radiator it would take some time for the engine to overheat sufficiently to seize up and stop.

Jane was finding it hard to concentrate. Only a few yards away throbbing traditional Mbube music boomed. Going outside she found a badly placed speaker and yanked at the connecting cable; it came free in her hand and the speaker fell silent. The level of sound dropped markedly. In the background she heard the crowd that was assembled in the amphitheatre cheer. She couldn't see that the crowd were roaring in approval as Mandela stood and danced for them. She brought her mind back to the task at hand and returned to the table in the cabin, shutting the door behind her as best she could. Now at last she could think.

The pile of papers was getting smaller. She was getting scared in case she'd missed the significance of any discarded scrap. A small business card caught her eye; she picked it up and turned it over. There was a handwritten address on the back. It looked wrong, out of place and somewhere in the back of her mind it struck a chord. She thought for a while before picking up a pile of bank statements and thumbing down the entries until she found what she was looking for.

Tracy Shapiro was still asleep when the phone rang; she stretched over to the bedside table and picked up the receiver. She would have preferred just to let it ring. She'd been having a wonderful dream, the first good dream for a long time, and didn't want to abandon the thought, but she knew, it was inculcated in her, a missed call was a missed opportunity. She had to pick up.

Tracy Shapiro was born Tracy Wellington. She'd married Arnold, a quiet man, eight years before and it had been good at first. If you could have asked Arnold he'd have told you that in the beginning he'd loved her ambition, her style and her go ahead nature but that didn't last for long. It soon turned out that ambition meant constant pressure, her style cost a lot to maintain and her 'go ahead' nature made her constantly pushy. Arnold didn't like arguments, so he didn't argue. One day he just upped sticks and left, leaving Tracy with three things; a new surname, a son called Randy and a heap of debts.

One quality that had gone unnoticed by Arnold was that Tracy was not a quitter. After the initial shock of his departure she'd knuckled down to doing what she could to give Randy a good life and keep the large Long Island apartment that had been the family home. As a *'commission only'* realtor, in the rental market, it was a tough world but she never stopped looking for or believing in the lucky break, and now she thought she'd found it. The diplomatic core attached to the United Nations in New York was huge and they were always coming and going, there were always fresh customers. She'd tried to break in for a long time and now finally in the last weeks she'd done it; secured her first diplomatic let to a newly accredited Italian.

Jane knew that an American realtor was not that much different than a British estate agent – they are all a pretty mercenary bunch. Only the prospect of more commission was going to achieve co-operation.

"I'm calling from London. I understand you are able to relocate overseas clients. Am I right?" Jane had begun.

Tracy's mind immediately went into full alert mode. "Yes, I specialise in that kind of work," she'd exaggerated.

"Good. I represent a number of people that are relocating to New York and you were recommended to me. I was wondering if you'd be interested in helping."

Stupid question thought Tracy. "Of course I would. Are they people for the United Nations? I've recently relocated an Italian diplomat."

"That's exactly the type of thing."

Jane picked up the business card and flicked it over. "Is that the one on Roosevelt Island?" she asked reading the hand written address again.

"Yes, it is. Do you know Mr Rossi?"

"I haven't had the pleasure of meeting him. But can you tell me how that placement went."

"No problems. It was all handled by phone. I got a great apartment. It's on the fourth floor of Martin Luther House on West Road. It's got a great view. Mr Rossi was really pleased when I told him he would actually be able to see the United Nations building from his window; it's just across the water. I think that clinched the deal for him, that and being able to accommodate his special requirements."

"What special requirements were those?" asked Jane.

"Mr Rossi is not actually arriving till tomorrow, the 11th but his container of furniture arrived on the 9th. He wanted me to put it somewhere for the two intervening days."

Jane's heart was beating faster. "So what arrangements did you make for him?"

"I had a word with the block's janitor and got a spot in the service yard where it can stand for a couple of days. No problem. Of course there was a small extra fee. That's the kind of personal service I offer my clients" .Tracy didn't mention that she was giving the janitor twenty bucks up front and a another twenty when the new tenant arrived because she'd actually charged two hundred and fifty dollars for the service.

"So the container's in the yard now?"

"Yes it is."

"I got a call on another line, got to go sorry." Jane hung up not even hearing Tracy's last sentence.

"I didn't get your name……"

If Jane had dug a little deeper into the pile of paper she'd have found another piece of paper, a consignment note for a container sent from Cadiz to New York and she'd never know about what happened in the container terminal in Cadiz nearly three weeks before.

Cadiz is most remembered for its long and rich history. The cramped 'old town' is crowded with historic buildings on almost every corner separated by narrow cobbled streets, a tourist's paradise. Few people realise that the reason Cadiz became such a historically important place still exists today. All ships entering or leaving the Mediterranean Sea must pass Cadiz and its deep water port facilities and that is why today Cadiz has one of the busiest container transhipment terminals in the world.

Fernando Sanchez was eighteen and it was his first day as a trainee customs officer at the Port. Roberto Vieira, a senior customs officer of more than twenty years had been given the task of taking Fernando around with him on that first day. It had been a lot to take in but with his fresh young mind Roberto had absorbed every word spoken by his fatherly mentor.

"One last place Fernando, then we are finished for the day."

It was a gated and fenced area with only a dozen or so containers scattered around the yard, far different from the main marshalling yards with thousands of tightly packed containers standing in six high stacks.

"What is this place?" asked Fernando.

"This is the reserved compound," replied Roberto unlocking the giant padlock and leading his charge inside. "Some consignments we trust a little more than others. It isn't a rule, more an informal convention. Diplomats and embassies are constantly sending their staff around the world and they very often take their furniture and even cars with them. Unless we have a really bad suspicion we don't search these containers. The diplomats get upset."

"So these are containers our Government is sending to Spanish embassies around the world?"

"No not just our embassy. We also tranship diplomatic containers for other countries as well. Look at this one for instance."

Roberto walked over to a container at random and checked the papers inside a protective bag attached to the opening mechanism. "This container belongs to an Italian diplomat, a Mr Rossi, and is being shipped to New York."

"So it belongs to an Italian who is going to be a diplomat in the United States."

"I'd guess Mr Rossi is going to work in the United Nations. That's where they're based.

"So it's furniture inside?"

"I hope so."

Duncan and Stuart were retreating bit by bit as the Mamba got closer, stopping where they could to let off another shot at the grille but not knowing if they had hit the target. The Mamba was within fifty yards of reaching the track when they saw the first signs; steam coming from under the vehicle, a sure indication that it was overheating. But still it kept on coming.

Busy concentrating on keeping the vehicle on its intended course, Okra had not noticed the needle on the water temperature gauge steadily climbing, climbing in to the red section of the dial. Van Stardan was trying to re-load his M16 carbine so that he could take some more shots at the men outside.

Normally a Mercedes diesel engine will run for a couple of miles after the radiator has been punctured. But these circumstances were not normal; the engine was being run flat out in first gear, climbing a severe gradient over rough ground. The pressure on the engine was immense, more than the Bavarian engineers had designed it for. The fact that the Mamba was armour plated and more than twice the weight of the original Unimog didn't help either.

By the time the wheels broke the crest and got purchase on the gravel track, the fuel was already getting so hot that it was vaporising in the injector system, making the engine miss and sound very rough.

Any relief van Stardan felt at finally reaching the flat track was quickly overtaken by the strange noises and smells that permeated the cab, coming from the engine; the sound and smell of hissing steam and overheated oil.

"You must keep it going. You must drive it to the podium so that I can complete my mission. You must go faster!"

"If I go any faster the engine will overheat more quickly and will fail altogether. I must nurse the engine."

"Go faster." demanded van Stardan.

Stuart, Duncan and Burt back together, watched as the Mamba speeded up and disappeared down the track.

"It's got to go the long way around. We can try and go over the hill and get there before it," gasped an already breathless Duncan.

"They're going for Mandela directly. The bomb is somewhere else," said Stuart as he started to climb the hill in Duncan's wake. Burt, older and less fit, struggled to follow.

The Mamba trundled on, the trail of white steam now turning to black smoke. Okra's foot was flat on the floor, all care for the engine gone. As they rounded the end of the spur another vista of Pretoria emerged. Against a background of the high rises of the commercial centre, in the foreground, stretched out before them, in what were the normally ornate gardens, the crowds massed in their thousands. If van Stardan was closer he would have seen something unique in South African history, a joy to most but repulsive to him; black and white, united in hope for their country's future.

They were now only a hundred and fifty yards from their destination, the rear of the colonnade, the colonnade that was the backdrop to the dais where Mandela would take the oath of office. The Mamba had a six cylinder engine. At that instant two of the cylinders seized causing the crankshaft to shear. The Mamba stopped dead, it was going no further.

To its left the ground rose sharply, covered in dense shrub, to its right it fell away to the plain below. Van Stardan jumped out quickly and went to the back of the Mamba and opened the rear door. He worked quickly. Okra too left the cab but without instruction stood there helplessly.

Duncan was the first to reach the crest of the hill. He could only see parts of the track; the Mamba was not in sight. He guessed the vehicle had not made the colonnade yet. He started off down the slope just as

Stuart caught up with him. The two men slithered down the loose scree sections, bouncing off deep rooted trees and shrubs.

They didn't see it coming; the track was hidden by the vegetation. One second they were sliding down the slope and the next the ground went from underneath them and they were on the track. Okra stood fixed to the spot watching as Stuart recovered his footing and bounded towards him. He didn't even attempt to struggle.

Duncan got back to his feet as van Stardan came from the back of the vehicle. In one hand he held an AK47. He'd swopped it for the M16 because, despite it being highly inaccurate, the AK47 is a better close quarters weapon. In the other hand he held a plunger that was connected by cable to two military haversacks that he wore on the back and front of his body.

Duncan still held the Smith and Wesson but after shooting at the Mamba he didn't know how many rounds were left. Stuart held Okra in front of him with a paralysing arm grip around the throat.

"Put your guns on the ground," shouted van Stardan. "There are enough explosives in these sacks to blow us all to kingdom come."

"You won't hurt Mandela at this distance," said Duncan.

"Maybe not but it will be enough to stop the inauguration, I will settle for that. Put your guns down or I'll shoot you all."

"I don't think so. I believe you're mad enough to kill us but you won't fire your gun; it will bring a hundred armed guards swarming down on you. I know you want Mandela, nothing less."

"You don't know anything, replied van Stardan. This is only a side show. You believe I'm mad and that may be true but you should not confuse madness with stupidity, they are two different things.

"So where is it?" asked Duncan, "Where is the atomic bomb?"

" Ah so you know about that. Well it's too late now for you to do anything. I always knew it would be difficult to conceal and detonate an atomic weapon here. Right now this is the most protected and secure place in the world. I wanted you to believe this was the main target so I carried on planning knowing it would distract the people looking for me.

Don't you understand South Africa has not been won by the black man. It is the United States and their cronies working in the United Nations that have betrayed South Africa and it is they that will be punished and there is nothing you can do about it.

In less than an hour the heart will be ripped out of America's greatest city and when it disappears so will that loathsome building on the East Side. And what a delight that will be. How could I have known when I was planning this operation that the President of the United States, too scared to come here, would be in that city when the bomb goes off. What a beautiful irony. Van Stardan smiled. "Here I have only one intention. I will kill the leader of the Africans by my own hand, face to face equally, one man to one man."

"Except that you will have a gun and he will be unarmed," said Duncan.

"That is of no consequence. What is important is that leaderless the Africans will go back to where they belong and I will have had my retribution for what was done to me and my country!"

Burt was not giving up. He'd clawed his way to the crest of the hill, barely able to draw breath. With a determination of steel he didn't pause to get his breath back, just rolled over the summit to begin his descent. He'd followed the way he thought Duncan and Stuart had gone but soon became disorientated and lost the track. He tried to regain his feet for a better view but the loose scree stopped him getting a sure footing, the ground slipped beneath him and he tumbled downhill. He entered the shrubbery at speed and without control and suddenly the ground disappeared beneath him. He broke through the vegetation almost airborne in a flurry of broken twigs and leaves and caught van Stardan totally by surprise. Too late he tried to dodge out of the way. Burt crashed into Van Stardan with such force both men went flying to the ground. The struggle lasted only a second or two. Stuart seeing the opportunity released his grip on Okra and darted forward. He hadn't taken two steps when Van Stardan broke free and scrambled back to his feet, the plunger no longer in his hand. He managed to swoop up the AK in a single move and point it at Stuart.

Duncan's reflexes were quick. Not only did he have time to raise the Smith and Wesson and take aim at van Stardan's head he also found time for a quick prayer. "If there is a God please make sure there is a bullet in this chamber, this is for Elizabeth"

It was a clean shot, centre of the forehead. Van Stardan dropped like a stone.

Stuart turned to Okra who seeing his opportunity jumped over the edge of the track and disappeared into the undergrowth.

"Let the weasel go," shouted Stuart. "We don't have time."

"Is he right, is the President in New York now?" asked Duncan.

Burt was back on his feet. "Yes and Jack's with him."

"We need to get back to the cabin." The three men ran.

Thomas Jefferson High School, New York
7.10am (EST) 10th May 1994

There was nothing for Jack Carter and David Evans to do but wait for the President to arrive. With amusement they watched Eugene Forester run about like a headless chicken trying to organise things that had already been organised. Eventually Eugene made it over to them.

"The President's coming."

"I know that," replied Jack dryly. "That's why we're here."

"I mean he's coming now, ETA eight minutes."

"Okay, we won't start without him."

"I would prefer it if you'd take this a bit more seriously. You just make sure you're both ready."

"That guy is so far up his own arse," said David Evans.

"Yeah but his preferred position is up the President's arse. Let's go over to the control van and see what's really going on."

Parked out of sight, down the side of a building in the school yard was the control van, the place from which the event was being choreographed. It was a large trailer really. Half a dozen men were inside watching monitors and listening to radio communications.

One of the men, Chuck, pushed his chair back and stepped outside the van. He got a pack of Chesterfields out. "Just time for a few quick puffs before the President arrives," he said drawing deeply on the cigarette. "You're the hero getting the medal aren't you?" he said to David who smiled in reply. "And you must be the guy from Langley. No medals for you?"

"Get our satisfaction from the job," said Jack.

"I wouldn't mind doing a couple of overseas assignments myself. This stuff is boring. I could do with a bit of action now and again."

A voice from inside the van shouted. "Hey Chuck, Eagle One about to arrive: thirty seconds. Better get back in here."

Chuck stubbed out his cigarette. Perhaps you'd put a word in for me?"

Jack didn't have time to answer. His cell phone started to ring.

Duncan was the first to arrive at the cabin, Stuart second and Burt, drawing from previously unknown reserves of energy, immediately behind.

"The bomb is in New York," said Duncan.

"I just got there myself with that one," replied Jane. "And I'm pretty sure of the location too."

"That's fantastic but it may be too late by the time we convince anybody in the US and there's no possibility of an evacuation," said Stuart.

"We could at least give them a chance," threw in Burt, "if Jack has his cell phone turned on."

Burt didn't need to tell Jack it was serious, the tone of his speech was enough. I'm putting you through to Stuart."

"Okay Stuart shoot"

"Jack you got to believe this. The bomb is in New York. I've got the address." Stuart took the card from Jane and read out the address on Roosevelt Island. "You got less than an hour. It's in a container somewhere in the service yard."

Roosevelt Island is a mixed residential area about two miles long and eight hundred feet wide and lies in the East River between Manhattan Island and the Borough of Queens. Although the Queensboro Bridge crosses directly over the island there is no way for vehicles to get on or off the bridge. The only way vehicles can get on to the island is by using the Roosevelt Island Bridge which connects the island with Queens. If it wasn't for the subway it wouldn't be a great place to live and work. It does however have good views of Manhattan and, in particular, the United Nations Buildings.

"What the fuck you talking about?" said Chuck.

"I haven't got time to argue. There's a bomb; initiate your plan now," Jack shouted.

For a moment Chuck hesitated. David Evans didn't. He wasn't hanging around to watch Jack convince Chuck. He ran from behind the building, across the yard and through the gate to the road. The cavalcade had arrived and the President had just got out of his car and was waving to the crowd of children pressed up against the chain link fence. David ran with his hands high in the air so the Presidential Guard could see he was unarmed. "Bomb!" he shouted, "Get the President out of here!"

The Presidential Guard were trained to react to the unusual. They didn't take chances. They would argue the rights and wrongs later on. Their only concern was to protect the President.

"Get him off the Island," shouted David.

The President didn't have to do anything. Strong hands bundled him back into his car and the driver, well trained in this type of exercise didn't need any orders. The vehicle leapt forward surprisingly quickly for its size and the amount of armour plating it carried. The route had been pre-planned and was clear. Within three minutes the President was being herded into his helicopter that was standing at the north end of Central Park, ready and waiting.

Policemen surrounded David. "What's the problem?" one of them demanded.

"Get me back to the control van quickly."

Jack was in the control van, standing behind the men at the monitors.

"Of course I got a bomb disposal squad. It's two hundred yards down the road, ready to go," said Chuck. "Somebody give me a route to Roosevelt Island."

The man at the last screen responded. "It's bad chief. The only way onto the island is from Queens and that means a trip over the Queensboro Bridge and the traffic's all backed up there because of the Presidential visit. I guess it's going to take them an hour to get there. They're on their way."

"We haven't got an hour," replied Jack still holding the cell phone in his hand. "You got to have something better than that."

"We got a fire and rescue launch in the East River. It was there 'just in case' for the Presidential helicopter. It's just going off station"

"Get it back shouted Chuck."

Jack spoke into the cell phone. "Did you get any of that?"

"I got the gist of it" replied Stuart. "If you can get to the container Duncan can talk you through it. He says it's simple enough once you're there."

"We'll have a go. Call me back in fifteen. If we answer we're still here."

"Get me to that launch," said Jack.

"I'm coming," said David, standing outside the control van still being held by a police captain. "I did the ordnance course. I know a bit."

The police captain drove the squad car himself. It was only a couple of blocks to Sutton Place Park and the riverfront. The orange painted rescue launch was edging up to the wall as Jack and David ran the last few steps to the waters edge. They both jumped the last yard.

"As close as you can get to the piers on West Road," shouted Jack to the helmsman.

The bow of the boat lifted high into the air as the Packard diesel engine opened up on full throttle.

As the boat skimmed the water Jack shouted to a crew man above the roar of the engine. "You got any tools? We need to get into a container."

The crewman smiled. "We got everything."

"We'll need you to help."

"New York's finest here. We're with you."

The launch bumped along the pier, they didn't wait for them to get a line ashore. They just jumped: Jack, David and the crewman. A cop stood at the end of the pier waiting.

"We found it. That way," he shouted as the men ran past him.

A hundred and fifty yards across a green and a road, then through a gate into the courtyard. The container was in front of them. A cop was cutting through the steel wire seal with bolt cutters. He saw the men approaching.

"It's New York, we don't wait for people here. If you didn't show I was going to have a go myself."

Jack's cell phone rang. "We're here. The doors of the container are opening as we speak."

"What do you see?" asked Duncan."

"It just looks like a normal bomb, the type you drop from a plane. It's strapped into a wooden cradle and fixed into position with a wooden framework. The pointy end is facing us."

"Go to the right of the bomb. You will find……"

Jack stepped forward into the steel container. The line went dead. Jack looked at the phone display. The signal indicator was at zero. He stepped back outside and a bar reappeared and a second later another. The phone rang again..

"I'll go into the container," said David, "stay outside and shout the instructions to me."

"You gave us a fright!"

"Might still do that, what do we do?"

"Have you got a hammer and say a 12 inch screwdriver to hand?"

"Hammer and twelve inch screwdriver?" Jack looked to the fire and rescue crewman.

He pulled the tools from his tool belt and passed them to David.

Jack shouted the instructions as clearly as he could.

David Evans removed the three access covers, stopping only to wipe the sweat from his brow.

"Centre inspection hatch," shouted Jack. "There's a Casio digital timer held in by a circlip. Remove the circlip with a screwdriver and pull the clock out. There are four wires attached to the clock; blue, yellow, red and green. Cut the red one. This will stop the timer," shouted Jack. David followed the instructions slowly, carefully. "Done" he shouted "Now" said Jack "Duncan says we need to remove the detonators as well. Go to one of the other holes. Inside there are aluminium tubes, about an inch in diameter by four inches long. They are buried in the conventional explosive that surrounds the nuclear core…."

It took David seconds to remove the first detonator and less time to remove the second.

"Take care," shouted Jack, repeating Duncan's warning. "The detonators could still go off on their own if they receive a sharp knock. Put them down somewhere safe, outside the container.

"Well done," said Duncan.

The phone bleeped in Jack's hand and the line went dead. He looked at the display again. The battery indicator was reading empty. "Until they get the battery problem sorted out these phones are going to be useless," he said shaking his head in disbelief.

Around the world people watched as Mandela took his oath and made his historic address of reconciliation. In the cabin, behind the colonnade, nobody could see the spectacle but they could just about hear it on the PA system.

"Burt that was a brilliant idea of yours," said Stuart.

"Which idea was that," he asked.

"The coffee machine. I never thought I'd enjoy a cup so much."

"That's so true," added Conrad Skelly who'd joined them.

They sat quietly listening to Mandela's words. When the address had finished Jane turned to Conrad.

"It's going to be a big change for you here in South Africa. What are your hopes for the future?"

"Me?" replied Conrad. "I hope it stays the same for everybody."

"It's a bit late for that isn't it," said Stuart.

"I hope not. You see for us whites here in South Africa we have been brought up in a place where things only got better and better. I think those times are gone. The best that the whites could hope for are that things just stay the same."

"What about the black people though?" asked Jane.

"I want the same for them. You just have to look north, across the Limpopo. Every country there is independent now, all the colonies are gone. Yet it's the same story in every one of those countries. After independence the economies have failed, living standards fell and life expectancy has been reduced. A lot of the countries have also been racked by civil war and suffered horrible corruption. So even if in my heart I want things to get better for the blacks in South Africa in truth the best I can hope for is that things don't actually get worse for them."

"That's not a very positive view," said Duncan.

"I know said Conrad, "and I can't tell you how sad it makes me."

It was nearly three hours later that the President sat down in the oval office to watch a replay of Mandela's inauguration. He'd been busy making sure that the news of the bomb in New York got suppressed. He didn't want anybody to know that there were still South African nuclear weapons in existence when he'd rested his reputation on having eradicated them. A lot of people had been hurriedly sworn to secrecy and a lot of media favours had been cashed in but he thought he contained the situation.

The Secretary of State sat with him.

"We've done the best we can and at least the Mandela thing has gone okay." It was a feeble effort to improve the President's mood.

The President watched the television without responding. When the coverage from South Africa ended the picture flashed to the steps of Congress. Outside on the steps stood Congresswoman Sarah Plankton, the opposition's most critical voice. She spoke directly to the camera.

"Our President has insulted not only Mr Mandela and the South African people but also all Afro-Americans in the United States by failing to attend the momentous events in Pretoria. Even his feeble attempt at throwing a sop to the non-white minorities in New York has turned into a circus. Without explanation he failed to turn up for his scheduled appointment in Harlem – disappointing hundreds of hard working African children."

The picture switched to the hall of Thomas Jefferson School where the headmaster was handing out certificates to his own pupils.

"This was not Statesman like behaviour, it did not even achieve the standards of common decency," continued the Congresswoman.

The President clicked the television off. Get me Eugene Forester on the phone, I want to do this personally and after that I want to speak to that guy that was going to get the medal."

All had quietened down. Eugene was alone, he wanted to be alone. He'd started walking. He'd done the couple of blocks to the river and was now walking down the embankment. The sky had clouded over and he felt a light drizzle, almost a mist, on his face. With each step his depression deepened. His cell phone rang. He looked at the caller display. It was Eagle One. Until this morning he'd lived to receive calls from his boss but now he couldn't bring himself to press the green receive button. He didn't need to be told he was fired. He threw the phone into the river, put his hands in his pockets and with head bowed continued his walk as the drizzle turned to rain.

Camp David
Two Weeks Later

David Evans sat in the cane armchair on the porch of the visitor cabin. He wished his mother was there. He approached on foot. David didn't notice him until he was right there. He started to get up.

"No, no. Stay sitting. Mind if I join you?"

"No Mr President, I don't mind at all."

The President took the chair next to David. "David I want you to call me Ron today. I haven't invited you as the President, you're here as a personal guest. It's me the person who wanted to meet you. No cameras, no press release. If you don't tell anybody I won't."

"Why would you do that?"

"It's complex David. Perhaps I'm a dreamer but I believe everybody who became President started off with the idea of doing good things for this great country of ours, doesn't matter what Party they represent. But as you progress you get sucked into the machine, it's a meat grinder. You get involved in partisan politics, you give favours, you receive favours, you grovel for money and pressure groups lobby you all the time. Every day it appears you lose a little of your dignity and honour. You can't help it. Some Presidents get lucky and do a bit of good but most of us achieve very little in the end. You see we're too busy hanging on to power. This job isn't all it's cracked up to be."

"That's powerful stuff Sir."

"It's from my heart. I read up about you. That's a privilege of power. I can find out just about anything about anybody. That's why I invited you here. You see everyone in America wants to be President of the United States. I was like that and I made it and now that I'm here do you know what I want most of all?"

"No Sir I don't"

"Well I can't do any better than this, I'd love to be David Evans, I'd love to be you."

Foreign and Commonwealth Office, London
15th July 1994

Sir Basil Parker Smythe looked uncomfortable standing with the two Americans in their bright broad check jackets.

The room was packed with those in the know who wanted to get in on the act. Sir Basil thought his time might be spent better with others, but he wasn't going to spoil the occasion.

"Not often we get asked to a party in London," said Jack Carter.

"Strictly speaking it's not a party, it's a reception. And it is a special occasion. Private functions are very much the rarity in this place. Still I hope you are enjoying yourselves. We tried to lay on food that you like.

"You got ribs?" asked Burt hopefully.

"Ribs? I think we might have a rack of lamb somewhere," replied Sir Basil.

"No thanks," replied a deflated Burt. "I tried them."

Across the room, in a corner, were Stuart, Jane, James and Maggie. It was the first trip to London for James and Maggie; it was their first trip out of Africa. For three days they'd toured the sights with their father, Jane acting as guide, although at times it appeared she didn't know the way around herself very well.

The door opened. Ralph Foulkes walked in. "Can I have your attention ladies and gentlemen. Mr Murdoch has finished at Downing Street and will be with us shortly.

Seconds later Duncan walked into the room to be greeted by a round of applause. Sir Basil stepped forward.

"I won't speak for long. As you know some people do good things and they rightly receive recognition for their actions. However in our business we are often constrained in the amount of public recognition we can give – for obvious reasons. Mr Murdoch I want to say to you that this small private reception no way reflects the magnitude of the service you have freely given. I personally am grateful for your efforts, and millions others would be too – if they knew."

Ralph stepped forward, glass in hand. "A toast. To Mr Duncan Murdoch."

As soon as he could Duncan joined his family and close friends.

"So how was Mrs T?" asked Stuart. "As ferocious as they say?"

"No not really," replied Duncan. "She took me upstairs to her private apartment and made a cup of tea for me. We sat at the kitchen table and talked. Dennis joined us later."

"So what did she have to say?"

"Nothing much really, she just listened. She did give me a letter when I left. But it wasn't even signed by her."

Duncan withdrew the letter from his pocket.

"What does it say Dad?" asked Maggie.

"I think Stuart should read it first. He'll understand."

Stuart read silently. When he'd finished he stepped forward and hugged his friend. It would be hard for others to understand why.

Maggie grabbed the letter and read it herself. "What's a Royal Pardon and why is it signed Elizabeth R?

Jane lowered herself to Maggie. "The letter means that something wrong that happened a long time ago has been put right and the signature at the bottom of the letter belongs to the Queen of England."

That evening in the hotel Jane and Stuart joined Duncan and his children for a meal.

"Why didn't Tembo and Morgan come?" asked Jane.

"They wanted to stay and look after the business," replied Duncan. "Besides they said they'd feel out of place. Truthfully I can't get them off the hovercraft. They're like a pair of kids!"

"And what about Mary and Gus? They were invited."

Duncan smiled. "When they found out we were all going they were delighted. But not for us, it was the prospect that the two of them would be alone in the house for the first time. I think they stayed behind so they could play house."

"Really?"

"I think this is the last chance for Mary to re-live something she lost a long time ago and for Gus to taste something he's never had."

"There's hope for us all," said Stuart. "I suppose it's not a bad result really, after such a bad start."

"I'm not sure I'd want to go through all that again," said Jane. "I'm thinking it's time for me to try something new."

"What leave GCHQ?"

"Yes."

"What would you do?" asked Duncan.

"That's the problem. I'm not really qualified for anything else."

James gave Jane a mischievous glance. "Why don't you become a farmer's wife, you'd be good at that."

Jane blushed.

"Yes," added Maggie with a grin on her face. "I think Dad's got a vacancy in Botswana."

Stuart stood. "Time for me to go I think."

"Us too," quipped James.

Duncan and Jane suddenly alone looked at each other but were lost for words. Their hands met across the table.

ALSO BY THE AUTHOR

"The Valley of the Shadow"

'The Valley of the Shadow' is the first book in *'The Murdoch Wars'* series and details Duncan's early life and adventures from Aden to Zimbabwe.

As superpowers compete for dominance at the cutting edge of the Cold War the lives of three individuals converge. Duncan Murdoch a disgraced Scottish soldier, Elizabeth an African princess and Joshua the psychotic son of a radical intellectual clash in an epic conflict. The weeds of racism are being eradicated only to be replaced by the poisonous shoots of tribalism in infant Zimbabwe. Enemies become friends and friends become enemies in a ruthless power struggle. Betrayal, deceit and genocide combine in an attempt to suffocate the buds of hope.

This well researched fast moving book is based on factual events, historical figures and the recollection of participants. It weaves facts into a story that shames the major powers and exposes both the evil and inherent good that lurks within individuals. It is a dramatic story that goes as close to the truth as one dares.

REVIEWS

"Great story of the history of a country......"

Katherine Chand "book lover" (lumberton, texas)

The Valley of the Shadow (Paperback)

"Well written, historically accurate story of colonial Africa's struggle to become independant. Details both sides of the conflict weaving the fictional lives of the main characters with real life so well you can hardly tell which is which. I could not wait to finish and read the next book in the series."

"Phew! you want action? Here it is..."

Michelangelo Jack (Auckland, New Zealand)

The Valley of the Shadow (The Murdoch Wars) (Kindle Edition)

"This was a real page-turner, from beginning to end, it did not let up, at times I caught myself holding my breath. The way the author weaved several stories within a story was thrilling. This comes highly recommended, a damn good read...."

"Memories"

Pauline L. Cairns

The Valley of the Shadow (The Murdoch Wars) (Kindle Edition)

"The interweaving of fiction with fact makes for a splendid read. Duncan Murdoch's life through four countries made the story even more interesting. Also at the time of the bush war, one became more aware of the interests of China and Russia in the conflict. A time of great hardship and brutality, all with a happy ending for Duncan and Elizabeth in Botswana. A lovely reunion with Mary Scobie with whom Duncan kept in touch after her husband was killed in front of his eyes."

"The Valley of the Shadow"

Ms Beastle

The Valley of the Shadow (The Murdoch Wars) (Kindle Edition)

"Just finished this engrossing book. What a great plot, kept a tight story line with tension and surprises. Loved the descriptions of the places in Africa and the lead bad guy (oh, so satisfying to hate him!)...."

See more reviews on Amazon.

AVAILABLE IN PAPERBACK OR ON KINDLE

AUTHORS NOTES ON FEAR NO EVIL

To help people who have a deeper interest in the subject the notes below are included to indicate some of the events and places that influenced my story and plot development. They are not a concise history description, only guidelines. For those who really want to study the subject matter lots of information is available on the web.

ASCENSION ISLAND, ATLANTIC OCEAN. The Portuguese navigator Joao de Alburquerque is said to have discovered the island on Ascension Day 1501. It lies in equatorial Atlantic waters. It fell into British hands at the end of the Napoleonic Wars and has been permanently garrisoned by British forces since 1815. During the Falklands War in 1982 it became a major stopping off base for British Forces and it is said that for a short period it became the busiest airport in the world.

Today it remains part of The British Atlantic Territories and has an important naval and air base. The US air force shares some of the facilities as do other NATO countries.

BOSS. South Africa's Bureau of State Security was the equivalent of Israel's MOSSAD and the UK's MI6. It was considered by many to be a slightly inept organisation although it did have its successes.

BROTHERHOOD (THE). (Afrikaner Broderbund). Established in 1918 as an exclusively male Calvinist organization, it became an immense informal network.

Jan Smuts, statesman and former prime Minister of South Africa, is quoted as saying it was a *"dangerous, cunning, political fascist organization"*. Every leader, Prime Minister, President and member of the Cabinet belonged to the Broderbund from 1948 till the end of Apartheid, as did almost every person in a position of influence in every strata of life in South Africa. The remarks of the organization's chairman in 1944 offer a flavor of what the Broderbund was all about: *"The Afrikaner Broderbund was born out of the deep conviction that the Afrikaner volk has been planted in this country by the Hand of God, destined to survive as a separate volk with its own calling".*

The prime objective of the Broderbund was to wrest the country from the English-speaking British and place its future in the hands of the Afrikaners, whatever that might mean for the large black and mixed-race population.

Some of its members wanted to support the Nazis during WW2 others were in favor of neutrality. The organization had an important influence on South African politics from 1948 till Nelson Mandela's election in 1994.

CHRISTIAN BARNHARD (Dr). On December 3rd 1967 Dr. Barnhard carried out the world's first heart transplant on Lewis Washkansky in South Africa. The operation was a success but the patient died eighteen days after the operation from phenomena most probably connected with the lack of knowledge on anti-rejection drugs.

The operation and South Africa's pioneering lead in this field was seized on by many South African politicians as a demonstration of the technical advancement of their country not only compared to other African countries but also on the world stage.

DEMONA NUCLEAR FACILITY. Demona in the Negev desert is Israel's primary nuclear facility. It comprises a civil nuclear power station on the ground and weapons producing facility underground, directly below the reactor. Successive Israeli Governments have been secretive to the point of paranoia about this facility. The civil part of the facility was subject to periodic US inspection and surprisingly the US inspectors, over a number of years and several inspections, never found or suspected that a secret part of the facility existed.

The world came to know about the place when an employee, Mordechai Vanune, told the story to a UK national newspaper. The Israel Government was so incensed by the incident they turned the matter over to their secret service MOSSAD. Eventually MOSSAD lured Vanune to Italy using a female agent as bait, kidnapped him and smuggled him back to Israel on a freighter. He was subsequently tried for treason and sentenced to eighteen years in prison.

DIEGO GARCIA. This island group in the middle of the Indian Ocean was named after a Spanish explorer. It remained uninhabited till 1778 when French settlers arrived. It was ceded to Britain by the French in 1814 at the end of the Napoleonic Wars. When the Seychelles and Mauritius gained independence the island group became part of the British Indian Ocean Territories with a Governor based in the Foreign and Commonwealth Office in London.

London forced the civilian population to leave the islands when it signed a lease with the US Government for the establishment of a US military base there for ships and planes. It remains a strategic outpost for the US and the British maintain a smaller military presence.

GCHQ (General Communications Head Quarters UK). This vast complex is generally seen as the UK's prime electronic eaves' dropping facility. It is acknowledged worldwide to be in the forefront of military intelligence. It is based at Cheltenham near to Bristol in the West of England. Thousands of people work there including some of the finest minds in the country.

JERICO 2 MISSILES. Once the South Africans had developed a nuclear capability they needed a viable delivery system. They had enough difficulties in pinpointing potential targets. The only likely target that emerged was Cuban ground forces operating out of Angola. The problem was that the South Africans only had ageing Canberra and Buccaneer bombers that would have been no match for Cuban air defences. The South Africans tried to develop their own missiles but this proved to be too costly. For a time they are thought to have been in discussions with the Israeli Government for the supply of advanced Jericho Two missiles. In the end South Africa did not obtain the Jericho missiles and so never actually developed a credible method of delivering their newly acquired nuclear weapons.

PLAUSABLE DENIABILITY. This term was coined by the CIA in the Kennedy era to protect the President of the US from getting embroiled in events from which he'd rather distance himself. In *'Fear No Evil'* it is used in the context that the Israelis denied they had a nuclear weapons program (against all the evidence) and the President, in the absence of other evidence, stated he had no reason to disbelieve the Israelis declaration. The Israeli Government to this day officially denies a nuclear capability.

PORTUGAL: CARNATION REVOLUTION. A popular uprising, started by the military toppled the right wing dictatorship of Estado Novo. It started on the 25th April 1984. As well as changing forever the political environment within the country it also signaled Portugal's end as a colonial power. This had a major effect on South Africa as South Africa shared two borders with Portuguese colonies; one with Mozambique and the others with the South African protectorate of South West Africa and Angola.

Protracted wars followed with Eastern Bloc countries supporting the southern African 'black' guerrilla movements and eventually leading to South African ground forces coming into conflict with Cuban soldiers sent by Fidel Castro.

SIMONS TOWN NAVAL BASE: CAPE PROVINCE SOUTH AFRICA. The port was first established on the Cape by the Dutch East India Company in 1743 and named after Simon van der Stel the then Governor of Cape Town. In 1806 it was taken over by the British permanently as a naval base. In 1814 it was declared a naval Establishment and became home to the British South Atlantic Squadron. Interestingly its security was the responsibility of a special section of London's Metropolitan Police until 1957. In 1975 sovereignty of the base was handed over to the South African Government on the understanding Britain would have use of the facilities in war and peace.

It became the main base for the South African navy and home to the South African submarine force. The base controlled the strategically important sea lanes that joined the Indian Ocean to the South Atlantic. The Americans in particular wanted the base to stay in *'friendly'* hands for the duration of the Cold War.

VASTRAP. Vastrap in the Kalahari Desert was chosen by the South Africans as the site to test its nuclear weapons. Two shafts were sunk there, one completed in 1976 and the other in 1977. Before a test could be carried out Soviet Intelligence alerted the United States about the site's existence and this was confirmed by an over flight of a US SR71 spy plane. After pressure was applied to the South African Government the tests were cancelled.

In '*Fear No Evil*' I have chosen Vastrap as the major South African facility for the sake of simplifying the story. A nuclear weapons program by its very nature needs more than one facility. South Africa had in actual fact several facilities including Pelindaba and the Y-Plant as well as a large scale civil reactor.

VELA INCIDENT. The US Vela Satellite picked up a double flash in the south Indian Ocean near to Prince Edward Island, near Antarctica on the 22nd September 1979. A double flash is the unique signature of a nuclear explosion. The incident has been surrounded by controversy. One official report from the US says the double flash was actually caused by specs of space dust hitting the satellite's camera lens. If this was the case, most scientists conclude, the lens would have been marked and all subsequent photographs would be marked. They are not. Some think it might have been a test by South Africa but the good money is on the possibility of the Israelis carrying out a nuclear test far from home. The truth remains locked up in some country's secret archives.

VICTOR VERSTER PRISON: NELSON MANDELA. Many people believe that Nelson Mandela spent his entire captivity at the notorious Robben Island establishment off the coast of Cape Town. This is not true. He was at Robben Island from 1962 till 1982. Then he was transferred to Pollsmore Prison, possibly because of the influence he was having on other Black Nationalist prisoners. The famous pictures of him walking to freedom on 11th February 1990 were actually taken at Victor Verster Prison north of Cape Town.

In '*Fear No Evil*' I have only mentioned Victor Verster Prison as mentioning the other places of incarceration would have only complicated the story and added nothing to the plot.

'WIND OF CHANGE' SPEECH. This speech was made to the South African Parliament by the British Prime Minister, Harold Macmillan on 3rd February 1960. The speech was of dramatic importance as it signified British intentions to pull out of Africa as a colonial power and told South African politicians that the time of white European dominance of the continent was coming to an end. It was not well received in South Africa.

WINSTON CHURCHILL: IRON CURTAIN SPEECH. At a college in America's mid-West on 5th March 1946 Winston Churchill delivered a speech stating that an Iron Curtain had fallen across Europe from Stettin in the Baltic to Trieste in the Adriatic. This speech is regarded by many as the official start of the Cold War (although others would say that it had actually started some time before).

The end of the Cold War is considered to be the fall of the Berlin Wall on 10th November 1989. A view held by many, including myself, is that as long as the Cold War continued the United States was willing to accept the consequences of Apartheid in South Africa provided South Africa remained an ally of the West and protected the Cape of Good Hope, the waters connecting the Atlantic with the Indian Ocean.

4775646R00196

Printed in Great Britain
by Amazon.co.uk, Ltd.,
Marston Gate.